# DAMNATION SPRING

*A Novel*

## Ash Davidson

Scribner

New York   London   Toronto   Sydney   New Delhi

Scribner
An Imprint of Simon & Schuster, Inc.
1230 Avenue of the Americas
New York, NY 10020

Interior design by Wendy Blum

Manufactured in the United States of America

ISBN 978-1-9821-4440-1

*For my parents, Susan and Dean Davidson*

*. . . they are not like any trees we know . . .*

—John Steinbeck

*It's easier to die than to move . . .*

—Wallace Stegner

# DAMNATION SPRING

# SUMMER

*1977*

# July 30

# RICH

Rich nabbed the week's mail from Lark's box and swung off the Eel Road, bumping down the muddy two-track past a pair of show toilets. Thorns screaked against the Ford's side panels. Ferns tall as a man scrubbed the windows. The driveway was so overgrown Rich could barely read the signs.

DRIVE-THRU TREE! REAL GENUINE SASQUATCH!
CLEAN PUBLIC RESTROOM!

The two-track dead-ended in Lark's clearing, overlooking the river. Rich pulled up alongside the ancient International abandoned in front of the cabin, grass grown up through the truck's rust-eaten hood. The old hog nosing around in the weeds behind the outhouse didn't raise its head, but Lark's two lazy mutts stretched and moseyed over as soon as Rich popped his door.

"Banjo! Killer!" Lark called from the porch, carved Sasquatches posted along the railing.

Fifty degrees and here was Lark in a stained undershirt, gray hair and beard wild to his shoulders, rolls of toilet paper stacked in a pyramid on the parked wheelchair. He used the thing like a glorified wheelbarrow. Rich snagged the foil pan and six-pack of Tab riding shotgun and climbed out.

Lark sat back in his carving chair. "Saturday, already?"

"How's the shit business?" Rich asked, coming up the steps.

"Regular."

Lark scraped a chip off a hunk of driftwood where a shaggy Sasquatch head emerged, like the wood had washed up with the Sasquatches already inside, and all he had to do was shave off the extra with the ease of a man taking the rind off an orange in a single long peel.

"Had a gal out here yesterday, ass so round I wanted to take a damn bite." Lark lifted his chin toward the outhouse—the only pit stop for miles in this stretch of the redwood belt—as though the tourist might still be inside.

Twenty-sheet wads of toilet paper were piled on the chair beside him, enough to refill the basket below the tin can where tourists deposited their outhouse dimes. People were always pitching the rolls into the pit or stealing them, but no one took much interest in the individual wads.

Lark's flying squirrel sat on his shoulder. He'd found her as a pup, blown out of the nest. With her twisted hip, she and Lark were a matched set. Lark toed the half-circle of shavings at his feet, rotated the statue, and rubbed a thumb up the grain to feel the muscles underneath. Lark's own jaw was sunken. Rich eyed the upside-down crate piled with tools and empty Tab cans—no sign of his teeth—and spun the warm tin on his palm.

"That my last meal?" Lark asked.

"Still hot."

"Put it in the icebox." Lark tossed his head toward the door, always propped open, no matter the weather.

Rich ducked inside. Lark had built the cabin himself, back when men were smaller. The kitchen was just a sink and a two-burner camp stove, some cupboard shelves Lark had never bothered putting doors on. *What the hell for? Have to open them to find anything.*

"What time is it?" Lark called from the porch.

"Six?" Rich looked out the window at the gray sky. "Six thirty."

Empty pork-n-beans cans littered the counter. Rich pulled open the icebox: Marsha's tuna-casserole pan, one shriveled square remaining, a bottle of barbecue sauce.

"You coming in?" Rich asked, eye level with the door frame.

"Let's go see what else Kel is frying up." Lark took up his canes, one cut in the shape of a saw—the standard Sanderson retirement gift—the other a wooden rifle he'd carved himself.

"You want to go down to the Only?" Rich asked.

"There another place to get a hot meal in this town?" Lark asked.

"You going to put a shirt on first?"

Lark hobbled in, pulled open the top drawer of the hutch, dipped his shoulder so that the squirrel fell in, and slammed the drawer shut. The dogs would corner her if they ever got her alone.

"Those are yours." Lark grunted, pulling on an old work shirt and nodding at a pile of toothpicks on the kitchen table, sharp and even as store-bought.

"Appreciate it." Rich funneled the toothpicks into his front pocket. He'd quit chewing snus cold turkey the day he met Colleen. Stuck a toothpick in his mouth nine years ago, and that was it.

Lark took one porch step at a time.

"Since when do you want to go down to the Only?" Rich asked once they were in the truck, Lark panting from the effort. Besides a ride up and down the coast highway to pull his road signs—DRIVE THRU REAL LIVE REDWOOD! HOUSE INSIDE A TREE!—for repainting or to replant them, Rich couldn't remember the last time Lark had wanted to go anywhere.

"Since when do you ask so many questions?" Lark shot back. He squinted out at the river. Two Yurok men slid by in a boat. "Looking for fish."

"Early for salmon, yet," Rich said, backing up far enough to turn around.

Lark shrugged. "They've been fishing that river for a thousand years. They've got fish in the blood, those guys."

The truck juddered, swung around the Eel Road's washboard curves, as winding as the animal it was named for. Dark walls of second-growth rose up the steep sides of the gulch, alder and vine maple crowding in around old stumps large enough to park a pickup on. When they pulled into the gravel lot, there was only one other truck besides Kel's: a burnt-orange Chevy Rich didn't recognize. Rain dripped off the bumper, washing mud from peeling stickers.

KISS MY AX.

DON'T WORRY, I HUGGED IT FIRST.

MY BOSS AIN'T A WHORE, HE'S A HOOKER.

The sign out front—THE ONE AND ONLY TAVERN—was faded by rain, but the white high-water mark over the entrance was freshly painted, showing the river how far it would have to rise to impress anybody.

Rich held the door and Lark hobbled in, surveyed the place as though it were crowded, and made for the bar, maneuvering himself onto a stool next to an old guy watching baseball, his dirty plate pushed aside.

"Corny." The man acknowledged him. Only old-timers, guys who had worked with Lark when he was young, called him that.

"Jim." Lark knew every crusty old logger for a hundred miles and which side to butter him on. "Rich Gundersen, Jim Mueller."

"You're Hank's boy?" Jim Mueller asked. His white hair was buzzed, an old scar visible on his scalp.

Rich nodded, taking the stool beside Lark. Jim Mueller narrowed his eyes, searching Rich's face for some resemblance.

"Hank was a hell of a tree-topper. Part monkey. Damn shame what happened to him." Jim Mueller cleared his throat and glanced at Lark. Lark had been Rich's father's best friend; after forty-five years, he still carried his death on his back.

"Rich lives out at Bald Hill, Hank and Gretchen's old place," Lark said.

"Above Diving Board Rock there?" Jim Mueller asked.

Kel pushed through the swinging kitchen doors. "Who let you out?" he ribbed, wiping his hands on his apron.

"I like to look around once a decade," Lark said. "What happened to your hair?"

Kel ran a palm over his shiny head, as though he'd forgotten his own baldness.

"I'll take mine rare," Lark said. "And easy on the damn onions this time."

Kel looked to Rich, who shrugged.

"One burger," Kel announced, pouring them coffee before heading back to the grill.

Lark turned to Jim Mueller. "I hear you're looking to unload a couple of forties."

For a man who rarely set foot beyond the end of his own driveway, Lark had an uncanny knack for knowing who had land for sale, whose truck had been repo'ed, who was doing six months plus a fine for poaching burls off the national park.

"Might be." Jim Mueller cast a suspicious look at Rich.

"Don't worry about him," Lark said. "I've known rocks that talked more."

"Hazel's bleeding me dry," Jim Mueller confided, glancing back at the TV.

"How many's a couple?" Lark asked.

"Eighteen."

"Eighteen?" Lark choked, setting his coffee down.

"Seven hundred twenty acres." Jim Mueller scratched his cheek, eyes still on the game. "The 24-7 inholding—that whole ridge behind Hank's."

Rich's heart skipped. He'd walked 24-7 Ridge every morning of his adult life. His great-granddad had dreamed of buying it, and that dream had been handed down through the generations until it landed, heavy, on Rich.

"Some good timber in there." Lark took another swig. "If you could get to it."

"Sanderson's putting roads in next door, on the east side, to harvest Damnation Grove," Jim Mueller said. "Practically rolling out the red carpet to the 24-7."

Lark looked to Rich.

"Harvest plans finally went through," Rich confirmed.

"All this new environmental bullshit, it's just paperwork," Jim Mueller said. "You know they'll have to run a road clear down to the creek to get the cut out. The big pumpkins in that lower half are all down along the bottom of that gulch. Hell, it's spitting distance from there to the foot of 24-7 Ridge."

"A lot of board feet up the 24-7," Lark mused. Rich felt his eyes on him.

"A million bucks' worth, at least." A look of disgust crossed Jim Mueller's face. "I've been waiting fifty years for Sanderson to harvest Damnation, so I could get to mine. I told Hazel: 'Wait. Couple more months, Sanderson'll cut roads down.' But that bitch says she's done waiting on my ass. She wants her alimony now."

"Those big pumpkins aren't worth a nickel if you can't haul them out," Lark reminded him.

"She's steep, and she's rough," Jim Mueller admitted, "but as soon as those roads go in and Lower Damnation gets cleared out of the way, somebody's going to make a goddamn fortune."

"Merle doesn't want to buy it?" Lark asked.

"Merle's a goddamn sellout." Jim Mueller belched. "The big dogs let him keep the Cadillac so he can rub elbows with the buddies he's got left on the forestry board, but all the real decisions go through corporate now. You think those San Francisco sonsabitches give a damn? They bought Sanderson to bleed her. They'll harvest her big timber, then auction off every piece of machinery that isn't nailed down, lock the doors, and throw away the key. Look how they sold off the trucks. Like a goddamn yard sale."

Rich sipped his coffee and tried to slow his racing heart. He pictured the 24-7 tree herself: a monster, grown even wider now than the twenty-four feet, seven inches that originally earned her the name, three hundred seventy feet high, the tallest of the scruff of old-growth redwoods left along the top of

24-7 Ridge. He'd circled that tree every morning for the last thirty-five years, figuring the best way to fall her, but it had always been just a story he'd told himself, like his father before him, and his granddad before that. *Someday*, Rich remembered his father saying. As a boy, it had seemed possible, though generations of Gundersens had died with the word on their breath.

"You sure the park don't want it?" Lark asked. "Aren't they looking to expand?"

Jim Mueller pushed air out his nose. "Up here? You seen the clear-cuts? Looks like a bomb went off." Jim Mueller shook his head. "Tourists don't want to see that. They expand, it'll be down where they're at, Redwood Creek area. Humboldt County'll die of that park. At least up here in Del Nort, we still got a fighting chance." Jim Mueller inhaled. "I'd take four hundred."

"Four hundred thousand dollars?" Lark asked.

Rich's heart sank.

"Rich here has been saving his whole goddamn life," Lark said. "Give him another five, six generations." He leaned back to make room for Kel to set his hamburger on the bar.

"Timber's worth ten times that." Jim Mueller sulked.

Lark picked the bun off the burger and scraped away the onions. "You got equipment rental, plus a crew, plus contracting some gyppo trucker to haul your cut to the mill," Lark calculated, cramming in lettuce and tomato and a few rounds of pickle.

Jim Mueller shrugged. "Got to spend money to make money."

Rich nursed his coffee, trying to focus on the game, to ignore the itch of possibility. It wasn't possible, not at that price. He'd never qualify for a loan that size. The batter hit a line drive to left field. Lark finished his meal, took hold of his canes, and pushed himself up, in a hurry.

"Damn lettuce runs right through me," he muttered, hobbling toward the john.

The game went to commercial.

"You get in a fight?" Jim Mueller asked, eyeing Rich's split knuckles.

"Nah." Rich flexed his fingers, still tender. "Just from working."

"You a high-climber too?"

Rich nodded.

"Well, you got the height for it. How old are you?"

"Fifty-three."

"Christ. Aren't loggers supposed to be dead by fifty?"

"Still got a few lives left," Rich said.

Jim Mueller shook his head, the gesture of a man who'd worked in the woods, whose body remembered the way bark could bite, the wet of blood before the pain came alive.

"Hank sure got in a lot of fights as a kid, but then, he always was a runt." Jim Mueller chuckled at the memory. "I bet guys thought twice before starting up with you."

Rich rotated his mug. Plenty of nights at the Widowmaker, before Colleen, he'd tightened his jaw as some jackass heckled him. Certain type, when he got a few drinks in him, looked around for the tallest man to fight, and in any bar, any room, that man was Rich. Six six and a half in socks, six eight in caulk boots. Short guys pushed hardest—same daredevil taste that drew them to high-lead logging to begin with. As if falling the biggest timber on Earth could make up for the North Coast's smallest pecker. Rich had defended himself, but he'd never struck a man in anger. Couldn't remember his dad well enough to picture him fighting.

"Hank swore he'd buy that 24-7 off me someday," Jim Mueller said. "Died too young." He paused a long moment, then wrote a phone number down on a coaster and slid it over to Rich. "I'd take two fifty. I wouldn't offer that to anybody else."

"I'll think about it," Rich said. He'd been planning to use the twenty-five grand he'd socked away up at the savings and loan to build on when the baby came, but there wouldn't be another baby, not after how hard Colleen had taken losing this last one.

"Hazel's lawyer has got me by the balls. I need this done quick or that sonofabitch is going to garnish my social security. Garnish." Jim Mueller grunted. "Big piece of fucking parsley."

"Ready?" Lark asked, coming back. He hitched an elbow up on the bar— Rich forgot how little he was until moments like this—and thumbed a few bucks from his wallet. "That enough?" he asked Kel.

Kel nodded. "See you in 1987."

"If you live that long, baldie. Take it easy on the onions." Lark held out his hand. "Jim." They shook. Jim Mueller nodded so long to Rich.

"What do you think?" Lark asked once they were back in the truck.

"About what?" Rich asked.

"Nice to be your own boss for once, wouldn't it?"

Rich shrugged. A quarter-million bucks.

"You cut, replant, harvest thirty-year rotations. That would be some real money."

"I'll be dead in thirty years," Rich said.

"Yeah," Lark acknowledged, "but Colleen won't."

Rich tightened his grip on the wheel. Lark had a way of getting inside his head, limping around on that pair of canes like a cursing, wild-bearded incarnation of Rich's conscience.

"The real timber's gone," Lark said. "What's left, ten percent, including the parks? Two thousand years to grow a forest, a hundred years to fall it. No plague like man."

Rich pulled out of the lot. Drizzle speckled the windshield.

"Sanderson's almost out of old-growth. How long you think Merle's going to keep you around?" Lark prodded. "Another year? Two? Don't need a high-climber if all they're harvesting is pecker poles. You don't bet on yourself, nobody else will, Gundersen." Lark rolled down his window, stuck a palm out to check the rain. "I'll tell you one thing, String Bean, your dad wouldn't have let an opportunity like this pass him by, that's for sure."

"I don't know." Rich stalled, though he knew Lark was right.

"You don't know what? Listen, it might take a pair of fists, three balls, and a bucket of luck to make a life in redwood country, but you get a chance like this, you take it. Chance of a goddamn lifetime." Lark coughed, scratched the lump on his neck. "I need a smoke. You got any smokes in this truck?"

"Hasn't Marsha been on you to quit?" Rich asked.

"What, you afraid she'll sit on you?"

"She's already shot one man," Rich reasoned.

"I ain't scared of her." Lark jogged his leg like he was late somewhere.

They rode in silence up the crumbling highway along the ocean, asphalt potholed from the weight of loaded log trucks, winding along the narrow strip of coastal timber the park had annexed back in '68. Big trees hugged the road edge like mink trim sewn to a burlap coat, hiding the clear-cuts that lay just beyond.

"I remember the first time I saw your dad climb," Lark said when they hit the straightaway, coasting downhill toward Crescent City. "Never saw another guy like him, until you. You know he used to walk up to scout that 24-7 tree? They knocked our dicks down into the dirt working. Fourteen-, sixteen-hour days. And still, every Sunday, he walked, all the way from whatever logging camp we were at. Miles. Like it was church. He ever take you along?"

"Once," Rich recalled.

"You know what he told me, the day you were born? He said, someday, the two of you were going to fall that tree. You were just a scrawny little thing. Ugly too." Lark grinned, his affection for Rich's father warming his voice. "Not a lot of guys are born to do something."

# COLLEEN

Colleen held out Chub's new yellow slicker, long in the sleeves. She heard Rich pacing out back, talking to Scout. Rich wasn't much of a talker, but he'd been talking to that dog all week.

"Where are we going?" Chub asked, holding on to her shoulder for balance.

She stuffed his sock feet into his rain boots.

"Your dad wants to show us something." She pressed her thumbs into Chub's dimples, his eyes still sugar-crusted with sleep. "Where'd you get these dimples?"

"I got them at the dimples store." Chub yawned. "Wait! My binoculars!" He ran back down the hall.

She looked out at Scout pacing behind Rich in the backyard, as though man and dog were thinking through the same problem. She hoped this wouldn't take long. Melody Larson was due in a few weeks and the baby was still breech. Colleen had promised her she'd stop by; she was the first mother to ask for Colleen's help in months.

The damp-swollen kitchen door whooshed when she yanked it open. Rich stopped in his tracks. He toed the grass, as though he'd dropped a screw or a washer, some small missing piece that might hold a conversation together. They'd hardly spoken since the hospital at Easter. *Miscarried*, as if, five months pregnant, Colleen had made some stupid mistake, some error in posture, in loading or lifting. And now here they were, the first Sunday in August, Chub about to start kindergarten, an only child.

"Found them!" Chub reappeared, brandishing the binoculars.

"Ready?" Rich asked. Dawn light caught in the crinkles at the corners of his eyes.

The hospital nurse had set their tiny daughter in Colleen's arms, and Rich had laid a hand on her, as if to transfer his own life force. He'd taken Colleen to visit the baby's grave a few times. *It's nothing you did. Let it go, Colleen. The past isn't a knot you can untie.* Like grief was a sack you carried a month and then left by the side of the road, it was behind them now, he seemed to believe, like all the others. Five by Rich's count, three more she'd never spoken of. But her Easter baby hadn't been like the others, lost in the early weeks, the size of an apple seed, the size of a raspberry. She'd had ten perfect fingers, ten perfect toes, stillborn at twenty-two weeks, her poor sweet baby girl. And, unlike the others, this time people knew in town, she couldn't hide it—she'd been showing and then, as the weight melted away, she wasn't. Couldn't Rich see that was different? Who would trust her to deliver a baby now, if she couldn't carry her own to term?

"Ready," she said.

Scout raced up the path through the blackberry brambles, climbing the hill behind the house. Chub ran after him. Colleen followed Rich up past the shed where creek water ran down through half a mile of rusted pipe into the tank that supplied the house. She needed two steps to match his one. Every day before he left for work, Rich disappeared for almost an hour up this path while she made coffee, fried eggs, packed his lunch. He returned breathless, carrying the scent of the woods, having checked the screen catch on the mouth of their gravity-fed water line three ridges away.

At the top of their hill, where the trees began, Colleen looked back down at the house, the new Chevy crew cab a shiny white toy in the driveway. She still hated the sight of it. The weeping willow that marked their turnoff dripped morning rain, fog obscuring the coast highway and the wild ocean beyond it, though she heard the chop crashing against the base of the cliffs below Diving Board Rock. She took off her glasses and wiped the fogged lenses with the hem of her shirt, as though, if she got them clean enough, she might see back through time: Rich coming home, not late as he had been, but right at six, when the cramping started, in time to drive her to the hospital when her old truck wouldn't start.

"Want a ride, Grahamcracker?" Rich asked.

He swung Chub up onto his back and headed deeper into the woods, trees shaggy with moss, vines draped like strands of Christmas lights, forest so close grown Colleen had to turn sideways. Snatches of Chub's yellow slicker and Rich's checkered hunting jacket appeared and disappeared through the trunks, and, all around them, the trickle of running water. They rock-hopped across Little Lost Creek and climbed up through the ferns and over the ridge behind it, dropping down to the marsh along Garlic Creek, the skunk cabbage chest-high, Chub vanishing into its waxy leaves. If she turned north here and walked a mile up the draw, she would end up, eventually, at the garlic farm out Deer Rib Road, where she and Enid had been raised. Instead, they topped the next ridge, jumped the spit creek at the bottom, and scrambled up to the backbone of 24-7 Ridge, where old-growth redwoods rose like the comb of a rooster. Lower down had been logged at the turn of the century, but this section had been too steep, back when they'd hauled logs out by rail. The 24-7 herself was so massive it would take a dozen people holding hands to circle her. Men still talked about her in town: the 24-7, the big fish that got away.

Rich pressed a palm to the 24-7's bark. Chub did the same. Colleen's breath scraped at her lungs. After a moment, Rich stepped back and cleared his throat, pressed his thumb along his top lip as though he could smooth out the old scar that ran up to his left nostril. When Colleen had first met him, she'd thought the scar made him look mean. Now she knew the gesture well enough to under-stand there was something he wanted to tell her. She'd felt him turning it around and around in his mind all week, like a piece of wood he was deciding how to carve. He took her hand, squeezed three warm pulses. *I. Love. You.* Six months ago, it might have thrilled her, but now she knew there was no desire in it. The hospital had flipped a switch in him. As soon as she'd healed, she'd wanted to try again—the doctor had said: *Wait a few healthy periods, try again.* She longed to hold a living, squirming baby in her arms—but Rich refused. He'd stopped wanting her. *I'm beat*, he'd say, gently removing her hands, rolling onto his side, turning his back on her. Maybe it was age. She tugged her hand free from his warm, platonic grip and moved ahead down the path.

"You're it!" Chub tagged Scout, sliding down the far side of the ridge toward Damnation Creek, ducking into the brush to hide.

"Where's Chub?" Rich asked, sidestepping, favoring his bum knee. "Have you seen Chub?"

"Boo!" Chub yelled, jumping out, struggling to disentangle himself from the brambles.

Rich smacked a palm to his chest in mock fright. Chub beamed. Scout nosed his ear. Without brothers or sisters, the dog was his most loyal playmate.

Rich swung Chub across Damnation Creek: twelve feet wide, clear and deep, numbing cold. One of the last creeks salmon still came back to. Colleen stood on the bank, watching Rich wade over to check the catch on the pipe that ran water around the bend and downgradient, all the way to their tank. Satisfied, he sloshed toward her. She stood over him. He smiled at the reversal in their heights, his sheared brown curls silver around the ears. He set his hands on her waist, and although she knew better, her heart leapt: his callused thumbs on her hipbones, heat and pressure, his clean-soap smell. He tipped her upside down over his shoulder.

"Rich!" she shrieked.

He splashed across and set her down, flushed and laughing, on the opposite bank. He was blushing too, that goofy lopsided grin of his. She felt a surge of foolish hope. *Let's try again. Let's keep trying.* She was only thirty-four years old, why shouldn't she have another child?

By crossing the creek, they'd crossed into Lower Damnation Grove, company property. Old-growth redwoods as wide as houses towered overhead, shafts of morning light filtering down through the needles, casting a greenish tint over everything.

"Where are we going?" Chub asked, hushed. The big trees made them all lower their voices.

"Almost there," Rich said.

They climbed the steep rise toward the culvert, where Damnation Creek spilled out from under the gravel road that cut the grove in two, separating the lower half from the upper.

"What road is this?" Chub asked.

"No Name Road," Colleen said. "The way we go to Aunt Enid's."

The side leaving the woods was cratered with potholes, the roadsides overgrown with yellowing brush. The tank truck must have been by. The company did a good job of keeping the road sprayed. A company road was better than a county road, better than a Forest Service road. The government sprayed once, in the spring, but Sanderson's spray truck worked year-round. By tomorrow, alder and brambles, trash trees and weeds, everything the spray had touched that wasn't a needle tree, a cash tree—a redwood or a fir—would curl and die, leaving the road wide enough for two log trucks to pass in opposite directions.

"'What creek is this?' is the real question," Rich said, water gushing down from the upper grove.

Chub thought for a moment.

"Every Gundersen is born with a map of Del Nort County in the palm of his hand," Rich hinted.

Chub consulted his palm. The forest was a maze. Between the fog and the sound of falling water, it was easy to lose your sense of direction, rare to find a spot where you could see farther than the next ridge. Men who'd grown up in these woods still got lost hunting in them. Walk in one direction for a few minutes, and the forest rotated. Before long you stood dizzy, like a child spun in circles, blinking with the sudden disorientation of having a blindfold removed. But not Rich. Drop Rich in the woods in the pitch black and it would take him ten seconds to chart a path home. He was determined to teach Chub, the way he claimed his own father had taught him, though he hadn't been much older than Chub when his father was killed.

Rich ran a thumb up Chub's lifeline to orient him.

"Damnation Creek?" Chub guessed.

"Good," Rich said. "If you know your creeks, you can always find your way home."

A rusted sign was staked above the road:

PRIVATE.
PROPERTY OF SANDERSON TIMBER CO.
KEEP OUT.

Rich headed up toward it and Chub followed, Colleen bringing up the rear. "Where are we?" Chub asked.

"Damnation Grove, the upper half." Rich craned his neck, a penitent standing in the doorway of a church. "A hundred years ago, the whole coast was timber this size," Rich said. "Two million acres."

Redwoods towered, disappearing into the fog above. So that was why Rich had brought them. He wanted Chub to stand here looking up at these giant pillars, ferns taller than he was, rhododendrons jeweled with dew, ground quilted with sorrel, to breathe it in before it was gone. Rich scratched the spot where stubble smoothed out into the leathered skin of his neck. She would be late if they didn't turn back soon.

"Come on," Rich said.

He led the way up to the pour-over where Damnation Spring spilled off a ledge into a deep pool, bubbling like he'd tossed in a handful of Alka-Seltzers. Rich crouched, splashed his face, cupped his hands into a bowl, and drank, then offered some to Chub.

"It's sweet," Chub said.

*Drinking rain*, Colleen's father used to call good spring water.

"When you turn on the tap at home, this is where the water comes from," Rich explained. The spring fed Damnation Creek, their intake pipe downstream in the gravel bed, back on the downhill side of the road.

"There's a spider on you," Chub said.

Rich let the daddy longlegs crawl onto his finger. He could be stubborn, but there wasn't a mean bone in Rich's body.

Together, he and Chub climbed up onto the boulders and looked south, down the Eel Creek drainage, Rich teaching Chub a rhyme to remember its course, how it spit out, finally, at Lark's place. Chub held his binoculars to his eyes. Usually he played with a new toy for a week or two, then lost interest, but the binoculars—a tiny pair of high-powered lenses meant for hunting that Lark had given him for his birthday in May, too spendy a gift for a child, really— remained a favorite. Chub would have slept with them around his neck, if she'd let him.

Colleen crossed her arms, drummed her fingers on her elbows. Melody Larson was waiting. To quell her antsiness, Colleen started up toward the next ridgeline, a hundred yards off. She'd never been any farther east than the spring. Her breath came quicker, climbing. Her heart pounded. When she reached the top, she heard herself gasp: mud and slash, branches and trash trees piled into teepees to be burned, hills crisscrossed with debris as far as the eye could see—a barren wasteland. She'd seen clear-cuts all her life, but never like this.

"Mo-om?" Chub called from below.

She turned. "Coming!"

Chub stood in a clearing with Rich, examining three redwoods that had tipped over, root balls tearing swimming-pool-sized craters in the soft ground. The deadfall's roots stood thirty feet high, rocks bound up in their tentacles. Chub watched her pick her way down the slope.

"What's up there?" Chub asked when she reached him.

"Nothing, Grahamcracker. Just more trees." She took his hand, eager to put some distance between them and the destruction she'd glimpsed on the other side. "What should we make for breakfast?"

"Pancakes," Chub said.

Together they crossed the road, Rich ferrying them back across Damnation Creek. They spilled over the ridges toward home, Chub running ahead, chasing Scout, Colleen walking so fast that for once Rich, with his long legs, was the one struggling to keep up.

# *August 8*

# RICH

He lay for a moment, Colleen's arm draped over him, heavy with sleep: three thirty a.m. on the dot, his body its own alarm clock. He held his breath, trying to slip free without waking her, but the moment his feet touched rug, she sat up. He groaned, getting his shirt on. His back ached from carrying Chub up to the 24-7 yesterday.

"Want me to walk on it?" Colleen asked.

"Maybe tonight."

He rolled his shoulder, laced up his boots. Out back, he let Scout off his chain and loped up the hill after him, into the white dark. His headlamp turned fog to gold. His heart knocked at his ribs. Like some young buck sneaking off to the joyhouse.

*I'll think about it*, he'd promised Jim Mueller. True to his word, Rich had thought of little else. The kitchen light glowed in the fog behind him, Colleen getting the percolator going, cracking eggs, dropping store bread into the toaster. She wanted another kid so bad it hurt to look at her. He longed to tell her, to roll the plan he'd been drawing up in his head out on the table like a map, but she wouldn't want to think about letting go of the remodel money.

Brambles snagged at his denims. Hack them down to nubs, dig them out by the roots, burn them: blackberries would survive the goddamn apocalypse. Couple more weeks and they'd ripen: Himalayans, long and fat as the first joint of his thumb. First of September they'd bust open and bleed in your hand, bring out the bears. Colleen would bake pies, boil berries down to jam.

Scout trotted ten yards ahead, tethered to Rich, even off his chain. Dog came with a built-in tape measure, same as Rich, who'd never strayed more than a hundred miles from this exact spot.

Years ago, back in the fifties, when Virgil Sanderson had hired the company's first sprayer—the new chemicals kept the brush down, made it faster and cheaper to log—the pilot had let Rich ride along. He'd barely fit in the tin-can plane, knees pressed to rattling metal. They'd lifted off from the mill road, bottom falling out of Rich's stomach. The pilot had followed the coastline, turning inland at Diving Board Rock. It was Rich's first and only bird's-eye view of his life: the small green house with its white shutters set back on the bluff at the foot of Bald Hill, the cedar-shingle tank shed. The plane's engine noise buzzed inside his chest, a hundred McCulloch chainsaws revving at once. They'd flown over 24-7 Ridge, the big tree herself lit by an errant ray of sun, glowing orange, bright as a torch, and, for an instant, Rich had caught a glimmer of the inholding's potential—an island of private land in a sea of company forest. They'd flown over the dark waves of big pumpkins in Damnation Grove—redwoods older than the United States of America, saplings when Christ was born. Then came the patchwork of clear-cuts, like mange on a dog, timber felled and bucked and debarked, trucked to the mill, sawed into lumber, sent off to the kilns to be dried. The pilot had flipped a switch and spray had drifted out behind them in a long pennant—taste of chlorine, whiff of diesel—Rich's heart soaring.

Rich followed the memory of the plane east, slid down the steep back side of their hill to Little Lost Creek, running fast at the bottom of the first draw. If Eugene dropped a twig in up at his and Enid's place, Rich could pluck it out here an hour later. It was roads that turned a few creek miles into twenty. Scout dug his snout in, drank. Rich took a running leap, felt a tweak in his right knee, leaving his doubt on the bank behind him.

Up and down the first no-name ridge, choked with alder and piss-yellow Doug fir—even smelled like piss when you cut it—second- and third-growth redwoods. Nowadays, even the fir that shot up to fill the cutover ridge-sides—trees he'd fit two arms around growing up—was worth something. His dad could have bought it up for nothing.

Who ever thought piss fir would be worth shit?

Scout cocked his head at the question.

Rain rolled down Rich's slicker, creeks rushing headlong in the morning dark. Water: always looking for a way to the ocean. Still an hour until dawn. He'd be on the crummy by the time the sun rose, the old school bus jolting along rutted logging roads—just another Monday—but for now, the woods were his. The trail was a tunnel; the deer weren't cropping her back like they used to. Rich's caulk boots were good and damp, flexible. He'd set them in front of the woodstove to warm up last night; the secret was to never dry them out completely or they'd turn stiff as rawhide. Could use a new pair, but it would be cheaper to get them re-spiked.

In his mind, he'd been chipping away at Jim Mueller's price since he'd named it, the notion foolish but irresistible. Timber was a young man's game. At fifty-three, Rich had already outlived every Gundersen on record. Yesterday, Chub dozing against his back, a warm weight, he'd felt a surge of hope so alarming it had taken a moment to realize nothing was physically wrong. Rich's mother had died in her sleep at thirty-six. Valve in her heart just gave out.

He climbed the second ridge and from there it was up, up, up the steep rise of 24-7 Ridge. It would take every cent he had. A hell of a risk on paper. But stopping to catch his breath and looking up at the old-growth redwoods near the spine, the tallest the 24-7 herself, three hundred and seventy feet if she was an inch—the worry evaporated. A monster, the tallest tree for miles, dwarfing even the giants of Damnation Grove. Goddamn, he could sing. Scout nosed his knee. Rich sniffed: wet wood, needles rotting to soil.

Smell that, old man? That's the smell of money.

Rich inhaled deeper. He'd never have to work another day for Merle Sanderson, as he had for Virgil Sanderson before him, as Rich's father had worked for George and his granddad for Victor, all the way back for as long as men had felled redwoods.

The one time Rich remembered his dad taking him up here, his dad had stopped at about this spot, hitched a boot up on a fallen limb. *There she is. Twenty-four feet, seven inches across. Someday, you and me are going to fall that tree.* His dad had just turned thirty, but they'd lived harder and faster in those days, smoked, chewed, drank like mules. When they'd gotten up to the 24-7, his dad had pressed a palm to her bark: fireproof, a foot thick. A week later, he'd be dead, but that day he'd looked out over the ridges, dark with timber, one behind the other like waves in the ocean, breathed it all in. *Someday.* That breath swelled in Rich's chest now. His whole life he'd wanted her, and here she was.

Jim Mueller was right. Sanderson would have to run roads down into Lower Damnation Grove, if not to the creek itself, then close enough to spit across at the foot of 24-7 Ridge. All Rich would need to do is lay the big pumpkin down and truck her out. That, plus the two hundred other redwoods—close to a hundred million board feet, grand total. Even after the equipment, the crew, the mill taking its cut, it'd be twenty years' salary for a few months' work. Pay the land off free and clear. Rest would be gravy.

Forget her nails, Colleen would bite her fingers off to the first knuckle if he told her he was even thinking about it. Seven hundred and twenty acres. His dad had worked six days a week from thirteen until the day he died and never owned more than a damn truck.

Rich sidestepped down the ridge to Damnation Creek, low this time of year. He cleaned a few dead leaves out of the screen catch at the mouth of their water line, snuffed his nose on his arm, slicker spreading the wet around. He whistled for Scout, sweating by the time the yellow square of kitchen window finally reappeared below like a beacon. Winded, he stopped to catch his breath. Something glinted under the sweep of his headlamp. He stooped, picked it up: a red pinwheel mint in a clear plastic wrapper. Scout butted his leg, looking for an ear rub.

Come here, you mutt.

Down in the yard, he hooked Scout back onto his chain, got his caulks off before the pegs driven through the soles for traction tore the hell out of the kitchen linoleum. Inside, Colleen turned bacon with a fork.

"Smells good." He draped his wet socks over the handle of the woodstove and padded down the hall for dry ones, the red tail of Chub's rocket night-light glowing in the morning dark.

Colleen set his plate on the table, eggs steaming.

"I might stop by and see Lark after work," he said, testing it out. It didn't sound untruthful. He tucked into his eggs so he wouldn't have to look her in the eye. He rarely lied to her, usually only to play down an injury.

"Should I pack him something?" she asked.

"Nah, I'll stop at the Only." His back tooth throbbed with the coffee's heat. He pressed his tongue to it, mopped up the last of the yolk, brought his plate to the sink, lifted his slicker off the hook—rain puddled on the linoleum below—and grabbed his thermos and lunch pail. Colleen turned the lamp on so he could see to fish his keys from the burl bowl, half-filled with the pea-sized beach agates she collected, bright as candies.

"Gloves?" she asked.

"In the truck."

When they were first married, she would inspect his body at night, feeling along his neck, his ribs, his abdomen, until his heart was pounding. When she found a new scrape, a bump or a scab, she'd cup her hand over it, as though it were an insect she'd trapped there.

Now she pecked him on the cheek—*I choose you*—in a better mood since she'd started helping out the Larson girl, pregnant again, and still too poor for a hospital birth. It had taken her mind off it, finally.

"Want anything from the store?" she asked. "I have to take Enid down to the clinic. The kids need their shot cards before school starts."

"She can't drive herself?" he asked, pinching a toothpick from his front pocket.

Colleen shrugged, Enid more her child than her sister. She stood out front, hugging herself for warmth, watched him climb into his truck. Over her shoulder, the wooden plaque he'd carved and mounted on the door shone with mist. HOME IS WHERE THE ♥ IS.

"Be careful," she called.

His denims were cut off two inches above his ankles to keep a Cat tire from catching the hem and pulling him under, mashing him like a potato. But there were a hundred other ways to die in the woods. He'd seen a three-thousand-pound haul block land on a man's chest, choker chains snap and send logs as big as school buses bouncing downslope, felt their shadows pass overhead when he dove below an old stump for cover.

*Don't ever leave the house without kissing that woman goodbye*, Lark had said, knotting Rich's tie tight enough to hang him, on his wedding day, advice tinged with his own regret.

Rich thumbed the blower on full blast and cracked his window down a half inch. Rain tapped the hood. Up valley roads, across creeks, in town and the glen, men walked through this rain to their trucks, wives looking up from the dishes, pausing the length of a prayer. *Be careful.* What besides prayers kept any of them alive? Luck, the steady hands and quick judgment of men he'd known all his life, men who swung an arm up over the seat back, reversing down their driveways as Rich did now, fog eddying in his wake, rain-beaten yard sign listing below the weeping willow:

THIS FAMILY SUPPORTED BY TIMBER DOLLARS.

# COLLEEN

The rifle wasn't the first thing she noticed when she bounced down Enid's muddy driveway. What she noticed was Tice Whelan's tow truck, gleaming black with its bright blue hook. She set the parking brake, Chub's cue to undo his seat belt, and before she could register the rifle Enid held loosely at her side, a crutch too short to lean on, Chub was scampering across the yard, hopping the creek, and disappearing up the steps into the trailer house.

Growing up past the last telephone pole, Enid had always sworn she'd move down south, beyond where the redwood curtain parted, someplace you could buy a hot dog on the street at midnight or one of those big doughy pretzels that looked like it should hang on a door like a Christmas wreath. But here she was, way out Lost Road. She had a telephone that worked half the time, when she paid the bill and a tree hadn't fallen on the line, but otherwise it was about as far from San Francisco as you could get.

Tice Whelan didn't appear to have noticed the rifle yet either. He crouched, fitting a tow trap around the front wheel of her sister's new Wagoneer—red with veneered side panels.

"You're making us late," Colleen said, as though Enid could hear her through the windshield. The runaway roses were blooming, pulling down the fence meant to pen the climbing goats, who balanced in the branches of their tree, watching Tice Whelan work. Colleen's mother's old Mercury was a mound of blackberry brambles, unrecognizable except for a side mirror that hung limply, like the fin of a lethargic fish. She knew she should get out of the truck before Enid did something stupid, but first she wanted an apology.

They'd agreed to meet at the Beehive, but this morning Colleen had found the gravel lot empty except for the sweet scent of the blackberry bear claws Dot pulled from the bakery's oven. Colleen had even gone inside to check.

"Sorry, hon, haven't seen her. You want some coffee while you wait?" Dot had asked, circles of rouge making her look like an overheated doll in her sequined sweater, her hair a platinum beehive. She'd been a beauty queen young. Ms. Sanderson Timber. Ms. Del Nort County. Ms. Redwood Country. *Sweet as sugar and slower than molasses*, Colleen's mom used to say.

Next, Colleen had driven up to the turnout where Mill Road met the highway—the way Enid would have to come. She'd left a hole in her crossword, clue stuck like a kernel in her teeth. *Desires.* Four letters. Loves, wants, needs—she couldn't make anything fit. She'd picked at it the whole way, past Rich's pickup lined up in the mill lot with the others; out No Name Road, gravel popping against the truck's underbelly; past Damnation Grove; and down the steep hump onto Lost Road. And now here was her sister, holding the repo man at gunpoint.

Colleen sighed. Getting upset at Enid wouldn't change her. She closed her eyes, wishing she could open them and see the yard tidy. No Tice. No tow truck.

Enid raised the rifle—thirty-one years old and still, here was Colleen, trying to keep trouble from crashing down around her little sister. Colleen climbed out.

"Hi, Tice," she said.

"Don't talk to him," Enid snapped.

The Whelan twins were identical, down to the rattail Tice wore at the back of his shaggy hair, but Colleen could tell him apart from Lyle, who worked as a bucker on Rich's logging crew, by the topless mermaid tattooed on his neck. The only marks Rich had on his body were scars, decades' worth of nicks and gashes, hard white lines of healed skin like the skeleton of a fish on the inside of his forearm, where he'd been cut to the bone as a teenager, sewn up, and sent right back out to work.

"Take those things off," Enid ordered Tice, who was already securing the second trap. Enid's blue eyes flashed, her eyeliner making her short white-blond hair, long behind the ears, appear even whiter. Pretty, even in one of Eugene's old undershirts, still heavy around the midsection, baby weight left over from carrying Alsea.

"Enid—"

"Stay out of it, Colleen. I mailed the check."

Tice Whelan went around the other side of the Wagoneer.

"Whelan, I swear to God."

Colleen felt the slide of the bolt in her chest.

"Don't make me shoot you between your damn eyes," Enid threatened.

"You going to load that thing first?" Tice asked.

Enid checked the empty chamber, choked up on the barrel, and started toward him.

"I'll bash your skull in and eat your brain with a spoon."

Tice backed up. He was used to having guns pointed at him, but the stock was oak, and though he was missing an eyetooth, he still had a good straight nose.

"Enid," Colleen said.

"Over my dead body you're taking this thing. You have any idea what it's like to live out here with six kids? It's not called Lost Road for nothing. Have You Lost Your Mind Road, more like."

Three of Enid's milk goats jumped down from their tree and loitered, chewing air, waiting for Tice Whelan's answer. One bleated. Another nosed his bootlaces. Colleen thought he would finish the job, but instead he kicked the goat away, crouched down, and pulled out a pin, undoing the trap he'd just secured.

"All right," Enid said, meaning thank you. A habit she'd inherited from their father, although only Colleen was old enough to remember it.

Back in his tow truck, Tice Whelan raised two fingers from the steering wheel. *See you next time.*

"Go screw yourself, Whelan!" Enid yelled, watching him pull away.

"'I'll eat your brain with a spoon'?" Colleen asked.

"He doesn't have enough brains to fill a spoon. What are you doing here?"

"The kids' shot cards, remember?"

"Oh shit, was that today?"

Enid hurried inside to get ready. Colleen peeked in the Wagoneer's windows: seats already stained, though the thing wasn't even four months old. Eugene had bought it after Rich got Colleen the fancy white crew cab— as if a truck could make it up to her—pulling the showy red thing to the curb when Enid came out with the new baby in her arms. He hadn't wanted to be one-upped.

"Out of gas," Enid called from the porch now. She traipsed across the yard to Colleen's truck, Alsea swaddled in a tight bundle.

Wyatt streaked out of the trailer house, Chub in pursuit.

"Chub! We're going!" Colleen called.

"Leave him, Marla'll watch them," Enid said.

Colleen began to count. By four, Chub appeared, flushed, breathless, one overall buckle undone. She reached to help him, but he twisted away, turning circles after the overall strap like a dog chasing its tail. He hauled the buckle over his shoulder and fastened it with a satisfying click. His cowlick fell into his eyes, growing faster than she could keep it trimmed. He grinned, proud of himself, eyes turning from green to blue, Rich's eyes set in a small, round face. He'd grown out of his pudge except for his cheeks, the doughboy dimples. Every night, after she switched on the rocket night-light, she pressed her thumbs into those dimples. *My cookie-boy. My sweet Grahamcracker.* She'd been trying to get him used to Graham in time to start school. Graham Gundersen, she'd printed on his registration form.

*All set?* Gail Porter had asked without looking up.

She'd been the secretary since Colleen was in school. That Colleen was thirty-four, with a child of her own, hadn't changed things. She was still afraid of Gail Porter, a stern, no-nonsense woman whose raised eyebrow could lower the temperature of a room.

Colleen had hesitated, drawn a little caret. "Chub," she'd inserted. Gail Porter had taken the form back without a hint of friendliness, though Don Porter was as much Rich's friend as his crew boss; they'd shared a table at the company picnic on the Fourth. Colleen wondered if it was still the age difference Gail Porter disapproved of. It bothered some women, especially women Rich's age.

*Tell Enid I'm not letting hers in the door without proof this year,* Gail Porter had said, handing back Chub's shot card.

*I will.* Colleen had offered a weak smile that Gail Porter registered but didn't return. In school, Colleen had always been "Enid's sister." As though she had no name of her own.

There must have been a time, when Enid first started kindergarten, Colleen already in the third grade, when it had been the other way around. But it wasn't long before Enid punched a boy in the stomach so hard he vomited;

threw wads of wet paper towels at the ceiling in the girls' bathroom, where they gunked and dried like the muddy nests of birds; ate a cricket on a dare. For years, through high school, Colleen had slouched in a slick yellow bucket seat outside the principal's smoked-glass door, the kind of chair it was impossible to sit up straight in, waiting while the principals—they changed every few years—paddled Enid. As though her sass could be dislodged. Colleen had flinched at the muffled thuds, but Enid never let out more than a grunt, the principals dog-panting. Mrs. Porter would scowl and Colleen would sit up, tugging her skirt down over her knees, as if her bad posture were the object of Gail Porter's disapproval.

Chub clicked his seat belt.

"Let's go," Enid said, cramming her nipple into Alsea's mouth. "You're making us late."

Colleen set the parking brake and looked up at the low brown building. She hadn't been inside the Mad River Clinic since her five-month checkup, before Easter.

"Let's get this over with," Enid said.

Inside, the linoleum was pocked from the men's caulk boots. Enid argued over their missed appointment, as if the receptionist were the one in the wrong, then joined Colleen and Chub to wait in the seats lining the wall. Sanderson didn't give insurance, but so long as somebody in your family had worked in the woods, the clinic took care of you for life, however long that was.

"Which one of Gail's bees flew up her ass anyway?" Enid complained, as though she hadn't lost the shot cards to begin with. "It's not like they're rabid."

A nurse came out, holding a chart. Colleen recognized her from last time.

"That baby's still not crying?" she asked Enid.

"I wish I'd had six of her," Enid answered.

"Every baby's a miracle," the nurse reminded her—their mother's old line.

Their mother had never wanted children. She'd told Colleen flat out, near the end.

A cross-stitch of the saying hung in the little room at the end of the clinic hallway. How many times had Colleen sat staring at it, onionskin covering the exam table sticking to her thighs, where the gown didn't meet in the back? EVERY BABY IS A MIRACLE. Somehow, when the door opened, it was always a surprise not to see her mother.

If Colleen had stayed pregnant this spring, she'd have been sitting there now, legs dangling beneath the swell of her belly, counting down the days until her due date—August 14. It still blinked like a light in her mind. Even the nurses—women trained to feel nothing—felt sorry for her. Colleen could tell by their phony brightness, the way they avoided her eyes. But even after the bleeding, after laboring to deliver a baby she knew would never breathe, after the steady stream of bills, the bitter glue on the envelope flap she licked closed with a check inside each month, a taste she associated now with the hospital—even after all that, Colleen still felt the longing for another baby, an ache lodged deep in her chest.

*Desires.* Yearns? No, too long.

The nurse sighed. "Bring her back for a minute."

Enid disappeared with Alsea.

"Was Aunt Enid really going to shoot him?" Chub asked, swinging his legs.

"Shoot who?"

"The tow-truck man."

It was a good question.

"No." Colleen licked her thumb and wiped a spot off his cheek.

Chub tipped his head away, eyes settling on the gum-ball machine, though he knew better than to ask. Watching him peeled back the layers on what Rich must have been like as a boy: gentle, quiet, a terrible sweet tooth.

The door that led to the exam rooms swung open and Helen Yancy shuffled out. Colleen hadn't seen her in months, hadn't even known she was expecting. Helen's pregnant belly jutted through her coat, her hands large and pink from cannery work, her hair pulled back in a thick black braid. Luke trailed behind her, still small for his age. He'd been born small, barely five pounds. Helen's great-grandmother had pressed a dark paste inside Helen's cheek and rubbed salve on her belly. Her great-grandmother had raised her and wouldn't set foot in a white man's hospital—she said they sewed Yurok women up inside so they couldn't have any more babies—

and Helen had refused to go without her. Her great-grandmother had sung prayers—a rhythmic singing the old woman carried on for hours without seeming to draw breath, her tattooed chin wrinkling in concentration. *Not prayers*, Helen had corrected Colleen, later. *Medicine. To make the baby come easy*, which Luke had, landing slick and furious in Colleen's hands as she knelt on a shower curtain spread out on the floor of Helen and Carl's bedroom, herself six months pregnant with Chub, stunned and grateful, holding the first baby she'd ever delivered.

"Go sit over there," Helen told Luke now.

Luke climbed up beside Chub and swung his legs.

"You're starting kindergarten pretty soon, aren't you, hon?" Colleen asked him. Marsha called everyone "hon" and the habit had rubbed off on Colleen when she'd worked in the mill's front office. Enid said hanging around old people made her act like one.

Luke nodded.

"You and Chub will be in the same class."

The nurse handed Helen some papers.

"Can you do immunization records for the DeWitt kids?" the receptionist asked the nurse.

"Again?"

The receptionist shrugged. "She lost them."

The nurse sighed and accepted Enid's thick file—six kids' worth of earaches and broken bones, chicken pox and strep throat. Colleen pictured her own file: a thin catalog of disappointments. No, she shouldn't say that. Here was Chub, swinging his legs beside Luke.

"Luke, let's go," Helen said. Her eyes were red-rimmed. She gave Colleen a quick nod.

"Congratulations," Colleen offered. They'd been close, drifting apart after the boys were born. She thought Helen might offer her condolences, or some explanation—*I heard what happened, I wasn't sure you'd be up for it*. Colleen had delivered Luke just fine, hadn't she? Why wouldn't Helen want her there for her second? But Helen only touched her belly, as though worried Colleen's bad luck might rub off on her, and pushed out the double doors into the drizzle.

"Next time we're going to charge you," the nurse warned Enid, handing her the new cards.

"All right." Enid tucked them into her purse. "Is it true that baby came out with no brain?" she asked the nurse.

*Enid.* Colleen wanted to shush her.

"What's her name? Married one of the Cooney boys." Enid looked to Colleen for help, snapped her fingers to spark the name. "Beth."

The nurse gave Enid a stern look. "They still making noise up by you?" the nurse asked.

Hippies had been hitchhiking up from Arcata to protest the logging. Humboldt State was infected with them. A few weeks ago, they'd blocked No Name Road again, and Rich hadn't gotten home until dark.

"Can't mow your lawn without somebody showing up to protest," Enid said. "What do they wipe their butts with? That's what I'd like to know."

"Somebody ought to tell them trees grow back," the nurse agreed.

"Okay." Enid climbed into the front seat. "That's done." She adjusted the baby's swaddle. "Remind me to make Eugene sleep in another room from now on. Six is enough."

"The gown's almost finished," Colleen offered, to change the subject.

A pastor was coming down from Crescent City for Alsea's baptism in two weeks. There hadn't been a regular pastor in Klamath in years. People saved their gossip, their bolo ties and pearl-button dresses, for the Sanderson fish fries, free for employees, fifty cents for their families, all you could eat, every other Sunday. Alsea—still an effort to think of the baby by name. With Enid's kids, the baby had always stayed *the baby* until the next one came along, though Enid swore this was the last. Alsea, for the town in Oregon where Eugene had grown up—he'd finally run out of great-aunts to name her after.

"Why bother?" Enid yawned. "I've still got Mavis's lying around somewhere."

"Every baby is a miracle," Colleen said.

"Yeah. Right. Tell that to my tits. Down to my knees. You should sew me a bra. Or get Rich to carve me one, that's about what it would take."

"I'll bring it by," Colleen said. "I just have the roses around the neckline to do."

"All right."

The truck climbed into the bends, fog drifting up from the ocean and across the road like smoke. The radio dissolved into static. Chub slept, then Enid, breath ruffling in her nose. Colleen gripped the wheel. Finally, the sign emerged from the fog—WELCOME TO TIMBER COUNTRY—then the two gold bears, guarding the bridge.

*August 12*

# RICH

Rich hunched at the service-station pay phone, still in his work clothes. He dug the worn paper coaster Jim Mueller had given him from his pocket, thumbed a dime into the slot, hung up the receiver. He took a step back, palms sweating, and toed the ground. Finally, he thumbed the coin into the slot again and dialed.

"I'll meet you there," Jim Mueller said.

"Now?" Rich asked, chill seeping into the sweat-damp folds of his shirt.

"Half hour," Jim Mueller said, and hung up before Rich could change his mind.

Rich's hands buzzed with nerves by the time he pulled open the door to the savings and loan. The air was stale and musty. In the indoor quiet, he was suddenly aware of his odor, the mix of sweat and gasoline, the sweet nip of sawdust. He hadn't set foot in this place in years. Colleen deposited his paychecks; all he did was run through the account statements at the end of the month.

"Mr. Gundersen?" a man asked. He was short and stocky. He held out a hand hesitantly, as though wary of Rich's size. "We spoke on the phone the other day," the man said, to jog Rich's memory. Rich had pictured the loan officer older, in a suit and tie. This guy was in shirtsleeves. "We've got all the paperwork ready for you."

Jim Mueller sat with his back to the door. He nodded in greeting when the loan officer led Rich into his office and plopped down behind the desk.

"Mr. Mueller has already signed," he said. "All we need now is your John Hancock."

Jim Mueller slid the stack of papers toward Rich. Rich felt his front pocket for his cheaters but found only a stray toothpick. Here and there, a word jumped out: his full name, *24-7 Ridge Inholding, $250,000, interest rate 8.96 percent.*

Rich swallowed, rubbed his sweaty palms over his knees, denims rough, oil-stained.

"How much would I need to put down again?" Rich asked.

"Mr. Mueller, would you give us a minute?" the loan officer asked.

Jim Mueller grunted and got up.

The loan officer laid out Rich's accounts, as he'd done on the phone.

"That would leave you twenty-five hundred dollars in savings, after closing costs and the down payment," he explained.

That wasn't much of a buffer, with a $2,102.10 loan payment to make every month.

"What about the house?" Rich asked. "Could I use that as collateral and put less down?"

The loan officer shook his head, coughed, turned to the side to clear his throat. "No. Not with the park—" He paused, choosing his next word carefully. "Situation."

"I still own the place, don't I?"

"You were part of the legislative takings?" the man asked, as if Rich had had some choice in the matter. What he'd had was the bad luck of owning twenty acres in one of the slender necks of land Congress decided to use to string together a few state parks along the coast. People down in Humboldt got the worst of the takings, the body of the upside-down seahorse of land that became the national park. The Del Nort County piece was just a skinny tail of state parks, hugging the coast, Rich's house smack-dab in the middle of it. "What you have is more like a lease," the man explained. "They bought you out in '68? So, twenty-five years," the man calculated, "what's that, 1993?"

"Or until we die," Rich said. "We can stay in the house until we die. My wife's younger."

The loan officer nodded, like he was accustomed to people coming face-to-face with their own mortality on the other side of his desk.

"You have to own an asset to use it as collateral," he explained. "Excuse me a moment."

Jim Mueller came back in and sat heavily. In his mind, Rich saw Colleen watching him back down the driveway this morning. *Be careful.* His whole life, he had been.

"Got to take a risk sometime," Jim Mueller said, as though Rich had spoken the thought aloud.

The pen weighed ten pounds in his hand. Rich swallowed. Saliva refilled his mouth. The loan officer returned just as he was initialing the last page. Hard to believe a quarter-million bucks fit in a contract lighter than a pack of cigarettes.

"No reason to clear-cut," Jim Mueller said, chatty now that the contract was signed. "Once Sanderson clears the lower half of Damnation out of your way, go easy. Cut forty percent, let the rest grow. Your kid'll sit on the porch someday, watching your great-grandkids harvest."

"Used to be talking like that could get you killed," Rich said. Look what had happened to Lark, for preaching sustained yield—not cutting faster than the forest could grow back. It was just a hop, skip, and a jump from there to a union, pensions, vacation pay. Sanderson could smell a unionizer a mile off, snuffed that fire before it sparked.

Jim Mueller smoothed a palm across the desk, as though to wipe away Lark's whole sorry history.

"You're going to make a goddamn fortune," he said with a note of regret. "Well, you Gundersens have been lusting after that ridge for eighty years. Hank'd be proud as hell that one of you monkeys finally owns it." He stuck out a hand and Rich shook it. The loan officer walked Jim Mueller out. Left alone, Rich stared at the lacquered burl clock behind the desk. The whole transaction had taken less than forty minutes.

The loan officer came back with some dates—first payment due in October. Rich scribbled out the post office box number and handed it to him.

"What's this?" the man asked.

"Mailing address."

Colleen took care of the bills, wrote the checks, licked the stamps. He didn't want her finding out like that. He would tell her his own way, as soon as he got the details hammered out.

It was a relief to push out of the lobby into the early-evening air, rain freckling his face. Rich folded the documents into thirds, leaned across the truck's bench seat, and popped the plastic bottom out of the glove box. He picked up the key to the post office box he'd rented last week from Geraldine, silent and unfriendly, and, for those reasons, trustworthy. He weighed it in his hand, then tucked the papers into the secret space underneath, dropped the key in on top, and pressed the plastic back into place.

# COLLEEN

She walked Chub to the drugstore's toy aisle and took her list from her pocketbook.

"You stay right here, okay?"

Chub nodded, not taking his eyes off the rack of sixty-nine-cent Matchbox cars, his nose nearly touching the tiny hot rods. He was allowed to choose one.

"Look with your eyes, not with your hands," Colleen reminded him.

She picked up a quart of peroxide, Chub's wart ointment, Rich's foot cream, a box of sourdough pretzels, vitamin E. Rich had had the itch twice this season, a scaly mother patch on his rib cage that spread like beastly hickeys across his chest and arms and lasted six weeks: sweated-through clothes, rubbing for hours, that's what caused it. There was no cure, but vitamin E helped. She picked up cotton balls and rubbing alcohol, latex gloves, a shower-curtain liner, all the things she would need for Melody Larson's birth. She pushed the thought of her own due date from her mind.

"Colleen?"

She looked up. A man stood in front of her: pencil tucked above his ear, long dark hair, confident and upright, a half inch shorter than she.

"Daniel?"

As soon as she said it, she wanted to snatch the name back, as if she'd conjured him from the thin air of the past. He took her cold hands in his and squeezed. Her wedding band pressed into her flesh.

"Still freezing," he noted, reaching jokingly for the pad in his front pocket, as though to record the observation, and revealing the gap between his front teeth, wide enough to feed a coin through. She felt the strange urge to press the pad of her thumb to it, the way she once had.

"What are you doing here?" she asked instead.

"A little of this, a little of that." Daniel's eyes flashed. "Fish work, mostly."

"Guiding or gutting?"

Daniel chuckled—as if he'd run tourists or clocked in at the cannery like anybody else. "Both, I guess. Mostly catch-and-release. Depends on the study," he said. He'd been in his second year at Humboldt State when she'd seen him last, the only kid from their high school to go on to college. "It's good to see you." He cupped his hand to the back of his neck, as though trying to recall how many years it had been. Sixteen.

"What are you studying?" she asked, swallowing the bitter taste in her mouth. School had always come first for him.

"Water quality, silt load."

She heard it still, his refusal to dumb himself down. In a school full of Bills and Chucks, he'd never been Dan or Dan-O or Danny, always Daniel. "Even with the hatcheries, the coho run's down to almost nothing," he said. "And the chinook runs keep getting smaller. Every year." Daniel dropped his eyes. "I see what it's doing to my uncle. He's been fishing since he was nine years old—everything he has, it comes from the river. Not just him, the whole community. It's making people sick," he confided, quieter now. "It's not just food. It's not just a livelihood. It's our whole life, our whole identity, as far back as anyone can remember, you know?" His voice strained. "We can't be Yuroks, without salmon. And the water . . ." He shook his head.

"What's wrong with the water?" Colleen asked. She'd leaned in closer to hear, and smelled mint.

"Well, there's not enough of it, for one," Daniel said, as though this much was obvious. "All the ag upriver, and the dams—those warm-water releases are just cooking the salmon right there in the river. And then there's the runoff issue. What logging has done around here—you wouldn't believe what some of these drainages look like—no shade left, silt so thick the creeks are hot enough to take a bath in. And the contaminant levels—"

He went on, casting his eyes around the aisle as he talked, as though searching the shelves for items to offer her by way of explanation. She struggled to concentrate, to follow the tight turns of his sentences. Standing so close, his presence sent a tingle of electric current across her skin.

"We'll see what the fall run looks like, I guess. I'll tell you, I wouldn't be drinking out of those creeks anymore," he said finally. "It's not like when we were kids. But people don't worry about what they can't see, right?"

She nodded, though she'd been tuning in and out, only half listening.

"You're still living up in Klamath?" he asked.

Colleen felt the accusation underneath: *What happened to getting out of there?*

"North of town," she said. "Damnation Creek."

"Really?" His eyes widened a little. Or maybe she'd imagined it.

"Arcata——" she fumbled. "This just wasn't for me." As if those five months— her tiny desk at the real estate office, the water dispenser gurgling digestively, the rented room with the cramped twin bed whose springs squeaked so loudly she and Daniel had moved to the floor so her landlady wouldn't hear—were simply a shoe she'd tried on. "I was never—smart." At school, boys had baited him— *If you're so smart, how come you don't teach your uncle how to steal fish without get- ting caught?*—shoved him against walls, bloodied his nose when he fought back, and still, nine times out of ten it was Daniel the principal had paddled so hard he couldn't sit down. Colleen had once heard a teacher explain they had to beat Yurok kids like Daniel harder because their skin was tougher; they didn't feel it the same.

Daniel hummed in the awkward silence, the three short notes that indicated his mind was wandering off down a track she could not follow.

"How about you?" she asked, calling him back.

"I've been working up in Canada—BC. Salmon research. I got some funding to come down here for the year." Lines puckered in his forehead, as though there was more to the story. "With my uncle and everything—it just felt like a good time to come home, you know?"

She searched his eyes for a glint of the old anger. *I'm never going back there.* But it was gone. His uncle had been arrested dozens of times for gillnet- ting on the river, back when it was banned. But the Yurok had taken their case all the way to the Supreme Court and won. She'd seen his uncle in the paper when the decision finally came down a few years back: Yuroks had fished the river since time began, and they had the right to keep fishing, forty-five miles in from the ocean, plus up the creeks a mile on either side—the whole reservation—no matter what the state said. Colleen had had the map of it drilled into her head by every pissed-off weekend fisherman who sat down next to them at a Sanderson fish fry, hands tied behind his back by the state of California while Yuroks hauled out salmon the size of dogs. Rich seemed to think it was fair, but now you saw bumper stickers in town: SAVE A FISH, CAN AN INDIAN.

"How long have you been back?" she asked.

"A couple months," Daniel admitted. "I'm glad I ran into you. Actually, I wanted to ask—" He looked a little sheepish. "I probably should have asked you a long time ago—"

"Mrs. Gundersen?" Melody Larson came up the aisle, her two-year-old on her hip. "Guess what?" She grabbed Colleen's free hand and pressed it to the taut skin of her belly, low down, until Colleen felt the baby's head. "Feel him?" She grinned. She was only twenty-three, but there were crow's feet at the corners of her eyes. "It worked. Those exercises." She turned to Daniel. "She made my baby do a somersault," she explained. "Saved me from a C-section."

Colleen felt her face color.

"She delivered this one in four hours." Melody Larson bounced the girl in her arms. "I'm going to have this guy in three."

"I'll come by again on Wednesday," Colleen promised, anxious for her to leave.

"It's a date," Melody Larson said, and bustled down the aisle, leaving them alone.

"How long have you been a midwife?" Daniel asked, a word she never used herself.

"I'm not. I'm not trained or anything. I just kind of—you know. You do it once and word gets around. You know how this town is."

"I thought blood made you sick," he teased, and suddenly she was back at the movie theater in Arcata.

She blushed deeper. "I learned how not to let it."

He pushed air out his nose. "Good memory." His eyes dropped into her basket, then met hers with a flicker of playfulness too intimate for the bleached light of the aisle. "You know those pretzels taste like nothing, right?" He had a way of asking questions that made her feel both important—his attention so entirely on her—and stupid.

"They don't taste like nothing," she said. "They taste like cardboard." He laughed. A rush of warmth in her abdomen, the pleasure of making him laugh. "My husband likes them," she added.

"Ah." Daniel nodded. She was a married woman. Her pretzels were none of his business.

"Mama?" Chub stood at the end of the aisle, watching them, Matchbox car in hand.

She stepped back. Daniel cleared his throat.

"Did you pick one?" she asked Chub. "Let's see." She held out her hand to accept the baby-blue pickup, Rich's Ford in miniature, and her purse slid off her shoulder, something skittering across the floor.

Daniel retrieved the fallen earring: a garnet teardrop set in gold. Rich had given them to her in the hospital, as if the new truck already waiting outside weren't enough. All summer they'd been tucked into the side pocket of her purse, where she wouldn't have to look at them.

"Pretty," Daniel said, then glanced at her ears. "You should get them pierced."

She held out her hand and he dropped it in.

"Thank you." She took Chub by the hand. "Good luck with your research."

Daniel gave his old salute. Silly now, to think how it had once made her heart flutter.

"Who was that?" Chub asked as she unloaded her items at the register.

"Just a boy I went to school with," Colleen said, aware that Daniel was still behind them somewhere. She hoped the cashier hadn't overheard them talking. Gossip traveled quicker than water, ran through the creeks, out people's faucets into their coffee mugs. Colleen had to start over twice, counting change into the woman's waiting hand.

In the parking lot, she dug in the side pocket of her purse for her keys and felt the sharp backs of the earrings. She'd been meaning to take them to the jeweler to have them changed to clip-ons, but now she drove down to the town square instead. Chub played with his new pickup while the woman dabbed Colleen's ears with rubbing alcohol.

"These'll work," the woman said, examining the garnet studs, then loading them into the piercing gun. Colleen flinched when its cold nose grazed her ear.

"Fear's worse than the pain," the woman said.

Colleen felt her own power, sitting so still with a weapon so near. How long had it been since she'd done anything on impulse?

"Does it hurt?" Chub asked when they got back in the truck.

"No," she lied.

Her ears throbbed in time with her heartbeat. She tilted the rearview mirror to peek at them. They were pink and swollen, but Daniel was right: she felt pretty.

Colleen leveled the cup of flour with a knife and dumped it into the bowl. Rich came in the front door, already dusk in the yard.

"What took you so long?" she called.

"Stopped off to see Lark."

"How is he?"

"Still kicking." Rich came into the kitchen. "What are you making?"

"Lemon loaf. Chub and I ate. Your plate is in the oven."

"Let me get washed up."

Chub came running down the hall, catapulting himself into Rich's arms. Rich grunted.

She rechecked the recipe, though she made it almost every week—lemon was Rich's favorite. Enid grabbed handfuls of flour, ran the faucet straight into the bowl when the milk ran out, but Colleen did things by the book. She cracked two eggs, pinched her sore ears.

Rich came in after a few minutes, toweling off his hair as she stood mashing the lemon into the hand-juicer. He pulled her hair back and kissed her there, in the old spot behind her ear. She tensed, waiting for him to notice the earrings, but he was already opening the oven door.

"How was your day?" he asked, pulling out his plate.

"Fine." Acid juice marbled the batter. "We went down to Arcata. I got you more vitamin E."

He tucked in. She greased a pan, turned the oven up. Rich brought his empty plate to the sink. She gathered up the mixing bowl, the dirty whisk and measuring cups, and bumped him once with her hip. He shook water off his hands.

She finished the dishes, got Chub ready for bed, turned on his rocket night-light.

"Good night, cookie-boy." She pressed her thumbs into his dimples. "Good night, my sweet Grahamcracker." Chub yawned and snuggled in, rubbing the blanket's satin edge under his nose.

When she came out, Rich was on the couch, thumbing through a lumber catalog.

"You didn't notice anything different about me?" she hinted.

"What?" Rich asked.

She straddled his lap, the couch's old springs complaining. He leaned back to get a better look at her. It took him a moment.

"They hurt?" he asked, frowning.

She nodded. She wanted to tell him about Daniel. How he'd recognized her, after all these years. The first boy she'd ever kissed. The only one, not counting Rich. She waited for him to tell her she looked pretty.

"How'd a nice girl like you end up in a place like this?" Rich asked, tucking her hair behind her ear. Her heart skipped. Rich groaned, as if the weight of her bothered his back. "I'm beat." He yawned and patted her thigh, the way he patted Scout to let him know that was the end of the ear rub.

She'd shed the plumpness of pregnancy, but it had left behind cellulite dimpling the backs of her thighs, a stubborn handful of loose flesh at her belly. It brought tears to her eyes when she pinched it, this sad little roll of fat and skin, and no living baby to show for it. Maybe it was this new softness in her body that had made Rich start coming home late—he got off at five thirty, he should have been home by six—turning his back on her in bed, too tired to make love. He waited for her to swing her leg off and stood.

"Are you not attracted to me anymore?" she asked, Rich already halfway down the hall.

"Am I what?" he asked, tilting his head, waiting for her to repeat it.

His hearing was going, especially in that right ear, his saw ear, thirty-five years in the woods slowly lowering the volume knob on the world around him. She felt a wash of shame.

"Nothing," she said.

# *August 14*

# RICH

"Don't be long," Colleen warned Rich as he ducked out the kitchen door after Chub. "I'm making pancakes."

The baby had been due today. She'd kept herself busy all morning, hadn't mentioned it. He'd almost wondered if she'd forgotten, but now he heard the quiet plea in her voice. *Don't leave me alone here, Rich.*

"We'll be right back," he promised.

Rich let Scout off his chain and up the hill they went, Chub riding piggy-back, spurring him with his heels, giant sword ferns swishing in their wake.

"What creek is this?" Rich asked, splashing through the first crossing.

"Little Lost."

"You're sure it's not A Lot Lost?" Rich teased.

They crested the no-name ridges, then headed up 24-7 Ridge, steep as climbing stairs.

"There she is," Rich said as the big tree came into view. His heart surged. He'd forgotten how good it felt to have a secret. One minute he wanted to shout it at the top of his lungs, the next he was guarding it like a damn china egg. The 24-7. All his life she'd sat on a shelf in his mind like a trophy. Now she was his, and nobody knew it yet.

Rich let Chub slide down and sat back against the tree's rough bark. Scout threw himself to the ground, panting. Chub dragged an arm along the 24-7's girth, circled her, came around the other side, and climbed into Rich's lap.

"How do you cut a tree?" Chub asked.

"It takes a whole crew," Rich said, thumping a stab of heartburn—equal parts hope and worry—loose with his fist.

"But how?" Chub banged his head back against Rich's chest and looked up.

"I'll show you, when the time comes," Rich said. "You know your great-great-granddad Gundersen was a sailor before he was a tree-topper? They sent a bunch of sailors into the woods, so what do you think they did? They used the same pulleys they used to load cargo onto ships, and a high-climber to hang them. That's where high-lead logging came from. Your great-great-granddad taught your great-granddad to high-climb, and your great-granddad taught your granddad—my dad."

"And he taught you," Chub finished.

"Lark taught me."

"What about me?" Chub asked.

"What about you?" Rich tickled him.

"Stop!" Chub shrieked, grabbing his hands.

They'd cut Damnation Grove, upper and lower, the last of Sanderson's major old-growth holdings. Once that was out of the way, Rich would harvest the big pumpkins off the 24-7. The real timber would be gone by the time Chub was old enough to lift a chainsaw. Rich didn't like the idea of Chub logging anyhow. Too many ways to die. Chub's life would be different, with the money from the 24-7. Rich would be the last Gundersen to work in the woods.

"Let's go, Grahamcracker. Pancakes are getting cold." Rich lifted Chub by the armpits, setting him upright. "Which way home?"

Chub pointed.

"Good. Lead the way."

Scout ran ahead. Chub hummed, the same tune Colleen had been carrying on her breath all morning. Sounded familiar.

"What song is that?" Rich asked.

Chub shrugged and kept going.

It wasn't until they were on their way down the hill, almost to the backyard, that Rich recalled it.

*Hush, little baby, don't say a word.*

Colleen used to sing it to comfort Chub as a newborn. Rich hooked Scout's collar to his chain.

"Who's a good boy?" Chub asked, scratching Scout's ticklish spot. Scout flopped over, foot thumping in surrender.

At the kitchen door, Rich stopped, hand on the knob, watching Colleen through the glass. Her ears were still pink. He couldn't help but feel responsible: another hurt he'd caused. After they'd taken the baby away and told Colleen to rest, he'd walked, numb, along the hallways until he stood staring at the earrings in the window of the hospital gift shop.

*I guess I'll get my ears pierced*, she'd said when she opened the gray velvet box.

He'd seen her wear earrings, never occurred to him to turn one over. Earring's an earring.

Now he watched her pour batter into the pan. Seven hundred and twenty acres. Don't tell her. Not yet. Wait. Time it right. He inhaled, turned the knob, and pushed in.

"Smells good," he said.

She wiped the back of her hand across her cheeks, eyes red-rimmed. He'd interrupted her humming again.

# COLLEEN

From a distance, the crowd ahead looked like it was celebrating, gathered at the Mill Road turnoff, blocking the way to the community center. Rich tapped the pocket of his pearl-snap shirt, the shirt she ironed before every fish fry, to reassure himself his toothpicks were in it. His truck window was cracked for air, even in the rain. Through the half-inch gap came chanting.

"What is it?" Chub asked from the backseat.

Rich slowed to a stop, his turn signal ticking, windshield wipers clearing the view of the protesters, arms linked, four deep across the road: a bearded man in a tie-dyed bandana, a woman in an old surplus army jacket. Colleen flushed, realizing she was scanning the crowd for Daniel. All day, every time she'd thought of the baby, she'd forced her mind down a chute toward him instead.

They were close enough to read the signs: A painted planet Earth: LOVE YOUR MOTHER. Trees: LUNGS OF THE PLANET. A lone redwood: I WAS HERE BEFORE COLUMBUS.

"Stop sacrificing virgins!" they chanted. "Save Damnation Grove!"

Colleen clucked her tongue. "When are they going to give up?"

"What are they doing?" Chub asked from the backseat.

"Nothing," she and Rich answered together.

Chub had fussed when she'd dressed him in his yellow button-up shirt, complained the cuffs felt tight, but now he was leaning forward, straining against his seat belt. A truck pulled up behind them and honked. Rich checked the rearview.

"Don't get between Don and a free dinner," Rich said.

"Are they going to move?" Colleen whispered.

"I guess we'll find out."

Rich popped the clutch and the truck rolled toward the crowd.

"Rich—"

The protesters dropped their arms and parted, chanting louder. Colleen felt the urge to slide down in her seat.

Don Porter stood in the gravel lot with his thumbs hooked through his suspenders, watching the crowd block another truck.

"Remember when those tree huggers from the League used to come around offering to buy up timber to keep us from logging it?" he asked Rich when they got out. "'Save the Redwoods.' Those were the days. These jokers don't want to buy shit. They just want to shut us down."

"Somebody better call Harvey," Gail Porter said.

"What do they want to do with it anyway?" Colleen asked.

"Thirteen hundred acres of virgin redwood?" Don scoffed. "Not a damn thing. They had their way, the whole coast would be one big tree museum. They care more about trees than people."

Chub scampered toward the building, eager to see his cousins. A truck laid on its horn, blaring through the chanting.

*Stop sacrificing virgins! Save Damnation Grove!*

"You coming?" Rich asked Colleen, holding open the rec-room door.

Inside, cafeteria tables were arranged in rows, a line already snaking around the buffet.

"There you are," Marsha said as they signed in at the registration table. "Did you see those clowns out front?" Marsha rolled her eyes, tore three raffle tickets off the wheel, and handed them to Colleen. Marsha still worked in the mill's front office. She sent the crosswords from Merle's newspapers home with Rich for her on paydays, though Colleen had quit working before Chub was born.

Colleen watched Chub lead Rich across the room to where Enid, Eugene, and the kids took up a whole table. *I should be in labor right now. I should be flat on my back in a hospital bed. No. Think of something else.* She searched for a distraction—Daniel in the drugstore, going on about his research, the warmth in his eyes, the hint of possibility. More of his words came back to her.

*People think it's just about trees, or it's just about fish. By the time they realize it's about them, it's too late, you know?*

"We'll see who wins this thing," Marsha said.

Colleen looked at her, then down at the three blue paper tickets in her own hand.

*August 15*

# RICH

They stood on the road at the base of upper Damnation Grove while Don laid out the day's work and introduced the new guys.

"Everybody, you know Owen."

Merle's cousin's son from up in Chehalis. The kid had Merle's bull head and bulky shoulders, a top-heavy torso on bowed chicken legs: one hell of a resemblance. There'd been talk. But if the boy really was Merle's, he wouldn't have sent him to work in the woods, not if he cared two shits about him.

"Owen's going to run Cat for us," Don said.

The Sanderson kid puffed up his chest, cheek bruised from brawling with last night's protesters.

"And this here is Quentin Feeley, Tom's son." Don nodded at the tall, skinny Yurok kid. "Quentin'll be setting chokers. Rich, show him around, will you?"

Rich nodded and took up his gear, rain beaded on the chainsaw's casing. The Feeley kid shouldered the heavy coil of steel-cored rope without complaint.

"I knew your dad," Rich said as they headed up the steep slope. "He was a good man." The kid's denims were stiff with store creases. "How old are you?"

"Eighteen."

"Your mom know you're here?"

"She knows."

"She doesn't like it?" Rich guessed.

The kid shrugged. Tom Feeley had been quiet too. Tom had started out at the mill, a good way to go broke or lose a finger, and headed into the woods first chance he'd got. Hell of a hard worker, he'd busted his ass setting chokers, done everything right. But chains snap. His wife had been pregnant at the funeral—must have been this kid in her belly.

"This your first logging job?" Rich asked, stopping at the base of a three-hundred-footer.

The kid nodded.

"Well, you picked a good place to start. These big pumpkins are the big paydays." Rich surveyed the giant trees. "Solid heartwood, no knots, just clear-all-heart—highest-grade redwood God ever made." Rich dropped his gear. The kid lowered the rope. His shoulder would be sore later. "Come on, I'll show you."

They hiked up to Damnation Spring. Rich crouched at the water's edge, rinsed his hands, then cupped them, drank. "Those are some good-looking denims." Rich wiped his mouth, took the old lockback off his belt, popped the knife open and held it out, handle first. "Time to lose the cuffs. Stag off six inches."

"They're new," the kid objected.

"I see that." Rich stood up. "So, here's how this goes. First, we cut a road—can't get the equipment in or the timber out without a road. The Cats handle that—D8s, big piece of machinery. You catch the bottom of those fancy denims and don't get out of the way fast enough, one'll drag you under, roll you flat as a rug. Mash you into hamburger. Or say you trip trying to run clear, and pow: a log hammers you into the ground like a nail into sand. I seen it happen. Anything that can snag: hair, shoelaces, work pants"—Rich lifted his chin at the kid's denims—"can get you killed."

The kid took the knife, weighed it.

"Sharp enough to shave with," Rich said, seeing the idea of mutilating the new denims bothered him. "Now. Catskinners—guys driving Cat—cut road"—Rich traced switchbacks with his finger—"and clear out a flat spot up top, a landing for the yarder. Lew"—Rich looked around—"guy with the belly who was driving the crummy. He's the yarder operator. The yarder's a big diesel engine on skis. It's got a couple of big drums that spin around and reel the mainline cable in to pull logs up the hill. Like fishing, except that line's three and a half inches thick and the fish weigh a couple tons each. You follow?"

The kid nodded.

"This is a high-lead show. That means we use a spar tree, that big one, where we dumped the gear, as a center pole, like the mast on a ship. Spar's got to withstand a lot of weight. Our faller will drop a ring of trees around our spar. Once that's done, I climb up, trim off her branches, and cut her top off. Then we haul the blocks—big pulleys—up the spar and rig the cable system that maneuvers the logs. We'll tie guylines to that ring of stumps, use them as anchors, to take the pressure off, keep the spar tree from buckling."

The kid looked up, as though the work might be going on over his head.

"Since this is old-growth, there's not too much brush—shade keeps it down. But Sanderson will send a chopper out anyway. Chopper sprays places trucks can't. Forest Service hoses their timberlands once in March or April, then calls it good, but Sanderson sprays all season, wherever we're working. Spray kills the weeds and the trash trees—broadleaf plants—everything that gets in our way. It's a growth hormone—hops them up so they grow so fast they die." Rich batted at the chest-high ferns. "Now, redwood's soft. If she falls wrong, she'll bust. So the Cats push all the dead stuff into a pile at her base, and then piles every ten feet or so to give her some cushion—that's what we call a fall bed. It's an art, falling a tree this size. There aren't a lot of guys left can do it the way Pete can."

"Pete Peterson?" the kid asked, Pete's name a legend, up and down the North Coast.

"Down there in the chaps, the one with the big crooked nose. Pete nails his springboards into a big pumpkin and then he and the guy helping him climb up—six, eight feet off the ground. They cut the face on the side they want her to fall, like this." Rich held his hands together at a forty-five-degree angle, to show the shape of the undercut. "They pull out the mouthpiece—we're talking a slice twelve feet long—drive wedges in, and go around the other side and back her up, just a straight backcut. Then they run like hell."

Rich raised his voice a notch to be heard over the Cats below.

"Once she's down, Lyle comes along, saws off her branches, then bucks her to truck lengths. Slices up a three-hundred-footer just like he's cutting a carrot. Now, here's where you come in."

The kid straightened up.

"You and Eugene drag the choker chains around the logs—that means digging or setting dynamite so you can reach around under—and watch it, those logs can roll. You pull those chains tight enough to choke a man; that's why it's called setting chokers. You snug 'em and lock 'em." Rich pinched the fingers of one hand together into a choker knob and used the other to cap it like a bell. "Then you signal." Rich whistled through his teeth: three short— pause—two short. "Lew reels the line in, drags those logs up to be loaded. Got it?"

The kid nodded, though he looked uncertain.

"Eugene's been setting chokers for a decade and he's still got two arms and two legs. You can learn a lot from him. When I first met him, he was just a log-truck mechanic lying flat on his back fixing brake lines, but he smelled the real money. It smelled like the woods. Now look at him."

Rich had felt for Eugene back then—red hair already thinning, a wife and kid at home, young enough to be Rich's own son. He was from Oregon, logging country, small and strong, monkey arms long to his knees—arms made for setting chokers—but he still wore his dog tags, to show how tough he was. Rich knew Don would never hire a guy like that. So, for the first and only time in his life, Rich had climbed the stairs to the crow's nest above the mill floor where Virgil Sanderson kept watch over the saws, redwood boards dropping onto the conveyer belt red as raw meat. Virgil sat with a ledger spread out in front of him, white hair tinted yellow by nicotine, cloud of cigarette smoke surrounding him like his own personal fog. Rich had worked for Virgil Sanderson his whole life, but he'd never had a conversation with him.

*Gundersen.* Virgil had acknowledged him, as though he might be his father or his grandfather, any one of a long line of Gundersens.

Don never said a word about it, but every time Eugene did something stupid, Don looked to Rich: Eugene was his responsibility. Small price to pay, in the end. It wasn't long after Rich got Eugene hired on that Eugene's wife brought her sister to the company bonfire: the quiet girl from the front of-fice—Colleen. Flames reflected in the lenses of her thick glasses, and, without warning, the train of Rich's life had lurched onto a set of tracks he hadn't known existed.

"What's Don do?" the kid asked.

"Don? Don's the boss, but we're a small operation, so he's also the hook-tender. Hooker tells you what logs to choke in what order. Don's a fair guy, but he ever catches you without a hard hat, he'll fire your ass. Couple things to remember: every week, the scaler comes by to measure and mark our cut. We get paid by the foot and the grade, about a penny a board foot. A big pumpkin like these here pays five or six grand, minus breakage. The more we cut, the more we make. It shakes down different, based on your job, but bottom line, you slow the show down, you're costing us all money. Got it? Logging's a good living, but remember: these big pumpkins can kill you. Whatever's eating you, you leave it on the crummy. Pay attention. You let your mind wander, it can cost you your life, or somebody else's."

The kid dropped his eyes. Son of a killed logger, he still needed to be told.

"Look, my dad died in the woods too," Rich confided. "And my grand-dad before him. Doesn't matter how careful you are, a redwood's a monster. We've got to respect that. Don't be looking at the ground. Look up. A slacked cable, a widowmaker falling from the sky—even a branch four, five inches in diameter can break your neck if she falls from three hundred feet. Watch the wind." Rich tapped his ear. "Listen."

"What are those for?" the kid asked, nodding at the fistful of orange ribbons shoved into Rich's pocket. Rich had forgotten them.

"We need to stake off the creek. Fifty feet, on both sides."

"Why?" the kid asked.

"Good goddamn question. It's what they call a 'ri-par-i-anne corridor.'"

*What the hell kind of five-dollar word is that?* Eugene had asked the first time they heard it. *If you mean creek, say creek.*

"We have to leave a buffer zone. When I was your age, we filled streams that got in our way, but now there's rules. Makes things a little more complicated. Sanderson had a hell of a time getting these harvest plans through."

"How come?" the kid asked, suddenly more interested.

"Damnation Creek is a spawning creek. Salmon. Mud runs off, clouds the water, water catches more sun and warms up. Coho like it cool. I don't know." Rich sighed. "I just do what they tell me . . ."

"Quentin," the kid offered, seeing Rich grasp for the name.

"Any more questions, Quentin?" Rich handed him his share of the ribbons.

"I don't got a tape measure."

"Just pace it off."

Rich cut up around the top of the spring to the far side of the creek, tied a ribbon to a rhododendron, then loped twenty yards downhill and tied another. His throat was sore from talking. He got back down to the road first.

"You stag off those denims, when you're done," Rich called up, "then go get set with Eugene."

Rich got his climbing gear on, fed the steel-cored rope around the base of his spar tree, set his spurs to bark, pulled the rope taut, and started walking up the trunk. The climbing got easier as he went, the spar's diameter narrowing from eighteen at the butt, but the breathing sure as hell didn't. His heart double-timed. Used to haul ass up a three-hundred-footer, limb and top her in under an hour, but these days he was lucky to finish in two. He dug in his spurs, leaned back into the rope to give his arms a rest, and glanced up to gauge his altitude. First trick Lark ever taught him: look up.

*What's worse than a dumb, scared sonofabitch?*

*A dumb sonofabitch.*

He looked down at the kid below, sitting on a rock, sawing at his denims.

The spar dripped with condensation, Rich's clothes already wet where they'd rubbed. No staying dry in the woods. Paydays, guys used to strip buck naked in the mill lot to change after work, then hightail it to the old joyhouse above the Beehive, but those days were gone. The One and Only Tavern had become truly the Only—the Cutthroat and the Steelhead both boarded up. At the rate they'd turned timber into park, even the whores had packed up and left. Probably have to drive clear over the Oregon line just to catch a decent case of crabs.

The lightweight Husqvarna tugged at his belt, chainsaw swinging on her rope, tuned up. He was looking forward to the first cut: hot knife through butter. He flipped the rope up again, and like he'd pulled a cord, the lunch buzzer sounded, so loud Colleen heard it three ridges away. Almost a decade since Virgil had kicked the bucket and Merle sold out to the big-city dicks who switched them to the electric buzzer, but Rich still missed the old steam whistle. He looked up: the big tree's armpits overgrown with fern, lettuce-leaf lungwort, orange lichen.

*Different forest up there*, Lark said.

The lunch buzzer sounded again. Ten thirty a.m. on the dot, Don's regulation lunchtime thirty. Sonofabitch should have been a schoolteacher. Rich sighed. Just got situated, but now wasn't the time to piss Don off—short fuse on a long stick of dynamite. Getting into the grove had been hell from the start. First the longhairs barricading the road, then the timber harvest plans stalling—some environmental bullshit with the state forestry board. Merle had greased some hands and finally gotten the plans approved, but Don took that shit personal.

Rich looked off at 24-7 Ridge. He needed Sanderson to run roads down into the lower grove and clear those big pumpkins out, clear the way for him to harvest the 24-7. A need that itched worse by the day. But Don would sniff him out in a city minute if he started asking questions. He hadn't even told Colleen yet.

Rich lowered himself back to the ground and shed his belt and spurs. The buzz of killed saws rang in his ears. His hearing wasn't what it used to be. Sanderson had given out earplugs at the company picnic this year, earplugs when all that kept you from getting clubbed by a falling widowmaker or rolling-pinned by a runaway log was your damn ears. Back in the old days they got ball caps, aprons for the wives. Arlette picked that crap out, walked around collecting thank-yous, everybody trying to stay on Merle's good side. Now they'd been downgraded to earplugs not much bigger than a couple of aspirin and Arlette hadn't even shown up. Rich had tried them out, bucking firewood at the house—kept having to ask Colleen to speak up, figured he'd save what he had left—but the things were a pain in the ass to maneuver. Shoved one so far down his ear canal his head felt corked. Lucky he ever got the damn thing out.

Spit pooled in his mouth as he walked. Piece of lemon loaf would really hit the spot. When Rich got down to the crummy, he found Eugene hassling the big-headed Sanderson kid.

"Look at that asshole." Pete snorted. "Doesn't have two brain cells to rub together."

Rich wasn't sure what pissed Pete off more: that the kid had leapfrogged straight to catskinner instead of putting in his time setting choker chains like everybody else, or that he was Merle's blood. Rich hadn't learned to read until the fifth grade, Pete already multiplying three-digit numbers in his head, but, at the end of the day, they were both the sons of loggers. A high school diploma wasn't worth beans in the woods. They'd started out setting chokers together at fifteen, dragging cables thick as their forearms over giant logs, Klamath a timber kingdom and Merle its prince, away at private school.

Eugene clapped the Sanderson boy on the back and a grin broke across the kid's bovine face. Eugene had a way of shining a light on a person, making him feel important.

"Want to suck Merle's dick?" Pete asked. "Get in line."

Couldn't blame Eugene for hedging his bets. Six kids to feed. At least he was dancing with the ones that brung him. Not like some guys, shacking up with the first gyppo outfit that came along.

Pete shoved a plug of snus up under his lip and tucked the can into his back pocket, white ring worn into the denim. Best faller Sanderson ever had; Pete could drop a three-hundred-footer without putting a scratch on her. But even after he laid a big pumpkin down in a fall bed neat as a pen in a case—a skill maybe a hundred men in history had ever truly mastered—he looked dissatisfied. No wife, no kids, a habit of looking over your shoulder when he talked, such a skinflint he'd rigged his truck door with baling wire instead of shelling out to replace the rusted hinges, though he could fix radios, toasters, pop the guts out of a stopped clock, sort through the pieces, and set her back ticking in the time it took to drink a cup of coffee. Rich had known him all his life and still felt the itch to look over his own shoulder at whatever it was Pete saw there.

Pete spat a hot leash of juice in the direction of the Sanderson kid and dragged the back of his hand across his mouth. "Like to see the whore that shat out that piece of shit."

Hard to imagine Arlette putting up with it, if the boy really was Merle's—but she had missed the company picnic, first time in recorded history, as though even she wanted to keep her distance. Like to think it cost Merle some sleep, putting guys with twenty years under their belts out on their asses. But you didn't ride out shitstorms the way Merle had by letting things eat you. He'd come alone to the Sunday fish fries since, slapping backs, hitching his pants up over his belly.

Tom Feeley's son appeared, denims stagged off unevenly, and handed Rich back his knife.

"Hey, Rich!" Don called from up near the blowdown where three big pumpkins had gone over like dominos in the wind.

Rich looked toward the crummy, where his lunch was, and sighed. By the time he reached him, Don stood at the edge of a root-ball crater deep enough to bury a truck in, the hole Rich had let Chub scramble down into.

"That Feeley kid is so green I could plant him," Rich said.

Don didn't lift his head, just stared down into the hole. Boulders the size of TVs were bound up in the wall of roots, torn free when the wind tipped her, busted her to toothpicks. Deadfall. That's what happened when you let good timber get old: it went to waste. A human skull stared up from the bottom of the pit.

"What do you think?" Don asked, short arms folded across his chest.

Rich could hear the gears working in Don's brain. Don had a temper, but he'd work twice as hard for half pay to keep his crew together. That was why, with the downsizing, Merle had kept him and fired Bill Henderson, the other crew boss.

*Wish I'd been a fly in that shitstorm*, Eugene had said.

They'd all heard Bill in there with Merle while they waited on their checks. Bill was a tough guy to like, greedy, rode his crews hard. He'd stormed out, calling Merle a cock-sucking sonofabitch. Rich could picture Merle leaning back at his desk then, arms crossed over that big pregnant gut, knowing he had Don by the short hairs.

*Look, Porter, you can boss both crews or I can let yours go and assign you to Bill's. Your choice.*

Don so red-faced with rage he might bust a blood vessel.

*Goddamn it, Merle, that ain't a choice.*

Now Don coughed. He was the only guy Rich knew, besides Merle, who had any college. Started on a teacher's certificate, did a hitch in the navy, came home after the strike ended in '46. Barrel-chested ambition got him from choker setter to crew boss inside five years. Even guys who resented him respected him.

Don lowered himself into the pit with a groan. He ran a tight ship, chased every last board foot like it belonged to him. In twenty-five years, he'd only lost one guy, when a log slipped its choker and bashed Tom Feeley's head off like a rotted pumpkin. Made them triple-check every choker bell since. Wives all wanted their husbands on his crew. Don Porter didn't cut corners. He did things right.

Don stared down at the skull at his feet. Rich probed his gum, tasted rot. A breeze shivered through the timber.

"Shit." Don stooped, hooked two fingers through the eyeholes, and picked the thing up like a tiny bowling ball. Anybody could see it had belonged to a child.

# CHUB

Chub pressed his nose to the kitchen door, his breath fogging the cold glass. He wiped a peephole and stared out at Scout's snout, resting on the doorway of his doghouse. He reached for the doorknob: an electric spark.

"Chub?" his mom called.

She sat on the sofa, holding her sewing under the green lampshade. Light flickered on the lamp's bronze rabbit base. The painted saw stretched across the wall above her: elk in a meadow, a lake, a red barn. The tree-climbing spurs his mom had helped him cut from a cereal box lay adrift on the carpet by her feet.

He adjusted the slippery coffee can under his armpit. His new yellow slicker hung beside the front door. He hated its rubber smell. He tugged the doorknob, put the can down, and used both hands. The door whooshed open just enough to squeeze out. He pushed the can through first. Half in, half out, he smelled woodsmoke in one nostril, breakfast toast still clothespinned in the kitchen air in the other. He had a good sniffer. *Like a goddamn bloodhound*, Uncle Lark said, tapping his own nose with his stump-finger, bit off at the first knuckle. Every time his dad said goddamn, he was supposed to put a nickel in the jar. Uncle Lark carved wooden nickels.

"Chub?" his mom called again.

If she made him come back for his slicker now, he'd get stuck.

"Don't go far, okay, Grahamcracker? Stay where you can see the house."

Outside, it was misting. Scout lifted his head. Chub found two worms right away, satisfying *plonk*s in the can. He pulled up a fistful of grass and sprinkled it on them.

He held his binoculars to his eyes, pointed them up toward the big trees, and turned the dial the way Uncle Lark had taught him. He scanned the high branches for a flying squirrel spiraling down, furry arms spread, leather cape flapping. He would take him on a leash to visit Uncle Lark's flyer, who broke her hip when she was a baby and Uncle Lark found her. He'd already made a nest in his bottom dresser drawer, snuck a handful of peanuts from the jar. A flying squirrel was better than a kitten.

A breeze stirred the grasses at the edge of the yard. Beyond that, the hill was a tangle of brambles and ferns, thistles and stinging nettles, all the way up to where the forest started. *Stay where you can see the house*, his mom had said. But flying squirrels lived in the big trees.

He looked down at the map in his palm, cupped his hand to make the creeks pucker. Scout rested his snout on his paws, but as soon as Chub started for the path, he raised it, cocking his head, black ear sticking up higher than his gray one. Chub heard the metallic slither of Scout's chain, an almost-bark vibrating in his throat.

"Shh." He held up his hand, the way his dad stopped Scout in his tracks.

He pulled off Scout's collar. Scout zagged across the yard, nose to the ground, lifting his leg so high he almost toppled over, digging up fans of dirt, shoving his snout in, sniffing for moles.

Chub flexed his palm, felt his dad's finger drawing the map.

*Damnation Creek leaks down from the spring, water so clean you could almost sing.*

Scout snorted dirt and rocketed up the path. Chub hesitated—*one one thousand, two one thousand*—then bolted after him. The straps of his overalls yanked at his shoulders as he ran, his mom's voice in his head: *Don't.* Yank. *Go.* Yank. *Far.* Mist spritzed his cheeks. At the top of Bald Hill, Chub turned and trained his binoculars back the way he'd come: the ocean was out there, at the bottom of the cliff on the other side of the road, but he couldn't see it. Fog floated around the sides of the house. The kitchen window was crowded with geraniums, leaves soft like the velvet between a horse's nostrils, grasses swishing back and forth, back and forth, at the edge of the empty yard.

# COLLEEN

Colleen fingered the pink satin roses she'd stitched along the neck of the baptism gown. The ten thirty whistle sounded in the distance. She'd heard Chub open his dresser drawer before he went outside and made a mental note to inspect it. A few weeks ago, she'd found one of Enid's kittens nested in his socks. Rich had been sneezing.

*But Wyatt gave him to me*, Chub had wailed, throwing himself facedown on the bed.

She put away her sewing, got up, and went to Chub's room. Brownie leaned against his dresser, the old hobbyhorse threadbare in the ears. She'd have liked to take him to Enid's for the girls, but Chub still frowned when she suggested it. In the bottom drawer: twigs, a handful of strewn peanuts.

She dropped the nuts into the kitchen trash and cracked the back door.

"Chub!"

She opened the bread box, dropped a slice in the toaster.

"Chu-ub!"

She took out jam. Her unfinished crossword still sat on the table. *Desires*, four letters, starts with a Y. The toast popped up. She pinched it out and buttered it. That lone Y a wishbone, a fork in the road.

"Chub! Snack time!" She went out. Fog drifted up into the trees, rhododendrons lacquered with dew. "Chub! Let's go get eggs!"

She scanned the yard's overgrown edges. If he hadn't been hiding before, he was now. Rich had started it, smacking his hand to his heart when Chub leapt out. The coffee can lay abandoned in the grass. Chub lived for the moment Rich popped the lid off.

*Now we're cooking with gas*, Rich would say, tapping a worm out. Rich fished with flies, but he knew there was pride in work. Chub's face lit with the praise, the same naked joy as when Rich had given him sink baths as a baby. He'd loved water, kicked and squirmed like a chub in a net, so Rich had started calling him one, until it became his name.

There was Scout's collar, hooked to his chain.

"Scout?"

He still had scabs from the last porcupine. Ocean wind swept inland. She scanned the hill, a prickle at the back of her neck.

"Chub?" she called, forgetting the sadness she'd been holding off all morning.

"Scout ran away!" Chub yelled, bursting red cheeked from the brambles.

Colleen sighed. "He went to find your dad." Every time that dog got free, he lit out for Rich. "Go wash your hands, mister."

Inside, Chub licked jam off his toast. She took the wart cream from the kitchen drawer. In a few weeks she would lose him to school. The red lunchbox she'd bought was hidden in the coat closet. All summer, every time she'd pushed a pair of waders aside, it had stared back at her.

"Let me see your hand."

His shoulders slumped, but he held it out.

*He's too well behaved*, Enid complained. The wart was on his thumb, near the base. Colleen rubbed the cream in, her mind wandering back down the drugstore aisle. She twisted the cap back on, sealing the daydream inside, and tucked the crossword under the burl bowl for later.

They walked up their hill and over the next ridge to Garlic Creek, turning north up the draw. If they were lucky, Scout would be collapsed on the front stoop when they got home.

"What if he's lost?" Chub asked, as if she'd said it aloud.

"He's not lost."

Chub ran ahead. Soon he would leave her behind, the way Rich did every morning, coming home worn out and preoccupied by a world she could not enter.

*Kids are like puppies*, Enid said. *It's easier with two.*

Enid got pregnant the way other women caught colds. Well, the getting wasn't difficult, even for Colleen, if Rich would just agree to try. It was the staying. She gave her head a shake. *Think of something else.*

DAMNATION SPRING | 65

"What creek is this?" she asked. The water burbled.

"Garlic."

"Are you sure?" They'd made this trip a hundred times.

"Garlic is good with salt and bread," Chub recited. "It flows back and forth, all the way north. When you get to the farm, stretch out your arm. Go east over Deer Rib and far as it seems, you'll see Fort Eugene."

"Isn't there an easier way to Fort Eugene?"

Chub looked into his palm. "You can just follow the Little Lost."

"The whole way?"

He nodded. "But it's longer."

Finally, they came to the edge of the clearing. Eight years since she and Enid had sold it, but there was still something comforting about the first glimpse of the cabin. Their great-grandparents had cleared this land, at the foot of Deer Rib Ridge. Their grandparents had farmed it. To their mother, eating store-canned had been a sign of coming up in the world. She'd wasted away to almost nothing in the end but would still eat a canned pear if Colleen poured it in a dish of its own syrup.

Chub ran around front, charging the poultry flock. The birds separated, chickens scattering in a burst of clucks, ducks veering all one direction, a honking parade.

"Chub!"

"He's okay," Joanna called from the doorway. "They could use the exercise."

"So could he," Colleen admitted.

Joanna's sweatshirt hung to her knees. One of Jed's, though he wasn't much bigger than she was. They used to tease him about having to sit on his Bible when he drove for Sanderson. Merle had fired Jed or he'd quit. Either way, people had stopped buying Joanna's eggs in town. That was years ago, not long after the government swallowed up timberlands for the national park south of them, when jobs started leaking out of redwood country like blood from a lung shot and nobody wanted to get on Merle's bad side. Jed had found work up in Oregon, gone five weeks out of six, but he'd fared better than most. Sanderson had laid off all the truck drivers in the end.

*That park'll kill this town,* Colleen's mom had warned, though she hadn't lived long enough to see it. That was one lucky thing about cancer.

Joanna's skirt dragged, brown at the hem, pushed-up sleeves bunched at her elbows. Diesel hung in the air, a chlorine tang.

"They had a helicopter up there spraying all morning," Joanna said, thrusting her chin toward Deer Rib Ridge. She looked like a cherub with her big eyes and round cheeks, but she was made of rawhide. Last winter, when Joanna and the girls had caught the crud, Colleen offered to drive them to the company clinic if they walked down the draw to the house, mud a foot deep on the Deer Rib Road. Jed had been away on a run.

*You can still go,* Colleen had reminded her—*even if Jed doesn't work for Sanderson anymore* hanging in the air unsaid. The clinic was free for employees, their wives, and their kids, and five dollars a visit as long as somebody in your family had once worked for the company. Joanna had snuffed her nose. *Cut you with one hand and bandage you with the other*, she'd said, handing Colleen her change.

Now Colleen pinched an earring. "I hope we didn't wake you?"

"You'd have to get up pretty early in the morning. That baby's part rooster. How many?"

"Just a dozen." Colleen removed the egg carton from her bag.

Usually Joanna sent her oldest to gather the eggs. Judith was seven, homeschooled.

Chub had cornered the ducks against the side of the barn, near where Bossy—the last of Colleen's mother's Bossys—grazed.

"Chub, don't get so close," Colleen cautioned him.

"He's okay. That cow's half dog."

Joanna dragged her boot across the coop's ramp, clearing away scat. She'd done the bargaining when she and Jed bought the place. Pregnant with Judith, big as a barn, she'd marched Rich and Eugene around the cabin pointing out chinks between logs large enough to push a nail through.

Joanna ducked into the coop. Even standing outside, the bird musk was so thick it brought tears to Colleen's eyes.

"That should do it." Joanna came out, one arm bracing her back. From the posture, it struck Colleen suddenly—another one, already, the last still in diapers. She felt a pang of jealousy. Joanna looked out at the garlic fields and sniffed. "Really smell it now."

"Keeps the vampires away," Colleen said, her mother's line, though she couldn't smell anything besides chickens.

"The spray, I mean. Might as well spray us, the way the wind blows it," Joanna said.

The breeze carried the swish of pampas grass down from the Deer Rib clear-cuts. Colleen scanned the bare ridge for the half-built treehouse where, after her father had drowned, she'd gone to look for him, but even the stump of that tree was gone. Chub raced around the corner of the cabin, chasing the ducks straight at them.

"Chub!" Colleen scolded, ducks parting around their legs, rubber feet slapping up the ramp.

"There's something in the barn you'll want to see," Joanna said, and disappeared into the cabin.

"Did you scare those poor ducks?" Colleen asked.

"No." Chub toed gravel.

"I think you did. I think they're all hiding with their heads under their pillows."

Joanna emerged, towheaded Camber gripping her index finger, the toddler's steps jerky and mechanical, stopping to grin at Colleen. Joanna had labored alone through the night with her—just luck that Colleen had walked up to the cabin for eggs that morning and found Joanna squatting in the kitchen. The cord had been oddly easy to snip once Colleen had tied the ends off with string: a vein and a single artery instead of two, the placenta shriveled. But now here was Camber, fat and satisfied with herself, smug with life, with no memory of her difficult passage into it.

Joanna hoisted her up onto her hip. Leah and Judith flew down the steps next, as though they hadn't been allowed out of the cabin in days. Chub took Colleen's hand and they followed Joanna toward the barn.

"What is it?" he asked, his fingers squirming with anticipation.

"I don't know." She gave his hand three quick squeezes. *I. Love. You.*

Joanna pushed up the barn's brace board.

"Ready?" Joanna asked. Colleen's own curiosity swelled.

The smell of hay tickled Colleen's throat, barn lit only by the incubator bulbs. Leah mashed her face to the glass. Chub dropped to his knees, chicks and ducklings basking in the glow of a heat lamp rigged to a car battery.

Joanna handed Camber to Colleen. The baby squirmed, thunked her head against Colleen's breast—it felt so natural. Joanna slid the screen off the incubator.

"Gently now," she instructed the children.

Chub bit his lip, as though submerging his hands in water he expected to be cold. He touched a chick, darted his hand back.

Joanna scooped up a duckling. "Hold him close so he doesn't get cold."

"He's soft," Chub murmured, cuddling his duckling against his chest. He would have been a good brother. Loyal and protective, like Rich. A sweet, sweet heart.

The baby nuzzled Colleen's nipple through her shirt. She offered her finger instead. When it was time, Chub lowered his duckling back in with both hands.

"What's wrong with that one?" he asked.

Colleen saw the one he meant: small, with a crossed beak and a deformed wing.

"Oh," Joanna said. "That one's special. Watch your fingers." She lowered the lid.

"Why?" Chub crouched, his nose to the glass.

"Sometimes they just come that way, don't they? We love them a little extra."

"It'll die," Judith said. "The special ones always die."

"I'll take her. I know she's heavy." Joanna hefted Camber out of Colleen's arms.

They crossed the grass, heat evaporating from the spot where the baby had rested against Colleen's heart.

"That cow is fat," Chub said.

"We'll have another little Bossy running around pretty soon," Joanna said.

Joanna handed over the eggs, accepting Colleen's dollar bill without thanks or embarrassment. Chub lifted the carton's lid.

"Wouldn't that be something?" Joanna asked, palm on her belly, watching Chub's hands hover over the domes of the eggs, as though casting a spell to hatch them. "If you could just want them to life?"

Colleen kept a hand on the canvas bag as they walked. At the flat rock where Garlic Creek hooked south, they rested, Chub's head in her lap, his binoculars to his eyes.

"What do you see?" she asked. He lowered them to his chest. "Why do you love these things so much, cookie-boy?"

He shrugged, shy.

"What should we make with these eggs? Broccoli casserole?"

Chub groaned.

"Brussels-sprout cake?"

He wrinkled his nose. She pushed his bangs off his forehead.

"Where'd you get these beautiful green eyes?" she asked.

"I got them at the green-eyes store."

A branch snapped. Colleen turned. Up the ridge, an alder limb bounced, as though a bird had taken flight. Chub squirmed and she tickled him.

"Stop!" he squealed, grabbing her hands.

"Which way home?"

He studied her palm, then pointed.

"Why can't you read your map?" he asked.

"My dad never taught me," Colleen said, realizing it was true.

Rich was chopping wood when they got back. Scout trotted over, threw himself down for a belly rub.

"He found you," she said, no longer a question.

Rich swung, splits landing in the sawdust, half a cord of firewood scattered around the block.

"Lew almost ran him over," he said, winded, face slick with sweat.

Look up "careful" in the dictionary, and there was Rich with his handlebar mustache, head tilted ten degrees, favoring his left ear. Still, every day, she sucked in a breath when he left in the morning and held it until she heard his truck clunk up the driveway in the afternoon. She touched the top of Chub's head.

"You're home early?"

Rich's eyes followed her hand.

"Is everything okay?"

"Everything's fine," he said, and swung again, a loud crack, wood cleaving in two.

*August 30*

# RICH

Perched high in his spar, Rich leaned back into his climbing belt and rubbed the sore spot in his chest that had been there for two weeks, ever since Merle had pulled them out of the grove and sent them here to harvest the last of Deer Rib Ridge.

*Why didn't you tell me?* Colleen had asked after she read about the skull in the paper.

*It's just a stunt those longhairs pulled. We'll be back in the grove in a week,* Rich had promised. Now he was starting to wonder. He looked out over the ridge at the garlic farm, then back down the east sides, where they were cutting. One lousy skull and bingo: stuck harvesting Doug fir pecker poles eighteen inches in diameter, the legal minimum, a fraction of the board feet they should have bagged by now, harvesting the big pumpkins of Damnation Grove. It hurt. Small islands of old-growth like this one, up near the Deer Rib ridgeline, would pad a few last half-decent paychecks. After that, all bets were off. At this rate, he'd burn through what was left of the savings.

The chopper had sprayed again yesterday, blackberry canes curling up to die. The smell still hung in the air. The CB crackled in his pocket.

"All set?" Don asked.

"Yep."

"Good. Let's get her harvested before they dump another body on us."

Another crew boss might have tossed the skull aside, let the Cats crush it, or pitched it into the river, where Rich's mom had thrown her wedding band after his dad got killed. She used to slow the car on the old bridge, as if the ring might have hit the barrier and landed on the shoulder like a dropped wish penny. If he found that ring today, he'd put it toward the mortgage.

The lunch buzzer sounded. Yellow hard hats streamed across the muddy clear-cut below, beelining for the crummy. Rich lowered himself down the spar and shucked off his gear, caulks pulling up chunks of wet dirt, weighting him as he trudged down past Deer Spring.

Don had brought the skull to Merle. If there was one thing Merle was good at, it was making things disappear. Practically the company motto. But somehow the forestry board had gotten wind of it and pumped the brakes on both harvest plans. The board used to be all timbermen, but times were changing. It would decide at its next meeting, end of September, whether to let them go ahead. Don suspected Eugene and his big mouth, but whoever was to blame, if the rains came before Merle got it ironed out, it'd be a long, hungry winter for all of them.

Rich hadn't seen the survey maps, but he'd sidled up to the company's scaler, long-thumbed Mitch Danforth, who also cruised timber for Sanderson, figuring out where to harvest the most board feet at the least expense, long enough to confirm the harvest plan for Lower Damnation went pretty far down. How far, Danforth wouldn't say. Eugene had almost clocked the greaseball when he came out to tally their cut last week. Danforth was small and quick as a weasel, but writing up their cut he doubled in size, slipping his thumb as he measured—one thumb's width equal to a thousand board feet—to count less, pay less.

*Shit, Danforth,* Eugene had complained. *The way you're counting, you got a one-inch dick.*

Rumor was Merle was going to switch them to day rate instead of by-the-board-foot anyway, every day the same pay no matter what they cut. It would help them out now, stuck in the beanpoles on Deer Rib, but it would sure cost them later, when they got back into the grove. That was Merle, always two steps ahead. It gave Rich heartburn just thinking about it.

Guys milled around the crummy at the bottom of the hill, bus barnacled with mud, parked behind Eugene's rusted-to-shit Cheyenne. Eugene had stripped down to his undershirt. *You're at work, keep your damn shirt on.*

Rich still hadn't seen the two hundred bucks Colleen had loaned them at Christmas, when their stove quit. Money ran through Eugene's hands quicker than water. He just didn't take care of things. He hadn't waxed that Cheyenne since he bought her. Could use that undercarriage to drain pasta. Salt air would rust the springs out from inside a couch, rust a wedding band off your finger without wax. Sure could use that two hundred bucks back now.

Rich scrambled over a trough of rainwater.

"Lunch's over," Eugene called, Rich always the last one down. He'd put up with his share of shit over the years. Came with the territory: highest up, highest paid.

"You hear Chevy's putting heaters in their tailgates?" Rich lobbed back. "Keep your hands warm when you're pushing."

"You find a spar?" Eugene asked, snugging down the red Sanderson cap that lived on his head like it was glued there. "Took you long enough. Thought you might be picking out another wife."

Eugene had been nineteen when he chased Enid, eight months pregnant, up the stairs into a church. It was the redhead in him. He wanted something, he took it.

The young guys were using the hood of Eugene's truck as a table, drawn to him like moths to a porch light. Quentin sat off by himself. Someone had evened out his stagged-off denims. In the old days, Rich would have trained the kid up. Used to be guys looked out for each other. Old-timers—guys younger than Rich was now—wouldn't let him pay for a beer after Astrid moved up north and left him, just clinked bottles and nodded, as though she'd died.

Eugene was halfway through a Baby Ruth, a V of Slim Jims corralling a pickled egg. A married man who ate like he was single. *Enid should pack him a decent lunch*, Colleen would say, but those two still lived like teenagers shacking up. There were so many plywood additions tacked on to that trailer house the county would have had a field day: a five-bedroom single-wide, list of code violations thicker than a phone book.

Eugene had worked out a deal when Merle pulled them out of the grove and sent them over to harvest the rest of Deer Rib. Instead of riding the ten ass-numbing miles into town to catch the dawn crummy, then riding back out with the rest of the crew, Eugene drove himself, got the gate open, and locked up at the end of the day. First in, last out. And for two weeks, Rich had felt a twinge of envy at the sight of his brother-in-law sitting on the gate's top rung. Rich had missed the crummy once, his first week setting chokers; fifteen years old, he'd never felt more alone than he had that day in the mill lot. He'd been there by quarter to five ever since, catching a little shut-eye in the truck until the crummy roared to life. And every morning for the past two weeks, at the end of the road was Eugene, waving them in with the big-armed gesture of a man dealt an extra hour's sleep. There were days Rich would have traded a day's pay for another hour's sleep.

Rich knocked his caulks against the crummy's tire, removed his hard hat, and bounded up the stairs, stooping down the aisle. He pressed his tongue to his tooth to dull the ache. Colleen was on him to see a dentist. Rich must have been ten when his mother took him to Dr. Peine's wake. Peine was Swiss, but everybody said it Pain—a joke that stuck, given his profession. Even closed inside a coffin, Rich had been uneasy of the town dentist. Peine dug, and collected. Back in those days, every time they cut a new road, they uncovered some burial ground. They said Peine pickled heads in jars. He even had a letter from the Smithsonian, thanking him for the heads. He'd been digging by the river and drowned in the flood that took out the shingle mill, bloated so bad they had to shoehorn him into the box. Klamath hadn't had another dentist since.

Rich pinched sawdust from his nostrils. The crummy stank of sweat and gasoline, but it was nice to have a moment, just him and his aches. Even Pete, who'd once cracked a rib and still worked until the end of the day, was slowing down. Once the old-growth was gone, it'd be single-jacking: dropping, limbing, and bucking your own, a hundred trees a day. Guys their age wouldn't be able to keep pace. Sanderson wasn't what it used to be, and neither was the timber. Lucky Jim Mueller had wanted to unload the 24-7 when he did.

Rich pinned sandwiches to the side of his lunch pail to get at the lemon loaf underneath, pried off the top slice. Jackpot: double crumb-coated slabs of butter. Normally, Colleen was stingy with it, but she'd been preoccupied, the Larson girl due any day.

Rich polished off the cake, brushed crumbs from his mustache, grabbed his thermos and lunch pail, and stood. Outside, he popped a squat on a rotting log between Pete and Don, same order they'd sat in since grade school. The bruise on Pete's cheekbone had faded to a sick yellow. He'd rung some longhair's bell pretty good the night of the fish fry. He pawed at it like it itched, a tic from way back, when Pete had real bruises. Rich palmed the sandwiches from his pail—wrapped neat as a Christmas present—and tore open the wax-paper flap. A note flopped out. Rich tucked it into his breast pocket.

Pete packed a pinch of snus inside his lip, same ropy build he'd had at fifteen, Adam's apple that made swallowing look painful, nose so crooked if he turned his face far enough to the left, wouldn't know he had one. When they were teenagers, a limb rammed Pete's hard hat down and broke his nose, and guys started calling him the Big-Nosed Swede. Had a shelf in his house with every hard hat he'd ever owned, a few so dented you'd think they'd survived Normandy. As for Rich, he'd packed on a little paunch, a meatiness in his jowls that still surprised him when he shaved, but nothing like the couch-cushion gut Don had strapped on. Don's lunch was long gone. Didn't chew so much as inhale. Put away a tin of butter cookies in the time it took another man to get the lid off.

A breeze swept Don's balled-up wax paper off the log and Don stooped after it. He liked a clean work site, would hold the whole crummy hostage while he chased down a stray wrapper—don't shit where you eat. Forget schoolteacher, he'd make a good park ranger. Might be about the only job left around here, if those hippies got their way.

Rich took a bite and a flare shot up his jaw. *Sonofabitch*. He turned the sandwich sideways, slab of cheese slathered with peanut butter.

"What kind of cheese is that?" Don asked, lifting his chin at Rich's second sandwich.

"Orange kind." Rich nudged it Don's way.

"Nah." Don opened his fist to show the balled-up paper. "I had."

Pete spat a brown squirt of juice. "You seen Pacific started using steel spars down south? Hell, any monkey can climb those—don't need no high-climbers." Virgil Sanderson used to take Pete with him to look at new machinery, like a hound let loose on a scent.

"Rich hasn't been south of Scotia in his life." Don picked up the sandwich, took a bite, exhaled in appreciation.

"Gail still have you on that diet?" Pete asked.

"One percent's not milk, it's water," Don griped.

"Next you'll be sitting down to piss."

"That why you stay single, Pete?"

Pete turned to Rich. "What the hell are you smiling at, you cradle-robbing sonofabitch? Wait 'til Colleen gets to be your age."

"I'll be dead by then." Rich winced, cool air skimming molar.

"Fucking Merle." Pete shook his head. "Lets Arlette parade him around like a show pony and fucks the rest of us in the ass. He's got us digging our own damn graves out here."

"Want to survive, have to do more with less." Don crammed away the last of his crust. "Tree-farming's the future, once the big timber's gone."

"Any word on the grove?" Rich asked, hoping he didn't sound desperate.

"Watch those fucking longhairs get it turned into park." Pete spat at his feet.

"Damnation's an island, clear-cuts all around," Don said. "If the park wanted it, they'd have took it back in '68."

"If they expand, though?" Pete reasoned.

"If they do, and that's a big *if*, it'll be down south," Don said. "Merle heard it from the horse's mouth."

"More like from the horse's ass. I'd like to know how that joker ever got to Congress." Pete shook his head. "Can't trust a man who dyes his hair. Right, Rich?"

Rich shrugged, wishing he could shrug off the feeling of going behind everybody's back.

"You see clear-all-heart's up to six hundred bucks per thousand board feet for kiln-dried?" Pete asked. "That's a hundred bucks more than last year."

Don made a fist, straightened his swollen joints out slowly. "Ain't that much heartwood left. Market can smell it."

Rich's heart thunked. With prices rising, the 24-7 was worth more every day.

"You think they'll close the mill?" Pete asked.

"Once the grove is done." Don nodded. "Don't need a ten-foot bandsaw to mill pencils."

Rich would have to talk to Merle about getting his timber in. Sanderson's old-growth mill was the closest option; adding miles to haul it elsewhere would skim cream off his profits.

Downhill, Eugene guffawed, clapped the bowlegged Sanderson kid on the back.

"Look at that piece of shit." Pete spat. "What's he got, two dicks? Why's he stand like that?"

"You got anything left in that thermos?" Don asked.

Rich poured him some coffee. Guys packed up, cut behind slash piles to piss.

"Want some of this?" Rich asked.

Pete held out his cup. Rich's back had tightened up from sitting. He grunted, pushing to his feet.

"All set?" Don asked.

"Yep."

Don eyed him, gauging the distance between denial and discomfort. They all had their rusty hinges. Pete's white knuckle had gotten so bad he couldn't make a fist with his left hand. A bitch just to get his boots tied. Don tipped his cup back, draining the last drop.

"She brews this shit too damn weak," Pete complained.

"You can't taste shit with that shit in your lip. You're just jealous," Don ragged.

"Not all of us got an old lady we can live off, Porter."

A flicker of annoyance crossed Don's face. Gail didn't make much at the school, but Don had taken shit over her working for years. Most wives worked until the kids came, but Don and Gail had never had any.

"Is it my fault you never found a woman blind enough to marry your ugly ass?" Don asked.

"Marsha likes him," Rich offered.

"No thanks," Pete said. "I seen what happened to the last one. I'd like to keep all my fingers, thank you very much."

"Living alone gets to you," Don said, and swung his lunch pail off the log.

"Least I piss standing up in my own goddamn bathroom."

Rich felt for Pete, alone in that rattletrap house. Could have been him, if Eugene hadn't hounded him about Colleen. *One damn date. You afraid she'll want to jump in the sack? What's the matter, you forget how?* He should have saved a slice of lemon loaf for Pete instead of sneaking onto the crummy to hoard it like a kid. Colleen would tsk.

"What?" Pete asked, Rich's affection at the thought of her showing on his face.

"Nothing."

Pete went up the crummy's steps, tossed his thermos onto a seat.

"Crop lots. Farming trees like they're corn." Pete snorted. "Won't need us, that's for damn sure." The rawness in Pete's voice made Rich want to tell him. He'd need a good faller for the 24-7, when the time came. But it was too easy to kill an idea by saying it out loud.

"Hell," Pete said. "Not going to change it by bitching, am I?"

"Tried whoring?" Rich asked.

"That's Merle's department."

Rich offered Pete a toothpick and took one for himself, following the skid back up to his spar, skirting a spot where a log had slipped its chokers and gouged a pit deep as a grave. Uprooted stumps lay on their sides like giant molars. They would be teepeed with brush and burned. In the old days, they'd left them—redwoods sent up new shoots—but stumps got in the way of the replants. A farmer's problem.

He took Colleen's love note from his pocket. After an accident—Eugene couldn't keep his damn mouth shut—Rich wouldn't get one for months. Only when things were calm, when Colleen sensed he'd let down his guard, would she slip a note into the pocket of his denims or tuck one up under the cap of his thermos. *Come home safe to me, String Bean.*

He'd told her once how, without Lark watching out for him, he worried about falling. They were lying in bed. Something about the smooth slip of her leg against his made him talk. It was the thing that had most surprised him about being married: half the time he didn't know what he thought until he said it out loud to her.

Colleen never mentioned the notes. Still that shy girl behind the screen door, quiet voice he had to grab after to hear, sweet scent behind her ear—geranium—from a white bottle with a gold clamshell top. The first time he'd gone out to the garlic farm alone, he'd knocked, put his hands in his pockets. Big baseball-mitt hands, never knew what to do with them. How the hell had he let Eugene talk him into this? He'd started back down the steps, looked over his shoulder, and the sight of her almost took his feet out from under him. The way she dropped her eyes made him want to clap, whoop, sing—anything to regain her attention.

Downslope, he heard one of the new lightweight saws vibrating, rakers filed too low—the young guys were lazy about measuring their depth gauges when they sharpened their chains, and the hungry chains stressed their motors, made their tinfoil saws kick. Only old guys ran McCullochs anymore, saws so round and heavy they'd roll down a hill like a watermelon.

Deer Spring pooled in a gravel bed below his spar. He rinsed his hands, slurped a handful, wiped his mouth on his sleeve, and took out Colleen's note.

"Hey, Gundersen!" someone hollered. "Your mutt's back."

Scout bounded into him, almost knocking Rich onto his ass. Muddy and collarless, Scout lapped up water, then threw himself to the ground, panting, grinning his dog grin.

"You," Rich scolded, scratching his hackles. In a minute, he would have to walk him down to the crummy, make him lie under the seat until they were done, guys bitching about how the whole bus smelled like wet dog again.

Rich unfolded Colleen's note. But it wasn't a note, only a blank slip of paper.

*September 1*

# COLLEEN

Rich worked through three eggs over easy without lifting his head. Something had been eating him, ever since his crew got sent over to Deer Rib. Smaller trees, smaller paychecks. Enid would know. Eugene told her everything.

He mopped up the last of the yolk, drained his coffee. "That hit the spot."

He got his boots on, let her peck him on the cheek—*Be careful*—and ducked out into the rain.

*Every day of a marriage is a choice*, the pastor had said at their wedding.

She wedged the radio between the lamp and the wall, the sweet spot where the tinfoil-bulbed antenna managed to fish a tune from the air. She had one last satin rose to sew on. Four older sisters, a whole childhood of hand-me-downs; Alsea should start out with her own baptism gown. She was a good baby, no fuss. The kind of baby anyone would want.

She pinched her ears to relieve the itch. If it was itching, it was healing. What was it Daniel had wanted to ask?

She knotted the thread, snapped it clean, and held the gown up, satin catching window light. The red Wagoneer swung into the driveway, Enid laying on the horn.

"We're going to Bistrin's," Enid announced, barging into the house. "The girls need shoes. You coming?"

"Chub's sleeping."

"Chub?" Enid hollered. "Chu-ub!" And though Chub was normally unwakeable, crawling under the picnic table on the Fourth and sleeping through the fireworks, he wandered out from the hall in his pajamas, hair cowlicked. "There," Enid said. "He's up."

* * *

Chub sat in the backseat, chattering with Agnes, Mavis, and Gertrude, the girls lively and pretty with their red-blond hair and milk-blue eyes, despite being named after women three generations too old. Chub adored them.

"What did you do to your ears?" Enid asked, backing down the driveway.

Colleen touched the earrings. "Rich gave them to me."

"Lemme see?"

Colleen leaned across.

"Hm," Enid said. "What'd he do?"

"What do you mean?"

"I know Eugene has screwed up when he brings me something. I wish he'd screw up big and buy me a washer-dryer."

"He didn't do anything," Colleen said, pinching the earrings. A log truck barreled past in the oncoming lane. Besides her wedding ring, Rich had never given her jewelry.

"They look spendy," Enid said. "Must have been something bad. And he bought you that crew cab. Think what he must have done then."

Colleen knew it was ungrateful, but the truth was she hated that truck. She'd been alone at the house the Friday before Easter, Chub spending the night at Enid's. She should have called an ambulance as soon as she went out and found her old Ford wouldn't start. Instead, Rich came home late and found her in the tub—it was too much blood to stay in bed—head canted back over the rim, a scene from a horror movie.

When it was over, he'd gone straight out to the dealership and bought her the fanciest truck they had, though he despised Chevys with an intensity beyond the purely mechanical. She resented that truck every time she climbed into it—as if anything could make up for what she'd lost—but it was a family truck, a truck with seat belts, built for six. She clung to its promise: They would try again. They would keep trying.

"I'll make Eugene buy me a washer-dryer when he gets his first grove check," Enid announced, pulling up in front of Bistrin's, the store's windows plastered with back-to-school sales. *Stonewashed jeans $12.99.*

They went in, the girls heading straight for a display of fringed white cowboy boots.

"Those are like Dad's," Chub said, pointing to a pair of yellow work boots. He sat down obediently to try them on. "They fit!"

She felt the toes. "They're too big."

"Please?" he begged.

She checked the price.

"He'll grow into them," Enid called. "Do they have them in five? Wyatt needs a pair."

Enid had left Wyatt home and Colleen was glad. Wily, mean, he was the kind of boy she hoped Chub wouldn't befriend when he started school.

"You can't wear them until your feet get bigger," Colleen told Chub. He nodded eagerly, like he would sit there and wait as long as it took his feet to grow.

She bought him the too-big boots and two pairs of overalls—a size for now, and a size up.

"These are going to be filthy by the end of the day," Enid said, pulling the tags off three pairs of white boots so the girls could wear them out of the store. Outside, the kids hopped over cracks, sidewalk a novelty. She thought of Rich crossing the driveway this morning, one bootlace untied, in such a hurry to get out the door.

"Is something going on?" Colleen asked.

"What do you mean?" Enid asked.

"Rich seems—I don't know. Worried."

"Did you ask him?"

Colleen crossed her arms. *He doesn't tell me anything.* "Did they figure out where that skull came from?"

Enid shrugged. "Not that I heard."

"Eugene hasn't said anything?" Colleen pressed her.

"Just that they'll be back harvesting the grove by the end of the month," Enid said. "That's when I get my washer-dryer. You don't know what it's like, having six kids."

"No," Colleen said, pinching her ears. "I don't."

"Oh, come on. That's not what I meant."

"I know," Colleen said.

# RICH

Lark's driveway toilets gleamed, guarding the turnoff like two mismatched porcelain lions. Rich bounced along the rutted two-track, worry jostling in his chest. His whole life he'd been paid by the board foot, and though they'd heard day rate was coming, he wasn't prepared. He parked, snagging the six-pack of Tab and the covered tin off the seat beside him. The slam of his truck door radiated up the taut cords of his back. Killer and Banjo sauntered over, tails wagging.

"Where you been, String Bean?" Lark asked, leaning back in his porch chair, half-carved Sasquatch resting on his knee.

"Deer Rib."

"Didn't you clear the Rib a couple years back?"

"The west side. They got us on the east now."

Rich set a boot on the bottom step. Just a tweak, low on the spine, but the pain sang down his left leg to the heel. Working was fine; it was sitting still that hurt.

"How's the shit business?" he asked, coming up the stairs.

"Regular."

"Kel sent you some steak and onions."

"Onions." Lark humphed, then narrowed his eyes. "What are you doing here on a weekday? I told Marsha I don't need nobody checking on me."

"Those signs ready?" Rich asked.

"In the shop." Lark tossed his head toward the rusty-roofed outbuilding. Firewood Lark hawked to campers for a buck a bundle was stacked under the eaves.

Rich's shin pulsed, decent bruise over bone, split knuckle, gash on his wrist that could use a stitch. Through the shop door, he spotted a sign lying tabletop on a sawhorse. A paintbrush soaked in a bucket.

"They dry?" Rich asked.

"Half hour." Lark scratched his jaw.

Every year, Rich drove Lark out to collect his road signs, staked at two-mile increments on either side of the Gold Bear Bridge, up and down the 101 from Crescent City to Orick.

Rich spun the tin on his palm, meat warm through the aluminum. Lark sniffed. Ten bucks said he hadn't had a hot meal all day.

"Are you going to stand there like a damn undertaker?" Lark asked.

Rich cleared a Polaroid camera off a seat and set the six-pack and the covered tin at his feet, keeping his back straight.

"Who rammed a stick up your ass?"

The flyer dropped an acorn, which rolled across the porch and came to rest against Killer's back. The dog opened one eye, too lazy to investigate.

"What's the word on that skull?" Lark asked.

Rich shrugged, sweat-damp folds of his shirt itching where they touched skin.

"Heard the state bone collectors were out digging around. Those guys find so much as a damn fingernail clipping, they'll pull the plug on the whole operation. Who tipped them anyway? Merle?"

"Why the hell would he do that?" Rich asked.

"Who knows," Lark said. "Always playing some kind of angle." Lark spat over the railing. "You hear Jim Mueller unloaded those forties?" he asked, though Rich hadn't told a soul.

No phone, two canes, old two-tone International that hadn't budged in thirty-five years, and still Lark could tell you what was going on in the rooster comb of land between the Smith River at the north, clear south to the Eel, and as far east as the Trinity. As if news still traveled by river, and all he had to do was dip a finger in the Klamath to learn the latest.

Rich toed the tin. "Steak's getting cold." The dogs lifted their heads. The hog caught a whiff, grunted, and waddled toward the porch, but Lark pretended not to have heard. "What's the average life expectancy of a choker setter?" Rich asked.

It had been Lark's question to him, when Rich first asked about getting hired on at fifteen. Rich's father's best friend, Lark had sawed the branch that clubbed Rich's father dead, a true widowmaker. No one's fault but the wind's, but still Lark carried it. He'd hauled a stone up from the river to the stump of that tree every day until he got hurt himself, a mountain of rocks marking all the days Rich had lived without his father.

*High-lead's a ticket to dead, maimed, or crippled. Go to school, learn something*, Lark had said when Rich had fumbled for an answer. At fifteen, Rich was taller than his teachers. He hated ducking through the classroom door, hated all those eyes. The second time he'd asked, he'd walked all the way out to the muddy side where Lark's crew was working.

*What the hell are you doing?* Lark had screamed over the saws—everybody ran McCullochs back in those days. *You got a death wish?* A rage that shriveled Rich's voice in his throat.

*I want to work.*

*You know the average life expectancy of a choker setter?*

Again, Rich had searched for an answer. If he beat Lark to his own punch line, maybe he'd let him stay, but Lark had timed it perfect, the old steam whistle letting loose, blasting a hole right through Rich's heart.

"Lunch whistle," Lark said now, smiling at the memory, not looking up from his carving.

Rich watched a Sasquatch's bulky shoulders slowly emerge. Lark had carved a thousand of them over the years. After Rich's dad got killed, Lark used to take Rich fishing, set him up on the porch to whittle while steelhead fried in a pan, hogs nosing through the guts, then down to the Beehive for sweet rolls to bring home to Rich's mom. Lark's own wife had washed away when a logjam busted loose upriver and sent a pulse surging through in the twenties. When Lark came home from his logging camp a week later, she was gone.

*He never got over it. That was before your dad knew him*, Rich's mom had said.

Lark rarely mentioned his Karuk wife, except to say she came from upriver people, and always kept a toe in the water, that she would talk her own language at him when she was angry, and talked some Yurok too, that she could pull the fibers from a wild iris, roll them over her knee to make twine, and tie a gill net that trapped and held thirty-pound chinook half as tall as she was. Lark had made a grave for her, though there was no body to carry home. Rich had seen her headstone, not far from where his parents were buried, on the other side of the low rock wall that separated the white dead from the Indians.

"Where's your teeth?" Rich asked.

"In there somewhere."

Rich ducked into the kitchen, scrounged a fork, steak already diced. When he came back out, Lark was prying the lid off the tin, rooting out steak. The aroma brought spit to Rich's mouth.

"Too old to cut my own meat?" Lark grouched, forking up a mouthful. The hog grunted, watching through the railing. "Merle, sit your fat ass down." The hog lowered its rear. "Pigs are smart as hell."

Lark used to steal apples off the old Peine orchard to fatten the hogs, turn the meat sweet, but it had been years since he'd used the smokehouse. The old hog was a pet, though Lark wouldn't admit it. Lark used to keep two or three, all named after whoever had pissed him off that year. For two decades after Lark fell, muck-coated Virgils had lounged, waiting to be slaughtered. There was no one Lark hated more. Lark was sure someone had severed the rope's steel core enough to allow him to climb forty feet before it snapped, and if it wasn't Virgil himself, it was J.P., who ran a junk shop crammed with used saw parts down in Eureka but made most of his money doing Virgil's dirty work, though Lark could never prove it. Lark broke his back, his neck, both hips. *And just about every other bone, except my funny bone*, he liked to quip.

"You cut thirty percent, let the rest grow, Chub'll be harvesting long after you're gone," Lark said, like he'd been thinking about it. When Lark had first started talking about not cutting faster than it could grow back—sustained yield before there was a name for it—Virgil had ragged him.

*Somebody must be trimming your beard with a chainsaw, Corny. You've lost your damn mind.*

The real knock-down-drag-outs came later, Virgil calling him a communist, until finally Lark struck out on his own.

"Wish Virgil had lived to see you pull it off, that sonofabitch," Lark said. "Couldn't stand that I quit. Had to make me pay."

"Could have been an accident," Rich offered lamely. What was the use of dredging all that up again?

"Yeah. Accident. Steel-cored rope snaps like a damn fish line. Like that time Olin Rowley stuck his hand in the band saw? Running saw for twenty years and lops his arm off like a banana? Accident. He was helping himself to burls up Fatal Creek."

Lark pushed the tin—now mostly onions—onto the upside-down crate beside him.

"Are we taking these signs tonight or not?" Rich asked.

The outhouse placard could have used a repaint too: 10¢ (HONOR SYSTEM). WE APPRECIATE YOUR GOOD AIM.

"You got something better to do?" Lark asked.

Rich rubbed his palms over his knees, denims damp. Another half hour, he'd be stiff as a corpse. The flyer rooted around Lark's neck.

"Get off." Lark tossed his shoulder. The squirrel dropped to the floor, scuttling behind hunks of driftwood scattered across the porch as if deposited there by high tide.

"Ah, hell," Lark said. A dog's ear for engines. "What's that bitch want now?"

Marsha's Dodge puttered up the gulch to the drive-thru tree.

"You're blocking my customers," Lark yelled. There was a circular drive for tourists to pull through the tree and get their picture taken under the sign nailed above the tunnel: SURVIVOR TREE. HEIGHT: 301 FEET. DIAM-ETER: 16.3 FEET. SINCE 200 A.D.

"What customers?"

Marsha's Jack Russell spilled off her lap and raced over to yip at the hog, bouncing with the force of its own bark, all four feet off the ground. It zipped up the steps, on the flyer's scent.

"Get out of here, Gizmo, you little sonofabitch." Lark kicked at him.

"Hey, Rich," Marsha said, balancing a store-bought sponge cake on top of a casserole. Heavy as a sow, but still the same lilt in her voice. "What happened to you?" She eyed the cuts where the branch had caught him, worrying when he should have been paying attention—how was he going to make the mortgage on day rate?

Rich coughed. "Overdid it a little."

"Why don't you put some clothes on?" she asked Lark. "It's cold. I got more Tab in the truck." She took the casserole inside.

"Why don't you bring me some damn beer?" Lark called after her.

Rich heard her dropping empty cans into the trash, tidying up.

"You been smoking in here?" Marsha asked, coming out.

"I quit." Lark sucked his cheek.

"Why didn't you tell me you were out of soap?"

"Forgot."

"Here's your change." Marsha held out an envelope, which made Rich remember Lark's mail. He'd stopped at the box on the way in.

"Keep it." Lark waved her off.

She dropped the envelope onto the crate, along with a pint of strawberries.

"What the hell's that?"

"Fruit."

Lark crossed his arms, like she'd insulted him.

"See you Thursday. If you live that long. Gizmo!" The Jack Russell whizzed across the yard and leapt into the car.

Once she was gone, Lark picked through the onions for meat he'd missed, pushed the tin away. "That hit the spot. Now. Reach up under that seat."

Rich turned as though another chair might have walked out onto the porch. *Son of a*—it was twisting that killed you.

"That one you're sitting on," Lark said.

Rich slid a hand underneath, stood, turned the chair over, pack of cigarettes duct-taped to the underside.

Lark licked his lips. "Now we're cooking with gas."

Rich dug out a smoke. Lark fumbled a match, drew deep, exhaled.

"Quit, huh?" Rich asked.

"Tried it once. Got so damn hungry for a cigarette, I ate one. Tasted like shit." Lark took another pull. Mist hung over the river, gathering mass. "Merle really switching everybody to day pay?"

Don had broken the official news today.

"Starting Monday. Deer Rib's mostly pecker poles," Rich said. "We'd be paying Sanderson to work otherwise." His first payment on the 24-7 was due in a month.

"A lot can happen in a month," Lark said. "Get those signs loaded up, will you?"

Rich went out to the shed, looked up the gulch at the stripped pole of the Doug fir Lark had taught him to climb on after his mom died. He remembered Lark's voice rising from the ground.

*Cut from above. You cut from underneath, that branch'll strip down the side, suck your rope in, squeeze you so tight your gizzard'll come out your nose.*

For weeks, Rich had scraped and grunted his way up that pole, slipped, slid, started over, hands rope-burned, arms sore, until he could race to the top and touch ground in forty seconds, circle of flayed bark at the base.

Now Lark watched through a veil of smoke as Rich heaved signs into the truck bed, plywood nailed to sharpened two-by-fours.

HOUSE INSIDE A TREE! "House" was a lot to say for an old hollowed-out stump with a wobbly table and a couple of milk crates inside. In the old days, it might have made a good goose pen, but Lark had put a door in front and two pieces of tin over the top and started charging a quarter to go in. If there was one thing he enjoyed more than smoking, it was screwing a tourist out of a city dollar. Too rich to sweat for a living, too dumb to dig their own hole to shit in.

Lark stubbed out his cigarette. "Rich Gundersen. Won't risk a buck on a dice roll, up to his goddamn neck now. Welcome to the party, Rich. Congratu-fuckin-lations."

A grin tugged at the corner of Rich's mouth.

"How long 'til you're back harvesting the grove, you think?"

"Don't know," Rich admitted. "But I know that skull wasn't up there three weeks ago."

"You tell Merle that?"

"That I've been snooping around on my off days?" Rich asked. "No thanks."

"It'd give you a chance to ask him about using his roads to get your timber out. You want to nail him down on a milling contract, don't you?" Lark reached for his canes, knocking the saw over and using the barrel of the rifle to drag it into range.

By the time he got into the truck, the dogs had knocked the tin of onions to the ground, pushing it around with their snouts.

"Here's your mail."

"Cornelius Larkin," Lark read, as though the name belonged to someone else. He tucked an envelope into his pocket, ripped another in half and tossed it out the window.

Lark called the spots and Rich pulled over, Lark talking out the window while Rich sank the signs, occasional car whooshing past.

"Old long-thumbs Danforth still cruising for Sanderson?" They were stopped on the south end of Gold Bear Bridge.

"Yep," Rich said, driving a sign into the ground with the sledgehammer, impact ringing up his arm.

"Lucky somebody never cut his damn thumbs off," Lark said.

Rich slid back in behind the wheel. "I asked him how far down the roads'll go for the lower grove. He wouldn't tell me."

"Merle's been pushing through those harvest plans Danforth writes up for years," Lark said, "but that don't mean he can read them for shit. Most timber that cocksucker's ever handled is a pencil. Just ask him to give you a look."

Rich glanced over his shoulder. Three signs left. "Are there more of these than last time?"

They passed run-down houses along the coast, taken for the park. For now, they were rented, but once their twenty-five years were up, they'd be bulldozed to the ground, like Rich's own. You'd never know babies had been born here, dishes broken, that a man lay awake the whole night listening to a tree creak in a windstorm, worrying it might fall on the house.

"What's the use of putting a new roof on?" Lark lifted his chin at the last house, set apart from the others, bright white. The roofer reached into his hip sack and Rich saw it was Tom Feeley's kid.

"Would have made a good climber," Lark said. "Look at him."

"Would have," Rich agreed.


Rich hammered in the last sign, blood leaching from the hot lines where brambles had ripped flaps in the back of his hand.

"Merle'll find out sooner or later," Lark said, like he'd come to some decision. "Better it be from you. And tell Colleen. Nothing'll get you in hot water like lying to your old lady."

"I didn't lie."

"No. You didn't say a damn thing, did you?" Lark ran his stump finger along his gums, clearing out onion slime. He sighed. "Let's go take a look."

"Now?" Rich asked. It was near twilight.

"When you get to be my age, you don't leave things 'til tomorrow."

Rich turned at the dark mill. Back when loggers had marched like an army over the coastal range, Sanderson ran two shifts, every day but Sunday, the debarker's high-pressure blasts stripping logs clean, conveyers chugging bark out to be dried, sorted, bagged, Olin Rowley slicing logs lengthwise, edger sawing out defects, Yuroks on green chain, pulling boards, sorting and stacking them for the drying yards or the kiln, building rattling with the noise it struggled to contain. Now the place looked abandoned. Pecker poles got trucked south to

Eureka or up to Crescent City, where mills were retrofitted with saws small enough to handle them.

Rich slowed to a stop above where the culvert ran Damnation Creek under No Name Road and looked out at the timber along 24-7 Ridge.

Lark cranked down his window, let out a long whistle. "Don't make them like that anymore."

A guy in a backpack appeared at the edge of the upper grove, as though the whistle had summoned him.

"You know that's an Indian burial ground up there?" Lark called out the window, though the man was an Indian, handsome, about Colleen's age, a pencil tucked above his ear. "You're Dolores's boy," Lark said. He stuck his arm out the window and shook the man's hand, like they were comrades.

Rich didn't recognize him. Didn't remember Dolores—dancing with the radar boys who'd been stationed here during the war, throwing back her head to laugh—until Lark said her name.

"Daniel," Lark said. Lark had a memory for faces like a deck of cards tucked in his shirt pocket, one for every person he'd ever met in his life. "You a doctor by now?"

"Fish doctor," the man said.

Lark laughed. The man's eyes slid over Rich, as though calculating his height.

"Fish doctor, that's pretty good." Lark laughed again. "We're more than a mile from the river up here, aren't we?"

"We are," the man confirmed, but offered nothing more.

"How's George?" Lark asked. "Haven't seen him out on the water lately. Boat problems?"

"You could say that."

"Figures. I've seen him load her so full of chinook she wasn't riding two inches about the water line. Full enough to sink her," Lark recalled.

The man shook his head. "The runs aren't what they used to be. Half the creeks are silted in."

"There's still a good coho run up Damnation Creek, isn't there, Rich?" Lark asked.

Rich nodded. "Most years."

"Must be one of the last," the man said. "Not a lot of them are making it back, the way the offshore guys are harvesting them."

"Well." Lark slapped some dirt off his knee. "If there's one fish left in that river, George'll find it. Hell of a fisherman, your uncle. You want a ride?"

"I'm all set." The man adjusted his backpack. "Thanks."

"You be careful walking around out here, college boy. With that long hair, somebody might mistake you for a tree hugger, shoot you for the bounty. What's the bounty on a tree hugger these days, Rich? Twenty-five?"

"Sounds about right," Rich agreed.

"Used to get fifty for a mountain lion. But there were less of them around." Lark squinted ahead. "Empty stretch of road like this can be dangerous. You might want to stay off it."

"I'll keep that in mind." The man gave a quick salute and vanished into the brush. Lark watched the spot where he'd disappeared.

"What's he doing out here, you think?" Lark asked.

"Who knows." Rich rubbed his shoulder, ready to go home.

"Lucky somebody worse didn't find him."

Eugene had gone after those hippies outside the fish fry with a baseball bat. Would have bashed someone's head in if Harvey hadn't showed up when he did. Rich put the truck in gear.

"Hold up." Lark angled for another look. "How much Mueller take you for?"

"Two fifty."

Lark sucked air through his teeth. "Riding high on the whores in sunny San Diego, thanks to you." The 24-7 glowed golden-orange, catching the last rays. "Look at her. What's she now? 28-5?"

"Thirty and change. Been a hundred years since they named that ridge."

"Rich Gundersen. Betting on himself. Your dad'd be prouder than hell." Lark thumped the dash twice, the way he'd move a mule on. "About time one of you Gundersens had more than two sticks of firewood to your name."

Colleen sat under the rabbit lamp sewing when he came in.

"Where've you been?" she asked.

"Lark wanted to get his signs out." He dropped his keys in the burl bowl.

"Dinner's in the oven."

"Where's Chub?" he asked, getting his boots off.

She looked at him over her glasses. "Asleep. It's nine o'clock."

He shuffled into the kitchen, pulled the plate out. Meat loaf with those scalloped potatoes he liked. He heard Colleen go out, porch light aglow in the white dark. After a minute, a truck door slammed. Colleen swept back inside, banging the front door shut behind her.

"The new insurance cards came," she said. "I put one in your glove box." She pushed an angry puff of air out her nostrils. "Is there something you want to tell me?"

He thought of the papers, the post office box key hidden in the secret compartment. How could he explain that key? The future he hoped it would unlock?

"Colleen."

"Don't 'Colleen' me." She tramped across the living room rug without taking off her boots. "What are these?" she demanded.

He caught the packet of condoms she threw at him against his chest and cleared his throat, masking his relief. She wasn't mad that he'd cleaned out their savings, shackled them to a mortgage he might never be able to repay, risked his future and hers. No, she was angry about a pack of rubbers he hadn't even worked up the guts to bring inside. He tossed the condoms onto the kitchen table beside his dinner.

"Don't put those there," she snapped, crossing her arms.

He didn't know how much longer he could hold out. His whole body ached for her. But he wasn't going to put her through that. Not again. Not ever.

He ran his thumb along the lip of his plate. "I can't take another one."

"Oh, *you* can't?" She stomped down the hall and slammed the bathroom door.

He ate to the sound of bathwater glugging into the tub on the other side of the wall. When she finished, he took his shower. She was already in bed when he came in. He dropped the condoms into the bedside drawer. She lay on her side, turned away from him. He'd been hoping she would walk on his back. He eased himself into bed, traced a finger along her neck, down to her shoulder blade, felt her body tense, smelled her geranium lotion. He could tell her now—*I took a chance, a big chance.* He walked to the edge of it, so close.

He longed to pull her to him but stopped himself. He would never forget standing alone outside the emergency room doors after they rushed her in, hospital linoleum speckled with her blood. Left behind, helpless in the cold hallway, he'd bargained, promised, sworn. Never again.

He reached up and turned off the lamp. They lay there, separated by twelve inches of dark air.

*September 2*

# COLLEEN

"I want another baby," she said, setting his breakfast in front of him. She'd lain awake half the night thinking about it. "Can't we at least talk about it?"

Rich forked through his eggs.

She crossed her arms. "If you'd just come home on time, maybe—"

"Christ, Colleen. We've been over this. It wouldn't have made a goddamn bit of difference."

"How do you know?"

"There wasn't anything I could have done," Rich said, dropping his fork. "Even if you'd called the ambulance—there wasn't anything anybody could have done."

Tears sprang into Colleen's eyes. "But why can't we just try?"

An expression she couldn't read clouded Rich's face.

"Chub needs you," he said.

She waited for him to say more, to say *I need you*. When he didn't, she stormed out, crawled back into bed. She knew she was being childish. She heard him in the kitchen, washing his dish. When he came down the hall to say goodbye, she pretended to have fallen back asleep, which, after he left, she did. She woke an hour later with a cramp—the slow leak, the sick-sweet smell of her period. Her body asking, as it did every month, *Do you want another baby?* She brushed her teeth, peed, stared at the bloody tissue in the toilet.

"Mama?" Chub asked.

She reached for the handle and flushed.

After breakfast, she thrust the hand shovel into the snap pea bed. *I can have another baby*. She levered blackberry shoots out by the roots. Scout ran to the edge of the yard, barking.

"Scout," she called, but he didn't budge. She stood and crossed the yard. "Scout, quiet." She laid a hand on the dog's head. His barking dissolved into a low growl. She looked up the hill, watching the tree line for movement. The hairs on the back of her neck tingled. Chub played with his toy cars in the grass.

*Whoever killed that kid has been dead a hundred years*, Rich had said when Colleen had pressed him about the skull. Still, it bothered her. A hundred years ago it was still someone's child. Someone's little boy running through the ferns. She brushed soil off her knees.

Inside, she fished the truck keys from the burl bowl. Scout's barking had spooked her. Chub launched himself torso-first into the Chevy's footwell. The fog was so thick she could barely make out the guardrail running along the cliff edge like a fence. She hunched forward over the wheel. Every time the ground around Last Chance Creek crumbled off into the ocean, mudslide taking a section of the coast highway with it, Caltrans talked about rerouting this road inland.

*No fog, no redwoods*, Rich said. *No timber, no paycheck*. It wasn't as easy as people thought, being married to a man who never complained.

The road curved inland at the lagoon. Chub swung his legs. Another mile to Trees of Mystery—forever in kid time—the roadside tourist trap the last marker before town.

"There's Babe!" Chub cried at last.

The ox's boxy blue head, big as a Volkswagen, thrust through the fog, giant Paul Bunyan swallowed from the waist up, beckoning city people into the curio shop with its burl clocks and Sasquatch key chains, and a back room where other things were rumored to change hands—grave-robbed baskets and beadwork, burls the size of kitchen tables poached from old-growth trees. Pastimes people turned to when money ran low.

She turned off up the gulch toward Melody Larson's single-wide, set back from the dirt road, windows rattling when loaded logging trucks passed. Melody opened the door, pink in the face.

"Hey, Chub, you want to feed the fish?" Melody held the screen door open and walked him back to the tank. He sat down cross-legged to watch them. "I was doing my exercises again," Melody told Colleen. "I feel like he's moving around."

Melody's husband, Keith, worked in the cannery, not the woods. They had no insurance and no money for an ultrasound, but he wanted a boy, so she'd been calling the baby *him* from the start.

"Can you check?" Melody asked, sweat at her hairline.

She lay back on the couch and pulled up her shirt. Colleen rubbed her hands together to warm them and palpated Melody's hard belly, skin stretched taut. Here a foot, here an elbow. She felt for the head.

"Is he right?" Melody asked anxiously.

Colleen pressed again. "He's positioned okay, he's just got his head . . . tucked a little funny."

Melody sighed. "I hope he comes this weekend. Keith has it off."

Colleen felt for the hard curve of the baby's skull one more time.

"You call me when he does," Colleen said, and stood.


She and Chub drove by the old Peine farm, the school, the Beehive with its glass case of bear claws. Cream cheese in the dough, that was Dot's secret. They passed the post office; a boarded-up salmon-jerky shack—the fall run would be here soon, boats crowding the river's mouth; the One and Only Tavern with its white line painted above the door: the high-water mark from '64, the Christmas flood, when ankle creeks ran muddy to the waist and whole ridges slid out and buried roads. If her father had waited a decade, taken the skiff out Christmas Day 1964, he might have died a martyr instead of a drowned poacher. The white lines were everywhere: the base of the abandoned church's steeple, halfway up the attics of houses. For almost a year after the flood, the only way across the river had been by boat. The world might end in fire, but here in Del Nort County, on the banks of the Klamath, it would end in water.

She turned onto Mill Road, Rich's truck parked in its normal spot, sky reflected in the still waters of the empty millpond, once filled bumper-to-bumper with logs, enough to keep three bars in business. She'd dragged Enid from one to the next, looking for their mother's Mercury. When she found it, she'd let Enid scramble in, pull down the visor so the keys fell onto the seat, turn the heater on, and return with what was left of their mother's paycheck, usually in change. *Think of something else.*

"Four days until you start kindergarten, Chub," Colleen said.

Chub was unfazed by the idea, though it tightened the laces in her chest. The Chevy juddered over No Name Road's potholes, passing the grove. They'd found the skull, but where was the rest of him? The newspaper—a week old by the time she'd found it in the stack Marsha had sent home with Rich—said they'd recovered nothing else.

An eighteen-wheeler swung around the curve, bunks stacked with logs. It whooshed past, rocking them, the prow of Deer Rib Ridge, where the road forked, appearing through the passage torn through the fog. Colleen eased down onto the muddy two-track, Deer Rib Road carving along the base of the ridge, narrowed by brush, as though it led not only back through the clear-cuts but back through time. Her mother would have raised Cain with Sanderson, the county, anyone with a tank truck and a spray hose.

*Verne had a pair of lungs on her*, people said. *Pair of lungs and a pair of balls.*

The dashboard clunked, ruts knee-deep. The herby scent of last night's rain seeped in the vents. Saws buzzed down from the other side of the ridge, out of sight. Rich was somewhere over that ridge, on the Lost Road side, past Enid's.

"Tim-ber," Chub echoed, then grinned, his hair falling into his eyes—she needed to trim it.

Himalayans ripened along the hills, berries hanging in black clusters. Pockets of mist smoked across the road, undergrowth scrubbing the windows. At last, the farm appeared. They trundled up the long driveway between fields lined with knobby apple trees, past the pond where her father's pale hands had stretched toward her through the brown water—*Kick, sweet pea. Keep kicking.*

Chub leapt out as soon as she set the parking brake.

"Five minutes," she warned him.

Joanna emerged with Camber on her hip.

"Baptism?" she asked when she heard four dozen, and sent Judith into the coop.

Colleen wondered if it hurt Joanna's feelings that she wasn't invited. Joanna eyed the truck. Faster to walk, Colleen could see her thinking. She remembered Scout's low, throaty growl and considered asking Joanna if she'd seen anybody walk up the gulch, but that was silly. Who would be wandering around way out here?

Judith came out balancing the heavy tray. Joanna loaded the eggs into the cartons Colleen had brought, tucked the five-dollar bill into her waistband, and fished out a single. A helicopter's rotors thwacked over the ridge, spray plume drifting from its booms. A faint whiff of chlorine.

"Get inside," Joanna told the girls. Joanna snatched a dirt clod and hurled it toward the creek, where a raccoon hunched, drinking. The raccoon stood up on its hind legs, hands at its chest as though snapping an invisible pair of suspenders. "Get!" Joanna stomped toward it. The animal scurried off. "They're after the chickens," she said, straightening a hose Colleen hadn't noticed, running across the fields from Little Lost Creek. "Deer Creek stopped running," Joanna explained.

"When?" Growing up, they'd taken their water from Deer Creek, cleaner than the Little Lost, sweeter. Drinking rain.

"Friday?" Joanna narrowed her eyes as though to bring the date into focus. "It'll find a way out. Water always does."

# CHUB

The eggs were cold. No chicks moved inside. Still, Chub kept a hand on them, looking out the truck window at the sunlight dancing on No Name Creek. His dad was teaching him: the Lost, the Mad, the Mistake, Fatal, Starveout, Runaway, Last Chance, like learning the threads of a spiderweb. Roads dead-ended, but if you knew your creeks, you could always find your way home.

His mom turned onto Lost Road, the road to Fort Eugene. A tow truck came toward them pulling Aunt Enid's red Wagoneer, its windows smashed.

"E-nid," his mom scolded under her breath.

Across the swampy meadow a wind sock of smoke unspooled from the stovepipe of Fort Eugene. Goats stood in the branches of the goat tree, the trailer house balanced on cinder blocks, Little Lost Creek running right underneath it, dividing the yard into two separate territories: Aunt Enid's chicken-wire cat pen on one side, Uncle Eugene's junkyard on the other. Chub pressed his nose to the window. Add-ons mushroomed from the sides of the trailer house. Fort Eugene was damp-soft Oreos, hallways sloping like chutes for racing Matchbox cars, pocket doors that slid into the walls, his heartbeat cousin: Ag-nes, Ag-nes.

"Don't pet the cats, please," his mom said, pulling up in front.

Chub dropped down onto Uncle Eugene's side—a graveyard of rusty car skeletons and flat-tire bicycles—catapulted across the creek, and ran up the steps.

"Who's that?" Aunt Enid called down the hall, nursing the baby on the couch. "Hey, Chub. You drive yourself?"

Mavis and Gertrude looked up from their coloring books.

*Where's Agnes?* he wanted to ask, but he didn't want Aunt Enid to call him *lover boy* again. Aunt Enid teased mean and she never said sorry. She was loud, her blond hair chopped short like a man's, the opposite of his mom's quiet voice and silky mouse-brown ponytail. He slipped past Aunt Enid, past heights drawn on the wall in permanent marker. Agnes's room was empty. A cricket hopped down the hall and sailed out an open door that knocked against the outside of the trailer house. No stairs, a long drop, like one of those doors that opened up in dreams.

"Got one!" Wyatt yelled, popping up from the tall grass, shaking his cupped hands like he was trying to roll double sixes.

Agnes shot up nearby, red wisps working free from her braid, holding a jar. Wyatt stuck his hand in, jerked it out in time for her to clap the lid on.

Wyatt flicked the glass. "Kill it, stupid."

"Chub, look!" Agnes held up the jar.

Chub jumped down. A frog squatted behind the glass, grumpy, ignoring the crickets hugging the walls.

"He's retarded," Wyatt said. Wyatt liked watching the cats torture grass-hoppers to death.

"Frogs eat flies," Chub said.

"*Frogs eat flies*," Wyatt mimicked, bending one hand into a dinosaur claw and banging it against his chest. "Why do you always wear these?" Wyatt batted at Chub's binoculars. "Necklace boy?"

They rounded the corner into Aunt Enid. Agnes showed her the frog.

"Did you touch him? You'll get warts."

"Will not." Agnes squirmed. "Warts are gross."

Chub covered the hard button on his thumb, wishing he were brave enough to bite it off.

"Chub, don't run off," his mom warned him.

A tank truck lumbered slowly down the dirt road, a man walking behind, spraying with a hose.

"You're sure this is everything?" his mom asked Aunt Enid, reading the list.

"Hey, Carl!" Aunt Enid shouted. The man aimed the spray at the bushes, showering the nanny goat with the black ear eating weeds around the culvert. "How's Helen?"

"Any day," the man yelled back.

Chub coughed, a bad taste on his tongue.

"I wish he'd spray those Himalayans," Aunt Enid said, lifting her chin at the berry bushes. "Only damn thing that kills them. Chub, have you been picking your nose?"

His mom swooped down and pressed a tissue to his nostrils. He felt a pang of fear.

"Tilt your head back," his mom said when they got in the truck.

"Drive fast and take lots of chances," Aunt Enid called after them. "Ag-nes!"

Agnes scampered out of the brush.

"Where's your brother? Don't you feed that frog to the cats, you hear me?"

Agnes waved at Chub, showing her secret dimples. She opened her fist: two flies flitted out.

# COLLEEN

Gravel clattered against the truck's belly. A gnawing feeling, leaving the baptism gown behind. She'd gotten used to taking it out of her sewing basket, smoothing it across the burl table, as though it were meant for a different baby. Enid had tossed it onto the back of a chair when Colleen gave it to her, in a bad mood from arguing with Tice Whelan, crumbs of the Wagoneer's busted windows shining like crushed ice in the yard.

Chub rubbed his eyes.

"Ready for a nap?" Colleen asked.

He shook his head in heavy-lidded denial. Something quick for lunch: tuna. Brush blinded the curves, curling yellow on the side Carl had already sprayed. By tomorrow, the blackberries and ferns—everything the spray had touched that wasn't timber—would shrivel, leave the road wider. She swung around the bend, slammed the brakes: Daniel, a body's length from her front bumper.

"Ow," Chub grouched.

Daniel started toward her with such an air of purpose she felt the urge to press down the peg lock. She rolled her window down.

"Colleen," he greeted her sternly; she'd nearly run him over. "Hey, buddy," he said to Chub. He shifted the knapsack bandoliered across his chest. Glass clinked inside it. "The Knife still running back that way?" Daniel lifted his chin at the road behind her.

She nodded. "It's too far to walk." She wondered if he'd ask to hitch a ride back to town.

"You'd be surprised." A smile played on his lips.

"The Knife meets the Fork just shy of Starveout," Chub recited.

"Rich's teaching him," Colleen explained.

"You." Daniel pointed at Chub. "Have got your mom's good memory."

Colleen blushed. It had started out as a school assignment, eleventh-grade history: Daniel Bywater. Colleen Hinkle. Partners pulled from a hat. She'd wanted the lighthouse in Crescent City from the topic jar, the class giggling when the radar station came out instead.

*I can drive us to the library*, he'd said. So, that Saturday, they'd gone down to Arcata, to the university, her first time alone in a car with a boy. She'd buried herself in the books on the table instead of looking up at the high ceilings in a building she'd been afraid to walk into. It was on the way back that he suggested they go see it. *For research.* He'd parked the car at the make-out point and they'd walked down the coast in silence. There was only one reason you went to the radar station with a boy. Maybe because he was nervous too, Daniel had talked. He'd told her how his father had been stationed here, during the war, a white man with a wife and kids back home. How his mother had met him dancing at the Cutthroat, how nine months later Daniel was here, and his father was gone. He told her about eeling on the spit where the river met the ocean, how once, when he was thirteen, a sneaker wave had grabbed him by his ankles, how his uncle had hooked him in the back before the current could drag him out and drown him. About a canoe his uncle was carving from a redwood log he'd found floating near the mouth of the river, tied to the boat, and towed home. How his uncle would carve a heart, and lungs, and kidneys at the bottom, because redwood was alive, the canoe was alive. The way the river was. They'd sat, shoulder to shoulder, against the radar station's cold cinderblock wall. She'd wondered if he was thinking about his father, the way she sometimes thought about her own. Finally, Daniel had taken her hand, as if he had come all the way here to do only that.

*Good memory*, he'd whispered later, after she'd rattled off the dates she'd learned for their presentation and they were both back in their seats, her heart banging at her ribs. She'd wanted to reach over and take his hand again, but of course she hadn't. The next month he graduated a year early, and he was gone.

"There's nothing to see back here but clear-cuts," Colleen told him now.

"You trying to turn me around, Colleen Hinkle?"

"Gundersen." She pressed a hand over her turtleneck, as though to keep the red blotches of heat she felt on her clavicles from showing through.

They were stopped in the middle of the grove, creek water crashing downhill into the culvert under the road.

"What's in there?" Chub asked. He'd unbuckled his seat belt and stood in the footwell behind her.

"In here?" Daniel pulled a jam jar from his knapsack. Water sloshed inside. "Just some samples. I was hoping you might help me out." He met Colleen's eyes, hitched the sack up with a clank, and whistled. Scout burst through the brush, dripping.

"Scout!" Chub yelled.

She opened her door and Chub tumbled out after her, Scout bounding over, knocking Chub onto his butt to lick his face.

"He's all wet!" Chub shrieked.

Scout shook and threw himself to the ground, legs bicycling.

"He wants you to scratch his belly," Chub explained.

"I figured he belonged to somebody," Daniel said.

Colleen made Chub climb back into the cab.

"Good-looking dog," Daniel offered.

She shook her head. Scout looked like he was pieced together from parts of other dogs—gray-and-black brindle body, a bird dog's speckled legs, a shepherd's long coat, the white-dipped tail of a herd dog.

"He run off a lot?" he asked.

"He goes looking for Rich."

"Does he ever find him?"

"Usually finds a porcupine first."

"Dogs are the best judge of people. Must be a good guy. Tree-topper? Famous one, from what I hear."

The rain started again. She let the tailgate down and Scout leapt up into the bed. Her eyes stung.

"Really smell that spray now." Daniel pulled up the neck of his shirt and wiped his face. "Your water comes down off lower Damnation Creek, right?"

"How do you know that?" she asked.

"Do you filter it?"

"Rich takes care of it," she said. "He adds some chlorine, but the water's pretty clean."

"It looks it," Daniel said. "And cold. No wonder the coho like it. It's a hike to get out here to sample, though. I was hoping—if I gave you some jars, could you collect some from your tap once a week? It's pretty straightfor-ward." He pulled a smaller bag from his sack, the same gold-topped jars she used for canning. "Just label them with the date. I can stop by and get them."

"I can't," she said. Her eyes slid toward Chub, watching out the truck window.

"Come on, Colleen," Daniel pressed her.

The old refrain tugged at her. *Come on, Colleen.* As if he knew her, her secret wants and fears, the bridges she had to cross to reach them or to leave them behind.

"Daniel, I just—" She had a house and a child and a husband. "I can't."

"Well, if you change your mind . . ." His hand grazed hers as he swung the bag of jars up into her truck bed. He gave a casual salute.

She climbed back in behind the wheel. Chub slid the rear window open and Scout stuck his snout through.

"He's stinky." Chub clothespinned his nose.

She turned the key, grinding the starter. She'd left it running this whole time.

"Where'd he go?" Chub asked.

Daniel had vanished.

"I don't know, Grahamcracker."


Back at the house, she tightened Scout's collar a notch. Chub yawned, slouch-ing at the table, picking horseshoes of celery out of his tuna. She smoothed his bangs out of his eyes.

"Where'd you get those beautiful brown eyelashes?"

"I got them at the eyelash store," he answered, tuckered out.

She turned the water on full blast to fill the tub. It sputtered.

"Your dad'll have to fix that."

Afterward, helping him towel off his hair, she had to give her head a shake to cast out Daniel, the involuntary thrill when their hands had brushed.

Chub crawled into bed without any nap-time fuss.

"Where's Scout?" he asked, drifting.

"Outside, remember?"

"Oh yeah." He yawned.

"Sweet dreams, cookie-boy." He snuggled, rubbing his nose back and forth against the blanket's satin edging. She pressed her thumbs into his dimples. He turtled his head.

"Your hands are cold!"

"I got one miracle. And you're it." She kissed his forehead.


The dozen jam jars Daniel had given her clanked in their bag. She wasn't sure what to do with them, so she opened the cabinet under the junk drawer, where she kept her canning supplies, and stacked them there, in two neat rows.

She fixed dinner, watched the numerals click around on the stove clock: six, then seven. Rich must have stopped off at Lark's again, avoiding her. Outside, Scout barked. She went and got the fire poker. It was almost dark when Rich finally came in, meat loaf drying out in the oven. He turned on the rabbit lamp, shed his slicker in the pool of its light.

He sniffed. "Smells good."

"I think somebody was up on the hill earlier," she said. "Scout barked his head off."

"Bears are out," Rich said, watching her set the fire poker back against the wall. "Where's Chub?"

"Napping."

"Still?" Rich asked, glancing at the dark window. "Want me to wake him?"

Want.

"Let him sleep," she said.

# RICH

Morning mist blanketed Bald Hill. Scout shot up the trail ahead of them, Rich eyeing the path for broken ferns, trampled salal, a snagged thread. At the top, he cut sideways along the tree line.

"What are you looking for?" Chub asked.

"Nothing."

By the time they got up to the 24-7, Rich was panting. Chub pressed his palm to the big pumpkin's bark. It was only up here that the worry—a pain like indigestion—faded from Rich's chest. This was his timber. He'd find a way to get it out. He'd talk to Merle.

"How do you get to Lark's from here?" Rich asked, testing him.

Chub studied his palm. Rich held his own out beside it, like two books they were comparing.

"You walk up, up, up to the spring, then you zag along Eel Creek, you follow the sound . . ." Chub hesitated. "On one side is town, on the other Knockdown. When you start to Shiver—" He bit his lip, struggling to remember the rest of the rhyme.

Shiver was a spit creek that ran off Knockdown Ridge, through the parcel where Rich's dad had been clubbed to death. The stump was still there, a makeshift shrine, rock pile ten feet high, new shoot a tree in its own right.

"You're close to the river!" Chub exclaimed.

"Good. Now, which way home?"

Chub pointed.

"Well, aren't you just as bright as a dime?"

Chub ran ahead. From the top of their hill, Rich saw Colleen prying a fist of Himalayan roots from the garden. Chub snuck down toward her. Rich popped a squat to watch, and right there, in the dirt: a boot print. Smaller than his, larger than Colleen's. He touched the depression, a day old, weakened by dew. Down below, Chub leapt out, Colleen tickling him, making him squeal. Scout barked, feinting.

"What do you think?" she asked, out of breath, when Rich came down into the yard, Chub squirming in her lap. "Should we bake this cookie-boy in the oven?" Tickling had lifted the worry out of her, but now the shadow of it returned. "Anything?" she asked.

He shook his head, swept Chub up, blew on his belly. "What kind of cookie is this?"

"Chocolate chip?" Colleen guessed.

"No!" Chub howled.

"Peanut butter?"

"No!"

"Oatmeal raisin?"

"No!"

"Graham cracker?"

"That's what he is," Rich said, and set him down. Chub flopped onto his back in the grass.

"This cookie-boy needs a bath," Colleen said. Chub blew his hair out of his eyes. "And a haircut."

Rich glanced up the hill toward the boot print—deer-sense of being watched. A man had stood there, looking down at the house. At Colleen's geraniums in the window. At the back door, which didn't lock.

# COLLEEN

Chub strained against his seat belt, fiddling with his clip-on tie as they wound along the coast road toward town.

"It stinks back here," Chub protested.

"Hang tight, Grahamcracker," Rich said. "Almost there."

"How are my eggs doing?" she asked.

"I want to go home." Chub pouted.

"See any whales?" Rich asked.

Chub pressed the ends of his binoculars to the window glass and stared out at the gray chop. If he saw a whale, he got to make a wish.

At the community center, Wyatt jumped down from Eugene's rusty truck, followed by Agnes, Mavis, and Gertrude in velvet dresses with white collars, their white cowboy boots brown in the toes.

"Hold on a minute, mister," Colleen said, straightening Chub's tie. "You can't go in looking like a scarecrow." She licked her thumb and rubbed a spot off his forehead.

Sitting in a foldout chair in the church's rec room, listening to the pastor, watching Enid unwrap baby Alsea, water running off her head into the basin, Colleen breathed in her mouth and out her nose—*Don't cry, whatever you do, don't cry*—until it was over.

"She didn't even cry," Chub observed later, when Colleen sat in the reception room, holding Alsea.

"She never cries." She wiped the baby's chin. "She's a happy baby. Like you were, Chub."

"Can I have dessert?" he asked.

"Finish your food first."

Chub nudged cheese onto a cracker, avoiding the deviled egg.

"When are you going to have a little sister, Chubby?" Eugene's great-aunt, Gertie, the last living DeWitt sister, asked.

"I had a baby sister," Chub said. "She died."

Colleen shifted Alsea in her arms. She'd explained it to him, after she'd lost the baby, but she was surprised he remembered.

"What?" Gertie asked, glancing up at Colleen.

"My mom had a very tiny baby in her belly that died," Chub said. Colleen felt tears well in her eyes. "But I didn't die."

"Oh." Gertie cleared her throat.

"I'll be right back." Colleen excused herself, handed Alsea to Enid, and went out the double doors into the parking lot, gulping the cool air.

She'd been up late, mashing yolks, slopping the mixture into the icing bag, filling the rubbery white bowls. She'd woken tired, burned the toast, ironed Chub's shirt only to turn it over and discover it was missing a button. Even the drizzle had taunted her, like someone walking backward in front of her with a bowl of water, flicking it in her face. And of course Enid hadn't gotten here early and of course nothing had been set up. And now here was the third pan of deviled eggs, forgotten on the hood of the truck, tinfoil jeweled with rain.

*Take it easy on your sister. Someday you two will be all you have.*

She looked up, as if Mom might be standing there across the parking lot. Colleen had made it through dozens of parties like this one. Six kids' worth of baptisms and birthdays and school plays. She would make it through today. She would focus on what she had: Chub. She had Chub.

"How many of these did you make?" Enid asked when Colleen came back in, Enid's hand hovering over the deviled eggs as though she were deciding her next move at checkers. Even heavy in the hips, her pale skin a little pitted, she was beautiful. *Have to be pretty to carry off a do like that*, Mom had said the first time Enid hacked off her hair. Colleen had understood the warning.

Enid's kids swarmed the bowl of chocolates.

"Where'd all these redheads come from?" the pastor asked.

"You got me," Enid said, as though no more responsible for their behavior than their hair color.

Colleen's father's hair had been black, but his beard, when he grew one, had two orange streaks down either side of his mouth, like the hinges were rusting. Colleen wondered if Enid remembered this.

"Can you hold her?" Enid asked, unloading the baby into Colleen's arms again.

The doors to the playground were propped open and she saw Rich sitting on a stump outside, where the men were talking, bent paper plate between his knees.

"Tree-hugging welfare bums," Eugene said. "I'll tell you what really tears them up. Bunch of rednecks making bank. Virgin forest. Who the hell wants a virgin anyway? They show up again, we should shoot 'em all."

"You couldn't hit the broad side of a barn," Lew Miller ribbed him. "From inside it. What the hell did you use in Viet-nam?"

"My bare hands, Lew. My bare hands."

Colleen watched Chub chase Wyatt across the playground, bouncing Alsea in her arms. Latecomers slopped macaroni salad onto paper plates. The widow of a killed choker setter hurried her moonfaced kids along. Growing up, kids like these might as well have had the company stamp branded onto their foreheads. They used to get winter jackets, a Sanderson Christmas basket filled with tangerines. Once, Evelyn McCurdy, whose father had been cut in half in a rigging accident, had left a tangerine in her desk. Colleen had snuck in during recess, taken it into the girls' bathroom, and eaten it. She'd smelled the rind on her fingers long after she'd washed her hands. There were no Christmas baskets for girls whose fathers had drowned poaching mussels in a borrowed skiff.

Colleen shifted Alsea's weight.

"Have one more," Eugene's great-aunt Gertie said, leaning in, as though letting Colleen in on a secret. Gertie's white hair was set in finger curls. She smelled of talcum powder, something sour underneath. Colleen forced a smile. Gertie patted her hand. "Honey, you're like ice."

Colleen had the urge to swat her. Instead, she let Gertie fuss with Alsea's swaddle, tucking it up under the baby's rump. Gertie was almost ninety, a widow for over half a century. Her only son had died of polio. She still wore a locket with his picture inside.

A chorus of guffaws erupted across the room, Eugene carrying on, holding Enid by the hip. Rich never touched Colleen in public.

"Look at those two." Gertie tsked. "We'll be back here again before long. Well. You're young."

But when had Colleen ever felt young? Even as a teenager, Enid had seemed less her little sister than her wild and careless daughter. She looked out the doors at Rich, his head tilted, listening in the fading light.

"It's lonely with one," Gertie said.

"Chub has his cousins," Colleen answered, though it sounded hollow, even to her.

"Have another." Gertie patted her hand again. The old woman's skin had melted over her bones, speckled with bruises. "I never met a man who didn't enjoy that part, no matter how old he was."

Chub wandered back inside.

"Can I have cake now?" he asked.

The cake hunched on a platter like a wrecked sandcastle. Dot cut him a slice.

"Nothing wrong with a baby that don't cry," Dot said, smiling at Alsea asleep in Colleen's arms.

They found a seat, Chub licking frosting from his fork. She kissed him on the head. Her sweet boy. Her little miracle.

"Grahamcracker," she whispered. "Where'd you get that beautiful brown hair?"


"Marla!" Enid hollered. "Put this stuff in the truck."

Marla hefted the ice chest.

"She's got a date," Enid told Colleen. "She'd carry me to the truck if I asked."

There'd been a time, before Chub, when Colleen had so longed for a child of her own that just saying good night to little Marla had wrung her heart out like a wet rag. Now look at her: a teenager, white-blond hair, skin so pale it showed the little blue veins at her temples, an eerie beauty. *Looks will get you knocked up and tied down before you get a chance at life*, Mom had told Colleen once, in high school. *Better to be plain.*

"I need a beer," Eugene announced, tablecloths shaken out, card tables wiped and folded.

"What about the kids?" Colleen asked.

"They can share. I'm not buying them all their own beers."

The kids crammed into the Only's corner booth.

"I want cheese fries," Wyatt demanded.

"Me too," Enid said.

"We just ate," Colleen objected, spotting Daniel at the bar talking to Bessie McQuade, who had been in their class at school. Gone for years, and now suddenly he was everywhere. Bessie's husband had left her. She lived above Mill Creek with her harelipped son and about fifty cats. Colleen remembered the flare of disgust in Bessie's husband's nostrils when he'd seen the little boy's lip, how he'd backed away when Colleen set the baby on Bessie's chest, already distancing himself.

"Huh, Aunt Colleen?"

"What?" Colleen asked.

Across the room, Bessie McQuade smacked Daniel across the face. Kel stood behind the bar, arms crossed. Daniel rose. He dropped some bills beside his glass, shoved a notepad into his pocket, tucked a pen above his ear. But it was the look on Bessie's face that struck Colleen.

"Don't let the screen door slap you on the way out," somebody called after Daniel.

"Must have got the wrong idea." Eugene winked. Colleen wanted to press her finger to the corner of his eye, pin it.

"Those hippies screw like rabbits," Enid said, setting baskets of fries on the table.

"Enid." Colleen hushed her.

"What? It's true. They're out there humping trees, aren't they?"

"Hugging," Colleen corrected her.

"One thing leads to another."

*Don't fan the fire*, Mom used to say when Colleen let Enid needle her.

Conversation ratcheted back up. Bessie McQuade traced a finger along the rim of her glass, making it sing a high note only Colleen could hear. Daniel had been asking about her son; Colleen could tell by the slope of

Bessie's shoulders, the way she sat at the bar surrounded by people, totally alone.

"What'd I miss?" Rich asked, sliding into the booth beside her, jogging his foot.

What was he so nervous about? She touched his thigh under the table and his leg stilled. He laced his fingers through hers and brought them up onto the table, into plain sight.

# COLLEEN

Chub held her hand across the parking lot, but inside the double doors—whiff of sloppy Joes—he slipped free. She'd cut his bangs too short, his forehead white and vulnerable. She wanted to cup her hand over it. The bulletin board outside his classroom was covered with paper fish: IN THIS SCHOOL, WE ALL SWIM TOGETHER. She traced his name fish—*G-r-a-h-a-m*—but he'd already scampered in, red lunch box in tow, children swarming past her like water flowing around a rock.

She lingered in the lobby to hold off her own loneliness. She'd walked by the class photos thousands of times, but now she studied the class of 1942, the year Rich would have graduated, the year Colleen was born. There was Astrid Fitzpatrick: tall, proud. *That Astrid was so cold*, Marsha said. *She was sharp*, Rich had explained once. Neither a compliment nor an insult. Rich never said a bad word against anyone.

Beside Astrid, chubby, smiling, unrecognizable but for the glasses: *Gail Maloney*—before she'd married Don. Colleen looked toward the front office; Gail Porter stared back. Colleen studied the photo a moment longer, feeling the pinch of Gail Porter's regard.

"Did you hear?"

Colleen turned, Gail suddenly beside her, pinning a notice to the bulletin board.

"Elyse lost the baby."

Elyse had been only a few weeks behind Colleen. She lived past Gail and Don's, a few mailboxes up from the Larsons. It was her first baby, so she'd wanted a doctor, not a home birth. Colleen had driven her down to the clinic once, to show there were no hard feelings.

"There's a sign-up sheet in the office," Gail Porter said. "If you want to bring them some food."

The truck felt empty without Chub. She crossed the road and drove up Requa Hill to the top of the headland, a whole sad day ahead. She'd lain awake most of the night, listening to Rich breathe. He'd gone up the hill in the dark, as if today were no different from any other day, while she'd fixed two lunches for the first time.

She stared out at the ocean. The truck's engine ticked, cooling. Mist smoked up into the dark spires along the narrow strip of coastal park. Sunlight reflected off a patch of shoreline in the distance, a tide pool maybe, or broken glass, winking like a signal mirror. She sat and watched it for a long time. It was cold in the truck by the time she started it up again. When she got back down to the stop sign, she let the truck idle. Left would take her home to the silent house. She was supposed to have a baby to feed and burp and sing to sleep while Chub was gone at school. Instead, she turned right, crossed Gold Bear Bridge, and turned off onto the river road, soft with dead leaves, littered with fallen limbs, hemmed between water and timber, the kind of road you shouldn't drive without a chainsaw. She passed the two tarnished bears where the old bridge had stood, before the flood. A logjam had bashed against the footings, pounding until they gave way. She'd forgotten these bears, still guarding their invisible bridge. She leaned across and rolled down the passenger-side window. If she could hear the river, maybe she wouldn't drive into it.

Old logging two-tracks cut up the ridge past the dump, and then, like a curtain swept aside: the river's mouth, the sandbar, the wild ocean. A black truck was parked in the make-out spot where the road elbowed downcoast. She heard a shriek, then laughter. She slowed, straining up out of her seat to peer down the steep drop. A girl stood on a blanket, a boy pulling the corners. She watched the girl twirl, taunting the boy until he lunged, swung her around, kissed her, a whirl of white-blond hair: *Marla. Marla, out here with a boy.* Colleen hit the gas, the road downcoast barely wider than a path. She plowed through, thorns screaking.

Enid's voice jabbed like a finger into her chest. *Why don't you stop them?*

*They look happy.*

*Horseshit.*

*You only get one life, Enid.*

*Exactly.*

Her tires slammed something solid and the truck lurched back, landing with a jolt. Colleen got out, kicked through the brush until she found the downed log, hidden by brambles. It wouldn't budge. She wiped hair out of her face, looked back the way she'd come. She'd have to reverse all the way to the bend just to turn around. She scanned a slow circle, as though there might be another way. Below, she spotted roof shingles worn tawny gray: the radar station.

She sidestepped down through the ferns. The bottom windows were concreted in, attic windows shattered. The radar had been hauled away, but the shell of the phony house remained. It had done its job, fooled German U-boats into thinking there was a farm hanging from this cliff. Colleen had gone to school with half a dozen kids like Daniel, the unclaimed offspring of the radar boys who'd spent their war here, hunched and listening.

Daniel rounded the corner. She froze, as though stillness might camouflage her.

"Colleen?"

"What are you doing here?" she blurted out.

He lifted a jug of berries, fingers inked purple. Couldn't go two steps without tripping over canes—they'd swallow the houses if no one fought back. He was three steps away, the time it took to draw a breath and hold it, to tuck a piece of hair behind an ear. His watch face caught the light. No bigger than a quarter. Had she spotted it all the way from the headland, signaling her?

"Chub started school today." Cold gusted off the water. She hugged herself.

He studied her. "You okay?"

She nodded. Tears spilled down her cheeks.

"What time does he get out?" he asked.

"Three thirty." Her voice cracked. She sat down in the wet grass.

"Hey." Daniel squatted beside her. She sobbed into his shoulder until he put his arm around her.

"I'm sorry," she said finally, lifting her head. "I don't know what's wrong with me."

"What makes you think something's wrong with you?"

Each time, after the warm gush of blood in her underwear, the cramping, the clots the size of plums slipping out of her into the toilet, after three emergency D&Cs she'd have bled to death without, and especially, especially after their little Easter girl, she'd spent weeks combing back through to locate her mistake. If only she hadn't lifted that bag of dog food, if only she'd drunk more water. If only, if only, if only. There must be something wrong with her, why else would it keep happening?

She sucked in snot, wiped her eyes. "I'm sorry," she said, "it's just— You don't have kids?"

He shook his head.

"Do you want them?"

He lifted his arm off her. "No."

"I wish I could be like that," Colleen said. "We lost two before Chub was born—" She shook her head, eyes brimming. "Why can't I just be grateful?"

"Hey, come on." Daniel hugged her. It felt good, to be held. To cry without hiding it. He released her.

"Rich won't touch me," she confided. "I lost a baby in April. A little girl. Twenty-two weeks. All the others, they were so early, but now—it's like he doesn't trust me anymore."

"How many have you lost?" Daniel asked.

"Oh." She let out a long breath. "One every spring, pretty much, except for Chub." It was a relief, to finally tell someone besides the nurses, to admit it outside the drab walls of the clinic.

"Colleen, that's—I'm sorry."

She shrugged. "Just not meant to be." *There must have been a reason. It's just nature's way. It's for the best.* How those empty consolations had stung and infuriated her when all she wanted was to know *why*.

"People always say the wrong thing, don't they?" Daniel asked.

She nodded. Something loosened in her chest. She inhaled, feeling, despite it all, better. "What can you do? You keep going. But Rich—he doesn't even want to *try* again."

Daniel ran his hand through the grass. She leaned, bumped her shoulder against his. He looked up. She felt the click and slide of bolts within her, an old combination popping open a lock. She should leave now, get back in the truck Rich had bought her, the truck that sat like a big white two-ton reminder in her driveway, morning, noon, and night. Instead, she pushed her glasses up onto her head, took Daniel's warm face in her hands. He slid his fingers up over hers, as though he might remove them, then slipped his hands up her forearms to her elbows, her shoulders, tracing slowly down her ribs. She straightened, so that he wouldn't feel the little bulge of flab at her waist.

*This is wrong.* The thought hovered briefly over her head as she eased herself back onto the damp grass. *What are you doing? You're just sad.* Daniel's heart thudded against her chest, the cold breeze on her bare stomach, her breath quickening, ankles hooked behind his knees. When he tried to pull out, she tensed, pulled him deeper. *Wait. Wait. Wait.*

He rolled onto his back and they lay side by side, panting, roar of the surf breaking against the rocks below. Colleen pulled her knees to her chest and hugged them, as the nurse had instructed, to increase the chances of conception. Who knew how many more chances she would get?

"What are you doing?" Daniel asked.

"Nothing." She turned her head to smile at him. "Why did you come back?" she asked.

"I told you." Daniel stroked her ribs. "Research."

"The real reason."

He stopped. "My mom's sick."

She looked over at him, but Daniel was looking up at the sky.

In Colleen's memory, Dolores Bywater was fearless, calling Gloria Adair a backward redneck for making her son, who was in Colleen and Daniel's class, kneel on gravel as a punishment. Sam was a stutterer, his knees pocked with bloody divots.

*Mind your own business, whore,* Mrs. Adair had sneered, a word Colleen had never heard a mom use. Mrs. Adair was a homely woman; a cluster of small moles clung to her neck. Daniel's mother was beautiful. Her dentalia-shell earrings, little bundles of delicate white icicles, had tinkled, though her face remained perfectly placid.

*What does your husband do to you, that you're taking it out on this little boy?* Mrs. Bywater had wondered aloud. *He cheats,* she'd guessed, *doesn't he?*—a flicker of victory in the corners of her beautiful mouth. How could a woman like that ever get sick?

"Why did you stop walking up to get eggs?" Daniel asked.

"How do you—?"

"I've been taking samples out of your creek for months. Your mutt's a real barker."

She toyed with a blade of grass. "He's Rich's dog." A pang of guilt, at Rich's name.

Daniel propped himself up on one elbow. "Couldn't you just run a little tap water into those jars for me? Come on. Just once a week. It takes me forever to get out there."

"Rich wouldn't like that." Colleen sat up.

"What is Rich like?" Daniel asked.

"Rich?" Rich was a man who caught and released spiders. Since Chub was born, he killed the poisonous ones, but always, before the smack, a sigh of regret, of duty. "There's not a mean bone in Rich's body," she said, pulling her turtleneck over her head.

Daniel reversed her truck the whole way, neck craned to see behind him, humming to himself, mint clacking against his teeth. Colleen was quiet. She'd never been unfaithful, in thought or in deed, and then a door had opened, and she'd walked through it. She pinched her ears. *Think of something else.*

The black truck was gone. Daniel backed into the empty pullout. She wanted to go home and strip off her clothes, to huddle in the shower. He killed the engine, sat back, and sighed. She smelled the mint.

"It's too bad," he said.

"What's too bad?" The giddy lightness she'd felt earlier was gone.

Daniel traced the edge of the steering wheel with one finger. "That you left."

"I didn't leave," Colleen said. "I came home."

"Right."

"You're the one who never called me back," Colleen protested.

"You didn't have a phone."

"I drove all the way to Crescent City to use that pay phone," Colleen shot back. "I must have called your dorm a dozen times." She choked back the rush of shame the memory still produced.

"You said you'd be gone for the weekend," Daniel said half-heartedly. In truth, she'd packed all her things, tucked the rabbit lamp under one arm, and slid the keys under the landlady's door, secretly relieved. For five months she'd stuck it out, homesick and lonely, Daniel consumed by his courses. He'd prop a textbook up on his bare chest to read in bed, humming to himself, leaving her behind. "You were the one who never came back," Daniel reminded her.

"You knew where I was."

Daniel tilted his head. "Come on, Colleen. You were just looking for a way out, admit it. You saw your chance and you took it."

"My mom was sick." Her voice trembled with anger. "You know what that's like now, don't you?"

"Look, I'm sorry I didn't show up at your door so your mom could call me your 'little half-breed boyfriend' and blow smoke in my face again, is that what you want to hear? I told you I wasn't coming back here. You made your choice, don't try to pin that on me."

"I'm perfectly happy with my choices," Colleen said.

Daniel scoffed. "Are you sure about that?" He elbowed out of the truck, disappearing into the undergrowth, the way they'd come.

Colleen slid over behind the steering wheel—*what had she done?* She turned the key in the ignition, gunned the engine, the bend so blinded by brush she barely had time to slam the brakes: there was Marla in a thin T-shirt and jeans, lips blanched with cold.

Colleen opened her door. "Get in," she said.

Marla went around to the passenger side and climbed in. They sat for a moment, Marla's teeth chattering. Colleen turned up the heat.

"Where's your coat?" Colleen asked.

"I forgot it."

Colleen went slow, Marla swaying with each bump in the road.

"That boy just left you out there?" Colleen asked when they were almost back to the highway.

Marla looked out the window.

"Marla," Colleen said. "I saw you."

"I saw you too."

Colleen's cheeks burned. She shifted into second gear, then third.

"Are you going to tell my mom?" Marla asked when Colleen pulled to the curb outside the school.

Colleen still smelled the cool burn of mint as she drew in air. "Are you?"

Marla gave a little shake of her head and reached for the door release.

"Marla, honey," Colleen said. "Be careful."

Marla got out.

"Don't do something you might regret later," Colleen said aloud, watching the double doors close behind her. She wanted to follow her in, to run down the hall to Chub's classroom. The truck idled. She couldn't remember the last time she'd felt so alone.

# RICH

House a sauna, windowpanes smoked with steam, it was still a relief to be home, to sniff the sweet air. His knee throbbed. Colleen tonged a jar out of the stockpot and set it on the counter with the others, solid black, seeds strained, the way he liked it.

Chub rattled off his first day: nosebleed, class fish, recess—*and then, and then*—and disappeared to his room.

"You been at it all day?" Rich asked.

She nodded.

"So how was it?" After today's close call, he wanted to hear her voice. "First day off in five years?"

"Fine." She pinned a jar under the roiling water. It knocked the bottom of the pot.

"Any left over?"

She clanked a mixing bowl with some jam at the bottom onto the table along with the cracker tin. Canning always put her in a bad mood.

"You pick all these today?" he asked. Her hair was up, streak of blackberry crusted across her nape. He sat with a groan, picked up Chub's art project—dried macaroni glued to construction paper. "Crafts. What happened to learning to read?"

"It's only the first day."

He spooned jam onto saltines, sighed with appreciation. "The way to a man's heart is through his stomach."

She ignored the compliment. Chub came back, nosebleed tissues still stuffed up his nostrils, a stick poking up from his bib pocket. Colleen hadn't noticed it yet, or she would have made him surrender it. She worried about him tripping and poking himself in the eye.

"Trade you." Rich swapped the stick for a saltine.

Chub licked the salt off the cracker, handed it back, and scampered out.

"That's the second nosebleed he's had in a week," Colleen said.

"I got them too, as a kid," Rich said. He polished off the sleeve of saltines, washed them down with a swig of cool water, hissed through his teeth.

"Let her fill that tooth," Colleen said, exasperated.

The clinic had a new lady dentist. He shook his head, took the ice-cube tray from the freezer, grabbed a dishcloth, and limped into the front room, keeping the leg straight. Goddamn. He'd been listening to the clock tick inside his head, counting down the days until the first loan payment came due, when the rotted-out branch broke, cracked him in the knee so hard it almost knocked him loose. He lay back on the couch, sank into the cushions.

Rich squinted, shielded his eyes against the lamplight. Colleen stood by his feet.

"Dinner's ready." She waited, making sure he could stand, his pants wet where ice had melted through the dish towel.

At the table, Chub chased a mushy carrot across his plate.

Rich tugged at one of the tissues sticking out of Chub's nose. "That sniffer still bleeding?"

Colleen set a slice of roast on Rich's plate, ladled juice into the crater atop his mashed potatoes.

"I think it's time to take those out," Rich said. Chub tipped his head back as Rich removed the tissues. "Make a dent out back?" he asked, jam jars lining the counter.

"Can't hardly tell." She hadn't met his eyes all night.

"Is the pie done?" Chub asked.

"We'll have it tomorrow," she said.

Chub dragged his fork through his potatoes, plate a landscape of his disappointment.

"Go brush your teeth. You have school tomorrow."

Rich cleared their plates, limped to the faucet. The water sputtered.

"Been like that all day?"

Colleen nodded. He needed to clean out the water line again. He stopped up the sink, let it fill, rolled up his sleeves, nabbed a deviled egg from the pan on the counter—nice tang of mustard.

"Those are for Robley and Elyse," she said.

He'd heard they'd lost a baby. He hadn't mentioned it to Colleen, but women had a way of passing bad news around.

"You're keeping those chickens in business," he said.

"Somebody has to." Colleen elbowed him out of her way, rinsing the plate he'd soaped. "Go put that leg up."

"Stain of guilt," he said, catching her hand, fingers purple to the first knuckle, nails black crescents. His mother used to say that when he came in for dinner with blackberry seeds stuck in his teeth.

Colleen blushed and slipped her hand back into the dishwater, as though she would stand at the sink until it soaked clean. She'd get used to having the days to herself. He ran a palm up the face of a cabinet. The first one they'd lost, a few months after they were married—wash of blood, clot the size of a lemon—she'd stayed in bed for a week while he tore out the old cabinets and built these, pecky cedar. He'd taken the sledgehammer to the old frames, planed the cedar, everything square, everything level. He'd tried, the best way he knew how, to build a life for them. She would get used to the idea of it being just the three of them. They had Chub. They had each other.

"Can you walk on my back?" he asked when she finally came into the bedroom. He'd been dozing, but now he rallied, lowering himself stiffly onto the carpet.

She sat on the end of the bed and pulled off her socks. He groaned when she stepped up, her cold toes pressing into the flesh above his tailbone.

"Were you really going to leave?" Colleen balanced, muscles along his spine rolling.

"What?" he asked, his voice hoarse, pinned by her weight.

"Marsha said you were going to Oregon."

She stopped, toes gripping his shoulder blades. Marsha talking about Astrid again, dredging the river of their lives.

"I was just a dumb kid."

When Astrid had finally emerged from the back room of the Millhauser house, she'd looked smaller, drained of color. After Colleen had lost their first, she'd looked the same way and he'd almost told her then, this thing he'd never told a living soul. He'd breathed in, and there was the sweet iron musk, water boiling on the stove, Astrid whimpering in the next room, the eerie music of the cat walking across the piano.

*It's not a baby, stop calling it that*, Astrid had said on the way there.

He'd touched a key on the piano.

*It's a dollar a lesson*, June Millhauser had said, staring at him with her mismatched eyes, one blue, one brown. She gave him the pot to refill at the tap outside—*You got her into this, you're going to help get her out.*

But he'd breathed out, and the urge had passed. Hadn't told Colleen then. No reason to tell her now. At least there were some stories she couldn't read on his body.

"Why didn't you?" Colleen asked, pivoting, tightroping slowly back down his spine.

"Lark fell."

He could have shown up at the dormitory at Oregon State, knocked on every door until Astrid's opened. But the days went by and he didn't, and when she came back she was engaged to a man studying to be a dentist. She'd told him straight, as though she were simply closing an account at the bank. He'd carried the caddis she'd given him in his breast pocket for a year afterward, fished with it every chance he got, watched it play on the surface— peacock-herl body, elk-hair wing, grizzly hackle—pulled trout half the length of his arm, until finally, one day, coming out of the tank shed, he'd slid the fly up on top of the wall frame.

"Do you ever wonder what your life might have been like?" Colleen asked, stepping off. "If you'd left."

"Things worked out pretty good for me." He sat up. "What made you think of that?"

"I don't know."

He waited for her to say more. But whatever it was, she held it.

*September 7*

# COLLEEN

She heard Melody screaming as soon as she opened her truck door. Keith met her in the yard.

"How long ago did it start?" she asked, grabbing her bag.

"Couple hours? I worked a double. I'd just got home when I called you."

Colleen pushed past him. Inside, Melody lay on the bed, panting. Her little girl sat on the pillow beside her, petting her head.

"This is it," Melody gulped.

"Ready or not," Colleen agreed.

She washed her hands and arms, gathered towels. Down the hall, she heard a contraction seize Melody. Colleen looked at herself in the dim mirror, her heart racing, though she'd done this two dozen times. *Breathe.*

"Breathe with her," she told Keith. He'd stayed for the first child's birth, which not a lot of husbands did, but Colleen wasn't sure he'd make it through this one, by the looks of him. She went into the kitchen and started a pot of coffee. "Let's see how we're doing." She felt Melody's belly, a lurch in her own chest. Melody's eyes were wild with fear—the baby was breech again.

"Why didn't you—" Colleen checked her watch. It would take an ambulance an hour to get here.

"We can't go to the hospital," Melody pleaded. Another contraction. They were three minutes apart now, and a minute long.

Colleen spread the shower liner on the bedroom floor.

"Get her up," Colleen told Keith. "She needs to squat."

"Why?" Keith asked. The little girl began to cry.

"Help her. Hold her up," Colleen instructed, keeping her voice calm. "Now, kneel down behind her. Support her back."

Colleen raised the thermostat to 85, turned on the television in the front room and cranked the volume. The little girl sat on the floor, sobbing.

"You take her," Colleen said to Keith. Keith stood up and Colleen slid into his place. "Leave that heat up," she told him. "And turn the oven on. It needs to be hot in here."

She counted, listening to Melody's shallow breathing.

"Can you sit on the end of the bed for a minute?" Colleen asked. Melody wore one of Keith's T-shirts. Colleen checked that she was dilated. Melody trembled through the next contraction.

"It's time, hon," Colleen said.

She waited for Melody to squat down on the shower liner, then crouched behind her. She hooked her arms under Melody's armpits, straining to help hold her up, and hugged Melody's back to her chest.

"Okay, you ready to push for me?" The room narrowed around them. "Okay, Melody. Here we go. One, two, three—"

Melody's slick skin slid against hers, spatter of blood on the shower liner, the smells. Currents of worry ran through Colleen—all the things she knew could go wrong with a breech baby. She drilled through them, pushing away her own sadness. She was here, holding Melody up, her sweat-stuck shirt pressed to Melody's back, but she was also standing in the doorway. Melody's baby would be here, she was pushing him out into the world, and after Colleen had cleared his airways and swaddled him and laid his pink form against Melody's bare breast, she would go home, empty and exhausted and alone. She tried to root herself to her body, holding tighter, coaching Melody to push—*push*—her own back aching.

Sweat dripped down Colleen's face. She pulled a clean towel from the stack and wiped the sweat out of Melody's eyes, one arm still hooked under Melody's, holding her up.

"Okay, hon, another one. Come on, another big push—"

Melody's body heaved. She groaned. "I can't do it," she panted.

"You have to," Colleen said.

"I can't," she wailed.

"You can. Come on, I'm going to push with you." She wiped sweat from Melody's neck. "Okay? Another big push. Come on, push. Push!"

Colleen felt the clench of Melody's body against hers and yelled, matching Melody's pitch.

"There we go, good girl. Another one, let's go."

She checked her watch: quarter after two. Melody panted.

"Big push, come on, one, two, three—"

At last, Melody screamed and a foot appeared.

"Keith!" Colleen called.

He appeared, drowsy, shaking his head to clear it. He saw the legs dangling and lunged.

"Don't touch him!" Colleen yelled, thrusting out her arm to block him. "You touch him, he'll gasp all that fluid in. You come in here." They traded places again. "Okay, Melody, honey, another big push. There we go!"

Melody screamed. The baby's bottom appeared.

"It's a little boy!" Colleen announced, tears streaming down Melody's face. "He's a little acrobat. Big push. Good. Again." Colleen crouched down, getting into position. "One, two, three, push!" And then the baby was in her hands. "Oh God," she said.

Melody sank down onto her butt, trembling from the pain. Colleen tilted the baby, pure muscle memory, her attention fixed not on clearing his airways, but on the missing top of his skull, the small, misshapen mound of exposed brain. She felt his little animal heart fluttering, but he wouldn't cry. His pink face was scrunched and perfect up to the eyebrows. She wiped his nose and mouth, rubbed him. She should cut the cord first, but there might not be time.

"Take her shirt off!" she ordered Keith, the baby's heartbeat faint but unmistakable, a flicker compared to the thud of her own, as she laid him against Melody's damp chest.

She was hosing her dirty clothes off in the driveway when Rich came home, Chub playing with Scout out back.

"What happened?" Rich asked, water splattering the rocks around her bloodstained pants. She walked over and turned the spigot off, as though she could twist off the tap of her emotions with it.

"Melody had her baby," Colleen said.

"Is she okay?" Rich asked.

Colleen shook her head. "He."

He waited, like he sensed there was more. If she told him now, she would come apart. She needed to wait until Chub went to bed. She followed Rich inside. He set his keys in the burl bowl. He'd carved it for her years ago, after she lost their second one. Each time, he'd made something: new kitchen cabinets, a checker set, the carved sign for the front door— HOME IS WHERE THE ♥ IS. He'd compressed each loss down into something physical, contained, something he could finish and set aside. After holding that little baby boy today, she wanted to hurl the bowl against the wall. She'd watched him die and there wasn't a darn thing she could do about it except clean up the mess, try to make Melody comfortable, sit in the truck in the school parking lot afterward and sob. How could she ever make Rich understand how much that birth had felt like giving birth herself, how losing that baby had been like losing her own again?

"The fish are back early," Rich said. "I thought I'd walk up." He let his words linger, an invitation.

"Take Chub," she said.

# RICH

They crouched on the bank, about level with their intake pipe, staring into the water, Damnation Creek clear enough to read the date on a sunk wish penny, cold enough to freeze the air in their lungs to powder.

"There's one!" Chub yelled, stumbling backward into Rich. "There's another!" Chub scrambled into Rich's arms.

Rich laughed. "They're not going to get you."

Chub was breathless, watching the coho muscle upstream, twelve inches around and as long as house cats, their jaws grown huge with their ocean teeth. When Rich was a boy, this run had been so strong it turned the creek red, made of salmon, not water.

"Where are they going?" Chub asked, though Rich had explained the spawning on the walk up.

"They're coming home from the ocean to lay their eggs before they die," Rich explained, careful not to scare him. "Their bodies will fertilize the soil, help the trees grow tall. They're coming back to die in the place they were made, where their parents were made, and their parents before them."

"But how do they know?" Chub asked, feeling brave enough to stand a little apart now.

Rich shrugged. "They learned their creeks. Same as you."

"Can we catch one?" Chub asked.

"No. You have to have a license. Yuroks can fish them, but only a mile up from the river"—Rich lifted his chin at the fish—"these guys have made it too far already, look at them."

"Three, four, five. There's too many!" Chub ran along the bank, the way

Rich had as a boy, the first salmon he'd netted so heavy and strong, it might have yanked him in and drowned him if Lark hadn't grabbed on. "They're fast!" Chub trudged back, out of breath, and flopped down beside Rich to rest. "I wish Mom came with us," Chub said.

"Mom's seen them before," Rich said.

"I just wish," Chub said.

"Me too, Grahamcracker. Me too."

*September 12*

# COLLEEN

The old tires leading up to Robley and Elyse's front door were planted with irises, some dead, some blooming lush as hothouse flowers, here at the bottom of the narrow, shady gulch, a few doors up from Melody Larson. Keith had taken Melody down to stay with his mom in Eureka, so she wouldn't be alone.

Colleen lifted the tuna casserole off the seat beside her and shoved the truck door closed with her hip. Rain speckled the tinfoil tented over top. A child's wagon sat on the porch. Last time she'd left the deviled eggs on the mat, but now Robley came out to meet her, shutting the front door behind him. His face was red and chapped from working on open water.

"How is she?" Colleen asked, coming up under the overhang.

Robley shrugged.

Colleen had pressed on Melody Larson's abdomen to help deliver the afterbirth. By the time it dropped into the bucket with a wet smack, the baby had already stopped breathing. Tomorrow she would go to the graveside service.

"Doctor said she was perfect," Robley said. "From her toes to her eyebrows. Just no brain to tell her to breathe."

It took Colleen a moment to understand. "Oh," she said. "I'm so sorry. I didn't know." She looked down the road toward the Larson place. She wondered if someone had told Robley about Melody's baby, its missing cap of skull, if maybe he and Keith had stood out on the porch and drunk a beer together. A terrible thing for two neighbors to have in common.

Robley scrunched up his nose, as though to keep himself from tearing up. He toed a rusty nail head sticking up from the porch. "Elyse kept telling me I needed to fix these, that the baby would get hurt. I figured I had time, you know? It'd be a while before she was crawling around." Robley sucked air in his nose, turned his ear toward the door, listening for Elyse. "You seen Daniel Bywater is back? You know he's a doctor now? PhD. Went to college and everything."

Colleen felt her face redden, but Robley didn't seem to notice.

"His mom's pretty sick, I guess," Robley said. "He came out to the house. He thinks it might have something to do with the stuff they're spraying. It's true, when they use the helicopters, especially in springtime, when the season starts up, it's pretty bad. You taste it when you run the faucet." Robley shook his head. "I don't know. He seemed like kind of a nutcase. Had some petition to stop Sanderson from spraying." Robley snorted. "As if anybody ever stopped Sanderson from doing exactly what the hell they want."

For a moment, he seemed lighter. Colleen knew there were times when you forgot, even just for a few seconds, and the grief lifted.

"Makes you wonder, though. Did you see Elyse's irises, out by the road?" Robley asked.

Colleen turned to look.

"Truck came by spraying the shoulder weeds, and it drifted down. Gail Porter, down the way, all her bees died." The windows began to rattle quietly in their frames, a loaded log truck swinging around the bend. Robley waited for it to pass. "I ain't afraid of those sprays," he said, the truck's vibration fading, squeal of its wet brakes in the distance. "But what if? What if there's a whole raft of shit they're not telling us?" The aroma of cooked tuna rose off the pan. "Here, I can take that off your hands," he said, accepting the casserole. "Elyse hasn't been outside in a week. I go to work and I come back three days later and it's like she hasn't moved."

"That's normal," Colleen said, her own sadness rising in her chest. "It can last a while, especially when—it's a big loss."

"Thanks for this." Robley raised the casserole in his hands. "And for driving her down to the clinic that time, when I was working. I never thanked you for that."

And then Robley was gone and Colleen was back in the truck, trundling down the driveway, past the irises standing dead in their planters, past Melody Larson's empty single-wide, past the rusting white bee boxes in Gail Porter's yard.

# CHUB

Uncle Eugene chopped wood, his chest so white compared to the rest of him it looked like he was wearing an undershirt made of his own pale skin. The longhaired mama cat meowed in the chicken-wire cat pen, udders dragging in the dirt.

"Where's her kittens?" Chub asked Wyatt. The new kittens had been squirmy and warm. Chub had wanted to open a little door in his chest and shove one inside.

Wyatt smeared a mosquito up his arm. "She ate them."

Aunt Enid's cackle rang out from the bonfire around back, where Agnes and the girls were racing leaf boats.

Wyatt tromped across the road, whacking dead ferns out of his way.

"How do you know she ate them?" Chub asked. He was pretty sure Wyatt was lying, but Wyatt was ten. He could knock Chub to the ground and pin him until his heart frogged in his throat.

Wyatt shrugged. "Who cares? She'll have more. Cats are sluts."

The creek was backed up, still as a pond. Chub wasn't supposed to go in water unless an adult was watching, but Wyatt waded across to the other side.

Chub found a stick, cracked bark off it in satisfying hunks as he walked, and ran the silky wood under his nose. When he looked up, he stood at the edge of a road that held the creek pond back. He crossed to Wyatt's side, perfectly dry. Wyatt fought his way out of the reeds. Cattails stood dead, water covered in algae. Chub dipped his stick in and lifted a hairy slime tail. It smelled like rotten eggs. He flung the algae and it whapped Wyatt's chest.

Wyatt shrank back, clawing it off.

"You're dead!"

Chub stepped in the water, his boot filling.

"I'm going to kill you!" Wyatt yelled.

Chub ran. His wet sock squelched in his boot. He heard Wyatt crashing through the brush behind him. He grabbed ferns and they opened like a curtain, revealing a water balloon with a curled pink baby inside. Wyatt spun Chub around, knocking him onto his back, and landed, heavy and panting, on his chest.

"Get off!" Chub bucked.

Wyatt dug his fingernails into Chub's pinned wrists, looming over him. His freckles looked scary. Then Wyatt spotted the balloon. He poked it. Liquid inside sloshed the baby around.

"Stop!" Chub yelled, surprised by his own voice. He rolled, breaking Wyatt's hold, and sprang up.

Wyatt wagged his finger like he was going to wipe it on Chub's face.

"Don't."

"*Don't*," Wyatt mimicked. "It's just a deer, retard. Look at its legs."

Chub peered closer. A tiny baby deer. He touched the sack: it felt slick, like a Jell-O mold in the refrigerator—irresistible and terrifying in its wobbliness.

"Come on." Wyatt grabbed the thing and led the way back to Fort Eugene. The nanny goat with the black ear lay on her side in the yard, bleating, covered in sores.

"What's wrong with her?" Chub asked.

"She's sick." Wyatt tromped up the steps.

Chub struggled to pull off his muddy boots. His wet overalls rubbed, cold and stinking. Chub's mom sat in the kitchen, shucking peanuts from their cardboard fingers. She wore her soft pink sweater. He wanted to press the cold tip of his nose into it.

"Why are you wet?" She frowned.

"What the hell is that?" Aunt Enid asked, catching sight of the deer baby in its balloon. "Wyatt John DeWitt. Take that outside right now."

"What is it?" Mavis and Gertrude asked.

"Baby deer," Wyatt said. "It's dead."

"Why?"

"It fell out before it was ready," Aunt Enid said. "Wyatt, take it all the way up the hill. Don't leave it in the yard, it'll stink."

Chub's dad and Uncle Eugene came in, shrugging off the chill.

"One more week," Uncle Eugene said. "The forestry board'll send those jokers and their 'human remains' packing. And if they don't, we will. You going to help beat the shit out of some hippies, Chub?"

His mom tsked and held out Chub's slicker.

"I'm sorry. Did I say 'shit'? I meant 'crap.'" Uncle Eugene's eyebrows danced.

"What's 'remains'?" Chub asked, shoving an arm down a sleeve tunnel.

"Bones," Aunt Enid explained.

"Enid," his mom warned her.

"What? He'll find out sooner or later."

"Find out what?" Chub asked.

"Nothing." His mom smoothed his hair, smoothing the question right out of him.

*September 23*

# RICH

Marsha had done Sanderson's books for thirty years, right here under this burl clock, ticking just loud enough to get under your skin. Rich would be fit to be tied, cooped up inside all day.

"Time for the big bucks," Marsha said, slapping the voucher and a pen onto the counter. "You the last one?"

"Eugene stopped off home," Rich said.

"Well." Marsha eyed the clock, her purse already on the counter. "He's got nine minutes."

Rich signed, slid the voucher back. Marsha yanked open the file-cabinet drawer, thumbing through the Gs.

"Lot of Gundersens in here."

"I'm the live one."

"Big plans this weekend, Rich?" She pinched the check from his folder and slammed the drawer shut with her hip. "Come on. You can tell me."

It was Marsha's routine, teasing the guys. If either of them were younger, it might have been called flirting. Marsha had two grown sons by different fathers but no husband. Jacob, the one she'd shot, was the only one she'd had no kids by. She'd spent a few weeks in jail, and men in town were still careful of her, though the judge had ruled it self-defense. After all, she'd only shot off Jacob's pinkie. Plenty of guys had lost worse to the mill's saws over the years.

She pushed the check across. He reached around for his wallet.

"Don't forget these." She heaved a stack of newspapers onto the counter. Marsha still saved the crosswords for Colleen, though she hadn't helped out in the front office since before Chub was born.

The first time he'd spoken to Colleen had been right here at this counter, their fingers accidentally brushing when she handed him his check. *Cold hands, warm heart,* he'd said. She'd turned beet red, grabbed a stack of folders, and disappeared down the hall.

*Wallflowers don't need much sun, do they, Rich?* Marsha had teased.

Now Marsha thumbed through the drawer, refiling the voucher.

"Merle around?" Rich asked, hoping it sounded casual.

Marsha tipped her head down the hall. "Need something?"

"If he's got a minute."

Marsha reached for the phone. "You got Rich Gundersen out here."

Rich rotated his shoulder.

"Go ahead," she said.

He'd come into the front office once a week since he was fifteen, but in thirty-eight years, he'd never had a reason, good or bad, to venture past the counter, until now. He swallowed, insect buzz of fluorescents reverberating in the wood-paneled hall. A phone rang through an open door.

"Yello," he heard Merle answer.

Framed black-and-whites lined the walls, loggers—arms crossed, wool pants stiff with paraffin, suspenders—standing on stumps as big as dance floors, faces a mix of pride and bashfulness at having their picture taken. Even then, they knew timber that size wouldn't last forever.

"Hang on a sec," Merle said. "Rich?"

Rich stuck his head through. Merle waved him in, receiver pressed against the front of his shirt. "Gail's busting my balls. That school's not keeping her busy enough." He slid the phone back up to his ear, pinning it between his chin and shoulder, freeing both hands to rustle through drawers.

"No, I hear you just fine."

The room was cramped, paneled in redwood. Even the desk was small. Typewriter, red Sanderson mug of pens, a picture of Merle and Arlette, hair dyed the same purple-brown, kneeling on either side of a fresh-shot five-pointer: a Christmas-card shot. Merle rolled his eyes at Rich and leaned back in his chair, scratching his belly through his polyester shirt.

"I can't fire those guys, Gail, they don't work for me. Why don't you give the county a call?"

Merle sighed. The glow of the desk lamp caught dark circles under his eyes. A painted crosscut saw was mounted on the wall behind him: a lumberjack swinging an ax, white pennants of smoke blowing from the mill stacks, logs in the pond, all framed by timbered ridges, a red banner—WELCOME TO SANDERSON COUNTRY. The saw's teeth were thick. Bought new, just to have it painted.

"Well, now, I don't know." Merle opened another drawer, shuffled some papers, dropped his cheaters down onto the tip of his nose, leaned back. "I don't see what-all I can do about that." He waggled his head.

Rich swallowed the saliva pooling in his mouth, resisting the urge to pull at his collar, top snap already undone, exposing a white triangle of undershirt. He smelled the rankness of his own body—sweat, gasoline. Sawdust sprinkled down on the carpet from a fold in his sleeve.

Merle switched the phone to his other ear.

"Well, listen, county's one thing, but if it's Forest Service, I've got no more sway than you. You know how those piss firs are—have to fill out three forms just to talk to somebody on the phone. Yeah. Yeah, I hear you. Okay. You have a good one, now." Merle dropped the phone back into its cradle. "Jesus H. Christ. That woman don't give up."

Rich looked down at his hands rolling the bill of his cap into a tight tube. Gail was no picnic, but she was still Don's wife.

"One of the piss firs' tank trucks went by her and Don's place." Merle rooted around in the drawer. "Would she rather they let the brush go wild? You'd need a chainsaw just to get out of your driveway. Well, she goes running out, yelling about those damn bees of hers—bees are *sensitive*. Hell, that stuff is special-engineered—only kills weeds. And what's she doing keeping bees so close to the damn road if she's so touchy about them?" He pinned something to the side of the drawer. "Anyway, you know Gail, can't keep her damn mouth shut. Before you know, guy turns the spray on her." Merle chuckled at the thought. "Just hoses her. This was months ago. April. And she's still mad as a damn hornet. Got a hell of a nosebleed, I guess. Wants the guy fired. You ever try getting a piss fir fired? Quicker to let them die off. How does Porter put up with that woman? No wonder he's got a belly full of ulcers."

Merle being Merle, pretending to confide, tricking you into letting your guard down.

"Where the hell'd I put that thing?" He slammed the drawer shut. "Ah well, there's this." He slid a Polaroid of his speedboat across the desk, THE ARLETTE stenciled on the hull, Merle's vinyl-sided two-story in the background. "She's for sale. You interested?"

Rich remembered watching that house go up on the Requa headland, looking down on the sandbar where the mouth of the river dumped into the ocean, lording over the whole coast.

"Hell of a smooth rider," Merle said.

The boat looked small compared to the house. It was that big yellow house that had set Merle strutting around like a prize cock, Arlette coordinating his shirts to match her outfits so everybody could see they were living high on the hog on their buyout money. Virgil had held on, kept the company in the family even when it meant tightening his own belt, but Merle had sold out first chance he got, happy to spend his time playing fishing guide, toting San Francisco bigwigs around on the river. But it'd been years since they'd produced enough board feet for corporate to visit. Every big pumpkin they felled was a step closer to Sanderson closing shop for good.

"She's a real looker." Rich pushed the photo back.

"Yeah, she is," Merle agreed with a tinge of regret. Maybe Arlette had finally walked out on him. There'd been rumors for years. Whores in Eureka. A married woman over the Oregon line. "What can I do you for, Rich?" Merle asked.

Rich rolled the bill of his cap tight, let it spring free, cleared his throat.

"So long as it's got nothing to do with any damn bees."

Rich's palms were sweating. He eyed the little anthill of sawdust, resisted the urge to tamp it down.

"I, uh—" He cleared his throat again. "Was wondering what the roads'll look like, going into the grove?" Rich swallowed, saliva immediately refilling his mouth.

"Into Damnation?" Merle leaned back, folded his arms behind his head, and narrowed his eyes. He was going to ask, *Why?* The pits of his shirt were sweat stained. He got a whiff of himself, dropped his arms.

"You know what? Forget it." Rich pressed his palms onto his knees, ready to stand. "It's Friday."

"I got the surveys here somewhere," Merle said, rolling over to the file cabinet and pulling out a few cardboard tubes. "It's one of these." He examined them. "Here." He set a tube on the desk. "Knock yourself out."

Rich pried the end off, hands clumsy with Merle watching, extracted the rolled-up map and spread it out over his knees.

"Pretty close to the 24-7, isn't it?" Merle asked.

"Yeah." Rich looked up.

"I watch out for my people, Rich, you know that." Merle leaned back, smug. "Hell of a steep job. It was anybody else, I'd say they were crazier than a shithouse rat."

Rich swallowed. "Colleen doesn't know."

"Won't hear it from me."

Rich nodded. "Appreciate that."

"Take your time." Merle picked up the speedboat photo, sighed, pushed back in his chair, and wheezed up the hall.

Rich bent over the map, memorizing the harvest zone so he could walk through it in his head later, carving out where he knew skid roads would have to deviate from what was here on paper. The cut ran all the way to the bottom of the lower grove, to the foot of 24-7 Ridge. Rich's heart soared—as soon as they got back in, they'd bring the roads to his doorstep, his timber good as sold.

Merle came back, dropped heavily into his chair, and tossed a stack of flyers on his desk, edges leafing up in the breeze of their fall.

"Well, what's the verdict? Mitch dicking me around?"

Rich let the map snap back into its curl. "Looks good to me."

"Yeah? Mitch wasn't too sure about going all the way down into that lower section. I told him there's a guy across the creek has some timber he might sell us." Merle winked. "How's that sound?"

"Sounds pretty good." Rich swallowed. "I wanted to ask, you know, about milling it."

"You mill it here. We'll cut you a fair deal. Listen, we need you on the grove, Rich, but after that, you decide to go your own way." Merle shrugged. "Nobody'll blame you."

"How soon you think we'll get back in there?" Rich asked.

Merle leaned backward. Rich had gotten too friendly, like they were in this thing together, no longer boss and employee. "We'll see what the board says Monday," Merle said.

Rich knew Merle was taking Don down to the forestry board meeting with him, to tell the workingman's story. If they got the green light and got back into Damnation by first week of October, that'd give them six weeks to cut roads in and start harvesting before the rains turned the ground too unstable to work. Rich's mind raced, running the numbers again—he could hold on, as long as he got his cut out by summer.

"That skull wasn't up there before," Rich said. "Somebody would have noticed it."

Merle narrowed his eyes again, nodded. Rich tried rerolling the map to fit it back into the tube, but his hands wouldn't cooperate.

"Keep it. I got another copy around here somewhere."

Rich stood. "Thanks."

"Here, take one of these." Merle held out a flyer. "Take that boy of yours out, do some real fishing."

Rich smiled, accepting it.

"He start school?"

"Couple weeks ago."

Merle nodded, eyed the middle distance. He and Arlette had never had kids.

"Hey," Merle asked. "How's Porter?"

Don was stretched like a two-pound line hooked to a twenty-pound fish running his own crew plus the one Bill Henderson had left behind, a two-man job on a one-man salary, and Merle knew it.

"Holding up," Rich said.

"Good. Don't be a stranger now."

Merle opened the folder on his desk, as though Rich were already gone. Rich ducked out, pulled his cap on, rolling the flyer and the map into a tight tube, loping up the hall. He hitched the stack of newspapers under one arm. Marsha followed him out.

"Hope I didn't keep you," Rich said.

"You're okay," Marsha said. By her tone, he had.

The dead bolt slid closed behind him. In the old days, guys winked and nudged over Marsha's locking the doors, staying until Merle finished up. Hard to imagine now, heavy like she was, Merle with his teased-up cloud of hair.

The lot was empty except for Rich's truck, Marsha's Dodge, and Merle's gold Cadillac. Rich popped the clutch just as Eugene fishtailed in, spraying gravel straight up to the front office, almost onto the stoop. He threw his door open, engine still running, and leapt up the steps. He yanked the knob, then banged on the door itself, cupping his hands to the glass panel to peer in.

"Mar-sha!"

The girls were packed in the cab, Wyatt huddled in the bed with his back to the window, looking grim. Rich pulled up behind them.

"You okay, tough guy?" Rich called out his window.

Wyatt nodded, jaw set, like the indignity of riding in back had welded it shut.

"Hi, Uncle Rich!" Agnes yelled, crawling across the seat. Her lazy eye stared off the other direction. She pulled Eugene's door closed, waved through the glass.

Rich held up a hand. He had forty bucks in his wallet. Colleen didn't mind loaning them money, and Enid was her sister, so Rich tried not to have an opinion.

"Marsha, sweetheart, come on, I'm begging you!" Eugene pounded on the door. "Sugar, please. I got the girls with me. We got a shopping list." He fumbled in his pocket, slapped a piece of paper to the glass. "Don't make me beg in front of my kids." He yanked the handle, rattling it. "Marsha!" He dropped to his knees. "Marsha. Sugar, I'm on my knees." The catch in his voice sounded real.

"Damn it, Eugene," Rich grumbled, jamming the truck into neutral to get at his wallet in his back pocket.

Marsha appeared in the doorway.

"Thank you!" Eugene called. "Thank you, beautiful. Last time, I swear." He hopped up, flashing Rich a grin—*Women are so easy*.

Marsha opened the door, arms crossed over her chest with the surly attitude of a jailer, or a wife taking back a wayward drunk against her better judgment. Eugene said something and she laughed, stood aside to let him in.

# FALL
## *1977*

*October 15*

# RICH

Rich stared into the metal cubby. Thin like it was, hard to believe how this first envelope weighed on him. Squint-eyed Geraldine pushed a stamp across the post-office counter.

"I thought you were up to no good," the old woman said. "Most of them are." She lifted her chin at the wall of mailboxes behind him. "Magazines." She flared her nostrils, a burden to know everybody's business, and disappeared into the back, a cuckoo retreating into a clock.

Rich tucked the check inside the flap, licked the stamp, and slid the envelope through the slot. He scanned the bulletin board for log splitters for sale. Knew he was getting old when he couldn't split an honest cord of burnwood without paying for it later. The door swung open.

"Rich." Merle nodded.

He stood a full foot shorter than Rich and the white roots of his hair made his face look even redder, though he'd worked indoors his whole life. Ran in the family, Virgil's hair white by forty. A real sonofabitch, but at least Virgil had worked as hard as he'd worked you.

"Not like the old days, is it?" Merle asked, pulling down a public-comment-period notice. "'National Environmental Policy Act,'" he read, then crumpled it into a ball. "You missed a hell of a show, Rich. What a goddamn circus." Rich hadn't seen Merle since before the forestry board meeting. "Environmental impact. What a crock of shit. This is people's lives we're talking about."

Rich sucked his cheek, tasted rot. For years the board had handed Merle whatever he'd asked for on a platter, but the state had shaken things up, booted some of the timbermen off.

"They're shitting all over the American dream." Merle shook his head. "Where the hell are they getting the skulls from? It's like a goddamn Easter-egg hunt. I know Doc Peine dug up a mess of them, but shit. He never went around burying them where they don't belong."

"They found another one?" Rich asked.

"You didn't hear? State bagged it a hundred yards from the first. Should have seen those longhairs parading around outside that meeting, bullhorn and everything. Unrolled this big banner: 'Cathedral without a roof.' Cathedral. Funny thing for a bunch of atheists to care about. If Eugene wasn't keeping an eye on Deer Rib for us, there'd be sand in those gas tanks, I guarantee. Between the poachers and the monkey-wrenchers, turn your head for one minute and they run you out of business." Merle tacked his speedboat flyer where the comment notice had been.

"So what now?" Rich asked. Don had been tight-lipped, but three weeks had gone by and they were still stuck on Deer Rib.

"Now we wait. The board has ninety days to review our appeal. Water this, fish that. All that horseshit about silt. Hell, salmon'll swim through wet concrete if it means a chance to spawn. What the hell ever happened to private property rights in this country?" Merle stepped back from the board to admire his boat. "She's a beaut, Rich. I'd cut you a hell of a deal."

"Can't barely swim."

"Boat like that, wouldn't have to." Merle gave the boat a wistful look. "We need somebody to keep an eye on the grove, scare off those tree huggers before they plant a whole goddamn graveyard. You want to pick up a couple Saturday hours behind your place?"

"Eugene needs them worse," Rich said. "New baby and all."

"I said scare 'em, not kill 'em." Merle hiked up his slacks. The door swung shut behind him, leaving Rich alone. Ninety days. The rains would be here in less, which meant the grove was out of reach until spring, Rich's timber stuck on the other side of it.

"Can you start the grill?" Colleen asked when he got home, handing him a pack of hot dogs.

Chub slashed at the high grass with a stick, dropping into a crouch as soon as Rich came out.

"Chub?"

Scout sauntered over, his chain slithering.

"Scout, you seen Chub?"

"Boo!" Chub jumped out.

Rich staggered back. Eugene's truck labored up the driveway. Eugene and the kids came through the house and out the back door. Colleen brought out beers.

"Thanks, sugar. I married the wrong sister." Eugene winked.

"I heard that," Enid yelled from the kitchen, unbuttoning her blouse to nurse, no more private about her tits than a milk cow.

"You believe this shit?" Eugene pulled the rolled-up paper from his back pocket.

DAMNATION GROVE HARVEST STALLS, AGAIN. Rich held the paper at a distance to sharpen the print.

*The discovery of a second human skull comes less than two months after re-mains found nearby halted logging operations to allow state archaeologists*—Rich skimmed ahead.

*The 90-day pause follows months of protest amid concerns that harvesting vir-gin old-growth redwood on the private parcel could result in silt runoff that would contaminate creeks, raise water temperatures, and endanger a coho salmon run on Damnation Creek.*

Eugene rearranged the hot dogs, sucked heat off his thumb. "These are done." They went in. "What are you doing for money this winter?" Eugene asked.

Rich shrugged.

"You want to try crabbing with me? Lew's brother has his own boat," Eugene said.

"No thanks."

"I told him I'd drown him in the kitchen sink, save him the trouble," Enid cut in.

"We get into that grove money"—Eugene pointed his hot dog at Rich—"I'm buying a motorcycle."

"A washer-dryer," Enid corrected him. "You buy a motorcycle, I'll run you over with it."

"Bark's worse than her bite." Eugene winked at Rich, knocking the ketchup bottle against his palm. "She's crazy about me."

Enid raised an eyebrow. "Jury's still out on that one."

Colleen worried a hangnail.

"Aren't you going to eat something?" Rich asked her.

"I'm not hungry."

# COLLEEN

She was late. *How late?* Rich would want to know. Yes, Chub starting school had been hard. She'd forgotten how empty the days could feel. Yes, Melody's baby had weighed on her. Yes, she'd lost her period before. There could be half a dozen reasons. Her breasts weren't sore. But yesterday, when they'd gotten ready to eat, she'd thought of Daniel's fingers playing up and down her ribs and felt sick. She'd gone out and dry-heaved behind the rhododendrons. She hadn't thrown up, but live through something nine times, you recognize it the tenth.

Sixteen days since her cycle should have started, forty since Daniel, the radar station. *What if?* She barely dared to think it. A wave of nausea—what would Rich say? He hadn't touched her in months—but, despite everything, there it was: the low, undeniable hum of excitement.

"You know clear-all-heart is up another thirty bucks?" Rich called from the front room, leafing through a lumber catalog. "Prices just keep going up."

"Isn't that good?" she asked.

"Good for us," he said. "Bad for the guy building a redwood deck."

"I'm hungry," Chub said, climbing into Rich's lap.

She should have started lunch half an hour ago. Rich let the catalog flip closed and glanced up at Colleen standing in the doorway.

"Let's go see what Kel's frying up." He groaned, lifting Chub out of his lap and pushing to his feet. "Your mom doesn't feel like cooking." He took Colleen's slicker off the hook and held it out.

What else could he read on her face?

# CHUB

"The One and Only," his dad said, picking up the menu. When their food came, Chub took his bun off to count his pickles, and his mom snatched one.

"Watch her," his dad said, and the good mood got back in the truck with them.

"Fish Creek eats Fly, then pours into the Noose," Chub recited. "Dead-man spouts out . . ." He waited for his dad to teach him the next part.

"Rich . . ." his mom said.

His dad eased the truck onto the gravel shoulder, behind a pickup with a barking dog tied in back. Uncle Eugene stood with his baseball bat, yelling at a man with long blond hair. The dog perched on a pile of painted signs, barking. Eugene swung at the man and the dog jumped over the side, kicking air, strangling in its collar. His mom gasped.

"Stay here." His dad's door slammed.

Chub climbed onto his knees and his mom grabbed him around the waist.

"It's okay. Your dad's got him."

His dad scooped the dog up under one arm and unclipped the leash, tugging its collar to loosen it. There was a loud crash. Uncle Eugene wrestled the bat from a dent in the man's hood.

"Eugene!" his dad yelled.

Uncle Eugene swung again. Glass shattered out of a window. The dog barked. "Shut that dog up before I do," Uncle Eugene shouted.

"Eugene!"

Uncle Eugene backed up, small compared to his dad. The man let the dog in the truck, climbed in after him, and drove off. Chub's dad grabbed the bat from Uncle Eugene.

Uncle Eugene bent over, hands on his knees, getting his breath. He straightened up, reached back over his shoulder, and gripped his neck, like his head was on crooked.

"What's wrong with these people?" Uncle Eugene asked.

"What's wrong with you?" Chub's mom asked under her breath.

*October 22*

# RICH

Rich yanked the stuck ax, grunted, hitched a boot up onto the round. Too damn green. Blade would be duller than a doorknob by the time he got done. Nip in the air, season starting to turn, beard weather before long. They'd been working long hours on Deer Rib, racing to beat the rains. Rich's back, his shoulders, his knees: not a part left that didn't ache, burn, or creak.

Eugene's brakes screeched—never slowed down in time—and his Chevy roared up the driveway. Rich had asked him to help trim the access path to his water pipe; the line had stopped running again and the tank was low. Could have done it himself by now, in the time he'd spent waiting, but Colleen wanted him to talk Eugene out of that winter crabbing gig, and, after the run-in on the road the other day, out of some other things too.

Rich kept a hand on the ax, not giving up, only taking a breather. Eugene climbed out. He reached into his truck bed—metal rusted to filigree—and tossed a doormat at Rich's feet.

COME BACK WITH A WARRANT.

"Where'd you get that?" Rich asked.

"Whitey had them." Eugene smacked rust off his pants.

"Lark'll get a kick out of it," Rich said. "What were you doing at Whitey's?"

Eugene grinned. "We're getting a deer this season, aren't we? I needed ammo."

"You put a deer in that donkey cart, it'll fall through."

Eugene jutted his chin at the stump. "What's the problem there?"

Rich clamped one hand onto the round, rocked it, and wrenched the ax free.

Eugene yawned. "I'm so beat I sat down to piss this morning."

Another few weeks, the woods would be too muddy to work, whole operation shutting down for the season, as it did every year, winding to a halt in November and sometimes not starting up again until March. Then Rich could worry about the mortgage full-time.

"You serious about going out for crabs?" Rich asked.

"Enid says it's a sure way to die." Eugene rolled his eyes. Neither of them had known their father-in-law, but Rich could picture him: a speck on the sea, growing smaller. "See what she says when the money runs out."

"You busting up hippies for free?" Rich asked.

Eugene shrugged. "Merle offered me twenty hours a week to keep an eye on the grove. Not enough to live off. You got a pair of waders I can borrow?"

"In the house."

"Give me that, old man." Eugene took the ax. "Before you hurt yourself."

Rich went in.

"How's he seem?" Colleen asked, chopping carrots. The scene at the roadside had spooked her, but she wanted Rich to try, for Enid's sake.

"Same old." Rich slung the waders over his shoulder, a rubber thunk. Going out for crabs was risky—not a lot of second chances in the woods, but on open ocean there were none. "He'll need some kind of work for the winter."

"Did your father drown?" Colleen demanded.

Rich wrapped his arms around her. He felt her stiffen, then relax into him. He breathed in the geranium scent behind her ear, gave her cold hands a squeeze.

"Be careful," she said.

Outside, Eugene struggled to free the ax from the stump.

"Got your saw?" Rich asked.

"In the truck."

Rich retrieved his own, pushed aside a sheet of warped plywood to reach Eugene's forty-inch-bar Stihl, six months old, handle guard already cracked. Man, the thing was light, half the weight of Rich's McCulloch.

Eugene jerked the ax, stumbling when it came free. It bounced off the round again.

"Sonofabitch."

Rich kneed Eugene's driver-side door shut.

"Hey, take it easy," Eugene objected.

"You're lucky that engine hasn't fallen out. Enough damn rust holes to strain spaghetti." Rich led the way up Bald Hill.

"We get into those big pumpkins this spring, I'll buy a new one. Have to take us off day pay then, right? I don't get my roof patched, it'll piss through all winter."

"You got the shingles?"

"Don't worry. I got the winning numbers right here." Eugene tapped the lotto tickets in his chest pocket.

The path disappeared into the brush and berry canes. Rich ripped his cord. The McCulloch growled to life.

"I need that fucking grove," Eugene yelled, revving his saw. With both going, it was too loud to talk, about the only thing that shut Eugene up.

They cut a tunnel through the undergrowth until finally they were looking down from the steep prow of 24-7 Ridge at Damnation Creek. They killed their saws. The quiet took a minute to settle. The brush was thinner from here, blackberry canes dried to soft tan sticks where spray had drifted. And there on the overgrown path, like someone had left it there on purpose: a fresh sac, membrane slick with mucus, pink profile floating in fluid.

"Deer." Eugene toed it.

Rich hocked phlegm, sidestepped down the loose duff of rotting redwood needles. Creekside, he laid his jacket over a rock and set his saw on it, got his waders on.

"Don't look stopped up," Eugene said, parking his saw on the wet ground.

"Not two drips coming into our tank."

"Stinks." Eugene covered his nose with his elbow, air ripe with the stench of rotting fish.

After the coho run had come through, Rich had spent a day tossing the carcasses above their intake pipe out onto the banks or into the current to be carried downstream so they wouldn't taint the water. Eggs would hatch in the gravel beds. By Christmas, salmon fry would feed on each other.

Eugene stripped to the waist, wrangling the waders, hopping on one foot. Rich unsnapped his cuffs, rolled up his sleeves, and waded in. He let his balance adjust to the current, creek thigh-deep at the center, slackening when he reached the eddy. Eugene sloshed after him. Rich toed around underwater for the gravity line—usually when it stopped up it happened here—plunged an arm in to the bicep, maneuvered the latch that sprang the joint, and slipped his finger into the pipe, feeling for a plug of weeds, creek babbling in his ear. Clean.

"Must be farther down."

Rich picked his way along the bank until he came to an orange ribbon—rocks rolled downcreek, but timber stayed put. He waded in, felt along the pipe for the release, ran a finger around inside while Eugene watched from dry land.

"When's that crab gig start anyway?" Rich asked.

"Lew's brother's thing? December."

"Dungeness?"

"Yellow too. Maybe some slenders."

"Speaking of good ways to die." They walked downcreek, Rich keeping an eye out for the next marker. "What's he paying?" Rich asked.

"Hundred fifty." Eugene scratched his bare arms.

"A day?"

"A haul."

Rich spotted another ribbon, waded in. Water lapped in his ear. He thumbed the release, pulled out the prize: algae tangled like wet hair. His soaked shirt sucked his chest, his skin itching, chill of the water exposed to warmer air.

"If somebody offered a better deal, I'd take it," Eugene said. They trudged back upcreek. "Every time I turn around somebody needs new shoes. A washer-dryer. It don't end."

They rounded the bend and there was Dolores's son, squatting in the gravel bed, scribbling notes. Snooping around about something—Rich had sensed it the moment he'd laid eyes on him with Lark.

"What the—" Eugene stopped short. "What's that motherfucker doing? Hey, asshole!"

The guy raised a hand, as though accustomed to the greeting.

"You're trespassing," Eugene called, even with him across the creek now.

"So are you," Dolores's son shot back, sliding his pencil above his ear and tucking the notebook into his pack.

Eugene stepped into the water, slipped, the man already loping up through the lower grove toward the road.

"Next time I'll shoot your ass, fucker," Eugene yelled after him, clambering up the opposite bank. He picked something off the ground, waded back, and tossed it at Rich, who caught it against his chest: a pinwheel mint.

"Fucking unbelievable." Eugene shook his head. Running the guy off had put him in a good mood.

Rich peeled his shirt off, wrung it out, stuffed it down inside his waders. Eugene snapped his closed, warm and dry, an old repair at the elbow ripping. Eugene twisted his arm to examine it. "Enid can't sew worth a shit."

They started back up the path.

"They keep fighting these harvest plans, somebody's going to get killed," Eugene said.

"Not by you." Rich stopped walking, forcing Eugene to stop too. "You got Enid and the kids to think about."

"I know." Eugene pouted the rest of the way. Raised by a bunch of women.

At the house, Chub came barreling out the back door into Rich's legs. He felt the tweak in his knee but kept his balance. Chub climbed onto his back. In the dim tank shed, Rich pulled them both up the ladder and leaned far enough forward for Chub to peer over the lip. A steady dribble ran into the tank. Rich let Chub slip to the ground.

"What's that?" Chub asked, crouched over a fly in the dirt.

Rich picked it up, careful not to bend the wings, looked up at the ledge it had fallen from. Best trout fly there ever was—as good as the day Astrid gave it to him. Fish it dead drift, skitter it against the current, sink it, swim it to the surface.

"I'll show you, someday." Rich tossed the fly lightly in his palm. It weighed almost nothing, for all the memories it contained.

They found Eugene in the kitchen, hunched over chili with a hunk of corn bread.

"Back in business," Rich announced.

"I'll fix you a bowl," Colleen said.

Eugene drained his, stood. "See you later."

Chub crumbled corn bread into his chili and stirred the soggy mess around, spooning through the mush, like a jellybean might be hidden in it. Rich washed his hands.

"Well?" Colleen asked when Eugene was gone.

Rich shrugged. "Maybe Enid'll drown him before the ocean gets a chance."

"We could loan them," Colleen said.

"Might as well toss your money down Lark's shithouse hole."

She tsked. "You know these waders have a tear?"

"Where?"

She rotated them on the hook beside the kitchen door, stuck her finger through a slit in the calf. Just like Eugene to snag them and not say a word.

"Bath time," Colleen announced to Chub. "We've got water now, thanks to your dad."

"Me first." Rich pretended to rise. Chub raced down the hall and slammed the door. "Who knows? Crabs might not be such a bad idea." Maybe he should try it himself, stretch out what was left of their savings.

Colleen clanked Chub's bowl onto the counter.

"It's Lew's brother," Rich reasoned. "Those guys are professionals. They don't take chances."

"All men take chances."

"Mom!" Chub called. Colleen went to help him.

Rich scraped up the last bite, corn bread lodging in the base of his throat. He held a glass under the faucet, drank off half. It flashed in his hand and he fumbled, set it on the counter, water sloshing: a tiny fish, small and silver, like someone had folded a dime in half and dropped it in alive.

*October 26*

# COLLEEN

She read the clue again—*"Pleasure is first found in anticipation" author*—eight letters, ends in a T. She chewed the end of her pen, doing her best to cordon off her brain, ignoring the press of her bladder, resisting the temptation to rifle through her purse, dig out the kit, and rip it open. Not yet.

Seven weeks, each day another breath inflating the small balloon of hope. She hadn't said anything to Rich; how could she? *Don't jinx it.* She wanted to be sure.

She doubled down on the new crossword.

*Fastest way.* Three letters. Fly.

*Quick to* _____. Anger.

*Head over heels.* In love.

*"Pleasure is first found in anticipation" author.* F-L_ _ _ _R-T.

She filled the sink, scoured the milk pot, the press of her bladder almost painful now. She took the test into the bathroom and closed the door, even though she was alone in the house. *You know there's a test you can take at home now?* the nurse at the clinic had asked when she'd called to make an appointment. Ten dollars, but it was worth it, to be holding it here in the privacy of her own bathroom. She read the instructions once without absorbing them, started over, tacking each word to its meaning.

After holding it all morning, it took her body a minute to comply. She slipped the urine-filled tube into the slot in the plastic box. She opened the medicine cabinet and set the test on the shelf, memorized the instructions, and dropped them into the woodstove.

The house was quiet but for the tick of the kitchen timer, the silent pulse of the test itself. Her heart thudded. She focused on slowing it, as if it might affect the results. If she was, if she really was—Rich would know it wasn't his. Her cheeks burned at the thought of telling him. She filled the kettle and set it to boil, watched the tiny silver fish circle the bowl, physical incarnation of the anxiety swinging around in her chest. She'd promised Chub. *He'll be right here when you get home.*

Lying in bed last night, she'd felt the magnetic pull of the test hidden in her purse.

*What's wrong?* Rich had asked, her restlessness keeping him awake.

*Nothing.* She'd driven all the way down to Arcata, to the drugstore near the university, to buy it. EVERY WOMAN HAS THE RIGHT TO KNOW SHE'S PREGNANT! a poster had proclaimed. She'd taken a basket, built a small fortress—four boxes of Band-Aids, six rolls of toilet paper—but the clerk hadn't batted an eye. With all the hippies on campus, she must have sold a dozen a day. *Those hippies screw like rabbits.*

She tried not to think of Daniel, but he might as well have been sitting here at the table, listening to the tick of the timer.

*You sure?* Rich had asked, turning onto his side, which she knew aggravated his back, sliding his palm down her stomach. She'd laced her fingers through his, worried he might feel it, might know without being told, the way she knew now, silencing the furious timer.

She touched her abdomen. *Little speck. Little sunflower seed. Little grain of rice.*

She could hear Mom. *Maybe you'll get one miracle in life.*

Colleen's father had been missing a week, truck abandoned near the beach in Crescent City where he took Colleen to hunt for agates. Colleen remembered her father driving them up and down the streets nearest the water, the big houses with their lawns, their widow's walks, as though somewhere there was a house that was theirs, if he could only find it. Colleen had been sure he'd show up, eventually, which, in the end, he had. Not the miracle she'd hoped for, but then came Chub and now—the kettle screamed.

*Charity*, four letters. Alms.

*Jury, undecided.* Hung.

*Warning*, six letters. Beware.

*Which came first?* Egg.

*"Pleasure is first found in anticipation" author.* Flaubert?

Sunlight curved in around the geranium leaves, illuminating dust motes. Her blood sang in her veins, her chest full to bursting, as she met her own eyes in the medicine cabinet mirror. Her hand trembled. But she already knew. She was pregnant. She would have to tell Rich. She would have to tell him. She inspected the bottom of the test tube for the small brown ring the instructions promised. Where was it?

She sat down on the toilet's closed lid. Hot tears leaked from her eyes. She cried for a long time. Ashamed of her stupid hope, her disappointment, her relief.

*Maybe you'll get one miracle. But you won't get two.*

She blew her nose, pushed the used test down to the bottom of the bathroom trash where Rich wouldn't find it. She flushed the toilet, as though to put the whole thing behind her. In the kitchen she found the fish floating on its side, dead in the twenty minutes she'd been gone. She opened the back door, slung the water out, and stood holding the empty bowl.

# RICH

Rich stood at the base of the spar tree he would limb, cut the top off, and rig with cables. Don walked a wide circle around it, marking trees with blue cut lines. This steep and this rocky, the guy trees would be doozies for Pete to fall, but they needed their stumps to anchor the guylines that would keep Rich's spar from snapping under the weight of logs lifted into the air. This was the last stand of big pumpkins on Deer Rib's east side. If they were still being paid by the board foot, these babies would have been a good chunk of change.

Rich watched Don hesitate before a Y-shaped three-hundred-footer whose stump they clearly needed. Its trunk forked halfway up, growing out in a half U, giving the tree the aspect of a lopsided slingshot. She was a sucker all right—only a sucker would try to cut her—almost impossible to predict which way she would fall. Suckers half this size had been twisting off the stump, knocking down good timber and killing fallers, even experts like Pete, for as long as men had cut trees. But leaving a pile of money upright wasn't an option. Don painted a blue cut line across the sucker's bark.

Rich snuffed his nose on his wrist. Pete stood in his chaps, watching Don work from downslope, his left arm weighted by the custom seventy-two-inch-bar McCulloch. Teachers used to tie Pete's left hand behind his back. He'd cut himself enough pairs of one-legged pants over the years using saws made for right-handers that he finally jiggered himself a lefty. It was that or a peg leg. Pete ran a thumb up the side of his crooked nose, ready to fight.

Rich had seen his share of pissing matches over trees less risky, and though Don was ferrying between crews, he still had plenty of piss left.

"Let's get this over with," Don grumbled, Pete streaking uphill like he aimed to knock Don flat on his ass. It was now or never, before the rains rolled in and sent them home until spring.

"I'll give you a minute," Rich said, and headed down, leaving the yelling behind him. Might as well have a cup of coffee while he waited, but as soon as he rounded the corner to the crummy's fold-in door, there stood Tom Feeley's kid, Quentin, cradling a forearm, bleeding through a makeshift tourniquet. He'd been setting choker chains with Eugene.

"What happened to you?" Rich asked.

"Strand of cable snapped." The kid swallowed. Rich smelled the sick iron scent of blood.

"Hang tight a minute." Rich radioed Don. "Don'll stitch you up." Eugene should have radioed himself instead of sending a bleeding kid down to the crummy alone. "Can you bend it?" Rich asked, to keep him talking.

"Yeah." The kid demonstrated. "Shit." He grimaced. "I can't get hurt."

"Everybody gets hurt," Rich said.

"I promised my mom."

"That's a lot of blood," Don observed, out of breath from his screaming match up the hill. He disappeared up the crummy steps and came back with his kit, rolled up his sleeves. "Let's see what we got here."

Quentin hissed air through his teeth when Don unwrapped the blood-soaked shirt and doused the wound with peroxide, calm until he saw the needle and thread.

"Don's sewn me up plenty of times," Rich assured him.

"You going to hold this arm down?" Don asked.

Rich took hold of him by the wrist and the elbow. Quentin flinched—reflex, not resistance.

"You got a hell of a pain tolerance, kid," Don said when it was over.

"Where'd you learn to do that?" Quentin asked, examining the neat stitches.

"The navy," Don said, and headed back up to finish duking it out with Pete.

Quentin made a fist, winced.

"You okay?" Rich asked.

The kid nodded, surprised it was true. "Happened so fast." He shook his head, bitter with himself.

"Welcome to the club." Rich unsnapped his own cuff and pulled up the sleeve to expose the matching scar laddering up his forearm. "Pop a squat," Rich said. "Rest awhile."

"That's okay." The kid trudged back up into the woods.

Rich belted up, waiting on Pete to finish chewing Don a new one so he could get to work without taking sides. Pete wanted to leave the sucker standing, afraid to bust her. She'd implode if she didn't hit exactly right. Trick was to drop her at an angle so that the entire length landed at once. One degree off and you had half a million board feet of splinters. Rich had seen the blank stare on a faller's face after a drop like that—it could cost him his job, if it didn't cost him his life.

But Pete could bitch all he wanted; it was his own reputation he was up against. Drop a three-hundred-footer with his eyes closed and still hammer a stake into the ground with her tip. Don rested his short crossed arms on his gut like a surly pregnant woman. Finally, Pete spat over his shoulder.

"Damn it, Don."

Rich trudged back up toward his spar. Deer Spring should be around here somewhere. He'd lost his bearings, harvest changing the feel of the ridge.

Pete shook his head in disgust. "That sonofabitch's head is harder than his damn hat."

Rich chose the spar's best face, ran one end of the steel-cored rope through the eye of his climbing belt, around the base of the spar, and back through the eye on the other end. He tied the Husqvarna to his belt and rolled his shoulders. Then he backed up against his rope, pulled it into a taut loop he jockeyed up level with his sternum, and sank his right spur into bark—*Start right, that's your good-luck foot.* He flipped his rope up, walking until he gained back the slack: one, two, three, flip. Huffing, he dug his spurs in and leaned back into his rope to give his arms a break.

Widowmakers loomed overhead; any one of those high branches could have his name on it, ready to break off and crack his head like a nut. Below, the Cats had finished pushing brush into beds for the ring of trees Pete would fall. Now the machines lumbered over the rocky terrain toward the ravine, safely out of range.

Rich watched Pete figuring below. He could have been something—an architect, an engineer. The angle of the bed combined with the angle of the sucker, accounting for the limbs overhead, he had maybe a foot of leeway if he was going to lay the sucker down right. Pete backtracked to the first guy tree, a simple one. He'd start there. He radioed Rich.

*Nice knowing you.*

Any other faller, Don would have had Rich wait until the circle of guy trees was nothing but a ring of stumps before he climbed up the spar in the middle of them, rather than risk a falling tree twisting off the stump and knocking into the spar, shaking Rich off like an overripe apple. But Pete was Pete.

Rich's Husqvarna swayed. He felt the rope's creak in his locked knees. He'd learned to climb with an ax on one rope and a saw on the other. The tug of the single chainsaw rope still felt like he'd forgotten something. He pulled her up, little lightweight roaring to life, and brought her down on the armpit of a branch, limb swooping, crashing ten stories. He moved to the next, tilting his head away from the fountain of sawdust. He killed the saw, climbed, did it all again, until a tree crashed to the ground, impact vibrating up the spar. Pete had dropped the first guy tree. Lyle Whelan stood frozen. In a moment he'd snap into action, lopping off her branches and bucking her to truck lengths, but up close, a drop like that sucked the air from your lungs.

Rich wiped away sweat-stuck sawdust. His eyes still itched from yesterday's flyover—sonofabitch had strafed them with that spray. The strap of his hard hat rubbed, start of a helmet hickey. He snorted, spat, wished for a swig of water. This high, he should have been able to see over the spine of the ridge, but it was shrouded by mist that hung in the gulches the way cold clung in the folds of clothes when you first came inside. Inside his hard hat, his scalp itched.

The spar creaked. Rich double-checked his knots. The show had gone quiet below, wind carrying the distant drone of the crew south of them. He spotted two hard hats scrambling up out of the ravine, holding a barehead—long, dark hair—by the arms. Don plowed through the cluster, only scraps audible at Rich's height. *The fuck!—Property?* Don had had it out for anybody with hair over a regulation inch since Merle took him down to the forestry board dog-and-pony show.

The barehead said something and Eugene cuffed him. The guy hit him back. Dolores's son, had to be. They circled each other until the Sanderson kid came up behind and swept the guy's feet out from under him. The pair of them dragged him downhill, swinging him into Eugene's truck bed like a sack of cement.

*Goddamn it. Don't be stupid, Eugene.*

Rich flipped the rope down, hit duff, staggered, legs taking a moment to reacquaint themselves with solid ground. Eugene's truck fishtailed out, hooking left onto Lost Road.

"Gundersen!" Pete shouted. "You want to die? Get the hell clear before I drop a sucker on your ass."

Rich tucked his gear against the trunk of his spar and loped up to the backbone of the ridge to watch. Pete climbed up onto the two-by-fours stuck into the sucker's trunk and measured the angle. Then, balancing on the springboards, Pete cut the face—a fountain of sawdust, Lyle helping him pull the huge undercut free, leaving a mouth eight feet deep. Pete drove his wedges in, then belly-slid inside the cut to check for dry rot, like a man disappearing into the jaws of a whale. Satisfied, he hopped down, backed up twenty yards—the distance he'd be able to run before the sucker tipped— kicking aside anything he might trip on. Finally, Pete boosted himself up onto the springboards around the back side of the sucker and revved his McCulloch. Catskinners hung out of their cabs. Even Don stopped what he was doing, the air tight with anticipation.

Pete's body vibrated with the saw, keeping the blade level, backcut straight, and woodpeckering his head up every three seconds to check for widowmakers— branches the diameter of a man's arm quivering overhead. The sucker's whole top shivered. Pete pulled his saw free, jumped down, and ran, a creak Rich felt in his rib cage, then ground rolling underfoot. Somebody wolf-howled. He'd done it! Dropped the sucker onto her fall bed neat as a corpse in a coffin, her butt end twenty feet high. Pete snorted sawdust out one nostril.

The afternoon buzzer ripped. Quitting time. Guys streamed down toward the crummy. By the time Rich got there, Eugene and the Sanderson kid were back. Rich eyed the empty truck bed.

"He dropped her already?" Eugene asked, disappointed to have missed the sucker's fall. His rifle rack was empty. Never one for keeping things in their places.

"Where is he?" Quentin asked.

Eugene sniggered. "I told him I'd give him a ten-second head start. He started arguing, I started counting. Turns out that sonofabitch can run."

"Should have put one in his back," the Sanderson kid said.

Eugene grunted. Quentin caught Rich's eye.

"Trespassing is trespassing," Don agreed. "But next time, we're calling Harvey. Got it?"

Eugene cracked his neck. The young guys were anxious to call it a day, cash their checks, and hit the bars down in Eureka. Friday six-packs made the rounds, cans dangling from plastic rings.

"Where the hell did Porter go?" someone asked, looking around for Don.

"Trash patrol."

Pete came down, carrying his saw.

"Somebody give this man a beer," Eugene said.

Quentin fumbled one his direction, but Pete waved him off. His hands shook pretty bad after a drop like that, whole body humming with nerves. Eugene caught a six-pack against his chest, tore one off, and handed the last to Rich. Rich popped the tab and offered it to Pete. Pete scowled—didn't trust his hands yet. He wasn't much of a drinker anyhow. His stepdad drank. Used to beat the living shit out of him.

Eugene slurped foam. "What? You too good to drink a beer with us?"

"Turns your dick soft," Pete said.

"Hear that, Rich?" Eugene asked. "You old guys gotta worry about that." He set the beer on the hood. "She getting to be too much for you to handle, old man?"

"I keep up," Rich said.

"Oh yeah? How long you keep it up for, old-timer?"

"How old's that daughter of yours?" Pete interrupted. "Fifteen?"

"I already shot one man today, Pete," Eugene warned.

Quentin's eyes slid to Rich's. Rich gave a little shake of his head. *Just blowing off steam.* Though he felt a seed of worry.

"Fifteen's old enough to breed her, ain't it?" Pete asked, though he'd never chased a girl in his life.

Eugene's jaw tightened. "First one of you assholes comes sniffing around, I'll—" Eugene shook his head, took a pull off his beer.

"You'll what?" Pete asked. "Finish your goddamn sentence."

"You wouldn't know which end to stick it in if she was flat on her back and staked to the ground, you big-nosed Swede," Lew cut in. "Now, any of you assholes know the difference between jam and jelly?" Lew looked around. "You don't jelly a dick down a broad's throat."

Eugene rolled his shoulders and took another pull off his beer.

"You've been telling that joke for twenty years," Pete said.

"And it's still funny. Now, tell me. What's the best thing about sex with twenty-eight-year-olds?" Lew waited. "There's twenty of them."

Eugene spat out his beer, wiped his chin with the back of his arm, shook his head. "Jesus, Lew. What the hell's wrong with you?"

"It's a joke."

Don trudged in, dumped a handful of broken glass into an old weed-juice drum, tossed a muddy notebook at Pete. "You make heads or tails of that?" he asked.

Guys chucked their cans into the burn barrel. Eugene hung back.

"You drop him at the end of the drainage?" Rich asked.

Eugene nodded. "Told him next time we'd skin him, hang him from old Yancy's cat tree."

Rich climbed aboard the crummy. The bus reeked: BO, diesel. Legs bounced in the aisle. Eugene followed them in his truck, hopping out to lock up behind them. Lew stopped below the next gate and the second crew streamed out.

Rich's arms had gone to putty. They shouldered up onto No Name Road. Near the grove, Rich looked out and spotted the 24-7 in the distance, proud as a flagpole, ache of longing in his chest he'd felt properly only one other time, nine years before: out at the garlic farm, Colleen on the other side of that screen door.

# COLLEEN

Colleen stopped in the doorway of the Only, smoke and payday noise thick as a wall. Enid pressed in behind her. Eugene swooped in and took Rich away. Chub scampered off to the game corner. Colleen hadn't wanted to come.

"Long day?" Kel asked, dealing out coasters. Nice, always was.

Colleen slid up onto a bar stool and took the beer he set in front of her in both hands, like it was warm instead of cold.

"You keeping an eye on those two?" Marsha asked, raising her chin in Rich and Eugene's direction. "Up to no good."

Enid's nostrils flared, but Colleen had always liked how Marsha asked questions, then answered them in the next breath. She didn't seem like the kind of woman to shoot off her husband's pinkie. *Honey, you think I regret it? I'd shoot off one of the bastard's balls if he gave me another chance.* Marsha grabbed a handful of peanuts. Kel rubbed a circle into the bar.

"You seeing anybody?" Marsha asked him.

"I'm waiting for Colleen to put Rich out to pasture." Kel winked.

"Ha." Marsha clunked elbows with Colleen. "That'll be the day."

"Hey, sugar," Eugene called, shaking the dice. Five rolls for a dollar. "Bring me some luck."

Enid rolled her eyes, slid off the stool, and sauntered into the bright spotlight of Eugene's attention.

Colleen thumbed condensation off the side of her still-full glass. Rich caught her eye, the corner of his mouth tugged up by an invisible thread.

"You know he had his pick, back in the day?" Marsha asked. "He was a real looker. Could have had any of us, but he was waiting on you, we just didn't know it yet."

Lying in bed that night, listening to Rich breathe in the dark, Colleen thought about what Marsha had said. She sifted back through her brief life in Arcata: the rabbit lamp she'd spotted in the window of the junk shop and bought with her first paycheck, the movie theater she could walk to on Saturdays, where, her second week in town, she found Daniel waiting in the red-carpeted lobby, like they'd agreed to meet there, though they hadn't seen each other since high school. All that time, Rich had been here, waiting on her.

She watched his chest rise and fall as he slept beside her, his unfaithful wife.

After Enid had called, pregnant, and said Mom was sick, after Colleen had gone home, the weekend stretching into a month, she'd hoped Daniel might come see her. She kept a nickel in her pocket. Sometimes, to calm herself, listening to her mother's sputtering cough on the other side of the wall, Colleen would finger the coin, turn it over and over until it grew warm with the things she would say to him. Every week when she drove up to Crescent City for her mother's cigarettes, for the malt balls Enid craved, she deposited the nickel into the pay phone outside the Safeway. *Hello, may I please speak to*—and every week, the dorm mother's stern reply. *Message?* She wrote him a few short, breezy letters, and then it was Christmas, then a year, then four and a half, the cancer creeping from Mom's lungs into her bones and finally into her brain, spreading like fog through the trees. She'd smoked like a chimney, until the last day. She'd die when she was ready, damn it. *Verne was a tough nut*, people still said in town.

Colleen had brought her breakfast every morning—a canned pear in a bowl of its own syrup. That last day, she'd found her slumped in her chair. A cigarette still smoldered in the bear-paw ashtray, a long gray cocoon of ash.

*Mom?* Colleen had asked. Like Verne had left her body, like she might be hiding behind the door.

After she died, Colleen barely left the cabin except to feed the cows, Mom's Bossys, or to help Marsha in the mill office two days a week. Finally Enid came tromping over Deer Rib Ridge with Marla on her hip—she'd moved into Eugene's trailer house out Lost Road when she got married. She carried armloads of their mother's clothes out into the yard and burned them, like the tracksuits and slippers were all contaminated. *There*, Enid said, stirring the embers where bits of cloth still smoldered. Like she'd checked off the first item on a list and could now turn her attention to the second: getting Colleen out on the town.

Klamath wasn't much of a town, even back then, when the pulp mill, the plywood mill, and the old-growth sawmill were all running double shifts. But Enid had done her hair, dragged her to a Sanderson shindig looking like a painted doll, left her standing by the bonfire alone. She'd crossed her arms. If she hugged tight enough, she might transport herself home.

A man had pulled a toothpick from the corner of his mouth and tossed it into the flames.

*Cold?* he'd asked. She recognized him, one of the loggers who came in for his checks. He'd shrugged off his coat and held it out until she accepted it. It still held the warmth of his body. The sleeves hung past her knees. He cleared his throat—a nervous habit, she would learn—his blushing undetectable in the firelight. The wind stirred. She coughed, eyes watering.

*Smoke follows beauty.* He'd cleared his throat again and offered a hand-kerchief, embroidered RG, creases crisp, as though it had been kept folded, untouched for a long time. Without thinking, she'd wiped the lipstick off on it, stared at the red smear.

*That's better.* He'd smiled. The left corner of his mouth hung up, as though hooked. Later he'd confessed he'd repeated her name over and over under his breath, but somehow, in the gulp of air he took between reaching out his hand and her shaking it, he'd swallowed it. *You're Enid's sister*, he'd said instead. His callused hand felt rough enough to strike a match off.

He'd waited for her to say her name, then nodded. *Cold-hands-warm-heart Colleen.* He was quiet. She wondered what he thought of her.

A few weeks after the bonfire, Eugene had brought him out to the cabin for dinner. Enid hadn't told her they'd invited him, and then suddenly there he was, ducking through the kitchen doorway with a paper pie box. *Fresh lemons, only the finest.*

*Didn't want to come empty-handed*, he'd said.

*Colleen, you remember Rich.*

*Can I help?* he'd asked, eyeing the potatoes.

Enid had nudged her. *Let him peel a potato.*

He'd pushed his sleeves up and washed his hands, slow and methodical, the way a doctor might. A tall man, but it wasn't the first thing you noticed about him. The way he'd ducked in the doorway, headfirst, it was his eyes she'd noticed, how they seemed to ask permission.

*Nice place*, he'd said.

*It was my mom's.*

He'd nodded, as though he understood. There was a fresh scrape across his knuckles. *Logger works with one foot in the grave*, Dad had said when Mom pushed him to get a timber job.

Rich had peeled potatoes with a knife in silence and handed them to her to chop. Finally, he began to talk. *The park took the land my house is on*, he said. *I can stay twenty-five years, or until I die. I was born in that house. So was my dad. My granddad built it. You know how I found out? They sent me a letter. Thing was, I never opened it until today. It was just sitting on the table all this time. I'm glad too. I opened it up this morning, but I knew I was coming out here tonight. Instead of stewing over it, I just thought about you.* He handed her the skinned potato, slippery white chunk jumping out of her hands.

*All done?* Enid had asked, Rich standing over a sinkful of skins.

*Almost cut my damn thumb off, I was so nervous*, he'd confessed later.

*More meat on the skins than in the pot.* Colleen's line, when they told the story together. *I thought, I better marry him before he starves to death.*

All through dinner he'd wiped at his mustache, like he was self-conscious of something stuck in it. Colleen had felt the same embarrassment, though she thought she'd concealed it a little better. Marla had a new pencil and spelled his full name right on the first try.

*Richard Gundersen*, he read. *Well aren't you just as bright as a dime?*

Marla climbed up onto Colleen's lap and Colleen bounced her on her knees—*giddyup*—covering her ears when Eugene cursed.

*Don't bother.* Enid rolled her eyes. *She hears it all at home.*

*Her first word was "sonofabitch,"* Eugene had announced proudly.

*Marla's first word was "sugar." "Sonofabitch" was Colleen's*, Enid had corrected him.

*Mine too*, Rich volunteered. Colleen had wondered if he was just being kind.

*Mom took her to the lunch counter at the Woolworth's in Redding*, Enid explained. *Had her all dolled up. Waitress comes over. Does she talk? No, she don't talk. Made a liar out of Mom.*

Everybody had laughed, even Colleen, embarrassed by a scene she couldn't remember.

*Well, where do you think I heard it?*

*From her!* Enid squawked. *Where else?* Enid could shriek and make a party, her laughter turning to confetti in the air.

Across the table, Rich had smiled. A spider had crawled across the counter earlier, while he'd been peeling the potatoes. He'd set the knife down, scooped the spider up, and taken it outside, a care Colleen had never seen a man—never seen anyone—take.

At the end of the night, she watched him crouch in the driveway, scratching Mom's old dog behind the ears, watched him thumb a toothpick from his front pocket. She'd wondered if he'd meant what he'd said.

*I like him*, Enid had announced, tilting her chair back on two legs and crossing her arms, challenging Colleen to contradict her.

*Shh*, Colleen had hissed. *He's still out there.*

*Don't you think Colleen ought to go out with him?* Enid asked Eugene.

Eugene sank back in his chair, the spirit that had animated him through thick wedges of store-bought lemon meringue, gooey and too sweet, drained away.

*Don't matter what I think*, he said.

Eugene had brought him to dinner a second time, then a third. Then, one night, Rich had turned up at the cabin alone. Afterward, she'd lain with her head on his bare chest as he recited all the times he'd noticed her before the bonfire—a teenager pushing through the crowd at the Only, looking for Laverne; standing off by herself, watching the fireworks on the Fourth—all these moments when she'd felt so alone. She'd listened to the vibration of his voice, the pump of his heart, his breathing regular as the tide.

*Your skin is so soft*, he'd marveled that first night. He'd made her feel that way. Like a marvel.

She turned toward Rich, an arm's length away in the darkness, breath catching in his nose. What would he say now?

*November 5*

# CHUB

The clinic smelled like picked scabs. Chub's dad tapped his foot. A lady came through the swinging door.

"Graham?"

His dad stood. Chub followed the lady into the room with the lie-down chair. She put on a paper mask with a nose and whiskers, like a giant rabbit with a ponytail.

*Your dad's afraid of the dentist*, his mom had whispered when he'd said goodbye. He'd breathed in her flowery smell. *Hold his hand, okay?*

When Chub came back out with a new toothbrush in a plastic wrapper, his dad stood again, in a hurry to leave.

"You hungry?" his dad asked.

Chub shook his head. Raindrops tadpoled across the windshield. He'd rinsed with water from the paper cup, but he still tasted cherry. The dentist smell had gotten into his clothes. His dad fiddled with the radio. The heat vents smelled like burning dust and old pennies. The radio fizzed. His dad clicked it off. The wipers scriff-scraffed. He thought about what Wyatt had said.

"Did Uncle Eugene ever kill anybody?" Chub asked. Wyatt had climbed up into Uncle Eugene's truck and dug the stamped metal tag out of the glove box. They'd taken turns holding it. Wyatt said it was from the war and that Uncle Eugene had killed three soldiers in tunnels underground.

"Maybe," his dad said. "Sometimes you have to in war."

"Were you in a war?"

"I never was."

"You never killed anybody?"

"No," his dad said.

"Would you?"

His dad sighed. "If I had to. To protect you and your mom."

Chub rested his head against the window. Woods blurred past. His dad pulled off at the cemetery. He dug some agates from his pocket. Chub picked four.

"Take one more," his dad reminded him. Chub picked a red one, polished and slippery.

The gate clanged behind them. They visited his mom's parents, then his dad's. Chub set one agate on each of their piles. He'd never met any of his grandparents. The last agate was sweaty in his hand by the time they came to the baby's grave. His dad tucked his chin to his neck, saying a prayer. When he was done, he nodded for Chub to add the red agate to the little pile for his baby sister who died. He felt a little jealous.

At home, Chub raced down the hall and catapulted onto the bed, landing with his face on his mom's stomach.

"Ouch," she said. "Let me see those clean teeth."

"Why are you in bed?" Chub asked.

"I didn't feel good, so I was resting," his mom said, pulling the hot water bottle from under the covers. She smiled but her eyes were sad. "Where's your dad? Did they fix his tooth?"

Chub shook his head.

"They didn't?" She groaned, pushing him off. "Ready for lunch?"

"You okay?" his dad asked her, coming in.

"Fine."

"You're not—?"

"Of course not," his mom snapped, her face turning red. "How could I be? It's just cramps."

His dad had stood a long time at the foot of his baby sister's grave, like he was waiting for her to come running up the path.

Chub dragged his sock feet down the hall carpet and across the living room to the dark rabbit lamp. He reached out to touch his fingertip to the lamp rabbit's nose, holding his breath for the one magic spark that might finally zap the bronze creature to life.

# COLLEEN

"'The early bird gets his own damn breakfast,'" Colleen read. The new cross-stitch hung from a nail above Enid's sink.

"Gertie made me that," Enid said.

Across the table, Eugene's great-aunt nodded, her white hair in curlers, though Eugene had never so much as fried an egg in his life. He'd barbecue, but indoor cooking was a woman's job.

Through the kitchen window, Colleen could see Rich standing off from Eugene in the yard, like he didn't trust him not to squirt him with the hose, resting all his weight on one leg. His knee was bothering him.

"Boys," Gertie said. "Always coming home hurt."

Enid dumped kernels into the air popper and lowered the hatch. "Legs heal. It's backs that do you in."

Eugene had Alsea's feet pinned in one hand, hosing off her bare butt.

"He's going to drown that baby," Gertie said.

Enid and Eugene had been fighting. Colleen could tell by the way Enid avoided looking at him; her glance would burn a hole. Colleen tidied a heap of unused disposable diapers. They cost a fortune.

"I can't do cloth without a washer. They stew in the bucket until Eugene has to bury them."

"I didn't say anything," Colleen said.

"You were thinking it."

"That water's cold," Gertie marveled. "Don't that baby ever cry? What's wrong with her?"

"Nothing's wrong." Enid's nostrils flared; she was ready for Eugene to drive Gertie home to Oregon.

The air popper bumbled. The first puffs shot from the maw onto the floor. "Shit." Enid grabbed a mixing bowl.

Gertie clucked her tongue. "I don't see why you need all these fancy contraptions."

Eugene dropped the hose, held the baby up by the armpits, and nibbled her toes.

"Better get some clothes on her," Gertie said.

"He'll bring her in." Enid plonked a stick of margarine into a skillet.

Colleen flinched—another stab of cramping. Her period had come yesterday, a heavy flow. She felt weepy. She wished she could lie down.

"You hear about Helen's baby?" Enid asked. "No brain in its head."

"Helen's?" Colleen braced her arm against the counter.

"There's a name for it. Mar-la! What's that thing called?"

"What thing?"

"What the Yancy baby had?"

"Anencephaly," Marla called back.

"Anen-what?" Enid yelled.

"Anen-ce-phaly!" Marla yelled back.

"Same as what's-her-name's, right? Its brain all shriveled up?" Enid looked to Colleen.

Enid hadn't pressed her for details, but she knew Colleen had seen Melody Larson's baby die. The tears Colleen had been holding back all morning leaked down her cheeks.

"That wasn't your fault," Enid said.

"I know." Colleen wiped her eyes. "Poor Helen."

"Evangeline's granddaughter had a baby like that," Gertie said. "Up near Five Rivers."

Eugene came in.

"You don't put that baby down, she'll never learn to crawl," Gertie said.

Eugene laid Alsea on the table, planted a kiss on Gertie's cheek, scooped up a handful of popcorn, and left before Enid turned around. The kids pawed into the bowl around Chub, each a mirror of a child Colleen might have had. Enid had never lost a single pregnancy.

Colleen shook the thought from her head, stepped over abandoned sweatshirts, and pushed out the back door.

"Colleen, tell your husband he's coming with me," Eugene said, as though she'd appeared to prove his point. "If I shoot myself in the foot, I'll need him to carry me out."

"Might shoot me by accident," Rich said.

"You're lucky I don't shoot you on purpose. Big high-climber here snags himself on a stub branch, drops his radio two hundred and fifty feet. Almost took my damn head off."

Rich poked the fire. He wouldn't tell her how he'd hurt his knee, torn his shirt nearly in half, and gashed his back, only that it was his fault and he was lucky nobody else got hurt. *Used up one of my nine lives today.*

"Come on. Sixty-forty." Eugene doused the grill with lighter fluid.

"Colleen doesn't like venison," Enid interrupted, coming out.

"Elk then. A nice Roosevelt."

"Norm'll jump so far up your ass you'll need fifty feet of line to reel him out," Rich said. The tubby game warden turned up at Eugene's every once in a while, sniffing around the burn barrel.

Eugene grabbed the flyswatter, snapped it, and examined the rubber webbing with the curiosity of a man inspecting the contents of a handkerchief after a productive sneeze. Enid wrestled open lawn chairs. Whatever they'd been arguing about—money, always money—Enid was still picking at it, telltale crease at the bridge of her nose.

"We could all be eating crab legs for Christmas," Eugene said, fishing cold beers from the creek.

"I'm already the orphan of a drowned man, I don't need to be the widow of one too," Enid snapped.

"I can swim."

"So could he."

The kids streamed out the back door to race leaf boats in the creek. Marla stood at the window—fifteen, a permanent babysitter, curse of the firstborn. She looked heartsick. The boy at the overlook, maybe. Colleen felt a stab of worry. Or was it guilt? She waited a few minutes, then went inside to find her. The shower ran behind the closed bathroom door and there, in the hallway, was Agnes, holding a glass jar, beam of sunlight setting her hair on fire. A pretty child. A shame about the eye.

"Who do you have there?" Colleen asked.

Agnes showed Colleen the salamander, slick and speckled. Colleen couldn't recall the last time she'd seen one. They used to be in all the creeks.

"Are you going to have a baby?" Agnes asked. Her lazy eye wandered off across the room.

"No, sweet pea. Why?"

"You're hugging your tummy."

"Oh." Colleen dropped her arms. "No."

Agnes looked up at her. Colleen put her hand on her head. The yellow legal pad with its waterfall of names still waited in her nightstand drawer. *Iris. Summer. Lily. Rose.* What would it have been like to have a little girl?

Outside, Enid was fiddling with a battery-powered radio.

"You're red as a lobster," she said when Colleen came back out with Agnes.

"It's hot in there."

"Tell me about it. That woodstove will cook us all in our sleep."

Johnny Cash crooned from the radio. *And my shoes keep walking back to you.* Enid dialed it up. Eugene pulled Agnes into a do-si-do, then wheeled Mavis in to take his place and pulled another cooled beer from the creek.

"Bring me one," Enid called.

He popped two more, handed one to Colleen, and clinked his own against Enid's, a peace offering. He put on a good show, but he was tired. If Rich's checks were small, Eugene's were smaller. He dropped into the grass, took his cap off.

"You need a haircut," Enid said.

"Why pay a guy to mow a dying lawn?" Eugene asked, running a hand through what was left of his downy hair.

"These are done," Rich said. Eugene hopped up.

"Where's Marla?" Gertie asked, sunk deep in a lawn chair.

"Washing her hair. She's got a date later," Enid said.

"A date?" Gertie asked.

"Talk to him." Enid raised her chin at Eugene. So that's what they'd been arguing about.

The seat of Enid's lawn chair sagged, her bottom an inch off the ground. The girls' dancing had turned to roughhousing. They veered, Agnes knocking over Enid's beer.

"Hey." Enid scooped it up and shook out the last drops. "Watch where you're going, lazy."

Agnes's chin crumpled.

"C'mere, sugar." Eugene held the tongs up in front of Agnes's good eye until she covered it with her hand, then drew a circle in the air for her slow eye to follow.

"Good girl. Now, go tell your mom you're sorry."

"Sorry!"

"Yeah, well. I can't drink a beer out of 'sorry.'" Enid nodded at Colleen's untouched bottle. "What are you, pregnant?"

"No." Colleen searched out Rich's eyes. *How could I be pregnant when my own husband won't touch me?*

Rich straightened. Under his shirt his arms and chest were still stamped with pink patches of sweat itch.

"Wy!" Enid yelled. "Come eat! Chub! Wy-att! Where are those two?" Enid went around to the front yard.

A droplet of worry welled in Colleen's mind. Then the yelling stopped.

"Found 'em," Rich said, and she knew he was right, the way you always knew when the missing had been found: someone stopped calling their names.

# RICH

He didn't see the doe, but he smelled her: musk, the sweet, metallic tang of blood. She was making a racket, crashing through junk alder grown up between rows of rinky-dink crop firs.

"Somebody's not doing his damn job," Eugene bitched.

Rich swatted air to silence him.

"Look at this." Eugene kicked brush. "You telling me they sprayed this?"

Rich swallowed a lump of frustration. Trying to shut Eugene up just made him talk louder. The crop firs were barely as thick around as a man's thigh, close grown. The sign at the gate slated this side for harvest in 1996, date already marked on the calendar—more farming than logging. Rich stopped, listening for the doe.

"Helicopter jackasses," Eugene griped, shouldering through another blind of alder. "A drunk could piss better."

Rich saw her in his mind: foam at the mouth, glossy black ticks beading the white tufts of her rump. His breathing was still ragged from jogging across the clearing. They'd belly-crawled a hundred yards along the soggy ground, downwind of the herd, hell on his back. All for a crackpot shot Eugene could have taken standing where they'd started.

*Wait*, Rich had breathed.

A few legal bucks, three- and four-pointers, had browsed near the perimeter, but of course Eugene had gone for the big 5x5 hemmed in by does. The herd had broken and they'd seen her, struggling into the brush. He'd had half a mind to walk, let Eugene clean up his own mess for once.

*Damn it, Eugene*, he'd muttered, Eugene already sprinting across the marsh. *Last time I hunt with that fool.*

Colleen would sigh. *That's what you always say.*

Wounded animals walked downhill, but the doe was lugging herself up toward the backbone of the steep ridge, pure animal terror, though Eugene had a better chance of beating her to death with that rifle than shooting her again. Her heart must have been double-timing, blood painting a trail through the undergrowth. The land was a patchwork of private, state, and national forest, hard to keep track of who owned what, but planting crop trees way up here? Only the Forest Circus was that dumb.

Eugene pushed ahead, turning to Rich to confirm he was still on track. Rich jerked his chin after snapping twigs, brambles combing flank. Eugene adjusted course, arms raised, wading through chest-deep brush, no ears in his head. A stick cracked under Eugene's boot—making more noise than the damn deer.

Eugene stopped. Jesus H. Christ. Couldn't he smell her? Salty sweet, sharp with adrenaline. Rich's clothes were soaked, muddy from neck to boots. His undershirt clung where marsh water had gone cold, sticking to his skin, itching to be peeled. He should strip it off, let the skin breathe. Pink wood hickeys had just started to fade off his torso. He scratched the scaly mother patch on his ribs. Sweat, rubbing for hours, that's how it started.

Almost to the ridgeline, Rich stopped to catch his breath.

"We lose her?" Eugene asked.

Rich squinted to sharpen his hearing, but the doe had paused too. If they didn't find her soon, it'd be a fight, Eugene wanting to cut and run, leaving the deer to die, Rich calling him a pussy—always a last resort. Rich inhaled. Somewhere nearby: twitch of nostrils, moisture beading muzzle.

*Where are you?*

He cleared the last ten paces to the spine and looked down at the clear-cut on the other side: a six-hundred-acre dump.

"Where the hell'd she go?" Eugene asked.

Pampas grass rustled in the breeze, six feet tall, slice you like a knife—some weed from Argentina nobody'd heard of twenty years ago; now it was everywhere. They retraced their steps, a burr of irritation working deeper into Rich's skull. If Eugene had just waited another goddamn minute . . .

*You know what he's like,* Colleen would say.

Eugene hollered. Rich grabbed brambles—sting in his palm, damn Himalayans. The doe was sprawled on her side, head canted back. She thrashed at the smell of them, raised herself onto her forelegs, collapsed. The wound was high on her flank, her fur matted with blood, but it was the swollen belly that set Rich's heart pounding. How hadn't he noticed? She thumped the ground as though strapped there, hyperventilating.

"Christ," Rich said. "Finish her."

Eugene raised his rifle, hesitated. Foam cobwebbed the corners of her mouth, her tongue caked white. She drove her hooves into the duff, wild-eyed, and, for a moment, it seemed she might get to her feet. Eugene's rifle barrel traced small circles, tracking her lolling head.

"Damn it, Eugene." Rich swung his rifle off his shoulder.

Eugene squeezed off a shot, recoil kicking. He rubbed the spot where a bruise would darken into a badge. Whiff of sulfur.

"Shit." Eugene spat. "What the hell's she doing that pregnant this early?"

Blood bubbled from the wound, trampled grasses a thick mat where the deer must have bedded down before, and Eugene stepped into the flat area, nudged a glassy brown eye with his rifle barrel. Rich blinked.

"Where's your tag?" Rich asked.

"Relax. I got it right here." Eugene patted the front of his jacket where there was no pocket, slipped the gunnysack off his shoulder, and handed Rich the rope. Ten years in the woods and Eugene still couldn't tie a knot worth a damn, couldn't tell a cat's paw from a boom hitch, raised by a goddamn bunch of women. Rich shoved his hands under her neck, lifted her: warm, heavy. Decomposing needles stuck to her tongue. He had the bizarre urge to wipe them off. Eugene tossed the rope up over a branch.

"On three."

She rose in the noose. Normally, they'd gut a deer, haul it home, let it hang two days, rot sweetening the meat, but this wasn't something for kids to see. They'd be in deep shit with Norm; he'd fine their asses for sure, gunning down a pregnant doe like a couple of lowlifes.

Eugene got out his knife. He was going to slit the doe's belly and pull the thing out, squirming and pink, still alive. Rich braced an arm against a tree, as though he were holding it up instead of the other way around. *Go half-assed, take the backstraps.* Then came the punch-grunt of Eugene stabbing throat, slitting a collar, skinning her proper. He stood back, undersides of his sleeves gore-smeared.

"Help me out," he said.

Rich yanked the hide down as Eugene slid the blade, Rich's ear pressed against the doe's wiry hair, his skin crawling with imagined ticks, until the heavy pelt dropped to the grass. Even with his head turned, the slip and plop of guts curdled Rich's stomach. Steam rose off the pile, stink of blood and shit, urine and bile.

"Look at this." Eugene shook a hose of intestine off his boot, stood back to show Rich there was no fetus, just some kind of growth. Eugene cut it loose.

Rich breathed through his mouth.

"What the fuck is it?" Eugene toed the lump, about the size of a baseball. He stepped around it and carved down the spine, taking the backstraps, the best cut.

Finished, Eugene dropped to his knees and dug hand-over-hand, like a dog chasing a mole, until he had a shallow pit. They heaved the carcass in and covered it. Her meat rested heavily against Rich's back, still warm.

At the bottom of the ridge, Eugene dropped the deerskin over the fence and hopped it, Rich searching out a low place to step over.

"What's the point of being seven feet tall if you can't jump a fence worth shit?"

With Eugene's jacket off, Rich saw his shirt pocket was empty.

"Where's your tag?"

"I got it."

"Let me see it."

"Relax, it's at the house."

Rich shook his head. Just like Eugene to skimp on the tag fee and risk the fine.

"Look, it was an accident, okay?" Eugene asked.

"I'm sure Norm'll be happy to hear that."

"Fuck Norm. All I see is a hundred pounds of good meat."

At the trailer house, they laid the cuts out on a tarp.

"Took you long enough," Enid said, coming out with a roll of waxed paper.

"Deafest poacher I ever met," Rich said. "Lose a cow with a bell around its neck."

Eugene tossed a scrap at him. "Who you calling a poacher, asshole? I got the tag."

"Sure you do." Rich smacked dirt off his hands.

"Take some of this." Eugene held up a backstrap.

"Keep it. Maybe Kel will give you fifty cents a pound."

Tourists paid a dollar extra for a venison burger at the Only, too dumb to know wild meat came cheaper than store beef.

An engine grumbled in the distance. Norm could hear an illegal shot for twenty miles. Rich headed for his truck. Agnes hopped the creek after him.

"Where's Chub?" she asked, balancing on one leg, scabbed-over cat scratches stitched up her shin.

"At home," Rich said. "Watch out, kiddo." She stepped back and he climbed in, rolled the window down. "See you around like a donut," he said, and she smiled, her good eye on Rich. He'd worried about raising a daughter, but maybe it wouldn't have been so different.

A black truck bounced down into the muddy yard and pulled up alongside him: not Norm at all, but the Sanderson kid, Owen, hair greased. Marla flew down the steps toward it, Eugene strutting around the corner, knife in his fist, like he'd been stabbing someone with it instead of cleaning it. Eugene wiped blood off his palm and shook the Sanderson kid's hand through his window, gripping to bust a knuckle. "You get her home before dark or I'll be on you like flies on shit, you hear me?"

"How old is that kid?" Rich asked after they pulled away.

Eugene shrugged. "Old enough to know I'd cut his dick off."

"Would you tell him his daughter's fifteen?" Enid called from the porch.

"She's a smart girl," Eugene said.

Enid crossed her arms. "What's smart got to do with it?"

# CHUB

From Uncle Lark's porch, Chub watched a family drive a station wagon through the tunnel tree. The dad used the outhouse, then came up the steps for the boy to choose a Sasquatch. The mom sat in the car with the windows rolled up. Killer and Banjo lifted their legs on the back tire.

"Chub here is learning to carve them Sasquatches," Uncle Lark told the boy, who eyed Chub.

He was a city boy, hair wet-combed like he was going to church. Chub felt proud, scraping a piece of driftwood with Uncle Lark's knife.

"There a restaurant around here?" the man asked.

"You can get a burger down at the Only." Uncle Lark tossed the man's money onto the upside-down crate, like it was junk. "By the bridge. Where you turned."

"Then can we swim in the ocean?" the boy asked his dad.

"That's not a swimming ocean," Uncle Lark said. "That's a drowning ocean. Sneaker waves'll grab a grown man by the ankles and drag him out a thousand feet."

The dad put his hand on the boy's head, steered him back to the car.

"How's that knife feel?" Uncle Lark asked once they were gone.

"Good."

Chub handed it back. Uncle Lark dug up the little notch that locked the blade straight and folded it closed.

"Lockback's a good knife," Uncle Lark said. "Won't snap up on you the way a pocketknife will. I had her sixty years. Old guy down at Hupa used to make them. Your dad's got her twin. His dad—your granddad—and me paddled all the way up the river to buy them." Uncle Lark weighed the knife in his hand. "A good knife is like a good woman: she won't cut you if you handle her right." Uncle Lark pushed himself to his feet and grabbed his fishing pole. "Let's see what's biting."

Chub stood on the stump, fishing line swaying in the brown water. His dad sidestepped down the riverbank. His clothes were bloody.

"What happened, String Bean?" Uncle Lark asked. "You finally kill one of those tree huggers?"

"Why do you always call him String Bean?" Chub asked.

"Who, him? 'Cause he used to be skinny."

"Eugene got one," his dad said, picking up a flat stone and skipping it across the water. It skimmed the surface, like a deer bounding away across a clearing.

"No shit." The flyer stuck her head out from Uncle Lark's wild hair. "You get some steaks out of the deal?"

"They're pretty hard up." His dad took Chub's fishing pole, reeled in, and cast a long arc.

Uncle Lark watched the hook sail out over the water and plop in above the riffle. A blue heron lifted off, flapping across the river. "Your dad's still got an arm on him."

"He's got two," Chub said, and looked down at Uncle Lark's hand, short index finger's skin cinched together at the first knuckle like a sausage casing.

"I ever tell you how I lost this?" Uncle Lark wagged it. "That damn flyer. Wow-wee, nothing like a squirrel bite."

"Nun-uh."

Uncle Lark frowned. "I told you that story already, huh? Bitch lion. I trapped her fair and square." He jutted his chin. Chub turned, as though the cage might still be there, though it had happened before he was born. "Tourists used to fork over a quarter just to get a picture with her. Hell, I gave her a fresh deer liver."

"Did she eat it?"

"Damn right. And took my finger for dessert. Would have took my whole arm if I let her."

"Did it hurt?"

"Not too bad." He held out the finger for Chub to grip, scarred skin like a rawhide drawstring pulled tight. "Got fifty dollars for her pelt. Sweetest fifty bucks I ever made."

Chub picked at the end of the rifle cane's barrel, looking for the door to the secret compartment inside it that Uncle Lark had popped open earlier to retrieve a hidden cigarette.

"I never seen anything like it," his dad said to Uncle Lark. "Big as my fist."

"Must have smoked too many cigarettes." Uncle Lark scratched the lump on his neck.

They followed Uncle Lark up the dirt path, his hip hitching like a broken puppet's. His face was sweaty by the time he collapsed into a plastic porch chair.

"Any customers?" his dad asked.

"One big shit from Frisco. You could smell it from here." Uncle Lark's body shook with his cough. "Chub, where are those field glasses I gave you?"

Chub pulled the binoculars from his bib pocket.

"Good. Keep a lookout for whales on the way home. And don't take any wooden nickels." Uncle Lark mussed Chub's hair, pulled a carved nickel from behind Chub's ear, and dropped it into his bib pocket.

Chub followed his dad down the steps.

"Watch out for potholes," Uncle Lark called after them. "And assholes."

*November 13*

# RICH

A rumbling, like thunder. He reached for the clock: 11:43 p.m. Nothing rattling, no water glass walking to the edge of the nightstand.

"What is it?" Colleen asked drowsily.

"Blowdown, I think." Even in the dark, Rich could make out the rolled-up map, propped in the corner. *Hope it's not ours.*

She scooted closer, burrowed her cold nose into his neck. He turned his head toward the bedside table, the rubbers tucked into the drawer, but she'd already fallen back asleep. He pictured the blowdown, his timber tipped by the wind, busted to pieces. He itched to walk up and check, but instead he forced himself to concentrate on the map, retraced its lines behind his closed eyelids. When he opened his eyes again, it was daylight. Sunday.

Outside, mist smoked off the ground. Scout rocketed up the path, Rich scanning for gaps, for trees lost to the wind. His heart pounded. Over the Little Lost. *Please.* Finally, weather-beat but proud, the 24-7 appeared. He surveyed his other big pumpkins. All still standing. Scout sat on his haunches, panting. A truck door slammed in the distance.

Rich waded across the creek and loped up through Lower Damnation Grove, to the road. Water roared from the culvert. Eugene's Chevy was parked on the shoulder, door ajar. Pete's truck too, mud-splattered bumper stickers peeling.

IF GOD DIDN'T WANT US TO CUT TREES, WHY'D HE MAKE THEM GROW BACK?

MY HOOKER'S BETTER THAN YOUR HOOKER.

Pete himself was nowhere in sight. Rich cupped his hands around his mouth.

"Ho!"

Pete hooted back. Rich caught up to him, standing at the roots of a wind-fallen big pumpkin, dry-rotted to dust.

"Imagine if I cut the face on that?" Pete asked. Could have killed him.

"You heard it out by you?" Rich asked.

"Nah," Pete said. "But that wind."

Eugene walked the log, measuring her. "Two eighty."

"Could have told you that by looking," Pete said.

"I'm working here." Eugene adjusted his rifle strap.

"Watch you don't shoot yourself in the foot," Pete warned.

"Wouldn't be the first time," Rich ribbed.

"You're a pair of assholes, you know that?"

A horn blared.

"Porter," Pete and Rich said together, but it was Merle's gold Cadillac, idling in the fog below.

Pete spat a steaming leash of juice. "Checking on his fatted calf."

Eugene went down to meet him.

"You see the paper?" Merle asked after Eugene explained the rotted tree gone over. "Stop by when you're done here," Merle told him. The Cadillac's tires threw fans of mud in its wake.

Rich followed Pete back down to the road.

"What did he want?" Pete asked.

Eugene shrugged. "Nothing."

Pete scoffed. "Since when did Merle ever want nothing?"

"Hey," Eugene called after Rich. "Take this mutt with you." Scout shot out from the brush, tracking a scent. "Dog thinks it's a pincushion."

Rich felt light with relief the whole way back—his timber still standing. He ducked into the house, snagged his keys from the burl bowl.

"Where you going?" Colleen asked.

"Get the paper."


"Hey, Rich," Dot said, bell tinkling over the Beehive's door when he came in. The bear claws were golden, just out of the oven. "How many you want?" Dot asked.

"How many you got?"

Dot smiled. Her cheeks were painted pink and she wore a sweater so full of sequins light bounced off her like off a fresh-caught trout.

"Better make it four," he said, handing over the money.

"When are you boys going to get back into that grove?" she asked.

"Not 'til spring, looks like. You spare a couple dimes?"

"It'll cost you." She punched a key and the drawer rolled out. Kids and drunks all knew Dot would slide an ugly—a bear claw whose filling had run out between its toes—across the counter for nothing. *What are we running, a soup kitchen?* Lew would grouse.

"Tell Lew I charged you double," Dot said, handing Rich his change.

The metal jaw of the newspaper dispenser screaked: log-splitting contest down in Orick, photo from low to the ground so the ax head looked larger than that of the man swinging it. Rich tossed the paper onto the seat, settled the sack beside him, and folded pastry into his mouth.


"Look at this." He tossed the paper onto the table for Colleen to see, setting the white sack of bear claws—an innocent three—beside it.

Chub rammed into Rich's side, reached into the sack.

"Ah-ah-ah," Colleen scolded. "Plate, mister."

Rich handed him one. Colleen wiped a palm across the ad. The whole back page, where the fishing report should have been, was redwood trees.

WE ARE THE LUNGS OF THE PLANET
SAVE DAMNATION GROVE

*November 17*

# COLLEEN

Joanna thwacked a soaked shirt over the side of the washtub. The girls spilled down the cabin's front steps. Even Judith seemed eager.

"It kept trying to stand up, but it couldn't," Judith said. "Its back end didn't work."

"We lost a calf," Joanna explained.

"Oh," Colleen said. "I'm sorry."

Bossy stood dumb, tail flicking.

"They say animals don't grieve." Joanna sighed and led the way to the coop. "How many?"

"Two dozen?" Colleen handed her the empty cartons. "I thought I might try making noodles."

"How's Chub like school?" Joanna asked, ducking inside the henhouse.

"He loves it. He's in the same class as Helen's—" The meal train hadn't started yet. Helen and Carl were camped out at the hospital, waiting for the baby to die. Joanna reemerged.

"I heard about that." Joanna handed down two full cartons and rested a hand on the swell of her belly protectively.

"It's the third one." Colleen had been thinking it, but this was the first time she'd said it aloud. Fourth, if the rumor about Beth Cooney's baby was true. "It doesn't seem—"

"Mama! Ma-ma! Camber has a bloody nose!"

The girls crowded around the baby. Blood dripped down her chin. She looked more terrified by her sisters crouched around her than by anything happening to her own body.

"Tilt her head back," Joanna instructed. "Pinch it. I'll get a rag."

The baby wailed.

"It's okay." Colleen pressed her index finger to the bridge of the baby's nose, bone barely there.

"It won't stop," Judith said.

Camber's eyes crossed on Colleen's finger.

"It will."

Joanna returned with a wet towel and whisked the baby up, tilting her head back.

"She's fine," she told the girls. "It doesn't hurt, you know that." Joanna turned to Colleen. "They sprayed a couple days ago. Again. Lucky I heard the helicopter coming this time, got the bathtub filled up. You should see the creek. Just a bucket of milk with oil scum on top. You can smell the diesel." Joanna rocked the baby in her arms.

The motion made Colleen's chest ache with longing. She took up her eggs.

"Good luck." Joanna lifted her chin at Colleen's stomach—no, at the eggs she held against it. "With your noodles. Tell Helen we're praying for her."

*November 19*

# RICH

Scout raced up the hill, Chub chasing him down the other side to the Little Lost. Chub flung a stick in, watched the wild runoff carry it. Rich pulled his waders on, tucking the foil-wrapped cookies inside, then hoisted Chub up. Scout launched himself into the water beside them, paddling madly. The big pumpkins of 24-7 Ridge loomed dark with moisture. When they finally reached them, Rich pressed a palm to the 24-7's berth. Chub squeezed between him and the trunk, pressed an ear to the bark, listening.

"You're not one of those tree huggers, are you?" Rich teased.

"No." Chub twisted in place.

"You go first." Rich nudged him along. "In case we meet Bigfoot."

"There's no Bigfoot."

"You sure?" Rich asked. "I don't want to share these cookies. Think you can find our pipe?"

Chub took off down the east side of the ridge after Scout.

Rich remembered watching his father's truck pull away; didn't want a kid slowing him down. Eugene was that way with Wyatt. But Rich took Chub along to Whitey's for chain oil, down to the old Lumberjack Hotel in Orick when they were tearing it down, to salvage the redwood to repanel the bathroom, Chub holding the coffee can, collecting the square-headed nails.

Now Chub stopped at the edge of Damnation Creek, across from their intake pipe.

"How'd you find it?" Rich asked.

Chub held up his palm and pointed to the spot on his map.

"Pretty good, Chub," Rich said.

"Can I help?" Chub asked.

Rich surveyed the fast, cold chop. "Not today."

"I never get to do the fun part."

"Water's too strong today. Dunk you under before you yell 'help.'"

Chub took a step back, as if the creek might reach over its bank and grab him by the ankles. Rich stripped to the waist and sloshed in. He windmilled, rocks rolling underfoot. Chub wandered downstream, poked a rotting salmon corpse with a stick.

Rich plunged an arm into the water, felt around for the pipe's mouth, removed the screen, cleaned it out, and waded back. He rebuttoned his shirt and they sat on a rock and ate the cookies. Rich dug two toothpicks from his front pocket and they cleaned their teeth.

"Let's go take a look at the spring," Rich said.

The rain had finally quit. Runoff thundered down from the culvert. Together they scrambled up across the road into the upper grove. Chub hid.

A gust washed through the canopy. "Chub?"

"Boo!" Chub jumped out.

Rich gave an exaggerated start, Chub's satisfaction lasting all the way up through the tattered yellow tape still fluttering from the stakes the state archaeologists had left.

"Why do these trees have potbellies?" Chub asked. Lark had taught him the expression, and he found it funny.

"They've got burls."

"What are burls?"

"You know. Tree tumors."

"Burl clocks."

"You bet."

"What happened to that one?" Chub asked, stopping.

"Which?" Rich asked, and then he saw it: the gouge in the base of a big pumpkin upslope, so deep it might kill the tree, a sunken set of poorly covered tire tracks, sawdust piled at the base. Must have been ten feet wide. It took some balls to steal a burl that size. Chub stared. "Somebody cut it," Rich explained. He needed to call Eugene, make sure he'd seen this. Keeping an eye on the grove was his job. Merle would hit the ceiling.

Rich spotted two more poachings by the time they got to the spring. Scout flopped down, panting. Chub slung an arm over his ribs, pressed an ear to the reassuring thump of his dog heart. Rich cupped his hands and drank, belched.

"Ready, lumberjack?" Rich squatted, letting him climb on.

Chub squeezed the knobs of his throat. "I feel your bobber."

Rich coughed, tossing his head to loosen Chub's grip. Getting too big to carry. Yesterday Rich had come home to find Colleen packing up his baby clothes to give away.

*Shouldn't we keep some?*

*What for?* Colleen had demanded, though he hadn't meant anything by it, just nostalgia for the younger Chub who'd once filled them. The list of names had vanished from her bedside.

Chub's warm cheek settled against his shoulder. He weighed more, asleep. When they got home, Colleen stood at the stove with a blanket around her shoulders, watching the kettle. He laid Chub in his bed.

"You okay?" he asked, coming into the kitchen. A sticky mass the size of a cabbage sat in a mixing bowl in the sink. "What is that?" he asked.

"Egg noodles," she said, her voice raw. "I can't do anything right."

"That's not true." He put his arms around her, sour scent at her nape.

"I don't want Chub to be an only child," she said.

The kettle whistled. Rich reached and turned it off. He was an only child.

"You don't think I can have another baby, is that why you won't make love?"

"Colleen. That's not fair."

"Oh, I'm sorry, am I not being fair?" She poured a mug of hot water and slammed the kettle back down on the burner. "Enid uncrosses her legs for two minutes and a baby pops out." She wiped tears away with the back of her hand. "Since when is life fair?"

# RICH

Colleen combed Chub's wet hair down into his eyes while Rich shaved.

"Hold still," she said. The scissors snipped, hair falling to the floor. "Where'd you get those beautiful eyebrows?" she asked Chub.

"I got them at the eyebrow store."

"Okay, Grahamcracker, all done." She went to get the broom.

Rich ran the razor under the tap, snapped up his good shirt, and held out Chub's yellow one. Chub shook his head.

"It's too tight."

"Mom ironed it," Rich countered.

Chub held out his arms in defeat, but he was right, the thing barely buttoned. Colleen sighed.

"He's getting so big. I'll have to make him a new one."

Colleen went to get dressed. She came out in a blue halter-top dress he hadn't seen before, her back bare, soft corduroy cinched at the waist.

"Where'd you get that?" Rich asked.

Colleen looked down at it. "Enid loaned it to me. Is it too skimpy? I can change."

"No. Looks nice." His hand brushed her shoulder blades as he helped her into her coat.

They had to park on the grassy shoulder and walk up the road to the Only, Chub flying across the parking lot in the sudden freedom of the cotton T-shirt Colleen had let him wear instead.

A roar of conversation and body heat hit them as soon as they opened the door, the Only packed so tight Rich put his arm around Colleen and steered her through the crowd, Chub worming through people's legs to get to Agnes in the kids' corner.

It was a tradition, company night at the Only, the Sunday before Thanksgiving. Colleen set her purse on the bar. Rich pressed in behind her, people jostling on all sides.

"What'll it be?" Kel asked, pouring with both hands.

Rich held up two fingers. It was hot.

"Can you see Chub?" Colleen asked, packed too tight to even turn around.

Rich turned his head. "Yeah. You want to take off your coat?"

She nodded and he helped her slip out of it, geranium scent coming with it. He piled it over his shoulder.

Kel set two beers on the bar. The glasses were cold amid the heat of all these bodies and Colleen drank hers, foam cresting her top lip.

"Can you still see him?" she asked.

Rich searched out Chub. "Yep." Her naked back pressed against him. Down the bar, men rolled the dice.

"You made it," Eugene said, shouldering through the crowd, doing a double take at Colleen's dress. "Merle upped hours, thanks to you. As soon as I told him about those burls, thirty hours a week this winter, no questions asked. Said when I catch the bastards to nail them to a damn tree. I'm going to buy them a beer first. Whoever they are, they're keeping me employed." Eugene signaled Kel for two more. "Must be sixty grand worth of burls they poached out of Damnation Grove." Eugene shook his head. "I almost admire the assholes." The beers arrived and Eugene clapped Rich on the shoulder. "Kel, pour this old man another round. On me."

Kel changed out their empties and Colleen stopped asking about Chub. Her cheeks flushed with the alcohol. She'd told him how her mother used to get off the first shift at the cannery, glare at the clock like it had insulted her until the hands aligned at five, gin splashing into a mug. Colleen worried that itch might be in her too. She rarely drank more than half a beer in one sitting.

A roar exploded down at the end of the bar, Lew holding the dice-roll jar up in the air like a trophy, then dumping the bills out on the bar to be counted.

"What happened?" Colleen craned her neck, trying to turn herself around. He shifted to allow her a better view.

"Five sixes. Lew just won the pot."

"Six hundred and eighty-eight bucks!" Lew yelled, holding the wad of cash in the air. He slapped it on the bar. "We're gonna drink it!"

Guys hooted and cheered, nobody talking about whether there'd be jobs next season, at least for one night.

"He's crazy," Colleen said, smiling. It was strange, to be alone together surrounded by all this noise.

Rich had to scoop Chub up at the end of the night; he was nearly asleep in his arms by the time they got to the truck, Colleen veering a little as she walked, waiting outside her door until Rich opened it.

"What?" she asked, smiling, holding on to his arm as he boosted her up into the truck.

"Nothing."

At the house, he put Chub to bed and came in to find Colleen topless, dress stuck around her waist. She puzzled over the zipper.

"C'mere," he said, the teeth slowly unhooking until the corduroy fell around her ankles. She pulled the band from her hair and let it fall around her shoulders. He moved it aside, clearing the space behind her ear, and kissed her there, in the old spot. Once, twice.

"That tickles," she protested. Rain gusted against the window.

His undershirt caught on his ear when she tried to tug it over his head. He felt colossal, her narrow body pressed into the mattress beneath him, her eyes squeezed shut, forehead creased, as though she was remembering something unpleasant.

"Am I hurting you?" he asked, clumsy, winded after all these months.

"No."

Her breathing quickened, fingernails digging into his back. She clung to him, cried out. Outside, rain drilled the roof. In the morning, the scratches on his back would burn where the shower's hot water touched, veins of bare dirt in the driveway where gravel had been washed away.

*November 21*

# COLLEEN

She heard the slam of a car door, squinted, confused by the daylight. Voices filtered through the bedroom curtains, a man talking to Rich out front. She felt a faint pulsing behind her right eyebrow and sat up. The pulse turned to pounding.

She swung her legs over the side of the bed and stood, head swimming. Out the window, the white face of a VW bus came slowly into focus. Rich stood before it, as though prognosticating over its mechanical future. She forced the window open, its damp-swollen frame resisting.

"No kidding," Rich said to the other man.

Daniel. Her heart thudded. Rich tossed the rag onto the hood of his truck, beside a tin of wax, and Colleen shrank back, a splotchy heat on her chest— *What's he doing here?* Their boots knocked the stoop. She pulled on clothes. The covers trailed off Chub's bed, but his room was empty.

"You know this guy?" Rich asked when she shuffled out into the kitchen.

Daniel ducked his head over a steaming mug. A flush crept up her neck.

"Colleen," Daniel said. "Long time." His eyes scanned the counter for cream. She saw Rich notice this, knew he considered a man adding milk to coffee a sign of weakness of character.

"You two went to school together," Rich said, repeating the explanation Daniel must have given him. Rich's eyes lingered on her. She wished he would wrap his arms around her, hold her as he had last night, send Daniel away, but instead he went back to pouring coffee.

"Had a heck of a time finding this place," Daniel said.

"Keeps the Bible salesmen away." Rich turned, holding two more mugs.

"Why aren't you at work?" she asked, her throat parched.

"Too muddy. Don called it."

"For the season?"

"For the day." Rich tipped his head toward the front room.

She sat in the straight-backed chair, the men settling onto opposite ends of the couch. Her hands trembled. She set her mug on a coaster. Rich sipped the top off his coffee, a slurp in the uncomfortable silence.

"You still do these things?" Daniel asked, studying the abandoned crossword pinned beneath the burl bowl, hole in its upper left corner. She'd forgotten it was there. "I remember this lamp."

Rich looked at the brass rabbit, then at her. She felt herself turning red. *Stop it*, she wanted to hiss, though Rich couldn't know that she and Daniel had knocked the lamp over once, fooling around in her rented room. Daniel turned to examine the painted saw.

The old crosscut had hung there every day of her married life: handles worn smooth, teeth resharpened so many times the points tapered to paper thinness. Some of the color had gone out of the red barn, and the emerald forest had dulled, as though the sun had set in the painting, a scene that had once taken place in late morning, the promise of a day ahead, passing into the low light of dusk.

"You a fish doctor for the tribe?" Rich asked Daniel. Rich gave everybody a chance. It was one of the things she loved most about him.

"No. I'm doing a postdoc. Fisheries biology."

Rich nodded. "You all have the right to gill-net now, since that Supreme Court deal."

"On the reservation we do. It's Indian Country. We have federally reserved fishing rights," Daniel explained.

Colleen saw the squint in the corners of Rich's eyes, struggling to follow. "I hear some of the commercial guys aren't too happy about it."

"No, they're not," Daniel admitted. "Sports fishers aren't either."

"No more sneaking around at night," Rich said.

"Still a long way to go," Daniel replied, glancing at Colleen. "Between the dams, the logging, and the stuff they're spraying—"

"Where you out of?" Rich asked. It wasn't like him to interrupt.

"I'm working with a lab at Humboldt State for the year. You ever make it down to Arcata?"

Rich grunted. "Too many to-fu shops for my taste."

"I hear you." Daniel dug a mint from his pocket, offered it. Rich watched him unwrap it.

"Where's Chub?" she asked suddenly.

Rich and Daniel turned, as though they'd forgotten she was there.

"Out back." Rich took another audible sip. "What kind of fish work you do exactly?" More questions than Colleen had heard out of Rich in a year.

"Research, mostly."

"You like to fish?"

"My uncle took me as a kid. You?"

"Sure. When I was younger. Used to be you could walk across some of these creeks—whole thing was fish. That what brings you up our way?" Rich asked.

"You could say that." Daniel took a breath. It occurred to Colleen that he was nervous. "I've been taking some samples from your creek."

Colleen shifted, her eyes darting toward the kitchen, the jam jars hidden in the cabinet.

"From all the creeks around here, actually," Daniel explained. "The whole watershed."

Rich tilted his head back. Daniel leaned in to close the distance.

"There are very high levels of two phenoxy herbicides—2,4-D and 2,4,5-T—in the surface water. They're common defoliants they use around here. I can give you some literature—"

"Literature." Rich set his mug on the burl table, beside the coaster, as though the moment for such petty precaution had passed.

"These herbicides they're spraying—not just Sanderson, the Forest Service, the county too—it's the same ingredients as Agent Orange, and they're contaminated with TCDD, dioxin. They're toxic, not just for plants, for animals"—Daniel glanced at Colleen—"and for people. They started spraying them in the fifties, and all this time they've been bioaccumulating, building up in the fish, in the deer, you eat the deer—"

"I'm going to have to stop you there, Mr.—"

"Daniel."

Rich stood.

"It runs off into the water. Whatever they spray ends up right there in your coffee mug." Daniel set his mug down.

"Sorry you can't take that for the road," Rich said, opening the front door.

"It's nasty stuff. We're talking birth defects, cancers." Daniel's eyes slid to Colleen. "There's a cluster of miscarriages up in Oregon. They'll tell you it's safe, it's safe. It only kills weeds. If they told you there was a safe kind of bullet, would you let them shoot your little boy in the head? I've seen your intake pipe. You might as well pour the stuff straight into your tank. There's a petition you can sign. Look, I'm sorry. I know that—"

Rich shook his head. "You don't know." He held the door ajar.

"You're private people, Mr. Gundersen. You mind your own business. I understand." Daniel rose. His eyes tracked to Colleen and back. "But if it were me, I'd want to know."

"You've got no right trespassing," Rich said.

"Sanderson—"

"24-7 Ridge, down to Damnation Creek, is ours."

Colleen frowned. It wasn't like Rich to lie. A current of worry ran through her. What if Daniel wouldn't leave? Would he say more?

"That's our land," Rich insisted, his voice tight. "We don't want you on it."

Daniel shot her a questioning look.

"Stop looking at my wife," Rich said. "She's got nothing to say to you either."

"Mr. Gundersen, I didn't mean to upset you—"

"You didn't," Rich said, standing beside the open door.

Daniel scooted the burl bowl a little to the right and tapped the blank spot in the crossword underneath. "Yens," he said, and went out. *Desires.* Four letters. Starts with a Y.

Rich shut the door. Colleen's heart pounded in time with her head.

"Shouldn't have let him in," Rich said.

"Why did you lie?" she asked.

Rich looked at her.

"About owning that land," she prodded.

Rich dropped his eyes. "I was going to tell you," he said.

"Tell me what?"

"I bought it."

"Bought it?"

Rich swallowed. "I was going to tell you."

"When?" Her raised voice reverberated inside her skull, her fear that

Daniel would expose her, that Rich would find out what she'd done, still rattling her.

"Sanderson is going to put roads all the way down into the lower grove, to the creek." He leaned over, drawing a map on the burl table with his finger. "We can use those to haul the timber out. I already talked to Merle about it. The old-growth alone will pay it off; we'll make back four times what I owe in the first year. It's seven hundred and twenty acres. The whole 24-7 Ridge."

"How much was it?" Colleen asked.

Rich sighed and stood up. "You know this place isn't ours, Colleen." He flung his arm out, as though he could sweep aside the walls of the living room and see out. "We've got twenty-five years, or until you and me die, then the land goes to the park. Chub can't inherit it. They'll knock the house down. It doesn't *convey*."

"What does that have to do with—"

"We could move the house up. Onto the east side of 24-7 Ridge, once I get it cleared. It's not that steep. It'd be dirt, up to No Name Road, but at least you wouldn't have to drive the highway anymore. Or—" Rich cleared his throat. "We could buy a place in town, if you wanted."

She knew he hated the idea of living in town, hemmed in by neighbors, cut off from his woods.

"How much did it cost?"

"A lot." Rich rubbed the toe of his boot in the carpet, like he was crushing a cigarette.

"Rich, I'm your wife. I have a right to know."

"I wasn't sure the bank would even lend to me," Rich said. "A thirty-year loan, at my age."

He crouched beside her—his knee hurt him too much to get down on it. He took her hand, traced a slow circle in her palm. "I signed the papers in August."

"When were you going to tell me?"

"I don't know," he admitted.

"You never tell me anything." Her throbbing head was making her sick to her stomach. "Sometimes I wonder why you married me."

"Colleen."

"Don't," she snapped, though she didn't move. "What if it's true?"

"What if what's true?" Rich asked.

"What if it *is* poison, what they're spraying—" What if all the babies she'd lost, what if it wasn't anything she'd done wrong? What if there was a reason beyond *Just bad luck. It just wasn't the right time.* As if bad luck were a medical diagnosis.

"They've been spraying that stuff for twenty years." Rich dismissed the idea. "Spray right over us when we're cutting. Turns your eyes red for a day or two, that's all."

"But Lark has all those cancers."

"He smokes like a chimney."

"What about Helen? Or Melody? Or Elyse. Or Joanna's chicks? What about—?" *Me*, she wanted to ask. *What about me?* She was crying now, braying sobs that made it hard to breathe.

"A chicken's not a person, Colleen," Rich said once she quieted. Her glasses were fogged. He took them off and began, slowly, to clean the lenses.

"If we own that land, couldn't you ask them not to spray near us?" she asked.

Rich snorted, slid the glasses back onto her face. "If Merle ever found out we even talked to that guy, he'd make sure no mill between here and Canada would touch the 24-7. He'd put us out of business before we ever got started."

"Mama!" Chub pushed in the back door. Colleen sniffed, wiped her eyes.

"That stuff is approved by the government," Rich said, as though arguing with himself. "Why would they approve something if it wasn't safe?"

"Ma-ma!"

"In here," Colleen called.

"That guy could be making it all up," Rich said.

"But what if he isn't?"

"Scout ate a mole!" Chub shrieked, a streak of mud across his forehead.

"What if he isn't?" she asked, sharper.

Rich bent over and kissed the top of her head, the way he might a child's. He would have been a good father to their daughter. Patient, fair, forgiving.

"I've got chores," he said, and ducked out the front door.

"What if he isn't what?" Chub asked.

"What if he isn't what-what, Grahamcracker?" she teased.

Chub climbed into her lap. "I heard its bones crack."

"Yuck."

"It was blind so it couldn't see him. It just felt his big wet nose."

She licked her finger, rubbed dirt off his cheek. Outside, firewood clattered, Rich's blows coming one after the other. He'd pay for it later. She'd have to take off her socks and walk the knobby ridge of his spine.

"I'm thirsty," Chub said.

"Scooch." She tipped him out of her lap and he padded after her into the kitchen. "What do you want? Milk?" She took a glass from the drying rack.

"I'm really, really thirsty."

She glanced out the back window at the tank shed.

"Juice?" She filled the glass to the rim.

Chub picked it up with both hands, orange pith floating at the surface, like he couldn't believe his good fortune. A whole glass, undiluted.

"Not so fast, you'll get a bellyache."

Chub tilted his head back, tongue waggling in the empty glass.

"Better?" she asked.

"Uh-huh." He caught his breath, then wiped his mouth on his sleeve.

She rinsed the glass, washing away the cloudy film, letting it fill and spill over. She dried her hands, but she still felt a residue where the water had touched. She had the urge to wash them again, to wash the water off.

*November 22*

# CHUB

Chub bounced in place, wishing for his dad to come. Luke sat on the school's low wall behind him, swinging his legs. The heels of Luke's sneakers thunked the bricks. All day Luke had lied and now he felt bad. He'd been absent for eleven days. He said a water balloon had exploded out of his mom's privates. He said his baby brother came out with the top of his head missing, that his brain got eaten.

*Is she going to die?* bossy Linda had asked, which had confused Chub because the baby was a he. *Well?* Linda asked, tall and a bully, the biggest kid in their class. *Is she?*

Luke had shrugged. Suddenly Chub understood *she* was Luke's mom.

*Maybe.* Luke's face had fallen, like he hadn't realized she could die until he'd said it.

Then bossy Linda had pushed Luke and shouted *Liar!* and they'd run. Like a dying mother was a cootie anyone could catch.

Chub shivered. They weren't allowed to sit on the wall, but there were no teachers to tell Luke to get off. Luke's heels thunked the bricks guiltily. There was a stink coming from his lunch box—browned apple, baloney, soggy bread—as if his guilt had a smell.

"Is somebody coming to get you?" Ms. Schafer asked. She was young and smiled more than the other teachers. She wore her coat and carried a big bag.

"My dad." Chub took a step away from Luke to show they weren't together. His mom had nothing to do with Luke's mom and her exploding privates.

"What about you, Luke, honey?"

"My dad." Luke stopped swinging his feet.

"Of course," Ms. Schafer said kindly, like she knew his mom was going to die. "Is there a phone at your house?"

Luke nodded.

"If he doesn't come soon, you go inside and call. Mrs. Porter is still in the office."

Fog swirled behind her station wagon. Now the parking lot was empty, except for one blue car. Luke's front tooth dangled by a thread. He twisted it, his heels drumming the bricks.

"Did he have any hair?" Chub asked, which no one had asked during recess, or at lunch, or during library time.

Luke stopped twisting his tooth. "No."

Chub backed into the wall and boosted himself up beside Luke, careful not to let their legs touch.

"Are you sad?" Chub asked.

Luke's chin crumpled. He nodded. He stopped swinging his feet. Chub heard a rattling behind them, and even though it was coming from inside, he hoped it was Luke's dad coming to pick him up first. But it was only Mr. Jorgensen, the janitor, pushing the rolling mop bucket down the hall. Tears rolled down Luke's cheeks. Chub wished an adult would come give Luke a tissue and take him to wash his face in the bathroom. He kicked his own heels against the wall, trying to make Luke start again. Luke sniffled.

"Your mom's not going to die," Chub said.

"How do you know?"

"Off that wall, boys," Mrs. Porter commanded. She nudged the wooden triangle loose with the toe of her tan old-lady shoe. The door banged shut.

"Both of you," she said. "Let's go."

They trudged across the parking lot.

"My mom had a tiny baby that died," Chub said. "But my mom didn't die."

Luke didn't say anything, but Chub could tell he was listening.

"She was sad, but she didn't die."

Mrs. Porter opened her back door. Luke climbed in first. Mrs. Porter's car smelled. The woolly fog was so thick, if Chub stuck his hand out the window, he could pull long white beards of it from the air.

"Look." Luke reached his fist across the seat. He waited for Chub to cup his hands, then dropped the tooth in, slippery and warm, still alive.

# COLLEEN

Helen and Carl lived in the glen, in a small, neat-kept house built after the Christmas flood washed out the old bridge, tore through two mills, and sailed most of the original glen houses downriver, like the whole neighborhood had decided to float away in a parade. Colleen hadn't been inside since the year she delivered Luke, but as soon as she stepped out of the truck, she remembered how open and exposed it felt compared to the woods, houses one on top of the other in the clearing, river hidden behind the grassy wall of the earthen dyke.

Carl was a hard worker and it showed: house freshly painted, an add-on room—making space for the baby. Vegetables spilled over railroad-tie beds. The raised red fists of roses reached skyward with the showy confidence of people who owned their house and the land it was built on.

A meaty aroma rose off the pan of stroganoff, still warm. She'd heard the hushed voices of the mothers who had stopped by the hospital to gawk. *Awful. I almost fainted.* Her throat tightened at the memory of Melody Larson's baby, the thrum of his little hummingbird heart—it was easier than thinking about her own. She closed the gate and the front door opened, as though connected by a string. She held the pan higher, barricading herself.

"Colleen?" Daniel asked, holding the screen door behind him to keep it from slapping.

"We—we signed up," Colleen stammered, handles of the casserole dish suddenly slick. What was he doing here?

He stepped off the pavers onto the grass, a bruise at his hairline, like he'd walked into the corner of something. His swollen lip looked tender as a plum. The stroganoff dipped in her hands, suddenly heavier.

"Smells good." He inhaled, then squinted upward. "You know, scratch a little gray off that sky, it might be blue." He showed the slot between his front teeth, skin wan with the salt of dried sweat. A fleck of fresh blood showed at the corner of his mouth. He saw her notice it, touched the spot.

"Hazard of the trade." He cleared his throat. "Sorry I just showed up the other day."

All the questions she wanted to ask swelled in her chest, but there was Helen, standing at the screen door. Colleen slipped past him, up the walk.

"Helen?" she asked, forcing brightness. "I'm sorry to get you up. I just wanted to leave this."

Helen pulled her robe tighter, pushed the screen door open. "I've been up."

She was solid and thick legged; with the robe, it was hard to tell Helen had just had a baby. She made no move to take the pan, her hair loose and unbrushed, but stepped aside to let Colleen in. There was the granny square thrown over the back of the couch, the burl clock on the wall, the bear-paw dish filled with yogurt-coated somethings, just as Colleen remembered. A car pulled into the driveway.

"Who the hell is it now?" Carl asked, still in his coveralls. "Oh, hi, Colleen." He thumbed up a slat in the blinds. "Christ. It don't stop."

"Did I get my day wrong?" Colleen asked.

Out front, Gail Porter lugged herself out of the driver's seat and opened her back door. Two small feet appeared underneath it.

"He's missing that bus on purpose," Helen said to Carl.

Luke shuffled across the wet grass. The car door slammed and there was Chub, holding his red lunch box.

"What——?" Colleen handed the stroganoff to Carl and went out.

"Dad didn't come get you?" Colleen asked. Luke brushed past her. "Mrs. Porter, I'm sorry, Rich didn't come?"

"Must have got held up. Well, this saves me a trip." Gail Porter got back in her car.

"Thanks for bringing them," Colleen called.

"Couldn't leave them."

Gail Porter backed out. Chub followed Luke inside. The cake. She'd forgotten the cake. She hurried out the gate, retrieved the Bundt cake and the bowl of frosting.

"Hello?" she called in the screen door.

"In here."

She followed Carl's voice to the kitchen. He was frying hamburger in a pan, sting of onions in the air, Helen at the table.

"Can I frost it real quick for you?"

Carl hunted around in a drawer, held a knife out handle-first. "This work?"

He turned back to the stove, swell of fat slopping over his belt. He'd been a few years behind her and Helen in school and she couldn't help but feel a little maternal toward him. Maybe Enid was right. Maybe being married to Rich did make her act old. Colleen uncrimped the foil from the bowl. Helen folded it in half, then in half again. Carl batted onions around in the pan.

"What did Daniel want?" Colleen asked, spreading frosting, trying to sound casual. How long had Helen watched out the door before she'd noticed her? She'd never told Helen about that first day in the movie theater in Arcata, how she'd cut her finger on the sharp mouth of the Coke can she'd been fiddling with, how, in her nervousness, the sight of the blood made her woozy. She'd never told Helen, told anyone, how Daniel had slipped her finger into his mouth and drawn it out clean, then pressed it until the bleeding stopped.

*Blood makes me sick to my stomach.*

*You just have to learn how not to let it.*

She'd never told Helen how there were days she'd stare out the window of the real estate office, unable to concentrate on anything but the clock ticking down the minutes until Daniel would vault up the back stairs, but Helen had once been her best friend.

"He wants us to sign some petition," Carl said.

Helen dipped her finger into the frosting, as though taking its temperature.

"Says the sprays are poison." Carl added salt to the pan.

"He came to our house too," Colleen confided.

"Oh yeah? Gets around. Lucky somebody hasn't shot him."

"I think Eugene tried."

Carl chuckled, shimmying the fry pan around on the burner.

"I did spray around here a lot, while she was pregnant. Kept the blackberries down. Better than her getting out there on her hands and knees. Those

Himalayans take over. They'll pull a fence down." Carl turned the burner off. "You know Helen can make a rock grow. Did you see her roses out front?"

Helen gave a weak smile. "One time I didn't get out of the way fast enough. Oh, I was itchy." Helen scratched her arm at the memory. "And my nose. Just bled and bled. You remember, Carl? He almost took me to the clinic. He's never had any problems with it though. Maybe a rash once in a while, but that's it."

"I never got pregnant," Carl said.

Colleen raised her head, listening for Chub.

"They're in Luke's room," Helen said.

Carl scraped hamburger onto plates and brought them to the table. Helen pushed hers away, like the smell sickened her.

"Guy cares more about fish than people." Carl shoveled crumbled meat into his mouth. "Kill a town to save some trees? Something wrong with that picture."

Colleen smoothed the last strokes of buttercream.

Helen stared at the cake. "I can't even cook."

Colleen set the knife in the sink. "A little rest never hurt anybody."

"That's what I keep telling her," Carl said.

Helen pushed back in her chair. Carl watched her go.

"Baby died Sunday night. They told us a day, but he was a fighter. Made it ten."

"Oh, Carl," Colleen said. "I'm so sorry."

He nodded, eyes brimming. "We're just a crying circus around here."

Colleen smiled. "I should go. I'm sorry I barged in."

"Nah. Don't be."

She followed the boys' voices and found Helen standing in the doorway of the nursery. A new swaddle, embroidered lumberjack in the corner, hung over the side of the crib. Colleen recognized it from the Sanderson gift basket. Chub had had the same one. Across the hall, Chub and Luke lay on their bellies, cards spread facedown on the carpet.

"They said something wasn't right on the what's-it-called," Helen said quietly. "That day I saw you at the clinic. Ultrasound." Helen snorted at the memory. "I wouldn't believe it. I told myself he'd come out fine."

Colleen touched her arm, but Helen gave a little shake of her head. *Don't upset the boys.* She dug a tissue from the pocket of her robe, her face crumpling.

"I'm sorry, I know you've—" She shook her head. "So caught up in my own pain I can't see anybody else's, you know?"

"I know." Colleen nodded. "Chub, honey, time to go. Help Luke clean up."

The boys sat up, turning over cards.

"I was going to guess that one!"

Colleen ushered Chub out the front door ahead of her.

"We're not signing anything," Helen said through the screen. "If anybody asks."

Colleen nodded.

"Thank you," Helen said, dropping the hook into the hasp, locking the door from the inside. "For the cake."

# RICH

Rich braced his good arm against the seat in front of him, gut clenched, back straight, ready to launch himself upright if the crummy hit a rut. Lew could load a five-ton log onto a truck without spilling a drop from a coffee cup balanced on the dash, but when it came to driving crummy, all bets were off. Jolt to the tailbone was about all it would take to put Rich out of commission. Wrenched his back pretty good, when he did his shoulder.

Don crouched in the aisle up front, on the lookout. There'd been a dozen hippies blocking the road that morning on the way in, like nobody had told them the rains were here. Today was their last day on Deer Rib, last day of the season; nobody would be harvesting shit until spring.

*What size are Dolly Parton's feet?* Lew had asked, letting the crummy idle. *She doesn't know either!* Lew had floored it, hippies scattering.

The whole thing hadn't cost them two minutes, but it had thrown the day off-kilter, right up until Rich had spotted the deer from above. He'd slipped his rope, the ten-foot free fall popping his shoulder out of its socket, leaving him dangling in the air, grunting like a one-armed gorilla. *One day that arm's going to tear off*, Pete said after Rich got himself down, rammed a fist into his armpit, and walked backward into the trunk of the spar he'd just finished rigging to pop his shoulder back in.

Now Lew slowed, approaching the curve. The road was deserted, muddy tire tracks in the brush, a few empties. That would get Don's goat—if there was one thing he hated more than hippies, it was their trash. Then came the high-pitched whine of wet brakes. The crummy lurched to a stop, stray thermos thunking down the aisle.

"Son of a bitch!" Don bellowed.

The morning's half dozen longhairs had swelled to a noisy throng of fifty or so, bobbing signs, plus a bullhorn.

"Gun it, Lew!" somebody yelled.

"Can't just drive over them," Lew said.

"Why the hell not?"

"Have to move those first."

The log truck they'd loaded with pecker poles a few hours earlier was stopped ahead, gyppo driver smoking near the back tire of his empty truck, his haul spread out across the road, like he'd been waiting on Don to show up and fix this. Don yanked the metal ball that folded the crummy door open and stormed out.

"He's going to give himself a heart attack," Lew said.

Younger guys jockeyed down the steps. Lew radioed Harvey, hung the CB back in its cradle, and turned the wipers on, clearing the windshield enough to read the signs: SAVE DAMNATION GROVE. Chanting rattled the windows. The bullhorn blipped on and off, Don shoving through the crowd, as though he meant to commandeer it.

"Better get out there," Pete said. Rich raised an eyebrow. "What are they gonna do?" Pete asked. "Break my nose?"

Rich got to his feet, careful of his shoulder.

"You coming?" Rich asked Lew.

"Nope." Lew crossed his arms over his big belly.

It felt good to step out into the fresh air, until the full force of the chanting hit. Don was screaming in the skinny bullhorner's face. A bearded guy held a boy on his shoulders a year or two younger than Chub, the boy and Rich the two tallest heads in the crowd. The kid squinted, as though the noise were being sprayed in his face.

Don grabbed the bullhorner by the shirt. A camera flashed. Suddenly, the chanting stopped. The mob went quiet. Even Don paused, red-faced, and in that split second of stillness a hoarse song rose from the crowd, voices swelling.

*This land is your land, this land is my land.*

Because he knew the words, Rich almost joined in. Don shook his head. *Look at these idiots.*

*From the redwood for-est.* The note hummed in the air, busted into a cheer.

Don cracked his neck, whirled around, and clocked the bullhorner. The child gripped handfuls of his father's hair. Glass shattered out of a crummy window. Something struck Rich in the head and his hand came away wet. He'd left his hard hat on the seat.

"Motherfuckers!" Pete yelled.

Two men cowered near the log barricade, attempting to cover their heads, chained there. Curses, shouting, the crunch of gravel underfoot, then the roar of a chainsaw cut through. Eugene stood in the bed of his truck, saw rearing up, an animal he wasn't fully in control of. Longhairs scattered, scrambling through brush, hoofing it for cars up around the curve.

Don was busy yelling at the two chained men, nose blood running down his chin, soaking the neck of his shirt. Eugene came up next to him, lowered the saw onto the log six inches from a man's hand, and lopped off the end, hippie coughing in the spray of sawdust.

"Somebody better unlock these guys in the next ten seconds!"

A cluster of hippies stopped; one had an eye already swelling shut.

"Ten, nine—" Eugene lowered the saw into the log and lopped off another two-inch round.

The chained men were yelling now.

"Somebody got the key to this thing?" Eugene called.

A man came forward, pulling keys from his pocket. "Calm down, man."

"Me calm down? Me calm down?" Eugene was so riled up if you threw him against a wall, he'd have bounced off it.

The hippie fit a key into the cuffs. The men rubbed their wrists, still crouched like prisoners. Eugene killed the saw.

"You're only hurting yourselves, man," one of the hippies said.

"Fuck you," Eugene spat.

"You think they give a fuck about you? You're working yourselves out of a job."

Eugene leaned into the man's face. "Fuck. You."

He made the remaining longhairs roll the logs to the side of the road. Rich wanted to get back on the crummy, but Lew stood inside the door.

Lew lifted his chin in Eugene's direction. "My brother wouldn't take that asshole out on a boat for a million dollars."

Eugene's saw got pinched in a log too heavy to budge and amid the swearing and opinion-offering it took to free it, the hippies made a break for it. Younger guys took off after them.

"Leave 'em," Don called.

Two longhairs remained, supporting a third, bell rung pretty good.

"Man, you have to take us to the hospital."

Don snorted, pressed a finger to one nostril, and blew out a plug of blood. "Town's that way."

"Come on," the other man told his friend. Together, the three limped off.

Rich and the rest of the crew climbed back into the crummy, picked up speed, gravel clattering. The mood rose, a team coming home from a big win. They'd have to haul the loader out to get those logs back onto the truck, but for now, they hooted and hollered, rattled the windows as they passed the three hippies, injured man walking on his own now. Harvey came flying up the road, siren wailing. Rich's head pulsed where a soft egg had risen.

Back at the mill lot, Rich dug out his keys, slip of paper coming with them. Shit. Colleen's voice rose from the note. *Chub, aftercare, 5:30. Don't forget.* School would have called her by now. He started the truck, leaned back a moment, head throbbing. Go home and get some ice on it. He put the truck in gear. *This land is*—a lot of work is what this land is.

# COLLEEN

Rain pelted the truck, windshield a blur, even on fast wipe. The downpour had let loose almost as soon as they'd left Helen's.

"You waited out front the whole time?" Colleen quizzed Chub.

Chub nodded. Rich had never forgotten him before. Should she check the mill lot? Gail would have said if something had happened, wouldn't she? Worry pulsed in Colleen's mind—*Please, please*—so consuming that when she bounced up the driveway and saw his truck parked out front, it took a moment for anger to leak in. Chub disappeared to his room.

Rich was laid out on top of the bedspread, still in his work clothes.

"You forgot Chub?" she demanded.

"I've got a hell of a headache." Rich squinted at her, dropped his head back onto the pillow.

"A headache? You forgot your son."

"I put my shoulder out," Rich explained. "They blocked the road off. 'Save Damnation Grove.'"

"Again?" she asked. He reached for the painkillers on the nightstand. "You're only supposed to take two." She picked the extras out of his palm, snatched the empty water glass, filled it at the bathroom sink, and thrust it back.

"Thanks. You okay?" he asked.

She should have been furious with him still—buying that land and not telling her—but here were the tears she'd been holding back since she'd seen the swaddle hanging over the side of the crib at Helen's.

He lifted his good arm. "Come here."

She crawled in. He raked hair out of her eyes. He smelled of sawdust and gasoline. He took her hand, guided it to the egg.

"What happened?" she asked.

"For a bunch of pacifists, they got a funny way of showing it."

She slid her hand down the side of his neck.

"Up on the Rib today," Rich said, "there were these three dead deer, just laid out in a clearing. Not a scratch on them—" He shifted uncomfortably, hissed air through his teeth. "I really did a number on it this time."

She helped him out of his shirt, cupped her hand over the swollen lump on his head, like she could heal it.

Once Rich fell asleep, she went into the kitchen, opened the cabinet below the junk drawer, and removed a single jam jar, a masking-tape label across the lid—Daniel's scrawl, handwriting she recognized from the lab notes she'd sometimes helped him type up, from the little pad he'd kept in his pocket to jot down things to look up at the library later, but never, not once, from a letter addressed to her. She'd thought the label would say her name, but it read only *DC-31*. She unscrewed the gold ring, pried off the canning lid underneath, filled it at the tap, closed it tight, and labeled it, *11/22/77*, then slid it back into the cupboard. If Rich could gamble on seven hundred acres of trees, refuse to tell her what it cost, she could do this.

# COLLEEN

She turned the engine off and looked up through the windshield at Whitey's. Paint peeled off the building's plywood sign: WHITEY'S SHOE HOSPITAL OR SAW REPAIR. Can't have both, the joke went.

She grabbed Rich's caulks and went in. There was a pause in Whitey's hammering. Whitey's had once been a bar—three people had survived the '64 tsunami on the roof here—and the moldy smell of spilled beer still off-gassed from the floorboards, counter stacked with ammo cans and jugs of chain oil, more storage unit than store. Whitey bellied through the saloon doors like a badger in Coke-bottle glasses, white mane combed back with its single black stripe.

Whitey took the boots and turned them upside down to examine the soles, as he did every year at the end of the season, when Colleen brought them in to have the plugs replaced. Beyond his appearance, there was his badgerlike gruffness, open 365 days a year.

"Thursday." He was of the generation that didn't speak to women except to issue a verdict on their cooking.

"Next Thursday?"

He lifted his chin toward the door.

"The Thursday after?" she guessed.

"One after." He looked over the top of his glasses at her. "Nose is bleeding."

Outside, mist spritzed her face. She tilted her head back, waited, checked her nostrils in the rearview, then drove over to the savings and loan. She'd tried asking Rich again this morning, but he'd sidestepped her, told her not to worry. She felt like a fool. All these years sliding paychecks and deposit slips into the slot at the bank, she'd never once stood in line to ask for the account balance. She managed the bills—truck insurance, house insurance, electric, the hospital bill from last spring divided into twenty-four monthly installments. By the time they finished paying it off, the baby girl she thought about every time she ran her thumb under the envelope's flap would be a toddler. She wrote checks, licked stamps, but when the bank statement arrived in the mail every month, she set it aside for Rich to open, cheaters sliding down to the end of his nose—it was his money, after all. For helping out with births she was paid in homemade jams and hand-knit sweaters. Loaves of banana bread weren't depositable in any bank.

Colleen waited in line, the teller a young woman in red lipstick and a tight blouse.

"I'd like to check the balance on a loan, please," Colleen said. She felt frumpy in her turtleneck.

"Driver's license?" the teller asked, checking her nails while Colleen fumbled in her purse for her pocketbook. The teller looked from the license to Colleen's face, then disappeared into a row of filing cabinets, reappearing a few minutes later, empty-handed. "It's in his name," she said.

"We have joint accounts," Colleen explained. "Checking and savings."

"Yes," the teller said, "but the loan is in *his* name."

"How much do we—does *he*—owe?" Colleen asked.

"You should speak with your husband," the teller said, tilting her head, as though taking stock of all Colleen's wifely failings.

Colleen felt her face go hot. The teller signaled the next person in line. Colleen hurried out. By the time she got to the truck she was close to tears, everything so far beyond her control, so completely alone without Chub. To calm down, she drove out to the agate beach. The wind was up, a struggle to open the truck door against it. She walked down to where the pebbles lay in beds, sudsy ocean throwing itself against the rocks, spraying foam. She squatted, picked through the stones until she had a handful.

*What's the matter, sweet pea?*

She closed the agates in her fist, squeezing them until it hurt. She wished, stupidly, for her father. She walked down the beach, hopping bedrock to the water's edge. The water licked her toes. The ocean doesn't care, she reminded herself. The ocean could give a darn about your problems.

*November 24*

# COLLEEN

Gail Porter dropped the folded tablecloths onto the bench and narrowed her eyes at Marsha's orange lipstick.

"Centerpieces are in the trunk," she said, blowing air out her nose disapprovingly, as though Marsha were responsible for the community center's stale scent of fish grease and mildew cut with lemon floor cleaner.

"We'll get them," Marsha volunteered, ignoring the pinch of Gail Porter's regard. "Who stings worse, her or her bees?" Marsha asked when they got outside, drizzle freckling their arms. She popped Gail Porter's trunk. "Bee must have flown up her ass this morning."

Colleen glanced back at the building, as though Gail Porter might be listening. "Is Arlette coming?" she asked. There were rumors in town—treatments down south, maybe some kind of drunk ward. Merle had been coming alone to the fish fries for months, but Thanksgiving was a different story.

"I hope so," Marsha said, arms loaded with plastic horns of plenty. "That'll really put a bee up Gail's ass." She slammed the trunk.

Inside, Gail Porter pointed out spots on the floor to Miles Jorgensen, who slopped his mop around as though it were remotely controlled by her index finger. She pinched a fake autumn leaf of centerpiece foliage, rubbed her fingers together.

"These are wet."

"Are they?" Marsha asked. "That's rain for you."

Colleen heard other wives laughing in the kitchen, baking hams in the industrial oven, plopping canned yams into aluminum trays. The sounds and smells of the season ending.

Gail Porter surveyed the room: drab brick, low water-stained ceiling. "Well," she sighed.

Colleen helped Marsha push cafeteria tables into rows. Gail Porter set up the raffle table.

"I'd like to win that." Marsha nodded at the goody basket—tinned meats, cheese logs, a fruitcake. "You been over to see Helen?" she asked.

Colleen nodded, slipped a tablecloth from the pile.

"Poor thing." Marsha tugged her end, cloth ballooning between them, settling over the tabletop. "I lost one once." Marsha reached for another cloth. "Before I knew enough to ask for a C-section. After that, I told them: gut me like a tuna." Marsha smoothed a wrinkle. "They said it was from drinking. I drank a few, but the other two turned out. Neither of them's got webbed feet. Got brains in their heads. May not use them, but they got them."

"Boy or girl?" Colleen asked.

"Boy. Mike knocking me around, that's probably what done it. He'd get so loaded he couldn't find our turnoff." Marsha chuckled. "He'd be out on the road, honking. I'd go find him and he'd lay into me like I'd up and moved the trailer on him. One time I just left him out there. In the morning, he was half spilled out of his truck. So much blood had gone to his head, turned his face purple. I thought he was dead. Scared the hell out of me when he woke up."

"You don't think Carl . . ."

Marsha flapped another tablecloth. "Who knows? They drink and they get mean. Or they get hurt. Even a nice dog'll bite when it's hurt." Marsha glanced over at Gail Porter, setting up the kids' corner—pin the feather on the turkey, coloring sheets of Pilgrim buckles to cut out and tape to shoes—and lowered her voice. "You know those hippies are trying to blame it on the sprays?"

"Those sprays killed my bees," Gail Porter called.

"You teachers got ears in the backs of your heads."

"They sprayed our road and killed all three hives."

"Well." Marsha picked up a centerpiece and fussed with the leaves. "I don't know about bees."

They set up the buffet, draped streamers from the bar. By the end, even Gail Porter looked satisfied. In the bathroom, Marsha checked her mascara. Colleen's own eyelashes were pale, almost invisible. Marsha reapplied her lipstick.

"Why do I bother? No men in this town." She offered Colleen the tube.

It was so bright Colleen laughed, reached for a paper towel.

"Leave it. Only get one life, right? That's what John used to say."

Colleen felt a snag. Strange how her father's name, spoken aloud, brought his voice back.

*You only get one life, sweet pea. Live it happy.*

The room filled. Colleen was glad to have a job, standing behind the buffet, tonging rolls onto held-out plates: scabbed knuckles, nail beds bruised black, curled saw-fingers, the stumps of pinkies. Enid's kids pushed through the line and claimed a table. Chub appeared, then Rich. A shy smile, the way he always looked when he spotted her across a room.

"Free grub." Eugene held out his plate. "Brings all the termites out of the woodwork."

Enid shushed him. "Stop yelling."

"I'm not yelling."

"You're talking too loud."

Merle came strutting in like a prize cock, Arlette in a red-flowered dress. Colleen nearly dropped a roll in the air beside Pete's plate. Arlette's usual plumpness had melted off. She looked sick.

"Look who the cat drug in," Pete said, roll landing in a puddle of gravy.

"Cauliflower?" Marsha asked.

"That sounds like a vegetable," Pete said, teeth brown from chew. He ran a knuckle up the side of his nose, as though to straighten it.

"Deep-fried, it's real tasty," Marsha said.

"No thanks."

Marsha dropped a few pieces onto his plate anyway. "That'll fatten you up."

He scowled, but Colleen could see he liked the attention.

"What about Pete?" she suggested, once he was out of earshot.

"Pete? He eats with that crap up his lip. Bet he even chews while he screws." Marsha laughed.

"What are you girls doing back there?" Merle asked. "Get yourselves something to eat."

Arlette's bracelets clanked. Her purple hair was teased into a beehive. She gave a strained smile.

"That's still alive," Marsha said, nodding at Merle's cut of roast.

"That's the idea." Merle winked, purple stain under his fingernails, like he'd been the one to rinse the dye from Arlette's scalp, scooping handfuls of water over the soft hairs at the base of her neck. Merle led Arlette to the banquet table. The noise dropped off, people digging in. Merle tapped the microphone, eyed his food getting cold. "This is some spread," Merle said into the mic. The talk died. "We've got a hell of a lot to be thankful for, starting with these ladies."

Arlette grimaced, as though the volume hurt her ears.

"We've had a tough run." Merle hitched up his slacks. "Had to cut a lot of good men loose. Going got rough. Lot of guys could have jumped ship. Gone to work somewhere else."

Colleen glanced at Rich, a head taller than everyone else, even sitting.

"But what's always set Sanderson apart? Our people." Merle panned the room. "Our people stick with us, through thick and thin. We've had our share of thin." Men grumbled. "Now these tree huggers are trying to set friend against friend, family against family. They don't understand Sanderson *is* a family. We stick together. There isn't a man here doesn't remember some hungry times. Somebody was even hungry enough to poach a few burls off Damnation Grove recently. Big ones." Merle sucked his cheek. "But not anybody in this room. Anybody in this room knows robbing a burl off that grove is stealing food off your own table. Off all our tables." Merle nodded. "We'll find out who it was. We'll make them pay. Don't you worry. Come spring, we'll make up for this season and then some." He raised a plastic cup. "Sanderson doesn't give up. And neither do you. Now, leave me a slice of that pineapple upside-down cake, will you? She never makes it for me at home."

Arlette smiled on cue. People tossed balled-up napkins onto tables, waiting for the raffle to be drawn. Colleen carried her plate over to Rich, sitting with Enid and the Porters.

"Where's Chub?" Colleen asked, surprised how hungry she was, after smelling food all day.

Rich tossed his head toward the craft table, where Chub and Agnes waited to have the headdresses they'd colored taped into crowns, a table of Yurok families nearby. Sanderson used to pay them half what they paid a white man. They made the same wage as everybody else now but still sat at their own tables.

Rich forked up a bite of pumpkin, winced. Why was he being so stubborn about that tooth? Arlette's smoker's laugh rang out, Eugene chatting her up while Merle shoveled in pie.

"Charm the warts off a toad," Don Porter said.

"Not that toad," Gail Porter answered.

Enid rolled her eyes. "That security job has gone to his head."

Merle had upped Eugene's hours patrolling the grove; it wasn't a lot, but it was enough to keep him off a crabber, enough for him and Enid to squeak by on through the winter. Rich said any poacher he met ran more risk of going deaf from the wasted cartridges than getting hit.

Enid sat back. "I'm stuffed."

The room thinned. Merle came over to shake Rich's hand on his way out.

"Come up and see me at the house on Monday. I got something I want to run by you," Merle told Rich. He snapped a suspender over his gut. "Hell of a meal, ladies."

Once he was gone, Gail Porter sighed, surveying the trash-strewn tables. "Always the same workhorses."

Rich and Don hauled bags to the dumpster, got the tables wiped and folded. Gail sent Miles Jorgensen home with leftovers, though he still looked disgruntled.

Rich drove, headlights spraying the front of the house. He carried Chub to bed, built a fire, sat on the couch leafing through a lumber catalog. She sat down beside him, close enough that their shoulders touched.

"I went to the bank," she said. Rich didn't lift his eyes, scanning redwood prices with the single-mindedness of a gambler checking the odds on a horse. "They wouldn't tell me anything. They said the loan is in your name."

Rich rested the catalog on his knees. "I figured, if something happened, you wouldn't be responsible."

"We're married." She worried a hangnail, willing herself not to say more. Sometimes, if she waited Rich out, he would fill the silence.

"I paid two fifty," Rich admitted. "I know it sounds like a lot—"

"Two hundred and fifty thousand?"

He nodded.

"Rich, that's a quarter of a million dollars! Can we afford that?"

Rich sucked his sore tooth. "We'll be okay, through the winter. I'll use my grove checks to rent the equipment. Once Sanderson clears the lower grove out of the way, we can take the timber off the 24-7 and pay the whole thing off."

"What if the grove takes longer?" She'd seen pictures of the road blockade in the paper, Don gripping a man by the collar, fist cocked.

"It'll be tight," Rich admitted.

"At least we have the savings." She tried to console herself.

"I used it, all but twenty-five hundred bucks."

Colleen's heart sank. She'd forgotten to ask the teller for the balance of their joint accounts. That $25,000 was supposed to be an extra bedroom for the baby, another bath, maybe even a playroom with a long bank of windows where she could grow tomatoes.

Rich hunched forward, tossed the catalog onto the coffee table. "I've waited my whole life for a chance like this, Colleen."

"A chance like what?" She felt warmth evaporating from the spot where his shoulder had been.

"A chance to make it on my own."

"You should have asked me. I'm your wife."

"You're my wife," he said, locking eyes with her in a way that set her heart racing, as if he could see Daniel, the radar station, all of it.

"Mama?" Chub asked from the hall, hair mashed where he'd slept on it. Sap popped in the stove. "I'm thirsty."

Rich got up. After a moment, she followed. In the kitchen, he filled a glass with water, held it up, then dumped it out, yanked open the icebox, poured them each a glass of milk. They sat in the yellow light of the kitchen. Chub rubbed white beads from Rich's mustache. Rich wiggled it, making Chub laugh.

Colleen took another sip. The milk was sweet, satisfying, but she was thirsty after she'd finished the glass.

*November 28*

# RICH

Rich turned the truck off and looked up through the windshield at Merle's house, perched at the top of Requa Hill. The yellow siding had faded, brown in spots. A wire brush would get rid of the stains, but it'd take what was left of the color along with it. The engine ticked under the hood, cooling.

Rich tugged at the snapped cuffs of his shirt to loosen their hold on his wrists and elbowed out of the truck. Years since he was last up here—the party Merle had thrown after they built it, Arlette showing it off: bacon-wrapped wieners, two girls serving booze on trays.

The deck was all uppers, tight-grained red heartwood that had held up, but the house had taken a beating—salt air was hell on siding. The latticework closing off the space under the deck was shaggy with vines, rotted out around the posts sunk into concrete footers. Where there were vines, there were rats. He tried to remember if there was a cat. Arlette was the type, one of those prissy kinds Enid had tried raising—all hair, no eyes. He sniffed, idea of a cat tickling his nostrils.

A chained-up old husky gimped out from under the deck, rasping, barkless. Rich held out a hand, shoulder still sore, rubbed him behind the ears. Lumps the size of Brussels sprouts clung to the dog's ribs. Rich wiped his hand on his denims, took a deep breath, loped up the steps. He raised a thumb to the doorbell, changed his mind, knocked. The dog let loose a hoarse volley. Rich turned to take in the view, waves lapping at the sandbar where the Klamath dumped out into the ocean below.

"Rich." Merle held the door open.

Rich raked his feet across the mat, dog still hacking. "That dog smoke too many cigarettes?"

"Cords are cut. Did it when they did his balls."

"What the hell good's a dog that don't bark?"

"Can't bark, can't fuck. You see the lumps on him? Like he swallowed a bucket of golf balls."

The hall carpet was a dull blue and the house smelled artificial, bowls of potpourri masking mold. A golf tournament played on TV, curtains closed, though it was nearly noon.

"Coffee?" Merle asked.

"I had, thanks."

The couch, covered in clear plastic, squelched under Rich's weight. He stole a quick look around: Arlette's fancy china eggs collecting dust. Merle dropped back into his recliner with a groan, white polyester shirt stretching over the swollen ball of his belly, red suspenders straining to hold up his khakis. He reached for his mug, nosed up against a bowl filled with tiny pinecones, like some kind of snack, their perfume stink making Rich's eyes water.

"Thanks for coming, Rich." Merle fixed him, but Rich knew the drill. Let Merle steer. "How's the family?"

"Fine."

Merle's eyes wandered to the TV. Someone—must have been Arlette—coughed from the back of the house. Merle turned his head, listening. Rich wanted to snuff his nose on his sleeve, cross the room and yank open the curtains, let daylight dilute the scent. His eyes itched; he looked around for a litter box. The TV went to commercial. Merle sighed, reached for the remote, and zapped the set off.

"Rich, I'll tell you, they don't make them like they used to."

A hard pit of dread lodged in Rich's gut.

"What do you think about the way we're headed?" Merle asked.

"How do you mean?" All these years of looking out for number one; had Merle's conscience finally caught up to him? Once the big timber was gone, he'd be up shit creek with everybody else.

"Well, how long you been with us?"

Rich shifted, remembered the plastic. "A lot of years."

"How many is it now? Can't fool me with that young wife of yours."

"Thirty-eight."

"A whole life."

A flush crept up the back of Rich's neck. Could he lay him off right here, phony pinecones masking the stink of cat piss?

"Cut the shit, Merle. If you're shooting, shoot. Don't make me dance."

Merle propped his sock feet on the burl coffee table. "That's what I've always appreciated about you, Rich. You call 'em like you see 'em."

Rich rubbed his sweaty palms over his knees.

"So. You worried about a little weed juice?" Merle asked.

Rich shrugged. "Not my business."

"Damn right," Merle agreed. "See, that's the difference between guys like us and those damn longhairs. County, state, Forest Circus, that's government land, that's forestry, okay, but what Sanderson does on Sanderson land? That's business. I'll tell you though, Rich. Doesn't matter how safe it is, approved by the EPA and all. Somebody convinces a woman those sprays are making her kids sick, it's like trying to talk sense to a damn bear, am I wrong?"

Rich tightened his jaw, but Merle was just winding up.

"It's gotten so you can't trim your grass without a goddamn environmental impact statement. Sustained yield might have worked back in the old days, but what are we saving for now? Why not let everybody make some money and move on? Meanwhile, the damn poachers are cleaning us out up on Damnation like it's burl season. Can't win."

Rich shifted his weight, couch plastic sticking. Merle turned on the lamp, lighting white bristle on his cheeks.

"Look, I'll level with you, Rich. We got our hands full. These hippies get their way, every tree between here and the Oregon line will be a goddamn national landmark."

Rich scooped some pinecones from the bowl and tossed them in his hand.

"Guys look up to you," Merle said. "There's not a guy left in Del Nort County can climb the way you can. But we both know that timber of yours isn't worth a red cent without roads. We need to know you're with us. No matter what."

Colleen must have let it slip to Enid—Eugene couldn't keep his damn mouth shut.

"There was a guy came out to the house a while ago," Rich admitted. "Said the sprays were getting into our water—"

"That asshole is selling his load of crap to any idiot who'll listen. Petition, whole nine yards. Riling people up. Those skulls, that was just a cheap trick to buy time. It's the spray angle they're banking on. You and me both know that stuff don't hurt a fly. Hell, they already turned half the timber around here into park. I'll be damned if we let them take the grove too. We need this. You need this." Merle leaned in. "They haven't announced it yet, but February, the forestry board's going to hold a hearing on those harvest plans—let everybody air their dirty laundry, and then decide if we get back in to harvest or not. You live the closest to Damnation. Your family is the only one drinking out of that spring. You stand up and explain your kid drinks that water and we could log from hell to breakfast, spray and all, and you're not worried one iota. They'll listen. Everybody knows you don't talk out your ass. You don't have to say much. Just"—Merle sat back—"call it like you see it."

Rich kept his eyes down. What would he tell Colleen? They owed thirty years on those lots.

"What's that 24-7 inholding, seven hundred acres?" Merle asked.

"Seven twenty."

Merle whistled. "You must have one hell of a mortgage." He tossed back the last of his coffee. "Thought you'd at least want to give it a shot."

"I'll think about it," Rich said.

"Good." Merle grunted, pushing up. At the door, he let Rich out. "Don't think too long now, Rich." The screen door snapped closed. "Your timber isn't worth beans without a right-of-way. Who knows? Company might get choosy about who uses those roads, once we're done with them. Be a shame to harvest that 24-7 for nothing."

Merle must have said something more—*See you around, Rich. Don't be a stranger, now*—but it didn't register. Rich dropped loose-legged down the porch steps, something cutting into his palm. He opened his fist: pinecones crushed to shards. He wanted to sit behind the wheel a minute, to let the tremble of rage settle. But even with the front door shut and the curtains closed, he sensed Merle watching. *Don't think too long.*

The dog stood under the deck, white-faced and bowlegged, barking its ghost bark.

# WINTER

*1977–1978*

# COLLEEN

Colleen reached into the box for the charcoal nubs and set them beside the other pieces. For $29.99 plus shipping, she'd thought there would be more to it.

"What is all that?" Rich asked, flipping through the rest of the mail.

"A filter." She held up the box, where a wholesome blonde displayed the fully assembled product—a ribbed plastic cylinder with a hose and spout. "It attaches to the faucet."

Rich grunted. Colleen pretended to study the pieces. It had seemed like a good idea in the catalog, but laid out on the table—rubber washers, baggies of rock, another of plain sand—she saw how foolish it was. Thirty dollars for sand. How could any of this junk fit together into something useful, much less the sleek contraption taunting her from the front of the box?

Rich tossed the mail on the table. "When did Whitey say my caulks would be ready?"

"Thursday."

She picked up a washer. Usually, if she puzzled over something mechanical, Rich would step in, the same way she'd bump him with her hip, once in a jokey way, a second time to show she meant it, until he shook dishwater off his hands.

*If I'd married a man who washed up, I'd let him,* Enid said.

But Rich didn't seem to notice the filter. He'd been distracted for days, ever since he'd gone to see Merle.

*What did Merle want?* she'd asked.

*Nothing much. Just politics.*

She forced the washer down into the hollow cylinder. It buckled, caught. She turned the cylinder upside down and whacked the bottom with her palm. Rich filled a glass, swirled the water around, eyeballed it, took a swig. She deposited the pieces in a defeated heap on the table, took the store loaf from the bread box.

"Tuna?" she asked.

"Got any of those pickles left?"

"A few."

He dropped heavily into a chair, but instead of fiddling with the filter, he picked through the mail again, holding it at arm's length, dropping it when she set the plate in front of him.

"I promised Chub we'd get a Christmas tree," she said when he'd nearly finished.

The untouched pile of parts irked her. He could at least put this mess together without making her ask. She picked up his plate as though her mood could be rinsed of frustration and set to dry in the drain rack with it. He held the last of his sandwich protectively, like she might take that next.

"I have to take care of a couple things." He got up. "Did you say anything to your sister about that guy coming to see us?"

"What guy?"

He jutted his chin at the jumble of filter parts.

"No," she said, a little too quickly. Her heart fluttered. "Why?"

He shook his head. "No reason."

"What's happening with the grove?" she asked.

"I don't know," Rich said. "It's hung up with the state. Merle says there'll be a hearing in February."

"Why do they have to wait all the way until then?"

Rich shrugged. "Too wet to work anyway." He pulled his slicker off the hook.

"I'm going to get Chub," she said.

Rich nodded and went out. She watched him disappear up the hill, then opened the cupboard and took out a new jam jar, filled it, labeled it, and loaded it into a canvas bag with two others. She pulled on her boots and fished her keys from the burl bowl.

Water washed down the windshield on the way to town. Just the short dash into the Beehive, cowbell clunking overhead, stuck her hair to her face.

"It's coming down," Colleen said.

"Like a cow pissing." Dot dropped a bear claw into a white paper sack. "How's Rich?"

"Keeping busy. How about Lew?"

"Oh, stir-crazy. He's fine for the first few days, then he's ready to get back to work. Can't do much, with this rain."

"Seems like all it does is rain," Colleen agreed.

"Three hundred days a year." Dot took Colleen's money, scooped quarters from the register, and stared into her palm at them before handing them over. "I told Lew he should learn to knit." Dot laughed. "I'd come home and find him all tied up in one big knot."

Colleen forced a smile, took the paper sack and folded the top down once, then again, sealing a sweet pocket of air inside.

The school lot was empty. A few miserable-looking kids crowded under the overhang, curtain of runoff pouring from the roof. Chub didn't emerge. She ducked out.

"He went on the bus," a girl volunteered. "With Agnes."

Gail Porter stood at her desk behind the counter, holding a stack of papers. She raised an eyebrow, as though, no matter how many centerpieces Colleen helped assemble, she still held her responsible for Enid's throwing clumps of wet paper towels against the ceiling of the girls' bathroom.

"Colleen," she said sternly, eyebrow raised over her glasses.

Gail, Colleen thought, though she felt eight years old, like she had a stomachache and was pleading to call home.

"I think Chub might have taken the bus by mistake?" Colleen ventured.

Gail Porter sighed, hefting the rotary phone onto the counter. Colleen pulled the numbers around, turned her back to muffle the ringing. *Pick up.* It clicked. Kids squealed in the background.

"Enid?" Colleen asked. "Is Chub with you?"

"What?" Enid yelled. "Hang on. Sorry. Cripes. This baby weighs a ton. Could you pick up some Cracker Jacks? I've been craving them all day."

"Is Chub there?"

"You want to talk to him? Chub! Come talk to your mom! Damn it, Wy, what did—" The line went dead. Colleen returned the receiver to its cradle.

"Enid's got her hands full," she said.

"Lucky her."

Gail and Don had never had children. Around kids all day, not exactly the motherly type—but then again, Colleen's mother hadn't been either, it was just what you did. Something about the way Gail Porter busied herself with the attendance sheets made Colleen wonder. *I've lost eight pregnancies. What does luck have to do with anything?* Maybe Gail Porter would look up from her papers then.

"Have a nice weekend," Colleen said.

"You too."

The teenager working the gas station register barely glanced up when she came in—lanky, pimple faced, one of the Shaughnessy boys. Daniel pulled his VW bus into the bay, waiting his turn. She ducked into the station's single aisle and picked up a box of Cracker Jacks, then another, building a barricade. Candied popcorn scuttled inside the boxes. She dumped an armload onto the counter.

"Want a bag?" the Shaughnessy kid asked.

Outside, a car pulled away and Daniel moved up to the pump, VW barnacled with mud. Her hair was damp and stringy. She fought the urge to tuck it behind her ears. She pushed out with the sack in her arms, a wash of cold air.

"All out," the attendant said to Daniel, holding the nozzle in one hand.

Daniel argued.

"I don't have to sell you anything." The attendant signaled the next car.

Daniel looked back at it too. Colleen ducked her head and hurried to her truck.

"Next customer!" the attendant yelled.

She set the paper sack on the passenger seat. It tipped, spilling. She leaned into the footwell, fishing up boxes. Four dollars' worth of crap. The last box was wedged between the passenger seat and the door.

"Colleen!"

She reared up, box in hand, hit her head, clamped her hand to the spot. Daniel had pulled up beside her.

"Some people are getting together tonight at Helen and Carl's," he called out his open window. "Six o'clock."

She dropped down onto the gravel, box of Cracker Jacks rattling in her hand. She shifted, blocking his view of the bag.

"You should come," he said.

"I can't."

"You know there are court cases up in Oregon, over the spraying? It's not like you're making it up."

"Making what up?"

"Colleen, come on. How many miscarriages have you had?"

"It's just bad luck."

"You don't believe that." He fixed her. "If I knew who else I should talk to—if we could show a pattern, prove—"

Colleen shook her head slowly, like she could make him disappear.

"Colleen. What are you doing?"

"Nothing," she snapped.

"You know something isn't right," Daniel said. "What are you *doing* about it?"

"What am I supposed to do?" She grabbed the bag of water samples off the seat and thrust it through his open passenger-side window. "This is all you wanted, isn't it? Go ahead. Take them."

He fished out a jar. His face lit up with surprise.

*You're going to get hurt*, she thought. *You might even get yourself killed.*

"If there's something in it, I want to know," she said. "I want to know."

Daniel nodded. She tossed the box of Cracker Jacks onto the seat and climbed in after it.

"Take it easy on those things," he said. "They'll rot the teeth right out of your head."


Runoff thundered from the culverts, mud thwacking the truck's side panels. Enid's front yard was soup, trash strewn around the overturned cans, bungee cord dangling. Raccoons.

"Oh, thank God," Enid said, nursing the baby on the couch, when Colleen came in, Chub and Wyatt wrestling on the rug.

A fire roared in the woodstove. Colleen dropped the sack beside Enid and closed the damper. "This thing is going to melt," she said.

"You buy out the whole store?" Enid ripped open a box of Cracker Jacks and tapped out a few hard puffs.

"I get the prize!" Wyatt yelled, popping up. The girls scrambled.

"Do not!"

"Yeah-huh. I called it!"

"Go wash up," Colleen commanded, lifting the sack. The kids tussled, not used to such edicts being enforced. "Go on." They pushed down the hall.

"If this rain doesn't stop soon, I'm going to take them all out and drown them," Enid said, picking through a handful to find the largest pieces, tapping candied popcorn into Colleen's hand. Hard caramel coating screaked against Colleen's teeth.

"Want to make jerky?" Enid nodded toward the hunk of raw meat defrosting on the kitchen counter. "That deer was part horse." They were short grocery money if she was making jerky.

The kitchen was a wreck, linoleum sticking to Colleen's socks, but it was calming to sit at the table slicing venison into strips, to feel the minutes passing. Colleen did her best to focus on slicing the meat thin, to ignore the timer in her brain. *Some people are getting together.* The kids tossed Cracker Jacks in the air, practiced catching them in their mouths.

At dusk the rain let up, fog rolling in. A black truck pulled into the yard. Marla dashed out to it.

"That boy's too old for her," Enid said. "No offense. Five years mean something when you're fifteen."

Colleen adjusted Alsea's sock. If she told her about Marla now, Enid would be furious.

She waited until it was long dark—past seven, she guessed—to roust Chub. The yard smelled of cat urine. Chub pushed aside the grease-stained bear-claw bag so he could lie down. They trundled back up No Name Road, past the mill, a hulking black outline, a single pane of light in the back office—Merle in his counting house.

*It's late. It'll be over by now. Everybody's gone home.*

The wet road snaked toward the glen.

* * *

She sat idling across from Carl and Helen's, their windows ablaze. Chub mumbled when she covered him with her coat.

"Shh. You stay right here, Grahamcracker. I'll be back in a minute."

She pushed open the gate and hurried up the walk. She hovered on the porch. Daniel's voice seeped under the door, and then it opened. Carl stood there with a pack of cigarettes.

Daniel interrupted himself. "Colleen."

Helen sat on the sofa. Robley, Elyse, Melody and Keith Larson, Beth Cooney and her husband, a woman Colleen didn't recognize, holding a notepad. Melody Larson smiled weakly. Colleen hadn't seen her since the funeral. Daniel stood up from his chair and gestured for Colleen to take it.

"I can't stay long." She leaned against the wall instead. "Chub's asleep in the truck."

"So what does that mean, en-do-creen?" Robley asked, turning back to Daniel.

"An endocrine disrupter interferes with the body's hormones," Daniel explained. "Endocrine disrupters can cause cancer, developmental disorders, birth defects like cleft palates—"

"Like, what ours had?" Robley paused. "All ours?"

Daniel nodded. The woman with the notepad looked up. She was pretty: wavy blond hair and a sharp nose. Colleen crossed her arms to quash the sudden pang of jealousy.

"Is there proof?" Keith Larson asked.

"There are studies," Daniel said.

"Like on rats and stuff?"

Daniel nodded.

"I fucking knew it," Keith said. "Something like that—" He shook his head. Melody wiped her eyes. "It don't just happen for no reason."

The blond woman scribbled, pencil scratching at her pad.

"We were just talking about the sprays," Daniel said, catching Colleen up. "There's a community up in Oregon trying to get an injunction against some of the same herbicides they're spraying around here—2,4,5-T in particular—until there's better science. And the EPA is studying it—

mother's milk, beef fat. In the meantime, we're asking for a voluntary moratorium."

All the eyes in the room turned to her. A clipboard sat on the burl table with a few scrawled signatures.

Robley asked another question. Colleen felt a tug on the thread that tied her to Chub, alone in the cold truck. She slipped out while Daniel was talking, pulling the door quietly shut behind her.

"Heard enough?" Carl asked, wreathed by a cloud of cigarette smoke.

"Tell Helen I said good night."

Carl nodded and took a long drag, orange dot in the dark.

The truck windows were fogged with Chub's warm breath.

"Colleen!" Daniel called, coming through the gate after her. "You should stay. You're not alone in this. Cynthia . . ." She could tell by his hesitation that Cynthia was the woman with the notepad. "She's a journalist. She'd like to talk to you. You know better than anybody what people have been going through around here."

"I can't."

Daniel looked down at his hands. "You can't? Or you won't?"

"Joanna had a calf that died," she said quietly. "At my mom's old place."

"Recently?" he asked.

"Not too long ago."

He reached reflexively for the pencil above his ear, gave a quick nod, and stepped aside to let her go.

She climbed into the truck and started the motor. Chub stirred in the backseat.

"Are we home?" he asked.

"Almost, Grahamcracker."


"In here," Rich called from the kitchen.

Noodles roiled on the stove, meatballs sizzling on the back burner. She and Chub had eaten so many Cracker Jacks she'd forgotten about dinner.

"Almost ready." Rich didn't ask where she'd been, why they were so late. He was wearing her apron, which made Chub giggle. She pulled Chub back against her legs as Rich lifted the pot and poured it into the sink, steam fogging the window. He rinsed the colander of pasta, letting her notice.

Rich didn't put stock in sorrys. His apologies were all in the things he did: in the hose running from the faucet to the filter's cylinder, in the jet of cold water shooting from its spout.

*December 17*

# RICH

He'd spent all day up 24-7 Ridge, clearing alder. Scout's collar jingled up ahead, creeks louder now that it was dark. Rain sluiced down his slicker, white clouds of breath eddying in the beam of his headlamp. Finally, he crested Bald Hill, kitchen window glowing gold. He hooked Scout onto his chain, mussed his wet hackles, and knocked his boots against the back stoop, bringing the McCulloch in with him. She'd rust to hell if he didn't dry her off.

"I'll clean this up," he said, tracking over to the table and pulling out a chair.

Colleen looked up from the spread-out newspaper. He shucked off his gloves and pulled a foot free, wet sock coming with it. Colleen pushed the paper across.

"These things weigh ten pounds," he said, working the laces on the second boot.

He missed his caulks. Needed to drive up and get them. His fingertips itched, coming back to life. He held the paper at arm's length until the print sharpened. Baby on her hip, braid, long skirt, she looked from another time, holding up a freezer bag of furry lumps.

*Joanna Roesch, 23, mother of three, with deformed chicks hatched at her farm off Deer Rib Road. Roesch believes herbicides aerially sprayed on nearby logging concessions are to blame.*

"What a crock," Rich said. "*Mad River Union*—communist bullshit paper."

"Read it," Colleen said, putting away dishes.

He cleared his throat and read aloud.

*"When Joanna Roesch first noticed a milky substance clouding the spring that supplied her family's gravity-fed water line, she didn't think much of it.*

*"'It cleared up after a few days,' Roesch said. 'But the kids got nosebleeds, after they sprayed. They bled and bled, sometimes for an hour.'*

*"Soon Roesch noticed other change too. Chicks that hatched in the weeks following aerial spraying on a ridge east of her farm had crossed beaks, deformed wings, and clubbed feet. The family's dairy cow gave birth to a paralyzed calf that later died. Roesch says she only began associating the birth defects with the sprays after water samples from a nearby creek showed high concentrations of the herbicides 2,4,5-T and 2,4-D, the two ingredients in the chemical defoliant Agent Orange.*

*"'I didn't think about them hurting things that weren't even born,' said Roesch, who is six months pregnant with her fourth child."*

Colleen bit a hangnail. Rich skipped ahead.

*"'People don't worry about what they can't see,' said Daniel Bywater, a fisheries biologist studying the impact of herbicide spraying and other logging practices on local salmon runs. Bywater, an enrolled member of the Yurok Tribe, believes the herbicides could also affect humans. The county has opened an investigation after it recorded three live births of anencephalic babies (born with sacs of fluid in place of brains) in the last year. Nationwide, the rare birth defect affects fewer than one in 2,500 babies. Health officials have also documented an increase in fetal deaths, though the total number of miscarriages in the county is unknown, since many women do not seek medical attention, and stillbirths are not always recorded, especially in rural and tribal communities where childbirth often takes place at home.*

*"'There are women in this community, women in good health, having two, three, four miscarriages,' Bywater said. 'You have to wonder, why is this happening here?'*

*"Roesch and her children still eat the eggs her chickens lay. Deer Rib Ridge, which overlooks the family's property, is scheduled to be treated with 2,4,5-T again in March. A concerned citizens group is circulating a petition asking logging giant Sanderson Timber, the county, and the Forest Service to temporarily suspend all aerial spraying of the chemicals.*

*"Helen and Carl Yancy—"*

Colleen clanked a plate against a cabinet door. Rich paused.

*"—of Klamath Glen lost their second child in November, shortly after Mrs. Yancy, also an enrolled member of the Yurok Tribe, delivered the baby, the most recent case of anencephaly.*

*"'They say it doesn't hurt nothing, we could shower in the stuff. We get it all over us when we spray,' said Mr. Yancy, who drives a tanker truck for Sanderson Timber,*

*spraying herbicides to keep logging roads clear of brush. 'I don't know. If they told me they'd invented a safe kind of bullet, I still wouldn't let them shoot my kid in the head.'*

"Stupid." Rich pushed back from the table, grabbing his boots. Talking to the paper—Merle wouldn't just let a thing like that slide.

"Do you think I should go check on Joanna?" Colleen asked. "She might not have seen it yet."

She held on to that woman, as if, just by living in the old cabin, she had become a relative.

"Stay the hell out of it is what we should do."

"Why are you so upset?" Colleen asked.

"I'm not upset!" Rich sighed. "If we get wrapped up in this, even if Merle thought we were being a little friendly to that woman—he'd yank those roads out from under me so fast my head would spin."

"What happened to your forehead?" Colleen asked, noticing the cut.

"Nothing." He pawed at it. "Let's just stay out of it."

Colleen pursed her lips, wiped her hands on a dish towel, drying each finger individually, like she was cleaning the command off them.

"There's a notice in there," she said, lifting her chin at the paper. "February twenty-seventh. The public hearing for those Damnation Grove harvest plans."

"I'm going to get cleaned up," he said.

His wet clothes slapped the bathroom floor. In the mirror, he saw the gash, the width of his pinkie, guttering the middle line of his forehead. The hot water of the shower stung, running down his face, draining the anger. He dressed, came back down the hall, forks scraping plates.

"Chub was hungry." She avoided his eyes, disagreement still hanging in the air.

He harpooned a baked potato, ladled meat juice over the roast.

"Rolls are in the oven," she said after he sat.

He forked up a mouthful.

"They said Luke couldn't sit with them," Chub continued.

"And what did you say?" she asked, making no effort to catch Rich up.

"I said he could sit with me."

"That was nice of you," Colleen said. "Did that make you feel good?"

"Uh-huh." Chub speared a carrot.

"Good," she said. "It's important to do the right thing. Even when no-body else is."

*January 6*

# COLLEEN

Colleen watched Chub across the school gym, thumb-warring with Luke, waiting with the other kids to be picked up. Chub wore the checkered black and red hat she'd bought him for Christmas, earflaps hiding the sides of his face.

"He's all Luke talks about."

Colleen turned. Helen's hands were red and chapped. She looked worn down, picking up extra shifts at the crab plant, since Carl had gotten laid off.

*Escorted him off the premises*, Eugene had bragged. Colleen had pictured Carl slowly getting to his feet in Merle's office, as though the conversation had aged him fifty years.

"Chub too," Colleen said, though this wasn't exactly true. Colleen had pried things out of him, enough to know Luke had been punched in the stomach by an older boy, called a crybaby.

Eleanor Riggs flashed a quick smile at Colleen—Colleen had delivered her twins—but gave Helen a wide berth.

"Chub this, Chub that. I'm glad he has a friend," Helen said, pretending to ignore the snub. She faced forward. To someone standing across the room, it wouldn't even look like they were talking.

"Remember when Mrs. Walsh wanted to hold me back a year?" Helen asked.

"Because you wouldn't talk in class." Colleen nodded.

"I knew I wasn't dumb, but still, it made me feel dumb. I remember Mrs. Bywater came to talk to my grandma about it. She said holding us back was just another way of holding us down. She made them give me that test, remember?"

Colleen nodded, recalling Helen's triumphant grin, her own joy that her friend was coming with her to third grade.

"Carl thinks I'm mixing one thing up with another, but it feels the same," Helen said. "Like someone's trying to convince me something's wrong with me. Like I don't see what I see."

Two teachers on duty chatted on the sidelines. A boy tugged a girl's pigtail and before she even wailed in complaint, one snapped her fingers at him and pointed to the opposite wall, the offender shuffling toward the designated spot, coat trailing in defeat.

"They've all got eyes in the backs of their heads," Helen said.

Sound reverberated under the high ceiling, which made it seem possible to eavesdrop on ten conversations at once, but Colleen couldn't single any one out.

"That was smart, freezing those chicks," Helen said.

Colleen had thought so too. Joanna must have walked out to the barn each morning, the dead still warm from the heat lamp.

"You have to wonder. If it can do that to a cow."

"Her girls are healthy."

Helen pressed her lips together. "I hope so."

Colleen felt a flicker of irritation. Everybody staring, pretending not to, was throwing her off-kilter.

"How's Carl?"

"You know how it is. When they're used to working."

"Pinned you!" Chub shrieked. Luke's hair was buzzed, making his eyes look huge. He was smaller than Chub, fine boned, the kind of boy who ran fast as a matter of survival.

"Luke!" Helen called. Luke looked over and his face fell. Chub turned too, lighting up when he spotted Colleen.

"I'm hungry," Luke said, dragging himself across the cafeteria.

"Your dad will make you a grilled cheese."

"I want you to make it."

"I have to go back to work tonight."

He shuffled, sulking. Chub launched his lunch box into Colleen's arms, trotting after Luke into the lobby, horsing around.

"Boys!" Gail Porter stood, hands on her hips.

Chub and Luke separated. Gail Porter locked eyes with Colleen.

"Better watch out, talking to me," Helen said, pushing out into the drizzle. Colleen hurried after her. "I'm sorry."

"Why?" Helen unlocked her door and herded Luke in. "We did it to ourselves, right?"

"We were all there," Colleen said. "It wasn't just you."

"They don't know that." Helen raised her chin at the meteor tails of eaten paint unfurled across the truck where eggs had hit. *He didn't hose them off in time*, Rich would say, yet another indictment of Carl's stupidity. Colleen had heard about her tires. What else had happened over the past three weeks for Helen to lock her truck in the school lot? Colleen searched for something more to say.

"Helen, I'm so sorry."

"Yeah, well. Sorry doesn't pay the bills." She slammed her door so hard Colleen's ears rang.

# RICH

Rich stood at the top of 24-7 Ridge, carving the roads with his eyes. Soggy ground sucked at his boots. The alder thicket he'd spent the morning falling was almost clear. Not bad for half a day's work. Drop the big pumpkins just fine, once the alder was out of the way. He ripped the McCulloch's cord—nothing. He tried again, hefted her—plenty of gas—dug out the spark plug. Insulator looked okay. He scraped crud off the electrodes, replaced the plug. Just cleaned the carburetor. Should purr like a cat. Damn ignition coil. Had to be.

Colleen was scrubbing the counters when he came in.

"Saw's busted. Need anything from the store?"

"No." She stopped, blew hair up out of her eyes. "Be careful."

He stood for a moment outside the front door, smelling the weather. It was raining good by the time he got into the bends. He cracked the window, canted the blower. Grab a couple gallons of chain oil from Whitey, while he was at it, finally get his caulks back. He swung around the Last Chance curve and the windshield darkened. He slammed his brakes, skidded, truck tipping onto two wheels, landing with the squeak of an old hide-a-bed.

Jesus—his chest heaved—Christ.

He set the parking brake—serious business—and climbed up onto the back bumper for a better view. Mud had slid down over the road, sixty yards across, a couple of redwoods snapped in the mix. Hope nobody's under it. No car horns, anyway.

Every year, the slides got worse. The more they logged, the less there was to hold the land in place. On the far side came a siren, then a wash of red pulsing through the mist. Harvey got out, climbed up onto the hood of his patrol car. Looked like a piss fir in that hat.

"You got flares?" Harvey yelled.

Rich set flares down the centerline, got back in his truck. His tires spun, spitting mud. He honked twice to Harvey. Driving back the way he'd come, it was hard to shake the feeling that any of these ridges might cave next.

Rich passed the house—he'd tell Colleen when he got back, no use worrying her now—hiss of wet road all the way to Eureka. Redwood Saw didn't have shit.

"Nobody runs McCullochs anymore," the kid at the counter said.

Nowhere left but J.P.'s.

Rich sat in the lot letting the truck go cold, took a deep breath, and went in. The place hadn't changed. J.P. was dead, but somehow Rich still expected to find him here. J.P.'s son—the rat-faced one—sat behind the counter, flipping through a skin rag. Rich plunked down a replacement ignition coil. He'd wait on the chain oil. Not lining these pockets any more than he had to.

"Anything else?" the son asked, silver incisor catching the light.

"Nope."

A phone rang. The son disappeared into the back. Rich took in the old guitars, eight-tracks, silver jubilee belt buckles and bolos. Guys used to pawn their saws at J.P.'s at the end of the season, hope they could afford to buy them back come spring. J.P. had done whatever Virgil asked—might have doctored Lark's rope, clipped the steel threads, restitched the weave right here in this room.

The son came back.

"Five fifty."

"Five dollars?"

"And fifty cents."

Rich paid and went out. Dolores's son stood waiting for him. He held out a hand and Rich shook it, let the man's name slip through his fingers again, though he'd just said it.

"I was across the way." The man lifted his chin in the direction of the mechanic's.

"She quit on you?" Rich asked. VWs weren't worth the tinfoil they were made from.

"Lost my brakes," the man said. "Whoever cut them knew what he was doing." He studied Rich. "I was hoping we'd get another chance to talk."

"Why's that?"

The guy jammed his hands into his front pockets. "I don't want those sprays running off into the creeks. You don't want your family drinking them."

"So, Sanderson stops spraying, you'd be okay with us cutting every tree in that grove?"

The man dropped his eyes.

"I didn't think so."

"Hold on, now. I'm trying to say that we could be on the same side."

Dolores had slunk out of town, pregnant by one of the radar boys, and returned a social worker; this was exactly the kind of self-righteous bastard she would raise.

"We could be," Rich said. "But we're not."

"Listen, I know Colleen—your wife," he corrected himself, "has lost a lot of pregnancies."

"She told you that?" Rich asked, a hitch in his voice.

The man shrugged. "A town this size, she didn't have to. Must have been rough on you, watching the woman you love go through that." The way he said it—*rough*—it struck Rich he was talking down to him, molding his speech to match Rich's own. "I don't think I'd be able to take it." The man went on. "I'd want to know why. I'd want to do something."

Colleen had had every test there was. If there was a reason, the doctors would have found it by now. What Rich could do was not get her pregnant again.

"If there's an answer, I want to help you find it," the man said, misreading Rich's silence.

"I judge a man by what he does," Rich said. "Not what he says."

"I hear you."

"See, that's the thing. I don't think you do. Stay away from my wife. You're not helping her."

"She knows something isn't right," the man said. "She knows it in her gut. Just like you do."

"Colleen has been through enough. She doesn't need you putting ideas in her head." Rich stepped off the curb onto the wet gravel.

"*I'll* stay away from *her*," the man baited him.

Rich stopped, his back to him.

"She wants to know why," the man said. "Don't you?"

Rich had never struck a man in anger, but here he was, fists clenched.

"Maybe you're afraid you won't like the answer," the man called after him.

Rich walked to his truck, climbed in, tossed the ignition coil onto the seat, backed out, pulled alongside the man and rolled down his window.

"You ever talk to my wife again, you and me are going to have a real problem," Rich said.

"Is that a threat?" the man asked.

Rich pushed air out his nostrils. "A threat? No. That's a promise."

He pulled away, the man growing smaller and smaller behind him.

## *January 14*

# COLLEEN

Colleen leaned over the wheel. The bulldozers still hadn't finished clearing the Last Chance slide north of them, cutting them off from Crescent City, and, after a rain like last night, there was no guarantee the road would still be where you'd left it. Chub kicked the back of the passenger seat.

"Stop, please."

Had she put noodles on the list? It poked up from her purse, a quick reach enough to send them careening off the cliff. She gripped the wheel tighter, until finally they were inland, passing the mill, juddering down No Name Road. The truck's tires spun in the mud.

"I hope we don't get stuck."

A mustard-colored VW bus was parked near the grove—not Daniel's—tents pitched above the road. She slowed, but there was no movement. They passed the Deer Rib turnoff.

"Aren't we getting eggs?" Chub asked.

"We'll get some at the store, Grahamcracker."

*Stay out of it*, Rich had warned. *Stay away from that woman.*

She pulled into Fort Eugene. The trailer house door swung open and Eugene himself appeared, still in his boxers. A cat slipped out through his shins, hopped up onto the carcass of a Corvette Eugene had been rebuilding since Marla was born. A goat bleated from its perch in the goat tree.

"They still camped out?" Eugene called, cocky, as though he hadn't noticed the bags under his eyes, his small mound of low-set belly.

"A few," Colleen called back.

Enid came out with the baby, plopped into the passenger seat, knocked her muddy feet together, and swung her legs in. "This damn thing." Enid pulled the seat belt out from under her.

"Tell them they got an hour to clear out," Eugene called.

"Ignore him," Enid told Colleen. "You leave it alone!" She slammed her door for emphasis.

Colleen backed out. When they rounded the bend below the grove, the hippies were breaking camp. A scraggly-haired man stood near a plywood sign: STOP KILLING OUR MOTHER.

"He's peeing," Chub said.

"Don't look," Colleen said.

"Not much to see," Enid announced.

The man zipped up, stuck out his thumb.

"Pull over." Enid reached across and yanked the wheel.

Colleen slammed her brakes. "Are you crazy?"

Chub looked alarmed when the man climbed in, bringing the smell of wet leather.

"Thanks," he said. "Cold out there." He blew into his hands, reached forward to introduce himself. "Nathan."

"We don't care what your name is," Enid said.

They surfed ruts to the paved road, so smooth Colleen had to remind herself to shift gears. They passed silently through Orick, Trinidad, McKinleyville, as though Enid had picked him up to avoid conversation. Chub traced shapes in the fogged window.

"Here's fine," the man said when they got to the outskirts of Arcata.

"Why would you do that?" Colleen demanded, watching him scramble down the shoulder.

"Better us than Eugene," Enid said.

Mud clung halfway up the truck doors. Colleen sat with Chub in the clinic waiting room with Alsea in her lap, a soft tuft of red-blond hair, rolls of pearly flesh. Finally, Enid emerged, smiling. Colleen had assumed it would hurt, the way Enid had described it, some little T-shaped device they inserted that pumped out hormones, tricking your body into not getting pregnant.

"Still not sitting up?" the nurse asked Enid, frowning at Alsea. "Bring her back for a minute."

Enid obeyed. Chub backed into Colleen's knees. She lifted him into her lap.

"Where'd you get these beautiful eyelashes?"

"I got them at the eyelash store."

Enid came out with her jaw tight, nostrils flared. At the store, she loaded the basket with a force to dent cans.

"How can you shop without a list?" Colleen asked.

"It's in my head."

"Just don't ask me to drive you back when you forget something."

"I didn't ask you to drive me here. You offered." Enid reached for the baked beans.

"I've got a coupon," Colleen said, grabbing the cans out of the basket and returning them to the shelf. "Two for seventy-nine."

Enid reached for two more to replace them. "Eugene likes this kind."

"It's the same thing."

"He'll taste the difference."

Colleen steered her cart down the next aisle, stood before shelves of canning supplies, loaded up three boxes of jam jars—she'd filled almost all of Daniel's—then checked out. Transferring her grocery sacks into the backseat, she felt around for the relish jar. She could picture its dark blue lid.

"Forget something?" Enid asked.

Chub was out cold by the time they passed Orick.

Enid squirmed. "It's only this big." She measured an inch between her thumb and forefinger, pulled her skirt away from her crotch. Pills didn't work for her; she forgot to take them. "What am I going to tell him about the string, though?"

"I could never lie to Rich about something like that."

Enid pushed an angry puff of air out her nose.

"What?" Colleen asked.

"When exactly were you planning to tell me you caught Marla at the make-out point? At their wedding? Or were you going to wait for their tenth anniversary?" Enid demanded.

How long had she known?

"It wasn't like that," Colleen said quietly.

"Oh really? What was it like?"

Colleen felt her cheeks color, tried to focus on the road.

"Marla only told me because she was scared of what I'd do when I heard it from you. But no, my own sister can't bother to tell me my daughter's out fooling around when she's supposed to be in school."

Had she already told Eugene? How long before Rich found out? What would she do then?

"What else did she say?" Colleen asked, heart pounding.

"Why don't you tell me," Enid challenged her. "You were the one who was there."

Chub turned over in the backseat but didn't wake.

She waited for Enid to spit Daniel's name at her. Was it possible Marla hadn't mentioned him?

"I'm sorry," Colleen said, popping the lid off the silence. She gripped the wheel tighter so that Enid wouldn't notice her hands trembling. "I just—"

"If you had a daughter, you would have told me."

"But I don't," Colleen said. "I don't have a daughter. Say it, go ahead."

"This isn't about you," Enid said. "Is it?"

*January 15*

# CHUB

Wyatt dropped down from the goat tree and stalked off into the grass as soon as Chub's mom pulled away. Chub looked back at Fort Eugene, smoke unfurling from the stovepipe, his mom's voice in his head.

*Don't go far.*

"Where are we going?" Chub asked, catching up.

"You'll see."

It was a long way across the marsh. By the time they started climbing up into the woods, Chub's overalls were wet, heavy, and swampy smelling. Wyatt cocked his head: a chainsaw, far away. They crossed Knife Creek, then another creek he didn't recognize. He checked his palm. Suddenly there was Uncle Eugene's truck, parked in the middle of the forest, and Marla's boyfriend with the big head. Uncle Eugene wrestled a chain around a burl bulging out from the base of a tree. The burl was so wide he had to stretch his body across it twice. Marla's boyfriend cranked something that made the chain tighten.

"What are they doing?" Chub whispered.

Uncle Eugene started his saw. It growled lower and lower, and then the burl dropped into a chain harness. The boyfriend cranked something else, Uncle Eugene jumped down, and the burl thudded into the truck bed.

"You coming to help?" Uncle Eugene asked, like he'd been expecting them.

The boyfriend moved the truck, then raked needles over the tire tracks backward to the cut tree, like he was sweeping up to a door.

"Where are you taking that?" Chub asked. He smelled sap and sawdust.

"I know a guy." Uncle Eugene winked, lifted Chub up by the armpits into the truck bed, and patted the burl. "Polish this baby up, people all over the country will want a slice of her. All over the world. She'll end up one slab in Los Angeles, one in New York City. Places nobody's ever seen a redwood."

Uncle Eugene shook out a blue tarp and tossed it over the top of the burl, hooking bungee cords to the corners. Then Uncle Eugene and Marla's boyfriend climbed into the cab, Wyatt scrambled up into the bed beside Chub, and the truck bounced downhill.

"That thing starts rolling around back there, you bail out," Uncle Eugene called back to them.

It was bumpy for a long time. Then they got to the road.

"If you tell anybody, I'll kill you," Wyatt said.

"Tell anybody what?"

Wyatt sighed, like Chub's stupidity exhausted him. He flicked the burl through the tarp, then slit his own throat with his finger, so slow Chub felt its ghost. He swallowed.

The tarp crinkled in the wind, truck picking up speed.

*January 16*

# RICH

He ran another quarter-inch groove up a salvage board, redwood felled and sawed a century ago, heartwood from the old hotel as solid as the day it was milled, graphite marks where a carpenter had figured his wages, silt lines from the floods of '64, '55, '53, '27. Colleen swung in, gravel popping in the wheel wells. She got out, hitched a paper grocery sack up on her hip, let the screen door slap behind her.

He turned off the table saw. Chub was splayed across the backseat, mouth-breathing. Rich smacked sawdust off his legs, caught the screen door behind him. He pulled a chair away from the table, just to make noise.

"You eat?" she asked, snatching a block of cheese, taking the store loaf from the bread box, pulling out the silverware drawer so hard forks jangled. She was in a bad mood from taking Enid down to the clinic again, second time in a week. She held the new peanut butter jar to her chest, twisted, turned it over to spank the bottom, grunted in frustration.

He held out a hand and she thunked the jar into it. The seal released with a pop.

"What's wrong with me?" she asked, tears streaming down her cheeks.

"Nothing's wrong with you," Rich said.

Her chin crumpled. "How do you know?"

"You don't have to be the one to drive her."

"She's my sister." Colleen sucked in her snot. "Could you carry Chub in?"

Rich went out to the truck. The glove box hung open, exposing a pinwheel mint in a plastic wrapper. The man's words echoed in his head—

*I'll* stay away from *her*. Rich smacked the glove box shut once, twice, until the latch engaged.

In the kitchen, Colleen set the four neat triangles of Chub's sandwich up on edge like the spines of a dinosaur.

"Tyrannosandwich rex," Chub said groggily.


A current of cold air woke him in the night. He found Colleen at the kitchen table, writing a list—names, addresses.

"What are you doing?"

Colleen laid her pen down horizontally at the top of the yellow legal pad. *You can come this close and no closer.*

"I couldn't sleep," she said.

# COLLEEN

She'd bought store eggs. She had stayed out of it, but now here was Joanna, huddled on the front stoop with her girls, behind a translucent curtain of rain, when Colleen came home from taking Chub to school.

"Can you drive us to town?" Joanna blurted out, hand on her belly.

"Is everything okay?" Colleen asked. The girls corralled the baby beside a wooden flat filled with eggs. They looked chilled. "Do you want to come in and dry off first?"

"We're fine," Joanna said.

The girls found the wool blanket and spread it over themselves in the backseat. When they got to the Beehive, the charity cases at the counter—old man Yancy, missing a leg; Olin Rowley, missing an arm—unshaven, hungover, turned around to stare.

"I hope you girls brought some sunshine," Dot said.

Colleen felt a surge of gratitude.

Jars of canned salmon gleamed in the refrigerated case beside a half-empty egg carton. Joanna laid a hand on Judith's shoulder, pulling her back from the bakery case. Judith's head bumped Joanna's pregnant belly, her nose print left behind on the glass, level with the cinnamon rolls.

"I have eggs." Joanna bounced the baby on her hip.

Dot glanced at the men's hunched backs, then gave a quick nod. Joanna went out to get them, bell jostling over the door. Leah banged her palm on the glass.

"How are you girls today?" Dot asked.

"Fine," Judith said, staring at the buns.

"Rainy enough for you?" Dot asked. "Even the fish are complaining. It's too wet!"

Joanna came back with a gust of damp, set the flat on the counter angrily, and counted out ten dozen. Dot tonged two cinnamon rolls from the case, dropped them into a sack, and pushed them across the counter with a ten-dollar bill.

"I can bring more," Joanna said, ignoring the sack.

Judith grabbed on to her mother's skirt. Colleen took the rolls.

*Thank you*, she mouthed.

Dot gave a false-stern look—*What in the world, Colleen?*

The girls stuck by Colleen, since she held the pastry bag. By the time the bell clunked over Colleen's head, Joanna was already halfway across the road. The tank truck idled, spraying the weedy strip along the stream. Colleen ushered the girls into the truck. The man aiming the hose wasn't Carl, of course not, but it took a moment to register the red cap. Joanna squared off in front of Eugene, baby on her hip, belly jutting.

"What's in there?" Joanna demanded.

"Just a little weed juice," Eugene said, glancing across at Colleen. "It's good for you."

The big-headed Sanderson kid hopped out of the cab and crossed his arms like a referee.

Colleen's nose itched: chlorine. The cowbell clunked.

"Lost our walnut tree. Just shriveled up and died," Dot said, coming out behind her.

"You want a taste, you nosy bitch?" the Sanderson boy asked Joanna. "Eugene, give her a taste, if she wants it so bad."

The Sanderson boy grabbed the hose and misted her. For a moment, the air was sucked from Colleen's lungs, from the whole street. Then it all came howling out the baby's mouth. Judith tried to climb out of the truck, but Colleen blocked her, her own eyes stinging, even from this distance. Joanna coughed, dripping spray.

"What's in here?" She banged the tank with her palm, spat. "I'm calling the police."

"Call 'em. Merle will fucking bury you like he buried your husband."

The baby screamed in Joanna's arms. Suddenly Joanna seemed to hear it. She came running back across the road, cradling the baby.

"You watch them," Dot told Colleen, the girls pressing their faces to the truck windows. "I'll take care of her." Dot hurried Joanna and the baby inside.

Colleen got in the truck.

"I want Mama," Leah cried. "Mama!"

"Hush now," Colleen said. "She'll be out in a minute," Colleen assured them, though her own hands were trembling. She reached for the pastry bag, forgotten on the seat between them, and tore off sticky layers. They chewed dutifully. Finally, Joanna reappeared with the baby, eyes red.

"Here she is," Colleen said to the girls, surprised at her own relief.

Dot opened the door, and Joanna climbed in, wearing a pair of Dot's polyester pants and a baggy cardigan studded with costume pearls. She looked like a child dressed in her grandmother's clothes. Dot watched them reverse out of the lot, eyes on Colleen. *Careful now. Some places you go you can't get back from.*

"I need to go to the store," Joanna said quietly.

They wove through the bends. The girls lay across the backseat, but it felt like Colleen and Joanna were alone, the baby asleep in Joanna's arms.

"Jed got fired," Joanna confided.

"When?"

"After that newspaper thing."

*Sanderson has long thumbs. And long arms*, people said in town.

"What's he going to do?" Colleen asked.

"I don't know. He's at my aunt's in Medford. He's looking."

When they got to the Safeway, Joanna took out a change purse.

"Could you hold her, while I go in?" Joanna asked, twisting for Colleen to take the baby. Joanna climbed out, careful of her belly. The girls dropped out after her. The perfume of Dot's clothes lingered in the cab. Camber fussed.

"It's okay, sweet pea." Colleen rocked her, the baby's warm weight pressing against her chest. "You're okay."

Colleen startled when Joanna climbed back in with her groceries. It felt like she'd only been gone a minute.

"All set?" Colleen asked. It hurt her heart, to hand the baby back. She felt the sadness even after she'd dropped Joanna and the girls off at the cabin and headed back to town alone. She idled at the stop sign, deciding.

She drove along the north side of the river, searching the brush for the turnoff, slowing a few times before she found it. She swung in. Weeds and berry canes blocked her view, branches sweeping the truck's roof, driveway dipping downward so suddenly Colleen worried she might be driving into the river itself. Brush whipped the windows and suddenly she emerged into a flat expanse ringed by trees. A few sheds and a smokehouse were still clustered at one edge, a stone's throw from the tidy cedar-shingle house, its new corrugated-tin roof shining. She wondered if Daniel's mother was inside, Dolores Bywater sitting perfectly still in her tinkling white earrings, cancer spreading inside her.

She heard a motor. The nose of Daniel's van shot up out of the brush that hid the driveway and pulled up behind her. Daniel got out, tucking a clipboard under his arm. She rolled down her window. He looked off toward the house, scratched the back of his head.

"What are you doing here?" he asked.

"Did you test it?" she demanded.

He narrowed his eyes, as though he suspected this was not her real reason. "Not yet," he said.

"I have more." She handed two jars out the window, but he didn't move to take them.

"It'd be good to get some samples this spring, when they start spraying aerially again. That's when the levels will be highest."

"We got a filter," she explained. "So I took one from there, and one regular. I labeled them. Could you test these too? Please?"

He nodded, accepting them.

She looked across the clearing at the house, remembering his uncle's bookshelves lining the walls. She'd only ever seen shelves like that in the library, never in a person's house. The uncle, when she'd met him, was gruff and serious like any other fisherman, speaking to Daniel in a way that sounded clipped, even in a language Colleen couldn't understand. As though he knew the album of recipes with the red and white checkered cover was the only book in her mother's house, and that Colleen would grow up to keep no books in her own. Aside from a few cookbooks and bedtime stories, he had been right.

Outside her window, Daniel cleared his throat, shifted the clipboard to his other arm.

Colleen fumbled for her purse. The list was in her pocketbook, shoved behind her driver's license: a yellow square. She watched him unfold it.

"That's every birth I've been at in the last six years where something wasn't right." Her eyes slid to the clipboard. "I don't know if they'll sign, but they won't shoot you."

"Are you sure?" he asked, half joke, half question, one last chance to back out.

She wasn't sure, but there they were, ten names, already in his hand.

*January 28*

# COLLEEN

Light filtered through the curtains, nightstand littered with bloody tissues. The rocker dipped on its runners when she pulled her sweater off the back.

Eugene stood in the kitchen, shoveling in hotcakes. Rich tipped the pan by the handle. Butter sizzled, batter slicking to the side. The kids sat at the table, their plates sticky ponds of syrup. Colleen kissed the top of Chub's head.

"There's sleeping beauty," Eugene said, as though he had nothing to be ashamed of.

"Who wants more?" Rich asked, flipping silver dollars onto plates. He slathered an unclaimed cake with jam and folded it into his mouth before he and Eugene disappeared up the hill with their saws. She finished the dishes, the kids migrating to the living room, petting the brass rabbit.

"Are you sick, Aunt Colleen?" Agnes asked, her lazy eye lolling.

"No."

"Your hair's messy."

"So is yours."

She undid Agnes's barrette, swept up her bangs—how natural it felt, to fix a little girl's hair. She sent them out to play. They flapped Scout's ears as though trying to figure out how he was sewn together, features twisting shut when he licked their faces. Alone in the house, Colleen dozed, startling when Eugene and Rich came in, shrugging off the cold.

"You keep driving that bitch around, people are going to start wondering whose side you're on," Eugene said, dropping onto the couch.

"Don't call her that," Colleen snapped.

"You don't pull that shit on Sanderson and get away with it. Merle—"

"Merle can go to hell," Colleen said. "And so can you, letting a baby get sprayed with that poison."

She went out the back door. Scout lifted his head. She was shaking. She rubbed her nose, loosing a rusty fleck—it had bled off and on since yesterday. She heard Eugene around front, calling the kids, then his truck sputtering away. Rich came out the back door.

"They're gone," he told her.

"He's a coward," she said.

"He may be," Rich acknowledged. "But he's not wrong."

# RICH

Lark sat on the throne he'd carved out of a stump the size of a kitchen table, fishing, saw cane leaned up against one side, rifle cane on the other. Rich side-stepped down the bank, toothache radiating, and looked out at the water.

"What happened to you?" Lark asked.

"Nothing."

"Yeah, looks like nothing."

Rich nudged the bucket with his toe. A few lampreys sloshed around, dead or close to it.

"I knew a guy got an abscess off a sore tooth once. Ate the brain right out of his head."

"You been talking to Colleen?" Rich tongued his gum, rot so strong it soured his stomach.

Lark shook his head. "Keep going like you're going, I'll have to take you around back and shoot you." He reeled in empty.

Rich picked up a handful of rocks and skipped one across the river.

"Yancy's old man was a hell of a shot," Lark said after a while. "I seen him hit a cherry pit at a hundred yards once, drunk off his ass."

"What happened to him?" Rich asked.

"Mainline snapped. Cable cut through his neck like hot wire through a slug. Pretty ugly, but it was quick." Lark wrinkled his nose at the memory. "Man alive, could he snore. One-man dogfight—shook the whole damn bunkhouse."

"What made you think of that?"

Lark held out a cherry, spat a stone. "Marsha thinks I'll get scurvy. How's that alder coming?"

"Grows back about as fast as I fall it." Rich thumbed the scabbed gash in his forehead, itching now that the skin was tightening up, healing.

Lark recast, hook plopping short, below the riffle. A throttle in the distance.

"What the hell does he want?" Lark asked. "Hear that piece-of-shit Chevy from the Oregon line."

Eugene's truck burst through the brush.

"You sonofabitch," Eugene yelled, hopping out and charging down the bank. "Nice toilets," he said to Lark. "I got to get me some of those." Eugene turned on Rich. "You goddamn Weyerhaeuser. You bought that ridge?" Eugene swiped a Tab off the ground, popped it, grimaced at the taste, like he'd expected beer. "You sneaky bastard." Eugene shook his head in jealous admiration. "You believe this guy? Whole 24-7. He owns it."

"I heard," Lark said.

"You heard?" Eugene turned to Rich. "I ask Merle what the odds are on Damnation Grove, he says ask you, you're the one's going to bring it home for us; you got your whole damn future riding on it. Made me look like a jackass."

"Since when do you need any help looking like a jackass?" Lark asked.

Eugene ignored him, crumpled Tab can smacking Rich lightly in the back. Eugene toed the bucket of lampreys. "What's with the eels?"

"Stick around, we'll fry them up," Lark offered.

"No thanks. Damn you, Gundersen." Eugene shook his head as though realizing he'd come all this way just to say that. "Well, you know where to find me when the time comes." He turned to Lark. "You know Rich needs a good hooker."

"Yes, he does."

Eugene loped up the steps to his truck.

Rich shot Lark a look. "Oh, you 'heard,' huh?"

"What? I got big ears," Lark said.

"Big mouth too."

"Set 'em straight at that hearing," Eugene called out his window. "And we're back in business!"

Rich grabbed the bucket by the handle.

"Lampreys used to be thicker than maggots on a dead dog around here," Lark said.

"Little far upriver for an ocean eel, isn't it?" Rich asked.

"I pulled a sturgeon the size of a man out of this river once." Lark took up his canes. "That kid come to see you?"

"What kid?"

"Dolores's boy. College type we seen out by the grove."

"Yeah." Rich switched the bucket to his good arm.

Lark hobbled up the dirt drive. "What the hell good is a petition on private property? Hell, you can pour strychnine down your well if you own it."

"You sign it?" Rich asked.

Lark farted with his lips. "Not worth the paper it's written on." He tilted his head, listening. "Aw hell. What does a guy have to do to get a little peace and quiet around here, die?"

Sure enough, after a minute, Marsha's car came trundling along the rutted two-track. Rich moved aside to let her pass, but Lark kept walking up the middle of the driveway.

"Quit riding my ass." He whacked her bumper with his cane.

Marsha veered at the fork, got out, and beat Lark up the stairs, like it was a race.

She peered into Rich's bucket. "You want me to cook these, you kill them first."

Lark settled himself in a chair. Marsha went inside without wiping her feet.

"Hey, can't you read?" Lark called after her.

"Why can't you just keep the door closed? It's cold in here," she called back. She brought out a knife, stopping to read the doormat. "Come back with a warrant? You're lucky I come back at all, the way you smell. You'd be eating cold baked beans for all three meals."

"Baked beans are better cold," Lark grumped.

Rich whacked the eels' heads against a porch pole, slinging guts across the yard. The dogs stretched, arched their backs, and moseyed over. The hog got wind and lumbered up, snuffling.

"You better watch it falling asleep out here," Rich said. "That hog'll eat you." He ducked through the doorway with the eels. "Where do you want these?"

"Table's fine. You been smoking in here?" Marsha called out to Lark. "You heard that doctor."

Lark grumbled, stirring, like if walking were easier, he'd have gotten up and left.

Grease crackled. Marsha brought out a plate, breaded eels shiny with lard. Lark picked one up by the tail.

"You're the only one who eats these," she said.

"Yurok eat them. Karuk too." Lark drew his lips back from his gums at the heat.

"Who got you in the habit?" Marsha asked.

Lark coughed. "My wife."

"She was from here?" Marsha asked.

"Upriver." Lark reached for another. "That's what 'Karuk' means—'upriver people.' But she grew up down here . . . Her grandma was washing one day— army was around then. Soldier come along, got some ideas. She brained the bas- tard with a rock. Come down here to hide. This was a good place to disappear in those days."

"Where'd you meet her?"

Lark smiled. "Fishing." He squinted, aiming a light down the long, dark tunnel of his memory. "She'd start yelling at me in her language. Hell, I didn't know what she was carrying on about. Never argued when there was a rock in arm's reach though, tell you that much."

"She pretty?" Marsha asked.

"You bet your ass."

"How come I've never seen a picture?"

Lark snuffed his nose on the back of his hand, as though to stop the rest of the story from leaking out. "Flood took care of all that."

*January 31*

# RICH

A horn blared. Rich tilted his head back on the pillow in the dark. "Who is it?"

Colleen went to the window. "Who do you think?"

"Rich!" Eugene bellowed, gave a two-fingered whistle. Scout barked. "Gundersen!"

Rich felt his way into the hall. Eugene swung the front door open so hard it banged the wall.

"Let's go!" Eugene yelled, flipping on the lights.

"Go where?" Rich blinked. "It's the middle of the night."

"Wait 'til you see it!" Eugene's boots were caked with mud, but he came forward on Colleen's clean carpet as if it were his own front lawn.

"See what?" Rich asked.

"Rich?" Colleen asked, a hand on Chub's head. Chub rubbed his eyes.

"Come on, all of you." Eugene flailed his arm. "Before Harvey tapes it off."

Rich cleared phlegm. "Let me get some clothes on."

Eugene went back out. They heard him pacing on the gravel.

"What do you think?" Colleen asked.

"Who knows," Rich said. Who the hell knew what Eugene had gone and done now?

"It's a school night." Colleen herded Chub into his room. Rich heard her getting him dressed.

Rich tugged on yesterday's denims, picked the alarm clock off the night-stand, squinted: 4:34—*sleeping in, old man*—and ducked out into the hall. Colleen led Chub by the hand, his slicker zipped to his chin.

"The roads are fucked," Eugene said. "Faster to walk."

Chub yawned. Rich stifled one of his own. He squatted for Chub to climb onto his back, let Scout off his chain, and followed the cone of Eugene's flashlight up the hill behind the house.

"Where's Mama?" Chub asked. Rich looked back at Colleen's bobbing flashlight, his headlamp casting ferns into relief.

"She's coming."

From the top of 24-7 Ridge, he spotted a wash of red and blue light pulsing in the mist. He took a step down, center of gravity shifting, caught himself, pounded downslope toward the swollen creek, Chub's small body thumping like a pack. He loped upstream a few yards, looking for the best spot to cross, then waded in, water hip-deep. Scout bumped against Rich's haunch, paddling furiously beside him. Rich set Chub down on the other side, then went back for Colleen until all three of them stood at the edge of the lower grove, on the farthest toe of company property. Scout shook. Damnation Creek thundered. Harsh pockets of gasoline fumes hung in the air. His headlamp slashed the dark, a spray of fresh sawdust, then a lens clicked one notch to the right and the whole side rushed at him in crisp focus: stumps, big pumpkins busted where they'd fallen, a sloppy maze of ruined timber. The ground was a muddy pulp of tire tracks and overturned boulders, a steep drop-off where the hillside had given way under the weight of the Cats.

"What the—?" Rich asked. He hauled Chub up onto his back again.

Colleen scraped mud off her boots on the sharp edge of a smashed rock. A laugh rang out. She started up toward it.

"Colleen," Rich called after her. "Colleen!" The downed logs were the size of school buses, but they could still roll. He counted five, ten, fifteen stumps, following her up.

A beam of flashlight, then Harvey's hat in the mist. "Rich?"

Rich shielded his eyes. Scout climbed up ahead of him, Rich emerging onto the road to find Colleen already facing Eugene, flanked by the Sanderson kid, Lyle, a few guys from Bill's crew Rich recognized from the crummy, a dozen others he didn't. Even dropping the big pumpkins cold—no fall beds, no nothing, using the buckets of Cats to lift guys into the air instead of driving in spring boards, not caring how many other monsters the trees knocked down like dominos when they tipped—it must have taken them all night. At least two dozen big pumpkins lay wasted, millions of dollars in timber massacred so badly Sanderson would be lucky to salvage a quarter—it was criminal. Merle must have really backed himself into a corner if this was the last trick he had to force the board's hand. Rich could hear him now. *Those trees are down, boys. No use fighting over spilt milk.* In the dawn light, the men's eyes were bowls of shadow.

"What's wrong with you?" Colleen demanded. "You just do whatever they tell you?"

"Works out pretty good for you, sugar. You sure you didn't put us up to it?" Eugene turned to Rich. "Have to approve those harvest plans now. No use letting good timber go to waste. Roads are coming to you, Gundersen. Lay that 24-7 down, you can practically roll her onto the truck."

"All you care about is money and you still can't poach enough to feed your own family," Colleen snapped.

Eugene did a phony one-two, bouncing like a boxer, getting too close. Scout bared his teeth, growling.

"You think this is funny?" Colleen shoved Eugene, Scout snapping at his shins, and he fell backward, slung mud off his hand. Rich stepped between them. Eugene showed both palms: *I'm fine* and *Get the fuck away from me.*

Scout was barking now, lunging as though to drive Eugene back. Rich held up a hand and Scout stopped, trotted back to his side. Men's eyes darted from the dog to him.

"We did you a favor." Eugene spat.

"We never asked you—" Colleen said.

"*You* never asked." Eugene looked to Rich.

"Harvey, aren't you going to arrest them?" Colleen demanded. Guys shifted, a few tipping their heads back, ready to fight.

"Yeah, Harvey," Eugene said.

Rich touched her arm. She shrugged him off. Chub dug his fingernails into Rich's neck.

"Hey, Harvey, remind me," Eugene asked, "what day is it today?"

Harvey consulted his wristwatch. "January thirty-first."

"January thirty-first," Eugene said. "Well, how about that."

"What's January thirty-first?" Colleen asked, searching Rich's face. He gave a little shake of his head. No idea.

"I'll give you a ride home," Harvey offered.

Colleen snorted, backed up, turned.

"Colleen," Harvey called after her. "Don't go walking through there!" He shook his head at Rich. "Roll some of those logs over with one finger."

"Tell Colleen she can thank me later," Eugene said.

"Tell her yourself."

"I ain't scared of her."

"That's one of us."

"See, that's the problem, Rich." Eugene smacked mud off his pants. "That right there is the problem."

Chub's cold fingers played up and down Rich's throat, timber creaking, Colleen's fury gusting like her own wind. Rich stumbled after Scout, Chub strangling him to hang on. When they got to the house, Eugene's truck was still parked out front. Rich clipped Scout back onto his chain, pulled Chub's boots off first, then, with an effort that brought a flush to his face, his own. The bronze rabbit's ears stood rigid, listening. Down the hall: the rush of the shower.

Rich cleaned ash out of the woodstove, teepeed kindling.

"You know how tall the 24-7 tree is?" Rich asked Chub, holding up a match. "This here is me." Rich crouched beside him, stood the match on the floor, a man in miniature, as his own father had done. "Now, see the top of the doorway there?" Together, they looked up. He couldn't summon his father's face with any clarity, but he could still see that match, its candy head. Rich struck the match, held the flame to newsprint until it caught.

"Is there poison in our water?" Chub asked.

"Who told you that?"

"Pancakes?" Colleen asked from the hall, towel turbaned around her hair. In the kitchen, eggs rang against the metal lip of a mixing bowl. He closed the damper. Chub lay down on the couch.

"Did you know?" she demanded when Rich came into the kitchen.

"Of course not."

"They think they can get away with anything. That dirt and whatever they spray on it will wash right down into the creek now. It's not right."

"Right. Not right. It's done." Rich sighed. "The past isn't a knot you can untie."

She clattered the skillet onto the stove.

"What?" he asked.

She turned and he saw: Colleen in that hospital bed, listing all the things she'd done wrong. If only she'd rested more, kept her feet elevated, if only, if only. *It's not your fault*, he'd said. *The past isn't a knot you can untie.*

Rich sighed. "I didn't mean—I've got a lot on my mind, Colleen. I don't see what I can do to fix it now, anyway."

"I'm not asking you to fix it. But would it kill you to just take my side for once? Why can't you just be on my side?" She was waiting for him to say it— *I am on your side.*

"Colleen. Come on. You know it's not that simple."

"Yes, it is," she said.

*February 4*

# CHUB

Wyatt dropped down from the tree with the nest in his hands: three bluish-white eggs, small as candies. Chub felt the strange urge to pop one in his mouth.

"No touchy." Wyatt elbowed him.

Chub followed him over the soggy ground, big burls wrapped in blue tarps at the side of the trailer house. They turned the corner by the chopping block, Aunt Enid knee-deep in a mountain of firewood, more cut wood than Chub had ever seen at Fort Eugene. She tossed a stick onto the pile nearest them.

"What are you doing?" Chub asked.

"Sorting. The ends are different colors, see?" Aunt Enid held two sticks next to each other. "This one's light. Here, let's find . . ." She rooted around for another. "Here, this one's medium."

Wyatt crossed his eyes, like Aunt Enid was retarded. A gold car came struggling down the muddy hump into the driveway. The door opened and Agnes spilled out.

"That one of yours?" Mr. Sanderson asked, getting out. His purple hair was combed back to cover his bald spot.

Chub crawled inside the empty washer-dryer box, hiding, a squeeze of excitement as Agnes walked by.

"So they tell me," Aunt Enid said.

"Found her by the turnoff, hunting frogs. Not shy of strangers."

"Should she be?" Aunt Enid crossed her arms.

"Make you sick what some people will try to get away with." Mr. Sanderson stared at the blue tarps. "These are all off Damnation?" he asked. "That grove's a goddamn goldmine. Where is he?"

"Doing his rounds."

"He comes back, tell him I've got a buyer waiting on him."

Chub peered through a crack in the box, watching Mr. Sanderson get back in his car and drive off. He twisted a stick, boring a peephole through the cardboard, then another.

"Chub?" He hadn't heard his mom's truck, but there it was in the yard now. She frowned. "Where's your coat?"

"Inside."

"Go get it, please."

When he came back, his mom was talking to Aunt Enid, who stood admiring her stacking job.

"You're just going to burn it," his mom said.

"So? You see it, Chub?" Aunt Enid asked.

He stared at the wall of wood. At first, he saw nothing, then two light circles with brown cores, two big eyes staring out.

"It's an owl." Chub walked toward it, the face disappearing as he got close.

"See?" Aunt Enid smiled. "You heard Last Chance slid out?"

"Again?" his mom asked.

"Worse than last time. All that rain."

"That whole road is going," his mom said.

Chub pushed his jacket onto the truck seat and climbed in after it. "Where are we going?"

"Home," she said. "Where else would we go?"

*February 5*

# COLLEEN

She flipped it back and forth in her mind, watching Rich work through his eggs. His cheaters slid down to the end of his nose.

MASSACRE AT DAMNATION GROVE! the newspaper headline shouted, photo of an old-growth tree busted into pieces taking up half the front page.

"Unknown vandals," Rich announced, skimming Merle's quotes. "'*We've been trying to do this the right way, following the laws. We've had to let a lot of guys go, waiting. I guess somebody got tired of it.*'"

Rich cleared his throat.

"*Two human skulls whose discovery in Upper Damnation Grove last fall halted two proposed timber harvest plans have been determined to have originated from another location. The skulls, locals speculate, may have been planted to delay the contested harvest of old-growth redwoods in one of the largest remaining unprotected virgin stands in the area, near Del Norte Coast Redwoods State Park.*"

Rich took off his cheaters. It had poured for days. Their creek line had stopped running and now their tank was nearly empty. Rich said part of the lower grove had slid out—with the trees down and the ground torn up, there was nothing left to hold the dirt in place—and Damnation Creek was backed up. It would take weeks for it to get itself flowing again. If they wanted running water, they'd have to clear the mud themselves.

"Eugene's poaching burls." There, she'd said it.

"About the one thing he could poach." Rich smeared a potato around in yolk.

"I'm serious. Chub saw him. Plus there must be fifty cords of firewood. He's just helping himself."

Rich shook his head, like he didn't believe her.

"There's a new washer-dryer," she said. "And a new TV."

"Maybe they got them on credit."

"What credit? Rich, he could go to jail."

She'd thought she'd feel better once she told him, but she felt worse.

*You've only got one sister*, Mom used to say when she and Enid fought. *Both of you. Remember that.*

"It keeps raining, we'll need a backhoe," Rich said, setting his plate in the sink.

Colleen slid sandwiches into a canvas bag. Rich carried the shovels and both sets of waders. Scout, let loose, rocketed up the path. Chub slipped his hand into hers.

*I. Love. You*, she squeezed.

When they crested 24-7 Ridge, Colleen gasped. The steep slope of the lower grove, company timber a mess of giant pickup sticks, had slid out into the creek, damming it just upstream of their intake pipe. Water had backed up into a brown lake, runoff slapping the surface like faucets running into a tub.

"Looks worse than it is," Rich said. "We cut a channel, gravity will take care of the rest."

"What happened?" Chub asked.

"Just water being water." Rich started down, sidestepping. Chub ran ahead.

"Chub, no running with sticks," Colleen called.

Chub stopped at the edge, watching Scout wade in to his belly.

"How deep is it?" she asked.

Rich got his waders on. "I guess we'll find out."

There was a divot in hers, where Rich had patched the hole.

"Chub, you're our lookout," Rich said. "Climb on up there."

Chub scrambled back up the ridge-side to a rock outcropping.

"Farther," Rich called. "Good. Now, when the water starts pouring, you shout, okay? Call Scout."

"Scou-out."

Scout raised his head from a decomposing salmon carcass and shot uphill.

"Hang on to him."

Rich walked out onto the exposed gravel bed, slung the point of his shovel into the wall of the mud dam. Colleen looked back at Chub, perched on the hill, holding Scout's collar.

"You're sure it's done?" she asked.

"Hasn't moved in two days."

"Rich——"

"Go up there and spot me, will you?"

Colleen leaned her shovel against a tree and clambered uphill. He speared the shovel's point into the mud. For a while he seemed to make no progress, sinking it, pulling it toward him, until finally he broke through. The lake poured out at his feet like water from a pitcher.

Chub yelled.

Rich raised his shovel in both hands.

"Rich!" she shouted. But it was too late.

Brown water swept him off his feet. He pushed up, still holding the shovel. For a moment, it was almost funny. Then, the mud: thick as wet cement, loud as a train.

"Rich!"

He went under, came up, and then he was gone, mudflow rounding the bend, out of sight. She screamed his name. Scout twisted loose, bounded up over the ridge. She swept Chub up and ran, struggling in the heavy waders. Chub's body thumped her chest. Mud and snapped trees had lodged in the bottleneck of the gulch, forming a makeshift dam. Scout was down there, barking at the mess.

"Rich!" She stumbled. Scout launched himself into the muck.

"Scout!" Chub screamed.

She hugged his face to her so he wouldn't see Scout struggle, turning as though to paddle for shore, sinking, doubling back, clawing in circles, digging his own grave.

"Rich! Ri-ich!"

She tried to pray. *Please, God. Please. God.*

A head shot up from the hole.

"Rich?!"

Scout clawed toward the bank, Rich dragging himself after him, vomiting. Chub slid down her side and she ran. Rich stumbled twenty feet and sank to the ground, scraping mud from his mouth. She dropped to her knees, grabbing his face with both hands. His shirt was torn, waders gone, one foot bare, eyes bloodred.

"I thought—"

Rich coughed, turned his head and spat.

"Daddy?" Chub's small voice asked behind her.

Rich raised an arm and Chub slammed into them both. When Rich was finally okay to stand, he looked down at his bare foot.

"Damn waders almost killed me," he said, voice scraped raw.

She squeezed his hand tighter. Three warm pulses. Scout snorted, pawing at his nose.

"I'd still be under there," Rich said, mussing the dog's filthy fur and staring down at the mudflow, as though part of him still was.

*February 9*

# RICH

Eugene loaded the shingles into the truck himself. About all Rich could do was limp the empty cart back to the front of the hardware store.

"How many lives you got left?" Eugene asked when Rich climbed into the passenger seat.

Rich sniffed, nose leaking. Nothing broken, but banged up pretty good. Rocks had played his ribs like a piano. Rich could still hear it, grinding, churning, like he'd fallen into a cement mixer. Mud was no joke.

When they got back to Fort Eugene, piles of cordwood sat out in the rain. Eugene turned the truck off.

"That's a lot of wood," Rich observed.

"You're telling me." Eugene rubbed his shoulder. "Thirty-five bucks a cord, fifty delivered."

"Does Merle know?"

"Know what?" Eugene asked. "That I'm hauling this shit out of the way? He ought to be thanking me."

"It's company property," Rich said.

"If I want to use my truck and my time, I don't see what the hell Merle has to say about it."

"If you were just using it around here, that'd be one thing. Soon as money's involved—"

"It's just a little burnwood. What do you care, anyway? You've got your own deal."

"Look, all I'm saying is, if Merle's going to hear about it, you want it to be from you."

"I can handle Merle."

Eugene got out and hoisted the shingles from the truck bed. Rich followed him inside. The buckets in the hall were an inch from full. Colleen got Chub's coat on.

"What's the rush?" Eugene asked. "Stay awhile."

Colleen flared her nostrils. Rich tipped his head. *A half hour.* She released Chub, who slipped away down the hall. She hadn't spoken to Eugene since that night on the road. Rich snuffed his nose on his kerchief. Colleen wormed her way in beside Enid, took over cutting onions.

"You getting free garlic now, Colleen?" Eugene needled her.

"Cut it out," Enid said.

Colleen tossed a handful of onions into the pan, an angry sizzle.

"Hell, newspaper ought to do a story on how ugly that bitch——"

Colleen spun around, onion knife in hand.

"Whoa now." Eugene spilled his coffee. "Gundersen, control your damn wife before she guts somebody."

"Cool it," Enid said. "Both of you."

"She's acting crazy."

"You stop baiting her and she'll calm down." Enid looked to Rich for confirmation. Blood leaked from one of Colleen's nostrils. "Cripes." Enid reached for a rag.

"Maybe we should get going," Rich suggested.

Colleen pulled the bloody rag away, pressed it back. "You came to fix the roof, fix it."

It was dark when they finished, but at least the rain had let up. The trailer house smelled of stroganoff.

"Didn't turn out half-bad," Enid said, handing Rich a plate.

In the truck, Chub took Colleen's hand. Rich saw him squeezing, spelling out a message Colleen didn't seem to hear.

*February 19*

# COLLEEN

"Why wouldn't we let him go?" Colleen asked, whisking cocoa into the milk pot.

The invitation sat on the table, Helen and Carl's address torn in half where Chub had ripped open the envelope in excitement. Rich picked at Chub's sandwich crusts, studying the spread-out timber-survey map. The scratches on his face had scabbed, one eye still bloodshot. Usually she liked how a beard looked on him, but there was something unsettling about this one: dense, woolly.

She whisked faster, raising brown foam. Rich sighed, picked up his coffee and took a swig. The top corner of the map curled where the mug had been holding it flat. The color, that's what it was—his beard was dark, making the gray in his hair stand out, a contrast that made him look, suddenly, old.

Rich drained his coffee, moved the saltshaker and the pliers off the map. It snapped into a roll. "You keep stirring that, you'll get butter."

She stopped. "I don't want us being part of it." The eggs, the tires. The way the other mothers parted around Helen, as though she stank.

"You bring Chub over there, we're part of it, whether you want us to be or not."

"It's just a birthday party. Anyway, it's not 'til next month." She turned the burner off. "It's not right, going after them like this." She dug a spoon into the sugar bag. "Chub! Cocoa!"

"I'm not saying it's right," Rich said.

Chub slid into the kitchen in sock feet. She set the mug in front of him. "Be careful, it's hot."

"Let's just stay out of it." Rich pushed back in his chair, rising stiffly.

"Out of what?" Chub asked.

Rich bopped him on the head with the rolled-up map. "I'm going to get cleaned up."

"Luke's having a treasure hunt!" Chub said.

"He is?" Colleen asked, loud enough for Rich to hear down the hall.

Chub blew a dip into the surface of his cocoa, slurped, sucked air. "Hot."

She scrubbed scalded milk off the pot, as though she could scrape her irritation away with it.

"Go get your binoculars," she told Chub. "Let's give your cocoa time to cool."

"Where are you going?" Rich asked, ducking out of the bathroom, towel around his waist.

"To look for whales."

"Now?" His hair, wet, was almost as dark as his beard.

"We'll be back," Colleen said.

She squeezed Chub's hand.

*I. Love. You.*

*How. Much?*

*Thiiis. Much.*

They crossed the road to the steep, rocky path hairpinning down to Diving Board Rock. She stood beside Chub while he surveyed the waves.

"See any?" she asked.

"No."

Wind whipped her hair. She raised her arms, sleeves flapping, chop crashing below. She revved her engine, tilted her wings, chasing Chub back up the path home.

"Ready?" Rich asked when they came in.

Chub barreled into him. "Ready!"

Rich groaned, jaw pink. He smelled of soap and aftershave. He eyed Colleen, shy, a look from before Chub, before they were married even, when he'd done something he'd hoped would please her—stuck a few rhododendron blossoms in an empty Coke bottle, snuck a spring-loaded wooden frog he'd carved beneath an upside-down mug, shaved off his winter beard.

The community center's lot was crammed, deep enough into the no-work rainy season that nobody could afford to turn up his nose at a free fish fry.

"You made it," Dot said, tearing three blue tickets off the wheel.

Colleen steered Chub toward Enid and the kids' table near the end of the buffet line. A burst of laughter erupted from the knot of men playing darts with Eugene. He tossed back a shot.

"Idle hands," Enid said.

"Doesn't he work tomorrow?" Colleen helped Chub out of his coat.

Enid rolled her eyes. "Try telling him that."

Colleen took Chub through the line, sat heavily. Chub nibbled breading off his fish sticks. A dial went down on the room's volume. Colleen turned and saw Helen at the ticket table with Luke, Carl a step behind, cap pulled low.

"Some people," Enid said.

Colleen bristled. "They've suffered enough."

"I'd say they got off pretty easy," Enid replied. "She's still got her job. Merle could have called the crab plant. Plenty of people have lost their shirts over a lot less."

Chub spotted Luke and started to slide off the bench.

"Finish eating first, please," Colleen said.

Rich tucked in beside her.

"Merle was looking for you," Enid said. Rich gave a little nod but didn't lift his eyes. Colleen watched Helen and Carl go through the buffet line and choose an empty table in the corner.

"I'm done." Chub pushed away his plate. "Now can I?"

Colleen watched him scurry past his cousins and tumble into Luke, their thumbs already warring.

"Imagine trying to make money off something like that." Enid snorted.

"I don't think it's about money," Colleen said.

"'Course it's about money. They want Sanderson to pay them off because of that baby."

Rich stubbed a fry into a puddle of tartar sauce.

"They should leave," Enid said.

"Where are they supposed to go?" Colleen demanded.

Enid and Rich exchanged a look.

"Rich!" Eugene hollered.

"Don't let him bet anything," Enid said.

"I'm more worried about getting a dart in the eye."

"Gundersen!" Eugene bellowed. "Come on, you old geezer."

"He knows how to get me," Rich said.

"'Least you didn't marry him," Enid answered.

Rich pinched a toothpick from his front pocket and got up. Across the room, Helen was gathering her purse, stacking plates. Colleen looked around for an excuse to stand. Enid laid a hand over hers.

"I have to pee," Colleen said, surprised how easily the lie came.

"You can wait one minute."

Colleen looked down at Enid's hand.

"Hey, chickenshit!" The cluster of dart players parted and old red-faced Yancy stood in the center, swaying drunk, yelling at his son, Carl helping Helen into her coat. "Where you going?"

Helen took Carl's arm.

"She got a leash around your neck?" Yancy demanded.

Colleen saw Carl bite the inside of his bottom lip. In high school, Helen said he'd drawn blood to keep from talking back.

"What's the matter? That fucking squaw cut your balls off and serve them to you for breakfast? No wonder that baby came out empty-headed."

"Carl, let's go," Helen said, taking Luke by the hand, as though the man following them were just some old drunkard, not Luke's grandfather, a man so hate-filled he'd shown up at Carl's wedding simply to spit in Helen's face.

"Yeah, Carl. Let your little wifey tell you what to do." Old Yancy staggered after them, knocking over cups.

"Yancy, lay off." Lew stepped in front of him, belly out, like the tired bus-driving logger he was, jokeless for the first time Colleen could remember.

"Mama?" Chub asked, his chin wrinkling.

"Christ." Enid released Colleen's hand and thrust a napkin at her. "She's okay," Enid assured Chub. "She's been picking her nose, that's all."

Colleen licked her lip. Salt. Tinfoil.

"That's what happens when you stick your finger up where it doesn't belong," Enid said. "Remember that."

# RICH

Whitey set Rich's caulk boots on the counter. They sat half an inch higher with the new spikes.

"What's the damage?" Rich asked.

"Twelve, plus this." Whitey lifted the roll of chain onto the counter.

Rich thumbed through his wallet.

Whitey jutted his chin at the caulks. "Was about ready to put them in the case."

"Had to wait on that slide to get cleared again."

"How's she look?"

Rich shrugged. "Wouldn't pull over long enough to piss."

"Law says I can sell a dead man's boots."

"Still got a few lives left in me."

Whitey snorted, punched numbers into the register.

"Looks like they're going to get it," Whitey said.

"Get what?" Rich asked.

"Park expansion. Down south, Redwood Creek." Whitey blinked behind his thick glasses.

"Better there than here," Rich said.

The door whooshed open.

"Charge him double." Eugene stomped his boots, flicked rain off his collar. "He's got his own racket now, didn't you hear?"

Whitey pushed the drawer closed; it dinged.

Eugene came to the counter, hefted the roll of chain, groaned. "You planning a clear-cut?"

"You need something?" Rich asked.

"Nah. Saw your horse," Eugene said. "Come on, let me buy you a beer."

Whitey butted through the saloon doors, leaving them alone.

"Little early to start drinking," Rich said.

"Since when's a beer drinking?"

Eugene tailed him over to the Widowmaker, Rich fighting the urge to peel off, lose him.

The Widowmaker was dim, windowless. Randy drew their beers. A lot of years since Rich was last in here. He'd watched the tsunami from the roof back in '64, wave lifting the dock, splitting it like a graham cracker, fishing boats bobbing: plastic toys in a bath.

"Where's Mabel?" Eugene asked.

"Hairdresser," Randy said. Never one to waste a word. Pushing eighty, but kept himself in shape.

Eugene drained half his beer and sighed, satisfied. Rich fingered his glass, took a pull, cold shooting up the root. The TV murmured, Randy leaning on the bar watching it, rubbing absent circles into the old lacquered burl.

"You ready?" Eugene asked.

"For what?" Rich asked.

"Next week. Those sonsabitches want to put us out on our asses, they're going to have to look us in the eye first. You thought about what you're going to say?"

Rich shrugged.

"Better get a handle on Colleen. Remind her who she's married to." Eugene slid his beer off the paper coaster.

"You don't have to worry about Colleen."

"*I* don't." Eugene downed his beer, set the empty glass on the bar. "Randy, you got a pen?"

Randy pulled one from his front pocket.

"Buddy of mine seen her talking with this guy. Said they looked pretty cozy." Eugene scribbled Dolores's son's name—*Daniel Bywater*—and a phone number onto the coaster. "I'd tell the asshole to stay the hell away from my wife. Show him an old lion can still roar." Eugene pulled his cap down, pushed out the door.

Rich slid a thumb up the side of his beer. He'd let that guy into the house, seen right away there was history there. The back-room door swung open and

Merle came out with the park super—clean-cut, upright, almost military in his government tan-and-greens—the congressman, and a few guys Rich recognized from the state forestry board.

Merle gave Rich a stiff nod, as he might any stranger. "See you, Randy," he said, and followed the other men out.

"What's that about?" Rich asked once they were gone.

Randy shrugged, retrieving Eugene's empty. Rich paid for both and nodded for Randy to take his half-full glass too, pushed off his stool.

"You want this?" Randy called after him, holding up the coaster.

Rich looked around at the empty booths—how many paydays had he spent in here, alone, before Colleen?—bar air stale with the dust of all those memories.

"Nope," he said, and ducked out into the rain.

# RICH

Rich swung into the service station, needle bouncing off empty. The attendant stood at the pump in the first bay, filling a black truck, speedboat loaded onto a flatbed.

Rich pulled up behind it, waiting his turn. A smack on his door and there was Merle at his window. Rich rolled it down.

"You putting in?" Rich asked.

"Sold her. Tooth snatcher Astrid married up in Coos Bay. Bought the trailer too. But no hitch on his Mercedes." Merle snorted. "Like selling my damn daughter." The pump clicked and the attendant smacked the gas compartment shut. "Eugene talk to you about next week?"

Rich nodded.

"Good. I knew we could count on you, Rich."

Pete pulled in, idled, waiting for a pump. Merle looked over his shoulder, a ripple of distaste passing over his face, as though, after all these years, he was still jealous of Pete. It was Pete who'd ridden shotgun with Virgil, headed up to check out some new piece of machinery. Pete who could take an engine apart and put it back together in the time it took the salesman to run through his pitch.

"What's the guy's name?" Rich asked, lifting his chin at the boat.

"Langley." Merle made his way back to the truck, heavy torso thrust forward like a toad walking upright, the name jangling like a key on the ring of Rich's memory. The boat lurched as Merle pulled away. Rich rolled up to the pump.

"Fill her," he told the attendant, and headed in to settle up.

"He after you about that hearing?" Pete asked when Rich came back out. "Going at it ass-backwards. It's the women he should be talking to." Pete looked past Rich, over his shoulder. "Woman'll lift a car if her kid's under it."

"You think there's something to these sprays?" Rich asked.

"I don't got kids," Pete said. "But if I did, they wouldn't be drinking out of no creek."

# COLLEEN

Colleen dug at the cornflake cemented to Enid's kitchen table. The raccoons had gotten into the trash again, rib cage of a roast chicken strewn across the yard.

"You ready for tomorrow?" Enid asked.

"I wish everybody would stop talking about it," Colleen said. She knew Rich was worried about the hearing too.

"You've got a dog in this fight now, don't pretend like you don't. I don't know much, but I know Rich didn't buy seven hundred acres flat out."

"How long has Eugene been poaching burls out of Damnation Grove?" Colleen shot back. Enid ran water over the dishes, as though she might wash them. "Enid."

Enid clattered plates. "What?"

"You have to make him stop."

"I can't make him do anything," Enid said.

"It's not worth it. It might seem like it is, but it's not. It's not right."

"How would you know?" Enid snapped. "When have you ever done anything wrong?"

"Enid—"

"You think Marla didn't tell me she saw you with him?"

Colleen's heart skipped, blood beating in her cheeks.

"With who?" She asked, fighting to contain her panic.

Enid crossed her arms.

Colleen's lungs tightened. "Does Eugene know?"

"Now, why would I tell Eugene? You know secrets just burn a hole in his pocket." Enid watched Colleen squirm. "You only get one life, huh?"

Colleen looked down at her hands, tugged at her wedding band. "It's not like that. I wasn't—it didn't—"

"Look, it's none of my business, Colleen. You live your life, me and Eugene, we'll live ours, okay? Just don't act like you're better than us."

"I'm not—" Colleen pushed a long breath out her nose. "You're not going to tell Rich?"

"If I was, I would have done it already," Enid said.

Colleen swallowed. "Thank you."

Enid shrugged. "You're my sister."

# CHUB

His mom's cold hand tugged him through the chanting signs. It was crowded inside too, rain rolling off slickers, cold air gusting in every time someone pushed through the doors, dads flipping their coat collars, moms lowering newspapers tented over their heads cautiously, like it might still be raining inside.

Uncle Eugene shrugged off the chill. "Fill a glass faster than you could pour one out there." He lifted the bill of his cap, then tugged it back down. His coat cuffs were frayed, like a cat had chewed them. "Hell of a turnout."

Chub's dad stood extra straight, like he didn't want to wrinkle the shirt his mom had ironed while he'd hunched in front of the mirror, trimming his mustache. Chub tugged at his dad's pant leg and his dad lifted him up.

"There's Merle." Uncle Eugene tapped a paper against his dad's front and shouldered away.

His dad unfolded the paper, scowled—he needed his cheaters—and tucked it into his front pocket. The doors opened—cold air, shouting.

"When is this thing going to start?" Aunt Enid asked, leaning to wipe something off Agnes's chin. Chub bounced his leg, but his dad didn't let him down.

Doors opened to a big room filled with folding chairs. They found seats. His mom pulled him into her lap. Up front, men sat behind a long table. Mr. Sanderson and his wife sat in the front row, wearing matching yellow outfits.

"Quiet down." A man read from a paper. "The goal today is to hear public comment on proposed Timber Harvest Plan 6817-1977 for Upper Damnation Grove, a six-hundred-forty-acre private inholding to which Sanderson Timber Company holds title, and Timber Harvest Plan 6818-1977 for Lower Damnation Grove, a six-hundred-forty-acre private inholding to which Sanderson Timber Company holds title, both located in Del Norte County."

"'Nortay,'" someone mocked him from the row behind them. "It's Del Nort. E's silent, asshole."

People lined up behind a microphone. Some shouted, some read slowly from papers. A man and a woman with long wavy gray hair took turns leaning in, telling a magical story.

"Imagine," the man said. "Two hundred years ago."

"This whole coast was covered in old-growth redwood groves," the woman continued, waving her hand through the air. "Murrelets nested in the treetops. Tailed frogs and spotted salamanders lived along the creeks. Every year the salmon returned to spawn."

"We've destroyed ninety percent of that old-growth," the man cut in. "We've chopped down the trees and sprayed the forest with chemicals."

"And all that's left," the woman explained, "is a tiny fraction, land private citizens banded together to buy and protect, land that became state parks. Damnation Grove is one of the last pockets of untouched primordial forest left in this part of California. It has giants three hundred and fifty feet tall, taller than the Statue of Liberty, grand as anything you'll find in the national park. But now"—she paused—"the greedy hands of industry are sharpening their saws, preparing to sacrifice these ancient living beings on the altar of capitalism."

"Trees a thousand years old," the man said. "They were here when Rome fell. When Columbus landed in America. They've weathered fires and floods and tsunamis."

"And they're still here," the woman marveled. "Noble. Strong. And we, all of us here today, we have the chance to save them."

"We might not agree on much," the man said. "But I think we agree we can't stop gravity. Water runs downhill. Look what happened in the lower section, where the biggest trees were, after it was vandalized—"

People grumbled. In the seat next to him, Chub's dad lifted one foot off the ground, then the other, as though freeing them from sucking mud.

"That's right," the man continued. "A mudslide, all those gravel beds where the silver salmon have spawned since time immemorial—washed away. There won't be another run this year, or next, or the year after that. If you tear up the rest of this grove, more silt will run off into the creeks. Frogs won't be able to live, salmon eggs will suffocate, murrelets will circle and circle, searching for a place to nest."

"Keep your damn birds," somebody called out.

"Let somebody else talk already," another voice yelled. People stood up, booing.

The man and the woman raised their voices in song. Mr. Miller came up behind them, took his handkerchief from his pocket, and wiped off the microphone.

"Don't want to catch what they have," he said. People laughed. He looked around the room, his black eyebrows raised so they almost touched his white hair. "My name is Lew Miller. I've been a yarder operator for twenty-some years. I started out setting chokers, same as everybody else. Roughest work, lowest paid. I worked with a lot of guys you see here today, and some you don't. They worked hard and when their number came up, it came up." Mr. Miller put his chin to his chest for a moment, out of respect. "We might seem simple to you. And I guess, in a way, that's true. We believe a man ought to have the right to work for a living. If your family's hungry, you work. We've always done that, around here. Then you people come in"—he gestured at the longhaired singers—"start nosing around, trying to blame this or that. Well, I got news for you. We didn't have no problems around here 'til you people showed up. Hell, they spray right over us when we're working and you don't see us complaining. I'm not afraid of some weed juice. I support the timber harvest plans." People clapped.

Mr. Porter came next. "Most people"—he brushed the wart under his eye, like he could flick it off his face—"when they look at a redwood board in the hardware store, all they see is a good piece of lumber. They see a picnic table, a deck, or a fence that'll hold up. They don't see the blood and the sweat. They don't see getting up at four in the morning, working in the cold and the rain, fingers so locked up it's hard to press 'em straight at the end of the day. They don't see the cuts and the bruises, the broken bones, the mother's tears when a guy like Tom Feeley—remember Tom?—a good guy, a family guy, gets up one morning and goes to work and never comes home. We've got Tom's son working with us now. Quentin, where are you at?"

Across the aisle, a skinny man shifted in his seat.

"Guys like Quentin and me, we risk our lives every day so that people can go to the store and buy their fence, or their deck, or what have you. And we're proud of that."

Chub squirmed in his mom's lap and she held him tighter.

"These woods aren't just a place we work," Mr. Porter said. "They're our playground. They're our pantry." Mr. Porter patted his big belly. "My wife makes a mean blackberry pie, if you haven't noticed. We care about this place. We take care of it. And we support the timber harvest plans."

People clapped. Uncle Eugene strode up to the microphone next, like the clapping was for him.

"You all work in offices?" Uncle Eugene asked the men behind the long table up front. "Well, let me tell you about my office. It ain't got no desk. No chair either. It ain't even got a door, but it opens at five a.m. Some days it don't close until dark. Summer, you might work 'til seven, eight, nine in the evening. You work, you go home, you sleep, you get up and do it again. You don't got a choice. You've got half a dozen other guys depending on you. No such thing as calling in sick. If you can walk, you can work. I got six kids at home, five of them girls, and they're depending on me too. Their dad never finished school, but you take a good look at them—Marla, Agnes, Mavis, Gertrude, stand up there, let them see you."

Heads turned, and Chub saw Marla, looking sick to her stomach, baby Alsea on her hip.

"Those girls are going to graduate high school," Uncle Eugene went on. "Every last one of them. And it's one logging job paying for all that. Every old-growth redwood tree we lay down, that's enough timber to build how many houses? We're contributing to society. We're paying our taxes. We're following the rules, no matter how fast they keep changing them. Please." Uncle Eugene took off his hat and held it to his chest. "These groves might not seem like much to you, but to these girls, they're everything. It's their future. Don't take it away from them."

"Thank you," the man said from up front, nodding once at Uncle Eugene. The singers started again.

"You people don't want to listen," someone complained. "This right here, this is opportunity. This is the American dream."

"You can't have your cake and eat it too," a man shouted from the back. "You want to cut it and *then* sell the land to the park. It's all money, money, money."

"Bullshit."

"It's true," the man insisted.

There was a tussle. A chair fell back, cracking against the floor.

"Back off," someone said. "Harvey! Where's Harvey?"

A woman stood up. "Where do you think toilet paper comes from?" she asked. "What would people like you wipe your asses with if it wasn't for people like us?"

An old man raised his cane in the air. "You bunch of freeloaders go chain your skinny asses anywhere you want, from a Mexican cactus to a Canada goose, but not here."

Suddenly, Luke's mom's voice boomed from the microphone.

"Good morning. My name is Helen Yancy." The microphone squealed and Luke's mom tilted her head back, until it quieted. "My husband, Carl, drove a spray truck for Sanderson for fourteen years, until they fired him. We had a baby in November. Eamon Paul. I was in labor eleven hours with him and when he came out, the top of his skull was missing. All these people here, they know. They came to see, like he was a circus animal. He came too." She pointed to Mr. Sanderson in his bright yellow shirt. "He brought us this." She held up an envelope. "He sat at our kitchen table and said he was sorry for our loss. Sorry. We can all see there's hardly any fish left in our river. Maybe that's the dams, I don't know. Maybe it's logging, or ocean fishing. Or maybe the sprays are killing the fish. Are they making us sick too? Are they giving people cancer? Are they eating the brains out of our babies' heads? You're all thinking it, but no one has the guts to ask." She looked around the room, pushed air out her nose. "Whoever said you can't buy loyalty never spent a day in Sanderson country. Well, you can keep your money." She dumped bills from the envelope onto the floor. Chub's mom hugged him tighter. "I may have buried my son, but his memory isn't for sale."

Luke's mom pushed up the aisle and out the doors. People whispered. Chub leaned back against his mom's chest. Man after man went to the microphone. Chub yawned. He kicked his feet until his mom touched his knee to make him stop. He arched his neck back over her shoulder and stared at the ceiling, imagining what it would be like to walk on it like it was the floor. He wished everyone would stop talking, so it could be over.

Then, at last, came his dad's voice, echoey and strange. His dad tried to adjust the microphone, but it wouldn't go high enough, so he hunched down and started over.

"My name is Richard Gundersen. My old man was Hank Gundersen. He started setting chokers for Sanderson at thirteen. That was back in 1916." Chub's dad dug two fingers into his collar and looked down at the paper in his hand. "His granddad was a high-climber, homesteaded up on the bluff above Diving Board Rock, back when the old wagon road went that way. His son, my granddad, ended up a high-climber too. Died climbing. So did my dad. I'm the fourth generation. I've been topping old-growth since I was eighteen. Seen a lot of timber. This grove, it's not like some of the big ones we worked. Those are all gone, except for what's park." Men nodded in their seats. His dad cleared his throat. "We've all got families. I got a wife and a son—they're sitting right there." Chub felt his mom shift. Heads turned their direction. "But you shut down that grove, it's not just us you're hurting. This town lives off timber. You might as well line us up against the wall." His dad folded the paper back up, tucked it into his chest pocket.

"Maybe there's some truth to what they're saying. Maybe the sprays are killing off some of the fish or the deer, I don't know. When you lose someone, you look around for something to blame, that's just human nature." His dad looked at his mom. "Especially a baby, who never got a chance at life. I understand that. But let's not confuse things here. I've lived in Klamath my whole life, never set foot more than a hundred miles from right here where I'm standing now talking to you, spent a good chunk of it up these sides. I've drunk out of these creeks for fifty years and never been sick a day of my life, except maybe once or twice, but that wasn't creek water I'd been drinking." People chuckled.

"It might not be popular to say, but I'm glad the government saved some big timber for a park. It's something to see. Ask any of these guys. You won't find a guy that loves the woods more than a logger. You scratch a logger, you better believe you'll find an 'enviro-mentalist' underneath. But the difference between us and these people is we live here. We hunt. We fish. We camp out. They'll go back where they came from, but we'll wake up right here tomorrow. This is home. Timber puts food on our tables, clothes on our kids' backs. You know, a redwood tree is a hard thing to kill. You cut it down, it sends up a shoot. Even fire doesn't kill it. But those big pumpkins up in the grove, they're old. Ready to keel over and rot. You might as well set a pile of money on fire and make us watch."

"That's right," someone called.

"It's not easy to make a living around here. We don't live fancy. But you grow up in redwood country, you learn how to make something out of nothing. We know how to feed our families. All we're asking is you let us do that."

His dad came back and sat down. Noise rose in the room.

"My name is George Bywater." An old man stood at the microphone. "My father—Lester Bywater, some of you knew him—he worked at the mill, pulling green chain. We're Klamath River people. First you killed us. Next you killed the salmon. And now you're killing yourselves." The old man's voice rose. "When you poison the land, you're poisoning your own body. The salmon come home to the river every year and you people, you don't give thanks. To you, salmon, that's just money, it's economics. Well, our people have been eating out of this river longer than it took these trees to grow. We've been eating the same runs of salmon for so many generations, our DNA is intertwined. We're part of the salmon and the salmon are part of us. Everything we have, it comes from the river. When the river's sick, we're sick, we're part of that too. You disturb a burial site, you don't care. You don't see us digging up your cemeteries, sending your grandma's head off to some museum."

"Those skulls didn't come from here!" Uncle Eugene yelled. "Read the newspaper!"

"No," the old man agreed. "Somebody dug them up and put them there." The man cast a long hard stare at Uncle Eugene. "You see, even our ancestors' bones aren't safe from you." Slowly, the man turned back to face front. "Yurok people, we've lived right here, along this river, for a hundred generations— longer, even—and we're still here. You hear about all these tribes that got moved off their land—but not us. Our reservation is right here: a mile on either side for forty-five miles up from the mouth of the Klamath River, that's Yurok Country. A lot of that land's been sold off now, but we still have our fishing rights. We're responsible for our river, for taking care of it. We've always been here. We've always been fishers. Always, always. It's like breathing air. If I can't fish, I can't live. My grandfather taught me that. Just like his grandfather taught him. I've had my nets seized by the game wardens. I've fished at night. I've been beat up, for fishing. I've been thrown in jail, for fishing. I've gone to the court in Washington D.C.—I've seen your Capitol Building, it's nothing compared to a redwood—it's just a little shrimpy, middle-sized tree." The man held his hand up chest-high, measuring. "The court said it: this is the Yurok reservation. This is Indian Country; we can fish. And still you're trying to find ways to keep us from breathing, from living our life here, caring for our river." The man crossed his arms. "I'm old now. My kids are grown. But if it was me, if it was my kids being born without brains in their heads, I'd be asking myself: Is it worth it? Just to get out the cut? But no, you won't rest until you've killed off every deer, every salmon, every tree, until you've poisoned all our springs. What will you eat then? Money? What will you build your house from? What will you drink when you're thirsting?" The old man looked around, as though waiting for someone to answer, but the room was quiet. He said something in another language, then turned and walked out, the door swinging shut behind him.

The man up front thanked people for their time.

"Wait." The man who had found Scout on the road stood at the microphone.

"We're done for today, son."

"My name's Daniel Bywater." The microphone gave a high electric whine. "I'm an enrolled member of the Yurok Tribe."

"Okay, but you're the last one."

Chub felt his mom's body tense.

"The herbicides Sanderson Timber is using to clear broad-leafed plants are toxic," the man's voice boomed. "The Forest Service is spraying them too, and the county. You've got healthy people getting sick, animals dying. You've got miscarriages, cancers. A lot of people right here in this room have suffered. We've got a petition here you can sign." He held up a clipboard and read from it. "'We, the undersigned, ask that the area known as Damnation Grove be preserved forever, free from chemical sprays that endanger our lives and the lives of the unborn.'" Boos skipped across the room. "Just ask Colleen Gundersen over there, she's seen what these poisons can do." The man held up a glass jar. "This is water from her tap. She collected it, and we had it tested. If you drink from a creek, and that creek runs downhill through sprayed land, I've got news for you: you're drinking this stuff. Ask Colleen how many birth defects she's seen, right here in this community. How many babies born sick, born deformed. Ask her how many miscarriages she's suffered herself, drinking this water."

Chub's mom dumped him from her lap. The man examined the jar. "It looks clean. Sure, it *looks* clean. But what is it doing to us? And how long will it take until you see it in your own house, in your body, in your kids?"

"Hey, buddy. You're done," a man with a beard said, coming up the aisle.

He shoved him away from the microphone, glass jar shattering, water mixing with a bright red worm of blood.

"Hey now, let's not—" a man said from the front, but it was too loud, everyone out of their seats, Chub's mom dragging him by the hand, adults crushing him.

"We'll bury you!" someone yelled.

"You tell 'em, Rich." A man shook his dad's hand, another clapped him on the shoulder, but others parted, staring.

When they got in the truck, the air felt tight. His dad shook his head.

"Goddamn it, Colleen." So quiet he might have been talking to himself.

"I told you," his mom said. "I knew something wasn't right."

"You don't know that."

"Weren't you listening?" his mom asked.

Chub reached for her hand, but she snatched it away. His dad started the truck.

"I've lost eight, Rich. Not one, not two, not five. Eight." Her voice trembled. "Don't you tell me what I don't know."

# RICH

Eugene's rust-shot Cheyenne was splayed crossways, gravel torn up where he must have hooked left just in time to avoid plowing through their front door. Eugene himself leaned back against a porch post, cords of his neck taut. Twenty-four hours gone by and still mad enough to kick over the wheelbarrow, judging by the arc of scattered firewood. Rich killed the engine and Eugene pushed off, bounce in his step. Colleen put an arm out in front of Chub, as though to shield him. Scout bayed from around back.

"Here we go," Rich said.

They'd steered clear of Eugene yesterday, churned out with the crowd. Rich had felt all right once they'd hit Crescent City, put some distance behind them. They'd wandered the supermarket aisles, Chub's fingers hooked through the side of the basket.

*Only the finest,* Rich had said, selecting a lemon pie. Chub had chosen a jar of fake cherries, sensing the normal rules had been suspended. It was better to be in a public place, Rich angry enough to clear a shelf with the sweep of his arm if he gave in to it. Colleen had walked ahead of him down the aisles, as she'd walked behind his back all these months. He'd waited for her to turn, to admit she still blamed him for the baby. To accuse him of being nothing but a bystander, a dumb witness to her grief. To say he didn't know what it was to lose a baby because he hadn't carried their little girl in his body, felt her move, because he'd gone on while some part of Colleen had stayed behind, trapped in that hospital room, feeling the warmth of her body heat on the child's skin cool, as if that tiny heart might incubate, because what was hope but belief, no matter how rare the miracle?

They'd gotten up early this morning and driven to the picnic spot on the Smith River, but the rain hadn't quit and they'd ended up huddled in the truck with the blower on. Now Rich wanted to get inside, get the fire going, but here was Eugene, worse for having stewed a day.

"What do you think?" Colleen asked, Eugene already at Rich's window, so close Rich could bash him in the kneecaps by opening his door. Eugene stormed around to Colleen's side.

"Just get in the house." Rich popped his door and went around, waiting for Eugene to back off enough for Colleen to get out, then putting himself between them. It felt good to protect her. Here, in the face of Eugene's anger, he could put his own aside. "What's the difference between a Chevy and a golf ball?" Rich asked, buying Colleen time to herd Chub inside. "You can drive a golf ball two hundred yards."

"Whose fucking side are you on, Colleen?" Eugene bumped against Rich's chest, trying to get around him. Rich leaned into him, then pivoted away, let Eugene stumble forward. "You're lucky Merle doesn't fire your ass." Eugene pulled the rolled-up baton of a newspaper from his back pocket and popped Rich in the chest. "You need this worse than any of us."

"They don't have to spray the grove to cut," Rich said. "Brush isn't that thick."

Eugene shook his head. "We're in a war here, don't you get it? They're trying to take it all away." Eugene dragged his fist across his mouth. "Merle'll find someone else, you know. If she doesn't get in line." Eugene jutted his chin at the house, Colleen already inside. "He's already got a climber down in Rio Dell ready to take over."

"I bet he does." Rich didn't bother to strip the bitterness from his voice.

"Look, Gundersen, don't make this hard on yourself. Sanderson gets its cut out, you get yours. Come on." Eugene held up the paper. "This is embarrassing."

There was Chub in the foreground in black and white, Rich and Colleen behind him in the parking lot outside the hearing, the three of them framed in the instant before Rich asked the photographer what the hell she thought she was doing.

"Colleen's messing with your head."

The screen door snapped, as though her name had brought her out.

"Go home, Eugene," she said.

Eugene shook his head. "You're un-fucking-believable. Both of you." He flung the paper at their feet. "You better watch yourselves. You're pissing off a whole lot of people. A whole lot of people." Eugene climbed back in his truck, revved his engine, and peeled off with a spray of gravel.

Inside, Rich dropped the paper onto the kitchen table, nabbed what was left of the pie off the counter. There they were in the caption, if he squinted: *Lifetime Sanderson Timber Co. employee Richard Gundersen, his wife, and his son, whose drinking water is threatened by the proposed Damnation Grove timber harvest plans.*

He scraped his fork across the gummy crust at the bottom of the pan. Colleen leafed through, cleared her throat, and began to read aloud.

*"A recent spate of mudslides, including this winter's Last Chance Slide, which closed Highway 101 north of Klamath for nine days, has sparked debate over the timber industry's slash-and-burn policies. The latest clash came Monday, at a public hearing on Sanderson Timber Co.'s plans to harvest two old-growth parcels known locally as Damnation Grove that drew over two hundred people. The logging heavy-weight employs fifty-eight residents in its mill and logging operations, nearly a tenth of the population in a town without stoplights, a gas station, or even a pay phone—"*

Colleen skimmed the next column.

*"Among those affected by the plan are Richard Gundersen, a fourth-generation high-climber, and his wife. Their land, known as the 24-7 after the diameter of the largest redwood tree on the property, borders the lower section of the disputed grove. Earlier this year, vandals felled several dozen old-growth trees in a section of Lower Damnation Grove, resulting in a mudslide that temporarily dammed Damnation Creek and destroyed important spawning habitat for coho salmon.*

*"'It's common sense,' one former logger said. 'You don't leave something to hold the ground, a whole mountain comes down on your head.'*

*"The sheriff's office is still investigating the incident.*

*"Meanwhile, Gundersen's wife"*—Colleen's voice cracked; she swallowed—*"a midwife, has documented nearly a dozen cases of abnormalities in babies born in the area over the last six years, and has herself suffered several miscarriages, fueling worries that the aerial spraying of herbicides to control weeds may be contaminating local water sources. The couple and their son rely on Lower Damnation Creek, in the harvest area, for their drinking water."*

Colleen skipped ahead, turned the page.

*"The timber harvest plans are expected to be approved next month, with cuts to begin later this spring."*

She pushed up, bashed the percolator into the sink so hard Rich thought it would shatter.

"What?" he asked.

"What do you mean, *what*?" She turned on him.

All the times she'd come home from a birth, carrying her sorrow like a package under her arm. She had a right to be mad at him. He could have stepped back off that porch, let her marry someone younger, someone who might have taken her away from here.

"Mama?" Chub stood in the doorway. "What's wrong?"

"Nothing's wrong." Colleen forced a smile. "Mama's just being silly."

"Why was Uncle Eugene yelling?"

"Oh, you know. He loses his temper sometimes."

"Why?"

"He forgets to count to ten." She stroked Chub's hair. "Could we sell it?" she asked.

"Who'd buy it?" Rich shook his head.

"Sell what?" Chub asked. "Sell what?"

"Celery sticks," Colleen said.

Chub bunched his lips, aware he was being teased, and flitted back down the hall.

"You don't think he'll do anything?" Colleen asked.

"Eugene? Nah." Eugene's temper flared like a match, burned out just as quickly. "What would he do?"

"What about Merle?" she asked.

"I'm not married to Merle," Rich said. He took the pinwheel mint—the first one he'd found on their hill, beside the man's boot print—from his pocket. "Am I?"

She looked down at it, bit her lip. "He asked me to collect some water. Out of our tap." She kept her voice low, not wanting Chub to hear. "So I did."

"Is that all it was?" Rich pressed.

Colleen pushed air out her nose, heat rising on her cheeks, splotching red across her chest. "Are you really asking me that?"

*March 3*

# COLLEEN

They sat down to dinner, the same tomatoes ripening on the table that had been ripening there for days. If she used them up, she couldn't buy more. She'd avoided going anywhere alone—to the store, even into the Beehive for bear claws—but she felt the looks in the drop-off line when she took Chub to school in the morning, and in the afternoons, when she picked him up. Not liar or traitor. *Whore.* Though no one said it to her face.

Across the table, Chub picked at his carrots, mashing one flat with his fork until she told him to go run his bath. She reached to clear Rich's plate.

"Did you?" Rich asked.

"Did I what?"

"Sleep with him."

A relief, in a way. The question had been hanging in the air all week. Water splashed into the tub on the other side of the wall.

"With Daniel?" She laughed, turning on the tap. "We were teenagers." The sink filled.

In eight years of marriage, Rich had never asked. He'd run his hands up her thighs, buried his nose in her belly button. She was his. He didn't need to know who there had been before. Now she saw him slowly retracing his steps, holding the question up to the light bulb of his memory.

"What about since?" he asked.

"Since when?"

"Since whenever he showed up." Rich's voice was level, but she heard him struggling to contain it. Her heart pounded in her ears. Chub chattered through the wall, water slopping.

She nodded.

He pushed up from the table, smacked his palm against the side of the refrigerator. She flinched.

"Only once," she said.

He shoved the fridge again and a ceramic magnet flew off, appliance settling with a heavy metal jostle. The valentine Chub had made her swished to the floor.

*Dear Mama. I hope the day is sunny and you are as pretty as a rose.*

"Damn it, Colleen!" Rich yelled.

She stiffened.

"Mama?" Chub called from the bathroom.

"It's okay, Grahamcracker," Colleen called back.

"What do you mean, once?" Rich demanded, not bothering to lower his voice.

"Shh. It just happened." Colleen shook dishwater off her hands. He was the one who'd refused to touch her. He was the one who'd turned his back. "It was wrong, I know that. I'm sorry, all right? But I can't make a baby on my own, Rich."

"What's that supposed to mean?"

"You know what it means," she said. "You barely even look at me."

"That's not true."

"You're not even looking at me now. You show the dog more affection."

Rich shook his head, stooped to collect the magnet pieces, pulled out the junk drawer, rifled through, tossed the tube of superglue onto the table, and shoved the drawer closed. It jammed. He banged it.

"Goddamn piece of—" he muttered, shoving a hand in to figure out what was stuck, then flinging open the cupboard to try from underneath, and there, like rows of crystal, were the jam jars, half a dozen more already filled and labeled, the rest waiting for spring. Rich stared at them, like this—not the arch of her back as she pulled another man into her, or her hands ripping grass from the ground above her head, but these jars—was the worst secret she'd kept from him.

Rich squatted, then sat back on his butt, staring at them. With one sweep of his arm, the jars clattered out onto the floor.

"Rich—" she stammered. "I—"

He picked one up and tossed it in his hand, contents sloshing. He threw it against the wall and it shattered: a spray of water, a burst of broken glass.

"Mama!"

Rich picked up another jar.

"You're scaring him," she hissed, and hurried out, her own heart galloping. She heard the second jar hit the wall just as she rounded the corner into the bathroom, Chub slipping over the side of the tub with a look of alarm. She shut the bathroom door behind her.

"It's okay, Grahamcracker," she said, assurance punctuated by a third burst of breaking glass. Would he break them all? She wrapped Chub in a towel and rubbed his arms, his back, his shoulders. "Where'd you get these beautiful elbows?"

"I got them at the elbows store."

She toweled off Chub's hair, listening with one ear for Rich. A door slammed and then, after a minute, came the steady thunk and clatter of the ax splitting firewood. She helped Chub into his pajamas, into bed. She turned on the rocket night-light.

"Can you stay until I fall asleep?" Chub asked.

"Sure, Grahamcracker." She lay down beside him, breathed in his clean smell. "Where'd you get these beautiful ears?" she whispered.

"I got them at the ear store."

She listened to the thump of the ax, blow after blow. When she started awake, Chub lay fast asleep beside her. She no longer heard Rich outside. The house was dark. She got up, tiptoed out into the hall.

"Rich?" she asked the empty bedroom.

She turned on the kitchen light, linoleum a field of puddles and broken glass. She crossed the front room—still and cold. The fire had gone out. In nine years, Rich had never let the house go cold. Her keys sat alone in the burl bowl. She pushed aside the curtains and looked out at the empty spot in the driveway. Her breath fogged the chilled glass; her wet cheeks smeared it clean.

She curled into a ball on the couch, pulled the crocheted blanket over her head. Her chest ached. He was gone.

# COLLEEN

Birdsong. She sat up, shivering. Weak gray light slanted in the front window. She pulled the blanket tighter, dug her toes into the carpet for warmth. Her eyelids were swollen. She stared at the cold woodstove. Finally, she stood and crossed the room to it, pulled out the ash drawer, and carried it outside, and there, in the driveway, sat Rich's pickup. The iron drawer dipped in her hands. She set it down, approached the truck, and peered in. The cab was empty.

"Rich?" she asked, her voice hoarse. She swallowed.

Gravel turned to wet grass as she rounded the corner. Rich sat on the back stoop, hunched over Scout, his face buried in the fur of the dog's back.

Colleen's nose ran. She sucked it in. Rich lifted his head but didn't look at her. She could see he hadn't slept. She sat down beside him.

"Where did you go?" she asked.

"Nowhere. Just drove around." He pressed his palms to his eyes, rubbed the fatigue from them.

She owed him an explanation, and yet she waited, afraid he might stand up and leave again.

"When I was living in Arcata, before my mom got sick, I just felt so— alone," she began finally. "Daniel—he had all these big plans." She shook her head. "But I missed Enid. I even missed milking the cows, that's how lonely I was." She made a fist, released it. "After I came back, I still felt alone. I guess I always had, even as a kid." She trailed off, realizing it was true. "And then you came along." She reached for his hand and he let her take it, let her lace her cold fingers through his big, warm, rough ones. "Every day, you got up and you chose me. And every day, even when you were gone, working, I just felt this love from you, like there was a rope tied around your waist on one end and around mine on the other. Like wherever you went, your heart beat for me. You used to do that thing, you know, where you'd talk right here"—she touched the spot behind her ear—"until we fell asleep? Like you saved it all up. And then Chub came, and our life was so full. I never thought my life could feel so full." She traced a circle on his palm. "I want to feel that again."

Rich exhaled and disentangled his hand. She let hers fall back into her lap.

"I'm sorry," she said. "I just—I wanted you to hold me and you wouldn't. I was so mad at you, and then—I dropped Chub off at school and I just felt so—lonely. I wasn't thinking."

Rich stretched his legs out in front of him. She felt a pain in her chest, like if he didn't raise his eyes and look at her, something inside her might snap.

"Do you wish you never married me?" she asked.

"Yes," he said. He pushed a long breath out his nose. "I want a divorce."

Her shoulders rose, then fell, the sob that had been clenched inside rising without warning or permission.

"Colleen, I'm joking. Don't cry. Honey. Colleen." His fingers were in her hair, his lips on her forehead, her nose, her eyelids, and she was in his lap, her legs wrapped around his waist, and she could smell his neck. She slid her hands down the collar of his shirt and he turtled his head. "Cold hands, warm heart," he said. He took her face in his hands, pressed his forehead to hers. "There are some things I would do different," he admitted. "But there has never been a day I wished I wasn't married to you. Not one. You hear me?"

She nodded, tears streaming down her face.

"I'll clean that up," he said, tipping his head back toward the kitchen.

His warm thumbs were still hooked behind her ears. He looked deeper into her eyes.

"I'd do the whole thing over," he said. "All of it, every damn day. There's nothing—nothing—that'd change my mind about you. You hear me? You get a miracle in life, you take it. You don't ask why."

# RICH

Lark's hog wallowed in the middle of the muddy two-track.

"Is he going to move?" Chub asked.

"I don't think so." Rich jinked around him. The cabin door was propped open with an old lard bucket. Rich went up the steps, Chub stopping to pet the dogs. Lark slumped in a kitchen chair, chin to his chest. Rich banged on the door frame with his open palm.

Lark's head bobbed up. "What the hell do you want?"

"I thought you'd be out catting around," Rich said. Better than *Shit, I thought you were dead.*

"Depends. That redhead still up at the Widowmaker?"

"You seen her lately?" Rich asked, steering Chub inside.

"You get to be my age, you can't afford to be too choosy."

Chub scooted onto a chair. Lark extended a mitt.

"Hey there, lumberjack." Chub shook. Lark pulled his hand free, wringing out his wrist. "Bust some knuckles with that grip."

Rich pulled out a chair.

"Hummingbird!" Chub pointed to the feeder hanging outside the kitchen window.

"Marsha put that thing too close to the glass. That hog plants his hairy ass right under it, opens his pie hole, and waits for them to drop in. You want something to eat?" Lark searched the counter with his eyes. "How about some hummingbird tongues on toast? I got fresh." Lark danced his eyebrows at Chub. "Let's see, I got some bread around here somewheres." Lark picked up his mug, like the loaf might be underneath. "You ever catch a hummingbird?"

Lark leaned over, clapped his hands behind Chub's ear, brought a wooden nickel back around, and dropped it into Chub's bib pocket. "'Course not. Too damn fast. Now, they bop into that window and *bam!* I hurry on out and cut out their tongues. I got to be quick though. That hog's greedy. Hard to talk without a damn tongue. You ever try?" He grabbed his own, a white crack down the middle that looked painful. "Ith almoth impothible tho thalk withouth yar thongue."

Chub smiled. "What happened to your neck?" he asked.

Lark looked down his nose at the gauze squares taped there like he hadn't noticed them.

"You don't want any hummingbird tongues, huh? Let's see what else we got." Lark hobbled over to the icebox. He tugged the cheesecloth off a cake, cut three crooked slabs, and slid the blade under to transfer them to the table.

"Damn good," Lark said, brushing crumbs from the patchy bristle around his mouth.

"Where's Flyer?" Chub asked, frosting on his lips.

"Around here someplace, 'less the dogs ate her. Go look in there." He jerked his head toward the sitting room. Chub slid off his seat.

"Take some of this." Lark handed him a hunk of cake. "Make her come to you. You got to learn that about women."

With Chub gone, Lark scratched at his bandages.

"How you feeling?" Rich asked.

Lark grunted, eyed the bags under Rich's eyes. "How about yourself?"

"Same." After he'd left Lark's last night, he'd trawled the streets of the Glen, driven up and down the gulches where houses were clustered, looking for that man's van, until he'd run the tank down.

"It'll blow over," Lark said. "Tree huggers stick around long enough to get their picture in the paper, then they're off to save the whales. Don't know about that one you're married to, though. You two smooth things over?"

Rich shrugged.

"You want to talk about it?"

Rich toed the floor. "Not really."

Lark hacked, cough racking his chest. "That doctor's a damn butcher. Should be wearing an apron. Says I smoked too many cigarettes. Hell, you ask me, I didn't smoke enough of 'em. I'd be dead. Speaking of. Hey, Chub, bring that lamp on in here, will you? That one, in the corner. Unplug it. There you go."

Chub carried the lamp in.

"Isn't she a beauty?" Lark admired the lacquered driftwood and yellowed paper shade, tipped it over, and pried a pack of cigarettes loose from under the base.

The pack shot out, skimming across the floor and under the hutch. Chub dropped to his belly, turning his cheek to the floor to make his arm reach.

"Got it!" He drew out the pack, turned it over like he'd expected something better—bubblegum, baseball cards.

"Well, aren't you just as bright as a dime?" Lark pulled the palmed coin from behind Chub's ear and tapped the pack against the table edge. "Want one?"

Rich shook his head.

"How about you, Chub?"

Chub grinned and slid back into his seat. Lark lit up, inhaled, shook the match out.

"Your line still running clean off the creek?" Rich asked.

Lark leaned back, considered his cigarette. "We get a real good rain it'll run brown for a day."

"Ours is more mud than water," Rich said. "That brush killer they're spraying—"

"She's really got you worked up."

"We're drinking it, whatever it is."

"You run a new pipe already?"

"Nah, just a hose lay for now. But nothing's growing. I mean, nothing—there's nothing to hold the soil. We haul that cut out of the lower grove, the whole hill will end up in that creek."

"Give it some time, it'll green up." Lark took a long drag, coughed. "Here comes the warden." He pocketed the cigarettes, pushing up from his chair, grabbing his saw cane, hobbling over to the sink to put his cigarette out, and tucking the wet butt into his front pocket, his speed startling. "Chub, open that drawer there. Yeah, that one."

Chub pulled open the hutch drawer. The flyer hopped out, skittering across the floor and up Lark's leg.

"How'd she get in there?" Chub asked.

"How do you think? I'd lock Marsha in there if I could fit her fat ass."

Marsha's Dodge labored up the muddy driveway. Lark hobbled back to the table and leaned his cane against the wall.

"Hi, Rich," Marsha said, coming in. "Heya, Chub. What are we, heating the whole county?" She pulled the door shut behind her.

"Leave that door open," Lark said.

Marsha sniffed. "You been smoking in here?"

"My damn house."

Marsha ignored him, set a sack on the table.

"What's this?" Lark asked, drawing out a bear claw. "Damn blackberry seeds stick in your teeth, worse than a wood tick in your crotch hairs." He drew out a turnover as big as a fist. "Ah, shit. What the hell do I need all this for?"

"You're welcome," Marsha said. "I've got groceries in the car."

Rich went out to help.

"He show you the pack under the lamp?" Marsha asked, handing him a sack. "I leave a few, let him think he's putting one over on me. He wants to kill himself, that's his business."

"He doing all right?" Rich asked, voice low, as though Lark might be able to hear from inside.

"Not great. But he's hard to kill." She led the way back in. "Good?" she asked Lark, flecks of pastry in his beard. "Sit down, Rich, I don't want to interrupt your visit."

"We should get going," Rich said. He held the door and Chub scampered out.

Lark tore off a pastry claw. "You see that redhead, you tell her I'm looking for her," he called after Rich.

"You'd be in trouble if you ever found her," Marsha said.

"You show me another eighty-three-year-old man can still do ten chinups before breakfast."

"Since when do you fix breakfast?" Marsha asked.

"What's a man got to do to get a little peace and quiet around here?"

"You tried dying?"

Lark waved her off. "Hey, Gundersen," he called out. "Don't let them push you around." The hog lifted his snout, catching a whiff of the pastries. "What are you looking at?" Lark demanded. "Your days are numbered, Merle, you old bastard."

Colleen's truck appeared at the edge of the clearing.

"Hey, isn't that your tree hugger?" Lark asked.

Rich watched the white pickup falter, negotiating around ruts.

That morning, dulled by sleeplessness, after he'd turned back up his own driveway, he'd sat in the dark for a long time, staring at the house. The anger had burned off and underneath it the thought of losing her, of coming home to an empty house, a life without her, without Chub—the notion gutted him.

Colleen turned her engine off. Chub ran to meet her. She got out and stood, casserole pan in her hands, as though the muddy path to the cabin's front steps were a long plank over a high river.

She found Rich's eyes and searched them. He let the corner of his mouth tug up. Colleen released her held breath, gathered herself.

"You think your dick is your dumbest organ," Lark said, watching Rich watch her. "But it's your heart. Every damn time."

# *March 5*

# COLLEEN

She took her keys from the burl bowl, morning light streaming through the windows.

"Roads are muddy," Rich cautioned her, seeing the week-old newspaper tucked under her arm.

They'd talked for a long time in bed last night.

*Eight?* he'd asked, thumbing back through the Rolodex of his memory. It hadn't occurred to her that it would hurt him, the pregnancies she'd lost without him.

The roads were soup, the Deer Rib turnoff so overgrown she almost missed it. Thorns screaked along the side panels. The company must have stopped spraying the road—*That's what you wanted, isn't it?* The truck jostled over ruts, brush thwacking the windows, and then came a dirt wall, so dark and high it took her a moment to understand it: the mudslide a mountain, casting its own shadow. She got out, the smell of turned soil filling her nostrils.

She trudged down along the edge, looked back up at the caved-in ridge. Blood beat in her ears. *The cabin—where was the cabin?* Even this far down from the road, mud stood ten feet high, too soft to climb.

"Joanna?" she yelled. Her voice boomeranged, taunting her. "Jo-ann-a-a-a?"

She tripped along the slide edge, until the mud was her height, then waist-high, then shin-deep, brambles catching her sleeves.

"Hello?" Her voice was hoarse. "Hello-o-o?"

She tried again to read the ridgeline, but the slide had changed the face of it. She sank a foot into mud, testing it, then trudged across, parallel to where she hoped the road was, though she no longer saw the truck. She was so focused on pulling her heavy feet free that she didn't register the first whiff of woodsmoke until it went up her nose. She coughed. She was farther down than she'd realized—she'd come up behind the cabin, a square island, river of mud carved around it.

"Hello?!"

The back door swung open, banged. Joanna teetered out over where the steps had been torn away, center of gravity thrown off by her huge belly, as though holding her balance over deep water. She scanned the tree line, reached out, and pulled the door in. Colleen felt a surge of fear, as though she might close the door and unmoor the cabin, sink down like a submarine.

"Joanna!"

Colleen waved her arms over her head. She tried to run, but the mud was too deep.

"Go around." Joanna gestured. "I shoveled." She disappeared inside.

A narrow, waist-deep trench tunneled around the cabin's side. Colleen's jeans were heavy, bogging her down. When she got to hard ground, she felt a strange lightness in her feet, as though she'd taken off skates. A square the size of a room had been dug out in front, mud sheared off like sheet cake on three sides, a patch of strangely green grass, a few pecking chickens.

"They said they'd bury us. I didn't think they meant literally," Joanna said from the doorway, streak of mud across her forehead.

Colleen looked over to where the chicken coop should have been.

"It ended up somewhere down there." Joanna pointed. "We found most of the chickens on the roof in the morning. Boy, were they grumpy."

The barn's roof had slid off so that one corner touched the ground.

"Are the girls—?"

"In here."

Colleen tried wiping her feet and crossed the threshold for the first time in years. The linoleum was patterned with brown fans where a rag had been rubbed in circles. The girls peeked out from the back room, standing on a triangle of wood where carpet had been pulled away. They looked cold. Sap popped in the woodstove.

Joanna poured water from a bucket into the kettle and set it to boil. One of Colleen's mother's old Blue Willow plates sat in the dry rack—they'd left everything behind when they sold it, as if the arrangement were only temporary.

"I should have known when the creek stopped running," Joanna said. "Water must have just built up, all this time, since they buried Deer Spring. Lucky I kept the tub filled."

Colleen rubbed her fingers together, mud crumbling off, ringing in her ears growing louder until it reached the pitch of the steam whistling from the kettle's spout. Joanna crunched dried chamomile flowers into hot water. Mud was streaked along the baseboards.

"I thought it was an earthquake. Good thing it happened at night or we might have tried running. You think something as big as a ridge will stay put."

"Where's Jed?" Colleen asked.

Joanna shrugged. "Washington? Idaho? He's getting spoiled by those truck-stop showers. All the hot water you want. He won't be back for three weeks. I'll have this place shoveled out by then. I thought it was the end, when it started coming in the door. We just prayed." She held a strainer over a mug and poured a stream of tea, clumps catching in the mesh. The house smelled of mold and earth, a gritty scent Colleen tasted in her mouth. She was waiting, she realized, for Mom to walk down the stairs.

"Honey?" Joanna handed her the half-full jar and sat heavily.

Colleen held her mug by its thick handle, cougar tracks imprinted on the side. The heft of it made her remember it in her father's hand—milk, two sugars.

"You can bury us, but you can't keep us from digging our way out." Joanna took a swig, winced. "Hot."

The tea was weak. Bits of flowers stuck to the back of Colleen's throat. She forced down a burning gulp. Camber toddled in. Joanna pulled her up onto her knee, against her pregnant belly.

"God took care of us, didn't he?" Joanna asked her, tucking the girl's soft curls behind her ear.

"Can you call Jed?"

Joanna made a phone with her hand, held it to her ear. "Dring! Dring!"

Camber giggled.

"From our house, I mean," Colleen said.

Joanna rose, pouring Camber out of her lap. The child gave Colleen a dirty look, as though she were responsible for this sudden eviction.

"I have to get the carpets out," Joanna said.

"You can't stay here."

"They stink like carcasses," Joanna insisted, as if she hadn't heard.

Together, they rolled the soiled carpet back and kneeled on the wood, catching their breath. Joanna stuck her arm under the bulky roll. Colleen's end was waterlogged, smell overpowering—wet dog, moldy earth—too heavy to lift, but it seemed bad manners to point this out.

"Ready?" Joanna asked.

They strained and grunted, rolling the carpet over once, loose and sloppy, then again, until it slumped near the door. Joanna struggled to her feet. Colleen sat back on her heels. The girls climbed through the jumble of stacked furniture, slipping between chairs and end tables in the boneless way of cats. Joanna yanked the last stapled corner free.

"There," Joanna panted.

"It's too heavy."

"We'll slide it out. Open that door."

Lifting wasn't good for the baby, but Joanna was already positioning herself. The door handle was cold. Colleen looked out on the field of mud and debris, the leaning barn. The next wind would wreck it. She wondered about the chicks in their warming bed, the central pillar with its square-headed nails, where her grandmother had once hung the desiccated feet of rabbits.

Joanna issued a birthing groan, pulling, forcing Colleen to hop down to avoid being knocked over, roll dipping down from the doorway like a melting bridge.

"I don't think—" Colleen caught the tail end, wet seeping through her shirt, struggling to settle it on her hip and follow Joanna through knee-deep mud, toward the woods.

Where the mud ended, Joanna veered and dropped her end to the ground, carpet scrubbing down Colleen's side. The dull tinkle of a cowbell: Bossy browsing at the edge of the woods.

"There," Joanna said, and then, as if the bell had triggered a release valve, tears.

"You can't stay here." Colleen lifted her chin at Joanna's belly. "That baby's not going to wait much longer."

"We can't just leave." Joanna sucked air in through her nose.

"You have to. It's not safe."

"Who will take care of the animals?" Joanna protested.

When they got back inside, she tidied the kitchen, like everything would be fine if she could just get this one room in order. Colleen scrounged a few paper sacks and went upstairs to the small bedroom that had been hers. The first night she'd spent with Rich in this room she'd tried to lie still.

*What's the matter?* he'd asked finally.

*I can't sleep*, she'd said, her voice dragging its own weight, his body, lank and warm, breathing beside hers. *I'm not used to another person.* She'd never spent a night with Daniel; he'd always slipped away before Eunice Hamilton, her ancient landlady, could discover him, returning to his dorm to study, and she'd had no other experience. Without a word, Rich had slid out from under the quilt and begun to dress in the dark.

*Don't go.* She'd touched his knee. *I'd like to get used to it.*

He'd climbed back in, lifted an arm for her to rest her head on his shoulder.

*I'd like to get used to it too*, he'd said.

Now, behind her, the bedroom door creaked.

"What are you doing?" Judith asked.

"This used to be my room."

"This is my room."

"I know, sweetie."

She removed a pile of shirts from a drawer and jammed them into a bag while Judith watched. She felt her own mother standing in the doorway. *Your father was a daydreamer. Look where it got him.*


Outside, the air was cooling, mist gathering mass when they reached the edge of the woods. Joanna carried Camber, Colleen the sacks. The light was weak. Colleen began to worry she'd left the truck too close, that mud had collapsed and buried it, until finally she spotted it.

"I'm hungry," Leah said.

"I know," Colleen answered, since Joanna said nothing.

"Where are we going?" Leah asked.

"You're coming to our house. We're going to have a nice dinner," Colleen said.

She waited for them to scramble up into the truck, then shoved the bags in. "Do you like grilled cheese?"

Joanna stared straight ahead, Camber in her lap. The girls squirmed in their muddy clothes.

"I want Papa," Leah whined. "Ouch! Judy pinched me!"

"Girls, be nice to each other," Colleen said. "Please." *Someday you'll be all you have.*

The shutters glowed white against the dark green house. Rich paused at the chopping block, taking in the mud barnacled to the side mirrors, the girls, Joanna.

"Who is that?" Leah demanded.

"That's Rich," Colleen said.

He leaned the ax against a stump, clapped his gloves, puff of sawdust like a cloud of magician's smoke. In her mind, Colleen saw the evening unfold: girls jumping down from the truck, filing into the house; Rich wiping down the ax head so it wouldn't rust, even-keeled, practical, keeping them warm and dry; Colleen running bathwater; sandwiches sizzling in a pan; Joanna phoning her uncle up in Medford; the horse trailer's brake cherries disappearing into the fog. How, after all that, when, finally, they were alone, Rich would simply raise an arm, let her rest her head in the safe space at his side. *That's the difference between you and him. Rich doesn't hold a grudge.* It was Enid who had first pointed that out.

The girls stirred: hungry, cold. Leah squirmed with the itch of her unanswered question.

"That's my husband," Colleen said.

She herded them into the house, seeing them as Rich must have: two stringy-haired, mud-streaked girls; a fussing toddler; Joanna eight and a half months pregnant, barely more than a girl herself.

In the kitchen, Colleen opened and slammed drawers.

"What are you looking for?" Rich asked, coming in the back door.

"The can opener."

He took it from the drawer beside the refrigerator and opened the soup cans, picking the lids off by their sharp edges. "This one's tomato."

She swapped it for another chicken noodle.

"What happened?" he asked, the girls' high voices chattering over the bathwater.

She rifled through a drawer. "Don't we have cheese?"

"Colleen."

"What?" she demanded. Rich stood two feet away, still holding the can opener. "Deer Rib slid out."

"How bad?" he asked.

"The whole ridge."

The girls appeared, hair wet, cheeks flushed, Colleen's T-shirts hanging to their knees.

She ladled soup. Joanna blew on a spoonful for Camber. The girls pulled their sandwich bread apart, cheese stretching. Chub and Rich watched silently, as though awake in the same dream.


In the bathroom, Colleen squeezed lines of toothpaste onto the girls' fingers. Their faces lit up at its sweetness. Joanna must have made them brush with baking soda. Colleen came back from tucking them into Chub's bed to find Joanna alone in the kitchen, standing with one hand on the phone.

"Did you get him?" she asked.

"He'll bring the trailer for Bossy. He's not my blood uncle." She rubbed her palms over her belly. "Jed kept saying we should move up there. Start fresh."

"You should get some rest," Colleen said.

"He said this place would kill you if you let it."


The uncle arrived after midnight. Rich carried the girls out. Colleen sent Joanna with a blanket for them, a jar of hot coffee for the uncle.


Chub sprawled out, asleep on their bed. Rich closed the damper. Flames flickered, starved of air. Colleen sank onto the couch beside him.

"You okay?" he asked.

"I keep thinking what my mom would say."

"'Here today, gone tomorrow'?" Rich suggested.

She shook her head.

"'Easy come, easy go'?"

She smacked him lightly in the gut.

He slung his arm around her shoulder, kissed the top of her head. "'You only get one miracle.'"

She pushed air out her nose. "Yeah."

The blur of Rich's undershirt ghosted in the bedroom dark. Outside, Scout barked, low throaty growls punctuated by loud volleys. Not a raccoon. Something bigger.

"What is it?" she asked.

"Shh." Rich hopped on one leg, getting his pants on. Underneath Scout's growling, a motor idled.

"Who is it?" she asked, thinking of Joanna's uncle—had they forgotten something?—Rich moving with a single-mindedness that frightened her. "Rich?"

She heard him bang his head on the threshold and curse under his breath.

"Are you okay?" she whispered. Scout barked again, then gunshots, breaking glass, truck doors slamming.

"Rich?!"

Light beamed through the windows, tires spraying gravel. The house went dark. Not even Scout made a sound. She smacked into the rocker. Rich stood in the hall.

"Don't go out there," she hissed.

"They're gone."

"How do you know?"

She opened the door to Chub's room, watched his chest rise and fall in the rocket-tail glow, still, miraculously, asleep. Her hands shook, pulling his door quietly shut again.

The front door stood ajar, cold air seeping in, porch light turning fog molten. Outside, Rich crouched on his hams, his hand on Scout's splayed body.

"Rich?"

He dropped his head. A sob rose from deep in his chest. She'd seen him cry only one other time: in the hospital at Easter. The gravel sounded strangely loud underfoot. She touched the small of Rich's hunched back and he let loose, his hand resting on Scout's neck, as though to comfort him. The dog's tongue hung out, blood soaking fur. She wrapped both arms around Rich's torso, pressed herself to his back. He brought an elbow up to wipe his eyes and raked his fingernails down his face, like it was a mask he could rip off. Then he gathered Scout's limp body in his arms and stood.

After she'd pressed her fingers to the bullet hole in the carving (HOME IS WHERE—the heart blasted away), swept glass into the dustpan, taped plastic over the broken panes, when finally Rich came in, his knees were brown. She smelled the soil on him. He went down the hall to their bed. She climbed in beside him, wiped the tender skin under his eyes. She needed to vacuum the glass out of the rug before Chub got up.

"Did you see who it was?" she asked.

"No. Colleen, you have to stop," he said. "What if—?" Chub's name pulsed between them.

*We'll bury you.* She'd thought they were talking to Daniel, but she realized now they'd meant her too, Joanna, Helen, anyone who stepped out of line. They'd meant her all along.

## March 6

# RICH

The wind swelled and sucked the plastic stretched across the busted panes, as though the house were breathing. He palmed the truck keys from the burl bowl, eyes sore. Stood under the shower too long.

"Where are you going?" Colleen asked.

He raked his fingers down his cheeks, itching from the shave. "Be back in a couple hours."

She followed him out. "Rich," she called after him. "Be careful."

He should have gone back, let her peck him on the cheek, but he knew the moment she touched him, he'd bawl—bawling over a dog—so instead he climbed into the pickup, pulled out north, and drove, putting miles behind him. He crossed the Oregon line. In Brookings there was a hardware store that carried prefab doors. Rich caught his reflection in the glass, as rough-looking and red-eyed as he felt.

"Can I help you?" The pimple-faced kid eyed Rich cautiously, like he might hoist a door under one arm and take a run at him.

"You got any without this cutout?"

The kid looked confused. "That's a dog door."

He bought a solid six-panel, no windows, twice what the lumber was worth, a peephole that made him think of a cheap motel. It would change the whole feel of the house. He loaded it into the bed alongside a new window, tubs of woodfill and plaster, felt the slam of the truck door in his bones, tooth eating its hole. Come this far.

He watched the miles tick up: a hundred twenty, a hundred forty, coast highway curving north, filling in the blank map in his mind the way a wave washed across sand. When he got to Coos Bay, he trolled the ritzy coast houses until he spotted the boat, a white sign trimmed with blue: STEPHEN LANGLEY, DDS.

He loped up the walk, rang the bell before he had time to change his mind, shoved his hands into his pockets, fingers stubbing bullet casings. Astrid opened the door: chin-length silver hair, reading glasses hanging from a chain around her neck, powder-blue collar sticking out from a white cardigan. As though she'd dressed to match the sign.

"Yes?" she asked. If she was surprised to see him, if it stirred any feeling in her at all after all these years, she didn't show it, just gave a quick nod of acknowledgment: *Yes, I remember you. Yes, we made a baby together once. What do you want?*

The side of his face throbbed in time with his heart. A hundred fifty miles, the farthest he'd ever been from home, and here she stood, impatient, as though he'd taken her away from a television program.

"I got a tooth needs to come out."

"Just a moment." She left the door cracked. He heard a burbling that, when she opened the door, turned out to be the pump on a fish tank. She led him around a staircase, toward the back of the house. She'd shrunk some, shoulders narrower than he remembered. She pushed open an inner door and stood aside. He found himself alone in a room with a chair like a barber's, a sink, a glass jar of tongue depressors.

A man about Rich's age came in. So this was Langley.

"Have a seat." The man went to the sink and washed his hands. Slight and severe, when he pushed the hydraulic lever and Rich's chair lunged backward, his pointed chin and sharp nose made him look like a rodent, overhead fixture lighting his thinning hair. "Let's take a look."

The man prodded along Rich's gums with a metal hook. Rich flinched, pain zinging. He opened and closed his fists, tasting the latex of the man's gloves.

The dentist sat back and removed his paper mask. "You need a crown."

"Can you pull it?"

"It's a molar. I don't like to pull a tooth you need."

Rich sat up. "I'd just as soon be rid of it. It's giving me hell."

The dentist's gaze tracked across the room. Rich scanned for needle-nosed pliers, a drill, some tool he recognized.

"Astrid?" the dentist called.

With both of them leaning over him, Rich's heart thunked. She avoided his eyes, stared at a spot on his top lip, as though he'd smeared some grease there. His palms sweated, extra saliva pooling.

"Take my sweet tooth out while you're at it."

The dentist sighed, as though the joke tired him.

"That's a nice boat you got," Rich said.

"Thank you."

"You take it out much?"

"We bought it for our son."

"What's he do?"

"He's an attorney." The dentist took the syringe from Astrid. "You'll feel a pinch."

Rich winced.

"Give that a minute to numb up."

They left him. Clammy with nerves—thought it was her, sitting so close, but it was worse alone. Pins and needles started in the gum, spread. Television in the next room. Fern in a china pot near the door.

"Okay," the dentist said. Astrid took a seat on the other side of his head. "You'll feel some pressure."

Flat on his back, Rich searched for something to take his mind off Langley, who was prying the tooth out as though levering a tree root free with an iron bar. He tasted blood. Every few minutes the dentist stopped for Astrid to suction it out. Rich stared at the ceiling, only half registered the slick lump passing through his lips.

"It'll be sore when that wears off." Langley peeled off his blood-smeared gloves and dropped them in the trash.

He washed his hands, gone before Rich could thank him, room spinning from sitting up too quick.

"That'll be forty-five dollars," Astrid said, putting on her glasses to write a receipt. She held it out to him, her hand reaching through time, the same hand that had once offered the peacock caddis, its tickling weightlessness landing on the water like a live insect, ripples circling out from the raised snouts of trout. The hand she'd once taken his in, to press it to her belly. At nineteen, he'd laughed to chase the fear. *I could teach him to fish*, he'd said.

*How do you know it's a him?* Astrid had challenged him.

There'd been no girl child in Gundersen history, but suddenly, because Astrid had willed it, it was so.

*Her then.*

Astrid had smiled, as though the idea pleased her, or maybe, looking back, it was only the satisfaction of winning. A day later, she'd changed her mind. After all of it—rain pelting the windshield as he fumbled for something to say on their way back from June Millhauser's in Samoa, settling finally on *We could still get married*. After her rage. *What makes you think I'd marry you?* After she'd forced him from the car, blood spotting through her wool skirt, and slid behind the wheel herself. After she'd left him there, at the side of the road. Even after he'd met Colleen, the guilt still lingered at the back of his mind—if only he'd said something, done something. But he saw now that Astrid didn't regret it, didn't think of him at all.

"Is that your grandson?" she asked, nodding at his open wallet, Chub all dimples in his school picture.

"Son." His tongue was numb and clumsy, gauze roll wedged in to staunch the bleeding.

"Oh." She stared at the wallet a moment longer, as though he might flip to the next photo.

"We've only got the one. Colleen—my wife—we've lost a few—eight." He corrected himself. "We've lost eight."

He waited, as though Astrid might say she was sorry. He still felt the weight of the small parcel June Millhauser had handed him to shove into the woodstove, a baby the size of an apple core. He'd wanted so badly to unfold the cloth. It felt wrong to burn what should be buried.

"I used to think about him," he admitted. "Her. For a long time, even after I stopped thinking about—" He cleared his throat. *You, us.* "I wanted a family." He'd been carrying it so long, it was a relief to set it down, finally, at her feet.

Astrid closed the account book. "I'm glad you found someone."

He pinched the fly out of his pocket and dropped it onto her desk. She lowered her hand over it, hovering, as though saying a prayer.

"Goodbye, Rich," she said.

He stood outside the closed door, holding the waxed paper envelope she'd put his tooth in. No one had asked if he'd wanted it. He patted his cheek, checking his face was still there. Fog rolled in. He drove slow, felt the curve of Last Chance in the pit of his gut. He passed the house and kept going, turned in toward Requa, up the roll-back hill. Pickups lined the road. Rich parked, got out, and walked up, passing Eugene's Chevy in Merle's driveway, sap gunked in the bed, a busted chain. Too lazy to even cover his tracks. Just as well. Needed to set things straight with both of them.

The debarked dog hacked. Rich pulled the blood-soaked plug of gauze free. He followed voices around the side of the house to the back deck, barbecue smoke itching his nostrils. They stood around the grill, Merle flipping steaks—Eugene, the Sanderson kid, a couple young guys from the other crew, a few more who looked familiar from that night on the road after they'd massacred the lower grove, though it had been dark.

"Rich, come on up here," Merle called, like he'd been expecting him.

Rich mounted the steps. Eugene's eyes slid away. Scout must have trotted right up to him looking for an ear rub.

"Grab a beer," Merle said. "We're celebrating."

Eugene slapped a bottle against his chest and Rich looked down at it, like this might be the fight starting. He saw it drop, explode at his feet. Saw himself clap the bullet casings onto the porch railing, shove Merle against it. But here was the beer bottle in his hand, slick and cool, still whole. Merle handed the steaks off. Guys headed in. Rich hung back.

"You don't look happy, Rich," Merle said, scraping burned fat off the grill.

"I don't know what to think anymore."

"You want to know what *I* think?" Merle closed the lid over the grill. "I think you're one lucky sonofabitch. I think you got a brother-in-law that looks out for you."

Eugene caught Rich's eyes through the glass, looked away too quickly. Rich set the full beer on the porch railing.

"I think you go home and tell your wife to keep her mouth shut," Merle said. "It'd be a shame if word ever got out that Larson baby came out stillborn because of her."

"It wasn't stillborn. It was born with the top of its head gone. How was she supposed to save it?" Rich demanded with a surge of anger.

Merle raised his eyebrows, not used to being interrupted. "I bet the state would be real interested to learn some backwoods housewife is playing doctor, pulling babies out before they're cooked."

"That's not true," Rich said, accidentally knocking the bottle off the railing. It shattered, foaming on the ground below.

"True, not true." Merle shrugged. "You know how rumors spread."

"She doesn't take any money," Rich said. "She never has. You leave her out of this."

Merle pressed his tongue into his cheek, suppressing a smile. "You coming in?"

Rich looked in the window at the men hunched over their steaks. If he looked at Merle, he would grab him by the throat, slam him up against the faded yellow siding.

Merle followed Rich's gaze. "They'll settle down. We were young once too, remember?" Merle gestured toward the door, but Rich didn't budge. "Suit yourself," Merle said. "Soon as this rain quits, we're going to work you so hard it'll knock your dick down into the dirt. Rest up. Get things straight at home."

"Or what?" Rich asked. "You'll have Eugene cut my brake lines too?"

"Go home, Gundersen. Go home to your wife." The screen door thwapped closed behind him.

Rich swallowed the taste of blood. Eugene shifted his weight, though his back was to the window. An animal knows when it's being watched. Quick shot of eye contact from Merle, letting him know Rich was still out there.

The husky growled, backing under the steps as Rich collected the pieces of the broken bottle so the mutt wouldn't cut a pad. A dog wasn't a man. It didn't choose which sonofabitch owned him.

# CHUB

His mom stopped chopping, listening without turning her head. Dad was home. Chub ran to the front door. His dad limped around the back of the truck and let the tailgate down. Chub waited for Scout to jump out. It was Chub who'd found Scout's chain abandoned in the backyard this morning and run inside to tell. *Scout ran away!*

*I know, Grahamcracker,* his mom had said, *I know.*

All day he'd waited: Scout had gone to find his dad. His dad would bring him home. Instead, his dad slid a door from the truck bed.

"Where's Scout?" Chub asked.

"Watch out there, Chub," his dad said. Chub moved out of the way.

"What happened?" his mom asked.

"Got it pulled." His dad patted his swollen cheek.

Chub walked out to the truck. Wet gravel poked the bottoms of his feet. He climbed up on the back tire and looked into the bed: no Scout. He jumped down and yanked open the truck's door, even though dogs didn't ride up front.

"Where is he?" Chub asked, coming in.

"Go wash your hands," his mom said.

They sat at the table. Chub dragged his fork through his mashed potatoes.

"What if he's lost?" Chub asked.

His mom looked at his dad.

"All he has to do is follow his creeks," his dad said. He took a bite, sucked air, and pushed his plate away.

Chub asked to be excused and slipped out into the backyard. Here was Scout's chain. Here were his bowls. Here was a marrowbone carved with his teeth marks. Chub carried the bone to the doghouse and peeked in the doorway.

"Scout?"

He crawled in. Here was the old rag rug from the kitchen, Scout's dog smell. Chub touched his cheek to the rug, hugged Scout's bone to his chest, and curled up to wait.

It was almost dark. His dad crouched in the doorway of the doghouse.

"You awake?" his dad asked.

Chub sat up.

"Come on, I want to show you something."

Chub followed his dad up the hill. It was strange to walk the path without Scout. No Scout running ahead, panting. No Scout doubling back to lick Chub's ear. They got to the trees and his dad veered off the trail to a spot where the dirt had been dug up and then stamped down. His dad squatted beside it and pulled Chub close.

"What's wrong?" Chub asked.

His dad sucked air in his nose. "Did I ever tell you about how I first found Scout?" he asked.

Chub shook his head.

"I went down to the beach to get your uncle Lark some driftwood. I pulled a log free from this pile, and there was this scruffy little puppy. Scared me. I fell back on my butt and before I knew it he was standing on my chest." His dad smiled. "When you were first learning to walk you used to chase him around the yard. When you sat down, he'd come over next to you so you could grab on and pull yourself back up and chase him some more."

Chub leaned against his dad's shoulder. His dad drew in a shaky breath.

"He was a good dog." His dad reached into his front pocket, and there in his palm was a yellow agate the size of a jellybean. Chub took it. His dad nodded at the turned soil. "It's okay," his dad said. "He had a good, long life. Now he can rest." His dad rubbed warm circles into Chub's back. "Now he can rest."

# RICH

"Maybe we shouldn't." Colleen stalled, staring across the community center lot at Eugene's truck.

"We're here," Rich said.

He held the door. The smell of battered fish wafted over them. Across the room, the Sanderson kid pinged a dart into the pocked board—bull's-eye. Eugene handed him another, caught sight of Rich, pretended not to. There were two kinds of men: guys who swung, and guys like Eugene, who looked around for something to hit you with first. The second dart pinged beside the first, so close it split the tail feathers. The kid could have shot Scout from a distance, but Eugene must have gotten out, pressed the barrel right to his head. Rich clenched his fists. *Eugene, you worthless piece of shit.*

"Enid isn't here," Colleen pleaded, as though this gave them permission to leave.

Pete, Don, and Lew all acknowledged him with curt nods, but Colleen kept her head down. Rich followed her and Chub through the line, watched Chub pick at his French fries. Eugene dug around in the cooler by the dartboard for another beer.

"I'm going to go talk to him," Rich said. "Before he gets too loaded."

"Rich," Colleen protested, but he was already up, tipping his head toward the door.

Rich went out and leaned against his pickup. Before long, Eugene appeared, loose in the knees.

"How much you up?" Rich asked.

"One sixty." Eugene raked his boot through the gravel.

Rich clapped the bullets and their casings onto the hood. "You have some-thing to say, say it."

Eugene glanced back at the door, rammed his fists into his pockets, cold air sobering him up. "You're the one who has shit to say."

Rich picked a bullet off the hood.

"I dug this out of my front door. We got a problem?"

"You tell me."

"You killed my dog."

"I didn't." Eugene shook his head.

"Who did then?"

Eugene shrugged.

"Cut the shit, Eugene. You're my fucking brother-in-law. You're the only damn family we have."

"I tried. I defended you. But then you let Colleen go off and do whatever she feels like, helping that guy sling shit at Sanderson. Shit, Rich, you might as well have hung a target on your back."

Eugene turned to go, but Rich grabbed him by the shirt neck and shoved him against the grill. Casings rolled off the hood, tinking at their feet.

"You listen to me, you sonofabitch."

"Get off me." Eugene struggled, went limp, outmatched, weighted down by liquor.

"I don't care what Merle tells you to do. I'll deal with my own wife my own way."

"He didn't tell me shit until after. You think I wouldn't have tried to stop them, if I'd known?"

Rich tightened his grip on Eugene's shirt. "Maybe there's something to all this spray talk if Merle's paying guys like you to sneak around shooting people's dogs. You've been drinking that stuff for years. We all have. If it can fuck up a deer, sure as shit it can fuck up a baby, you kiss-ass. Ever wonder why Alsea isn't crawling?"

Eugene jerked free. "Watch your damn mouth."

"And what do you think Merle would say about your little burl game?" Rich asked. "Colleen saw them out at your place—you think a tarp's going to hide that? You think Merle'll give two shits about you, once he finds out?"

"You don't know shit, Gundersen." Eugene snorted, beer on his breath. "You think I'm dumb enough to steal burls out from under Merle's nose?

Whose idea do you think it was? He had to keep some money coming in, how the hell do you think he could afford to keep us all on the payroll, waiting on those harvest plans to clear?"

"You're a fucking liar," Rich said.

"Who you calling a liar?" Eugene lunged. Rich caught him by the throat, felt the urge to hurt him—to really hurt him. It took Eugene a moment to start struggling against the chokehold, eyes sharpening, a glint of panic, hands clutching at the vise of Rich's knuckles.

"Richard," Colleen said.

Rich released him. Eugene coughed, sucked air, rubbed his throat.

"Go ahead," Eugene said, hoarse. "Tell Merle. Tell him I've made myself another two grand on the side, cutting cordwood off Sanderson land. At least I'm cutting something. Your timber is going to fall over and rot. You'll be so broke you'll be begging me to let you in on it." Eugene spat. "Sorry about your damn dog, but don't go blaming the shit you're in on me."

Colleen stepped aside to let him by, flinched at the door whapping shut behind him.

"My coat's inside," she said.

Alone in the parking lot, Rich spun a slow circle, eyeing the pickups. It could have been anybody, some guy from that night on the road when Scout had bared his teeth, growling, as though he already smelled him.

Colleen came out, dragging Chub by the hand and hustling him into the truck. Fog swirled in the headlights, rolling out over the rocky edge as they rounded the curves, Colleen inhaling sharply, unsure where the road was, if there still was one. At the willow, Rich turned in, flicked the headlights off. They stared at the dark house, silence where Scout's bark should have been.

# SPRING

*1978*

*March 16*

# COLLEEN

In the weeks since the hearing, Colleen had gotten used to the stares in town, conversations petering out when she drew near. *Give it some time*, Rich said. *It'll be a slow thaw.* Chub in school, she filled a glass at the filter spout, watched it spill over, sniffed it. She walked the mile up the gulch along Garlic Creek on her own. She sat on the front steps of the abandoned cabin and stared at the Deer Rib slide. Already plants were sprouting, life returning after disaster.

Walking back down the hill to the house, she heard the telephone, still ringing after she shed her boots and pushed through the back door into the kitchen.

"You heard?" Marsha was breathless.

"Heard what?" Colleen asked.


She smelled it before she saw it, smoke settled over the glen like fog. She got out of the truck: Helen and Carl's blackened fireplace a lone pillar, mounds of wet wood and ash.

"You a friend of theirs." A statement, not a question. The old man stood on his front lawn across the street, watching her. "Carl's hands are burned up pretty bad," the old man said. "Lucky nobody died. Hell of a fire. House went up like a bale of straw." The man scratched his scalp.

"Do you know where they are?" Colleen asked.

"Up at Hupa, with the rest of them, probably," the man said. "She's got family up there, on the reservation. They were always coming around."

"Are they coming back?" Colleen asked, hearing how foolish the question sounded. She wanted to sit down in the middle of the road.

Chub bounced up and down on the curb, waiting for her to come to a complete stop. He launched himself up onto the seat, chattering, and disappeared to his room when they got home. Rich sat in the kitchen, bank statements spread across the table, filling out their tax forms.

"They burned it."

"What's that?" he asked, not looking up.

"Helen and Carl's house. To the ground."

"What?" He stopped. "When?"

"Last night."

"Are they okay?"

"They're alive. Homeless, but alive."

"Did you tell Chub?" he asked.

She knew she needed to; he was looking forward to that party. But it surprised her that Rich had thought of it. She shook her head. Rich sighed and took off his cheaters, folded them.

"You're thinking that could have been us?" she asked. She'd felt a blinking light of panic, staring at the wreckage of Helen and Carl's house.

Rich was quiet. "They didn't have a dog," he said finally.

*How can we stay here?* she wanted to ask. But Rich's great-grandfather had chopped a clearing out of these woods, felled tree after tree until the call—*tim-ber*—had tolled like a bell in his heart, echoing down through the generations. Rich would chop off his own foot before he walked away from this place. And how long would she and Chub last without him? A week? A month? She sat down across the table from him.

"Things will calm down," Rich promised. "They'll calm down." As though repeating it might make it true.

*March 18*

# RICH

Rich idled. A fresh-painted sign, propped against a sawhorse, blocked the dirt two-track:

SORRY, WE'RE DEAD.

Have to be dead to pass up screwing a tourist out of a city dollar. Rich swerved around it, plunging into tall grass. The cabin came into view, Lark slumped in a chair on the porch. Rich punched the horn. Lark didn't budge, tuft of gray hair licked sideways by the breeze. He pulled up out front. The dogs came around the side of the cabin, followed by the hog.

*Shit. Lark. Don't do this to me now.*

He tossed Lark's mail onto the seat, pushed out of the truck, took the steps two at a time. Wood curls were strewn around Lark's feet, half-carved Sasquatch still in his lap. Two buttons held his shirt together at the bottom, as though he'd torn it open to breathe, growth the size of a plum swelling below his collarbone. Spittle cobwebbed the corners of his mouth. His freckled bald spot had a yellowy tint.

"Lark?" Rich asked. He touched his shoulder. Lark's head snapped up. Rich started. "You sonofabitch."

"'Closed' wouldn't fit," Lark said with a crooked grin, doing up his buttons. "You going to stand there like a damn tax collector? Pop a squat."

Rich wiped his boots on the mat, COME BACK WITH A WAR streaked with dried mud, and dragged a chair out from the kitchen.

"I knew a guy killed another guy over a dog once."

"Wish it was as simple as that," Rich said, splinter of grief still lodged in his chest.

"Pretty low blow."

"Least Merle didn't burn my house down."

"No kidding," Lark said. "Who do you think he had do that one?"

"Who knows."

They watched the river.

"Everything ironed out between you and Colleen?" Lark asked after a time.

"More or less," Rich said.

"You track down Dr. Fish Doctor?"

Rich shook his head.

"Afraid you'd kill him?"

Rich let out a long breath. "I don't know. I don't know what I'd do." He picked a squirrel statue off the crowded crate and ran a thumb along its tail, feeling every wiry hair, turned it over and examined the bottom, as though a message might be carved there.

"I wanted to hit her, when she told me," Rich admitted, the shame of it a lump in his throat. "I never would. You know I never would." He shook his head. "It's my own damn fault. I got so wrapped up in that whole 24-7 deal."

Lark tossed Rich a hunk of driftwood. "There's a Sasquatch in there wants free."

"That's your job," Rich said.

"Help a dying man out."

Rich popped open his knife.

"Any word on those harvest plans?" Lark asked once they were both finished.

"Not yet, officially." Rich rose to leave.

"How you doing on toothpicks?"

Rich tapped his front pocket. "All set," he said, and went down the steps to his truck.

"Watch out for potholes and assholes," Lark called after him.

Rich collected the mail off the seat.

"Almost forgot," he said, coming back up onto the porch and tossing the envelopes onto the upside-down crate. "Lot of mail for a dead man."

*March 20*

# COLLEEN

Daniel leaned against the brick wall of the Beehive, waiting, like they'd agreed to meet here. She walked past him.

"Colleen—" As though after humiliating her in front of everyone, in front of Rich, she was the one being unreasonable. "Colleen, come on." He stirred but didn't follow.

Inside, Dot's eyes kept sliding toward the window.

"How long's he been out there?" Colleen asked.

"A while. Waiting on a ride. Lost his brakes again, I guess."

In the refrigerated case: four white store-bought eggs, each stamped with a date.

"They'll be working right in your backyard," Dot said, as though trying to cheer Colleen up, to compensate for weeks of cold-shouldering. "Rich can come home for lunch." Dot dropped bear claws into a sack, set it on the counter, but kept her hand on it. "I lost one too," Dot confided. "Long time ago, now. When Lew and me were first married. You trust God, but still. You want a reason."

Colleen took the bag. The bear claws weighed almost nothing.

"My dad took me, once," Colleen remembered. "To see the salmon in Blue Creek, after they spawned. They were rotting up and down the banks. He said they died doing what they were born to do."

"You okay, hon?"

"I keep thinking about what this place was like when I was a kid. It's not the same."

Dot wiped an invisible smear off the counter. "Oh, I don't know. Still rains."

Colleen went out.

"Colleen," Daniel called after her. He held her truck door to keep her from slamming it. "Will you listen to me for one minute?"

"Oh, now you want to talk to me?" Colleen fumed. "You don't want to wait until there's a microphone?"

"Colleen, look, I only got those results the day of." Daniel dropped his eyes. "I should have told you first, before I—"

"Before you announced it to the whole town?" Colleen crossed her arms. "Well?"

He cleared his throat. "The lab found 2,4-D, 2,4,5-T, and TCDD—dioxin contaminant—five parts per billion."

"Is that a lot?"

Daniel looked off sideways. "There is no 'safe' level."

"You tested both?" Colleen asked.

"Both what?"

"The faucet water and the filtered?"

Daniel nodded.

Colleen snorted, shook her head.

"I never meant to drag you into all this," Daniel said by way of apology.

"Sure you did. From the very first day you did." How could she have been so stupid? "Where did you get them?" she asked.

"Get what?"

She rapped her knuckles against her temple. "You just woke up and decided, 'Today I think I'll dig up a child's skull and hide it like an Easter egg'?" Even as she lashed out, she knew the accusation was absurd.

"You think I'd have anything to do with—?" Daniel tightened his jaw. "All those preservation people think about is how they can use us to push their own agenda."

Colleen scoffed. "That's something you'd know something about." She jerked the door, but he held fast.

"Yes, okay, you're right," Daniel said. "You're not some here-today, gone-tomorrow choker setter's wife, okay? You bring babies into the world. It had to be someone the community respects. We have to show them we aren't just going to get in line."

"Who's 'we'?" Colleen shot back.

"Colleen, I see you. You want another kid so bad it might as well be written on your forehead."

"You don't even know me." She yanked the door.

"Colleen, come on, don't be like that. We can't give up now."

"*I'm* married." The look on Rich's face when she'd told him; the glass jars hitting the wall; the sick drop in her gut, still, whenever she passed the radar station turnoff; the worry at the back of her mind, even now, that someone would drive by and see her talking to Daniel—all of it contained in these two words.

"That's not what I meant."

A brown Datsun pulled into the lot and honked. The pretty journalist with the camera.

"Of course not." Colleen slammed her door.

"Look, I'm sorry," he said through the glass. "Colleen, I care about you."

"No, you don't. You didn't then, and you don't now."

She put the truck in gear. She'd made him angry. Her own hands were shaking with it.

# RICH

Rich rolled another round onto the chopping block, arms warm and loose. Ax work was honest work. He'd been out here since three, too antsy to sleep— first day of the season. In two hours, he'd be back on the crummy. Colleen cracked the front door.

"Coffee's ready," she called out.

He went in, took a sip, winced out of habit, tooth in his dresser drawer, still in its envelope. She worried a hangnail.

"It'll be fine," she told him, as though to convince herself.

Driving in, his hands were so sweaty he had to wipe them down the legs of his denims. A half hour early, he found the lot empty, crummy dark, mill silent, empty as an airplane hangar except for the ancient head saw—useless without the old-growth it was invented for. His head weighed twenty pounds. He leaned back.

A gunshot startled him awake. He hunched behind the wheel, squinting in the predawn. A second shot—no, only Pete yanking the handle of his jerry-rigged door and slamming it again to get it to latch. Rich scooped up his hard hat, grabbed his lunch pail and thermos, conked his skull on the rim of the door, hungover with sleep.

"Hey, Gundersen," Lew called. "Sure you still work here?"

Rich swung his McCulloch out, didn't raise his eyes again until he was halfway down the aisle of the crummy, talk going quiet. He slid in behind Pete and tried to breathe normally.

Mist poured over the ridges. His head lolled. Felt like he'd only closed his eyes for a second when the crummy jolted to a stop. Rich dropped down the steps, a creek thundering from a culvert.

"Circle up," Don said.

Most guys had the paunchy look of emerging from hibernation, winter spent bellied up at the Only, a few leaner and sun-beat from crabbing.

"We'll cut the track in first," Don said, pointing downhill: the lower grove, Rich realized with a surge of recognition, massacred timber crisscrossing the slope.

"Is it stable?"

"We'll find out," Don said.

"Did the plans go through?"

"How about we let Merle worry about that?" Don looked straight at Rich. "Anybody here doesn't want to work, town's that way."

"Pretty damn steep, Porter," Lew objected.

"You got a better idea?"

Lew's eyes tracked to Rich and back. "I don't want to end up at the bottom of a slide."

"Cats are waiting," Don said.

Lew shook his head, followed the others, until it was just Rich left.

"Look, I'll tell Merle the brush isn't bad, but if he says 'spray,' there's not a hell of a lot I can do," Don said.

"Appreciate it." Rich nodded. Blackberry shoots were already sprouting up between the downed timber, hungry for sun. Of course Merle would have it sprayed.

"Won't be anything left to hold this hill once we're done," Don said. "I was you, I'd get my cut out this season, before the rest of this slides out and takes the roads with it."

He was right. Most of this side would end up in the creek, trapping Rich's timber on 24-7 Ridge for good. He'd need to act fast.

Eugene climbed up into the cab of a D8, trying to get her going with the exaggerated frustration of a kid tugging a stubborn cow by a rope. The engine caught. Eugene grinned, shouting over the noise.

"Let's cut some damn roads!"

The road began as a nub, carving down through the wrecked timber of Lower Damnation Grove, skirting giant logs that lay broken where they'd hit, here a three-hundred-footer busted to toothpicks, here a trio of old monsters twenty feet in diameter that had knocked each other over like dominos. All day, Rich tracked the road's progress, watching the Cats carve hairpins into the hillside, switchbacks rolling down the steep grade toward the creek like a long, soft rug. In less than a week, they would reach the bottom, the very edge of Rich's property, a road he'd dreamed of all his life appearing suddenly at his feet.

At the end of the day, Eugene hung an arm out his truck window in the mill lot.

"Have a beer with us, Rich."

"I'm good."

"Wasn't a question, Gundersen."

*March 23*

# COLLEEN

She brought Chub home from school to find the phone ringing furiously, threatening to jump off the kitchen wall, the way only Enid could make it ring.

"Can you come get us?" Enid asked.

By the time Colleen got to Fort Eugene, Enid was waiting out front with Marla and the baby. A dead raccoon lay draped across the lid of the trash can, small hand hanging down, almost human. Enid climbed in the backseat with Chub, leaving Marla up front.

"Where are the kids?" Colleen asked.

"He took them to the store."

Marla looked out the window. Colleen felt the taut thread of anger tied between them and wondered what fight they'd had that Marla was being dragged along, made to sit up front where Enid could see her. They passed the mill. Colleen stopped at the T.

"Where are we going?" Colleen asked.

"Samoa," Enid said.

"Samoa?" Colleen heard her own voice reverberating inside a rusty can, traveling a string sixteen years long. She'd forgotten how a word could change the taste of the air. "I thought—"

"It's not for me."

Colleen looked to Marla—her baggy coat concealing her shape. "Does Eugene—"

"Don't talk to me about Eugene," Enid snapped.

Trees blurred past. South of Arcata, Colleen turned west and they crossed to Samoa, a strip of land a few streets wide latched to the coast by a rusting bridge. June Millhauser's white house stood exactly as Colleen remembered it: a covered porch, a swing, a chainsaw bear holding a burnt-wood sign: WIPE YOUR PAWS. It looked like the house of a spinster piano teacher, which, as far as Colleen knew, was what June Millhauser still was.

Colleen set the parking brake, sound stitching the two moments together: Colleen at the wheel of their mother's Mercury, Enid waiting to go in. Enid hadn't told Eugene then either. Colleen looked at Marla, wondered if she knew they were sitting in the exact spot where her own life might have ended. Enid got out, brought the baby around to Colleen, followed Marla up the steps. Marla's lashes were caked with mascara, but underneath she was still a scared little girl. Colleen's heart ached for her, for the second heart beating inside her. *Don't*, she pleaded silently. *Marla, honey, no!*

"What's wrong?" Chub asked, watching Enid knock, then step aside.

"Marla has a tummy-ache," Colleen said, hitching Alsea up on her hip.

"Is there a doctor in there?"

"Let's go see if we can see any whales, Grahamcracker."

They walked one street over and stood at the water's edge. Chub scanned the horizon with his binoculars.

"See any?" she asked, shivering.

When they returned, Enid was pacing on the porch. Alsea had fallen asleep, a warm weight on Colleen's chest. Chub boosted himself up onto the swing. The porch ceiling was painted light blue, as though, even on a rainy day, it was clear skies under the overhang.

Their teenage selves still sat in the driveway, idling in their mother's Mercury. Colleen had been terrified—it was illegal then. She'd let the car run, Enid unmoving. Finally, June Millhauser had come out onto the porch. They'd seen her in the supermarket with Mom once. Enid, five or six, had stared: June Millhauser's left eye white-blue, the other a dark brown that absorbed light.

*Why are her eyes different colors?*

*I don't know*, Mom had said, exasperated by Enid and her *whys*.

*But why?*

*Because she's the angel maker.*

*What's an angel maker?* Enid had asked.

Their mother had sighed. *She takes care of babies nobody wants.*

Then suddenly, they were teenagers, staring up at June Millhauser's house a decade later.

As if she'd needed to see the house to decide.

Colleen wondered if Enid remembered this—her childhood curiosity, the shakiness in her voice at fifteen, pregnant and scared—if she'd paged back through the album of her life while she'd been waiting here on the porch. The sea smell wafted in with the gull calls. Colleen followed Enid down to the far corner of the porch. She should have gone in with Marla. She was her mother.

"Eugene doesn't know?" Colleen whispered.

"He thinks that dumbbell will marry her."

"Would he?"

"That's not the point. I'm not letting her ruin her life." Enid folded her arms, scuffed the porch boards with her toe. "Eugene'll be so pissed. His little Sanderson grandbaby, flushed down the commode." Enid laughed, a heartsick laugh.

"Where'd you get it?" Colleen had seen the crisp bills June Millhauser had pinched from the envelope before letting Marla in.

"Merle. Where else does money come from around here?" Enid inhaled. "He's sending that kid back up north. That's the last she'll see of him."

Colleen rocked Alsea to calm her own restlessness.

Enid touched the baby's head. "Eugene drove me down. For that X-ray the nurse wanted."

The front door opened. Colleen hurried Chub off the swing. Enid tried to help, but Marla shrugged her off, raccoon eyed, fierce with pain. June Millhauser appeared in the doorway, her hair gray, her blue eye larger than her brown one, giving her the appearance of squinting. She shut the door. Colleen heard the first swelling chords of the piano.

In the closeness of the pickup's cab, Colleen smelled a musky iron sweetness. Marla squirmed. Colleen waited with her in the parking lot while Enid ran into the pharmacy. Chub lay down in the backseat.

"A hot water bottle will help," Colleen said.

"It hurts," Marla whimpered.

"I know, honey." Colleen would never, never end a child's life, but she knew what it felt like to have a dead one scraped out: how raw, how empty.

She took Marla's hand. She couldn't remember the last time she'd held it. This gangly teenager, once so small and happy, bouncing on Colleen's knees at the kitchen table, *giddyup*. Where had that little girl gone?

"I'm sorry, Aunt Colleen," Marla said.

"Why are you sorry?"

"For making you drive us." Tears spilled down Marla's cheeks.

"Oh, honey," Colleen said. "Don't you worry."

Marla started to sob quietly. "I wish I could have"—she hiccupped—"given it to you."

"Don't worry about me, sweetie." Colleen wiped Marla's eyes. "You just worry about getting better, okay?"

Marla nodded. "You're lucky." She sucked snot in her nose. "Uncle Rich loves you. Like really loves you. Not just saying it. He's always looking over, watching to make sure you're happy."

"You'll find someone like that someday," Colleen said. "You will. Just wait."

"No, I won't." Marla buried her face in her hands. "Nobody's going to want me now."

"Shh. That's not true." Colleen rubbed Marla's shoulder. "I used to think that too, before I met your uncle Rich."

"Did you ever—?" Marla grimaced, squeezed her knees together, and dug her palms into her thighs until the cramp passed.

"No," Colleen said. "I've never had a baby inside me I didn't want with all my heart. But that's different, sweetheart. I'm a lot older than you. Your time will come."

"How do you know?" Marla asked.

"I just do," Colleen said. "I've known you your whole life. Since you were a little bump in your mama's belly. You're smart, and sweet, and so, so beautiful." Colleen brushed aside the thatch of white-blond hair fallen into Marla's eyes. "You can have any life you want. If you want healthy babies, you'll have them," Colleen promised, tears welling in her own eyes, willing it to be true. "Later, when you're older. Okay?"

Marla dropped her chin to her chest and nodded. Enid emerged from the pharmacy. Marla hugged herself, blew air up into her eyes. Enid pulled open the truck door and climbed in with a bag of painkillers and three flavors of gum for Chub, who sat up.

"No eating it," Enid said. "Or you'll end up with a great big lump in your stomach and we'll have to take you to the doctor next."

\* \* \*

By the time Colleen pulled into Fort Eugene, it was dusk. The cab smelled artificially of watermelon. Chub dropped out of the truck.

"Five minutes," she called after him.

Marla climbed down gingerly.

"Enid?" Colleen asked. Enid got out, pretending not to hear. "Enid."

"What?" Enid flared her nostrils, clearing Alsea's hair off her forehead with one finger. "She's missing half, okay? They showed us. She might have trouble learning things, we'll have to wait and see, but she can"—Enid's voice cracked—"she can live fine with half."

"Half of what?" Colleen asked.

Enid cupped her hand over the baby's head.

"Oh my God." Colleen covered her mouth.

"I told you so, right? Say it. Go ahead."

"Why didn't you—"

"Why didn't I what?" Enid demanded. "What do you want me to do? We're just a dot on the map in the middle of nowhere. Even if it was the sprays. They don't spray, they don't log, and then where would we be, any of us?" Enid sucked air in her nose. "You should have seen Eugene. He blew a gasket, yelled at the lady and everything. Made them redo the X-ray." Enid shook her head. "When we got home, he just laid his head in my lap and cried. Like a little kid. He is like having a seventh kid, sometimes. But he's doing his best. He's trying to take care of us the best way he knows how. I know you don't think much of him."

"That's not—"

"Don't lie. I know he has his faults. But he loves his kids."

Colleen looked down at her hands. "Why didn't you tell me?"

"I've had other things on my mind lately. In case you hadn't noticed." Enid rattled the bag of painkillers. Colleen saw tears glistening in her sister's eyes, but Enid refused to let them fall. "No use crying about it," Enid said. "Won't change it. Anyway, I ask you for enough as it is. Thanks for the ride."

"Wait—"

"What?" Enid asked. "She's here, isn't she?" She bounced Alsea in her arm. "She's alive. What do I have to complain about, compared to—"

"Enid, you're my sister. We're all we have, remember?"

A tear rolled down from the corner of Enid's eye. She smiled, shook her head. "You have Rich. I'm not all you have. I haven't been for a long time."

The front door slammed and Chub raced toward the truck.

"Drive fast," Enid said. "Take lots of chances."

Chub climbed in, breathless, Enid trudging through the fog, mounting the trailer house's cinder-block stairs slowly, one heavy step at a time.

Rich was in the kitchen, crouched in the far corner, setting up a wooden stand.

"What is that?" Chub asked.

Rich took hold of the glass bottle and rose with a grunt, tipping it into the dispenser, five gallons of water gurgling. He held a mug under the spout, showing Chub how to press down on the spigot. Rich handed him the mug.

"How's that taste?" Rich asked.

"Good," Chub said, stepping up to refill it.

Rich set a palm on Chub's head. "Leave the empties out front and the delivery truck'll swap them out next week," he told Colleen.

She nodded.

He scuffed his boot against the linoleum.

"Thank you," she said.

"Nah. I should have done better." He cleared his throat. "I should have listened."

# RICH

Lark stood waiting out front in a denim shirt faded to white, red suspenders, and a bolo tie, scratching the hog with his saw cane. Rich pulled up beside him. Lark gave the hog a goodbye whack and limped around to the passenger door.

"Where's the party?" Rich asked.

Lark patted his pockets as they trundled down the rutted drive.

"Forget something?"

"Nope." Lark rubbed a spot on his chest like it pained him. "They didn't tar and feather you, I see."

"Not yet," Rich acknowledged. He'd felt the strain the first day, but once they'd gotten into a rhythm, work was work.

"What are you so happy about?" Lark asked.

"Road's about done." Rich couldn't keep from grinning. "You can spit across from the bottom of it."

"No shit?"

Sun streaked through the timber. Rich pulled off at the post office, left the truck running. He opened the box, dragged his pinkie under the flap of the mortgage bill and checked the amount, slid it back in carefully, like the numbers might get jumbled. Evangeline set his stamp and envelope on the counter, change jangling in his pocket, the sound of his savings dwindling. When he went back out, Merle had one arm braced above Lark's window.

"Don't know about that, Corny," Merle said with the air of humoring an old man.

"Pays to think down the road," Lark answered, bristling at the name, Virgil alive in it.

"I guess we'll see, won't we, now?" Merle waited for Rich to slide back behind the wheel, then patted the truck, giving it permission to move out. "Keep an eye on this guy, Rich."

Rich let the clutch out.

"Should have slacked the mainline on that sonofabitch when I had the chance." Lark spat out the window. "It true Eugene got his ass kicked by that Sanderson kid?" Lark asked, once they were on the road.

"How'd you hear about that already?" Rich asked.

Lark shrugged.

"It's his daughter," Rich said. Eugene had gotten himself two black eyes. Would have bit a chunk out of the kid's ear cartilage if Lew hadn't gotten between them yesterday.

"Merle sent him back up north?" Lark guessed.

"Came and picked him up himself."

"Girl got in trouble, Sanderson always could make one of their own disappear."

"Family business," Rich said.

Lark snorted. "You got that right."

They wound around the cliffs, coasting downhill into Crescent City, Lark leaning forward, nose lifted to catch the scent of the trouble he'd like to get up to.

"Where to?" Rich asked.

"Moneylender's," Lark said. "Why else you think I'm dressed for my own funeral?"

"Doesn't Marsha take care of all that?"

"Trust a woman with my money? I might be old, but I'm not stupid."

Rich pulled into the savings and loan. Just the sight of the building gave him indigestion.

"Want company?" Rich asked.

"You stay here." Lark maneuvered himself out, muttering. "Nosier than a goddamn bloodhound."

Rich massaged the wheel. He had eighty-six dollars left in his savings account. He'd be short on the loan payments for a few months, but as long as the lower grove stayed exactly on schedule, he could harvest the 24-7 this summer, dig his way out before they got around to foreclosing on him.

An hour went by before Lark hobbled back out, newspaper tucked under one arm.

"You seen this?" Lark asked, smacking the paper into Rich's chest as he got in. "It's official."

Rich squinted to make out the headline. DAMNATION GROVE HARVEST APPROVED.

"You ever seen Merle not get what he wants? Cheat, bribe, stab, or steal." Lark took the paper back, scrunching up his nose to examine the picture. "It's going to be a Damnation spring, String Bean. One hell of a last season."

Rich started the truck back up, his mind racing. He might be able to rent rigging and a yarder on credit. He'd have to find a gyppo trucker willing to work out payment-on-delivery.

"Tractor supply," Lark announced.

"What am I, a chauffeur?" Rich asked.

"Chauffeurs are paid to drive, not talk."


Lark banged the log splitters with his saw cane, as though he'd know the one he wanted by sound. The clerk—just a kid—showed him how to set the choke, drive the hydraulic wedge.

"Sure as hell beats ax work," Lark announced, satisfied.

"What happened to your finger?" the clerk asked.

"This one?" Lark raised the stump like he'd just noticed it. "Whore bit it off. Lucky my dick was too big around."

The kid grinned, hid it, helped them load the log splitter into the truck.

"That redhead still over at the Widowmaker?" Lark asked, climbing into the cab.

"She never was a redhead."

"When I knew her she was. The carpet and the drapes."

"You buying?"

Lark tapped his bulging breast pocket, buttoned shut. "Keep us drunk 'til next Sunday."

"That all in ones?"

"Ones?" Lark asked. "Try hundreds."

"Didn't know you were so loaded."

"Shit pays."

\* \* \*

Mabel's back was turned when they came in, hair a frizzy cloud. Lark looked around, as though not convinced it was the right place, almost to a stool by the time she slapped coasters onto the bar, her low-cut top exposing her sagging breasts, skin weathered like she'd spent too much time in the sun, though she'd spent most of her life right here, breathing other people's cigarette smoke.

"You still alive?" she asked.

Lark reached for the peanuts, tossed a few back. "When's the last time you changed these molar busters?"

"I've been saving them for you."

Lark held up two fingers, messed with his bolo—a lumberjack midswing, first prize at one of the big Oregon jubilees. Mabel set beers in front of them. Foam soaked into Lark's mustache.

"Where you been, Corny?" Mabel asked. "You got old. You still carving?"

Lark took a figurine from his pocket—a heron, legs fine as needles—and handed it to her. Mabel traced a long red fingernail along the beak, each feather perfectly scored. It felt like a private moment Rich had walked in on.

Lark cleared his throat. "How's Randy?"

"Still kicking. Up at Smith River today."

"Sounds like a raw deal."

"I'd rather work than fish."

"Well. If you ever get tired of him."

Mabel tried to hand the heron back.

"Keep it," Lark said. Mabel smiled, wiped the bar, her marriage band catching the light. Lark gulped down the rest of his beer.

"You want another?"

"Next time." Lark peeled a bill from the wad in his pocket, suddenly in a hurry, out the door before Mabel came to cash them out.

"Does he want change?" she asked, staring at the hundred.

"Guess not," Rich said, finishing his beer.

"He okay?" Mabel asked.

Rich shrugged. "He wanted to see you."

Mabel tucked the money into the register. "I'll open him a tab."

Rich made his way out to the parking lot.

"Looks like hell, doesn't she? Wrinkled up like a goddamn prune," Lark said when Rich got back in the truck. Lark shook his head, pressed at the spot on his chest again. "Would have spent my last dime on her."

"What are you doing, throwing that kind of money around?" Rich asked.

Lark pulled the folded bills from his pocket.

"What is that?" Rich asked.

"Eighteen hundred dollars." Lark held it out. "It's all I've got left. I know you're low. It'll tide you over."

"I'm not taking your money."

"Gundersen, you listen up and you listen good because I'm only going to say this once. This grove trouble, you couldn't have predicted it. Hell, nobody could have. I pushed you into buying that 24-7. You wouldn't be in this mess if it wasn't for me."

Rich shifted, preparing to protest.

"Hear me out," Lark said. "I made a promise, the day your dad died. I swore I'd look after you. I'd already lost my own boys—Ossian was about four, Henry was just a baby—their mom always had them out by the river with her, and the flood . . ."—Lark's voice clotted with emotion—"took 'em all. I made a grave for my wife, but not for my boys. Maybe they washed up on a beach somewhere. Maybe someday they'd find their way home. I kept that door open." Lark swallowed. "I never got to see a son of mine grow up, but because of you, I still got to be somebody's father. You're too damn careful. You take too long to make up your mind. But I'm prouder than hell of you. Like my own flesh and blood. So." Lark sniffed. "We'll call it a loan."

He opened the glove box, shoved the cash inside, and smacked the maw shut.

# COLLEEN

Colleen hung the dishrag from the faucet. Rich sat at the table with the staked-out timber survey, his cheaters slipped down to the tip of his nose. He moved the saltshaker off the corner and the map snapped up into a roll.

"Going to be a lot of long days," he said.

"Are they going to spray?"

He twisted his index finger in his ear, like he was dialing a rotary phone.

"Probably," he admitted.

*What do you mean, "half a brain"?* he'd asked when she'd told him about Alsea. As if it could mean anything else.

"It's not illegal."

"But it's poison," Colleen said. "We're soaking our dishes in it. We're washing our hair."

"So use that." He thrust his chin toward the water dispenser. "What do you want me to do?"

"What do *you* want to do?" she demanded.

"Get the grove cleared. Harvest the 24-7. You want to move, move."

"I don't want to move. I just—" The phone dringed. "If it's making people sick—"

"They can't prove that," Rich said, the phone ringing and ringing—Enid refusing to give up.

"You didn't see that baby—" The flutter of the Larson baby's heart, so faint. "That's all the proof I need."

"That's not how it works, Colleen. There's no law saying they can't spray."

The phone rang again. Colleen picked it up and slammed it back into its cradle. "Then the law's wrong, it's wrong!"

"I'm telling you, Colleen, there's nothing, there's not a damn thing anybody can do. Not me, not you, not—your friend—" The phone trilled again.

Colleen grabbed it off the wall. "Enid, what?!—Oh. Marsha. Oh. I'm so sorry. He's right here."

Rich held out his hand for the receiver, but she didn't let go. As long as she didn't let go, it wasn't true. Not yet.

*April 2*

# CHUB

Chub tugged at his clip-on tie half-heartedly, wishing he could turn the argument on and off with a pull-cord, like the pantry light at Fort Eugene, his mom's voice muffled by the bedroom door. They'd been arguing every day—water this, water that—though they stopped whenever Chub came into the room.

"Jesus, Colleen, how many times are we going to go over this?" his dad asked.

"It's not normal," his mom said.

"What's not normal is fighting about this on the way to a funeral."

The door flung open and his mom swept out, wearing a dress and her special earrings.

"Chub, let's go," she said.

In the truck, she crossed her arms. They shuttled over the bridge, leaving the golden bears behind. His dad turned the radio on, then off. The dashboard rattled, past the elk meadow, until finally they slowed, following a train of pickups.

The church was big, with benches, not chairs. Uncle Lark lay in his coffin. For a long time, they waited. Uncle Lark was dead, but it felt like they were waiting for him to wake up. Finally, the priest stood at the podium.

Chub didn't see Luke until they were outside, everyone waiting to shake Chub's dad's hand. Luke and his mom were in line behind Mr. Sanderson. Mr. Sanderson turned around and said something, and suddenly, like nothing Chub had ever seen a mom do, Luke's mom spat in his face. Chub's mom gasped. Mr. Sanderson wiped the spit on his sleeve, but the angry little smile didn't leave his face.

*April 3*

# COLLEEN

Rich stayed in bed, his eggs going cold. Finally, at half past four, she crept down the hall.

"Rich?"

"Yeah."

"Are you sick?"

"No." He groaned, hauling himself up. He'd stood at the head of the receiving line yesterday, the closest thing Lark had to family, shaken hand after hand. People had tried to talk to him, about Lark, about last Monday's big news—the park ballooning out around Redwood Creek—*Forty-eight thousand acres, how's that for an expansion?*—but none of it seemed to reach him.

Now she followed him out front, rose onto her tiptoes to peck him on the cheek. He looked still half-asleep.

"Be careful," she said. She watched him reverse down the driveway, willow swaying in the wind.

Chub dragged Brownie into the kitchen with him when he woke, leaning the old hobbyhorse against the table.

"Eat your toast. You'll be late for school."

Chub sat down and took a big bite, then another, doing his job. He glugged his milk.

"What's Brownie doing up so early?"

Chub shrugged, finishing his breakfast. She washed the dishes and wiped the counter, took a jar from the cabinet, filled it, checked the lid was tight, dated it, and loaded it into the canvas bag with the others. She found Chub already in his slicker and boots, holding Brownie.

"No toys at school, remember? He'll be right here when you get home."

"I want to bring him."

"Chub."

"I want to!"

She reached to take Brownie away.

"I want to give him to Luke!"

"To Luke? Why?"

"All his toys burned up. I want him to come back."

"I know," she said. "I know you do, Grahamcracker."

Chub started to cry. "I want him to come back to school." He collapsed into her arms.

"Oh, Grahamcracker. Sweetheart." She rubbed his back. "You are such a sweet, sweet heart. Where'd you get this sweet, sweet heart?"

Chub sucked in snot. "I got it at the sweet hearts store."


The nose of the truck dipped down ahead of her, then rose, pushing through the dense undergrowth into Daniel's uncle's clearing. A redwood log, split in half lengthwise, sat near the house. His uncle stooped inside it, and when Colleen turned the motor off, she heard the echo of steel biting into wood. She took the canvas bag off the seat and got out.

He didn't look up, so she crossed the yard to him.

"Excuse me," she said.

He was sweating, chipping away pieces of redwood, hollowing the log out. He collected chunks off the log's floor, pitching them out so that she had to move sideways to avoid being hit. The jars clinked in their bag and he looked up, brushed bits of wood off his hands.

"Looking for Danny?" he asked, straightening up.

Colleen nodded.

"He's not here." Up close, the man's hair was streaked with gray, and he was heavier and shorter than he'd seemed at the hearing, carpenter's pencil wedged above his ear.

"Do you know when he'll be back?" Colleen asked.

He tossed his head, so faint it might only have been to ward off a gnat. It was hard to imagine anyone handcuffing him, hauling him off to jail, again and again, just for feeding a net into the river.

"Is it all right if I wait?" Colleen asked.

He gave a nod and picked up his tools again. She went back to her truck and climbed in, sat watching him work. A rapping on the glass roused her. She jerked awake. Daniel stood out in the drizzle. She rolled down her window. His uncle was still chipping away at the log.

"I brought these. I had more but—they broke." She shoved the bag into his arms. "I have to do something," she explained. "I have to do something, or I'm going to lose my mind."

Daniel looked off in his uncle's direction. "They stole his outboard. He bought another one, so they sank his boat. They sink that canoe, he'll just carve another one."

"How's your mom?" Colleen asked.

Daniel dropped his eyes and jostled the bag. "Thanks for bringing these," he said, water sloshing inside.

*April 9*

# RICH

The cemetery gate clanged. Rich watched Chub hesitate, eyeing his feet, the way Rich had as a boy, as if a hole might open and swallow him, as it had Lark, as it had, years before, Rich's father.

Colleen took the gravel path toward the newer section, Chub trailing Rich to the willow sweeping the top of the double stone in the corner: HANK GUNDERSEN. GRETCHEN GUNDERSEN. Chub added an agate to each pile, then a red one for Colleen's father, John, buried a few rows away from Laverne, as though, even in death, she hadn't forgiven him for heading out onto open water, leaving her alone on shore with two little girls. Laverne's heap of stones was scattered. Chub spent some time scooping them back together.

Rich looked down the hill toward where Colleen crouched, hugging herself.

"You got any left?" Rich asked Chub.

"One." Chub held it out.

They followed the path around the side of the hill, through the opening in the stone wall to the old cemetery. At the funeral, Rich had laid a hand on both of Lark's, cold and strange, slipped a pack of cigarettes into them.

*Watch out for potholes and assholes.*

*No potholes in heaven.*

*Who said you're going to heaven?*

*I heard the whores are better.*

Lark was buried beside his wife. The heap of turned earth that covered the casket had already begun to sink into the ground.

*Back the hell up, you're on my feet. What's a dead man have to do to get a little peace and quiet around here?*

"You can talk to him," Rich told Chub. "If you want to."

Chub twisted his lips to one side, shy.

"Lark?" Rich's voice wobbled. He cleared his throat. "Marsha's taking care of your dogs. That hog's about ready for the smokehouse, but he's as stubborn as you. He won't go in. We're headed over to your place today, clean things up. Chub's going to sniff out your secret stashes and smoke 'em all." Chub brightened with the tease. "Anyway, we'll come by and see you again."

Chub dropped the single agate onto the turned dirt.

"Does it hurt to die?" Chub asked.

"I don't think so. Maybe for a moment, but then it's over."

"Like a shot?"

Chub's school shots were still sharp in his memory, the marker against which he measured suffering.

"Something like that," Rich said.

Chub toed the ground, Rich's own tic reflected back at him. They took the path toward Colleen. Chub ran ahead and slammed into her, hugging her from behind. She gave a little, turned her head to catch Rich's eye, tears streaming down her cheeks, the little pile of stones on the baby's grave a tiny memorial of his visits. A year's worth. He dug the agate he'd saved from his pocket and held it out to her.

"What's wrong, Mama?" Chub asked.

She added the agate to the pile, wiped her eyes, pushed to her feet, and held out her hand. "Let's go, Grahamcracker."

In the truck, Chub pressed his binoculars to the window, staring at the silver chop.

"I didn't know you'd kept going," Colleen said quietly.

"I try to swing by on my way home," he confided.

"A whale!" Chub shrieked. "A whale!"

"Where?" Colleen asked.

"There!"

Rich stopped the truck.

"Right there!" Chub pointed. "There!" He thrust the binoculars at Rich. The things were tiny in his hands. It took a moment to adjust them. "See it?" Chub asked.

"Where?" And then he did: a geyser of seawater, a dark hump of back.

"I get to make a wish!" Chub squeezed his eyes shut, then opened them, blinking.

"What did you wish for?" Rich asked.

"I can't tell you," Chub said. "Or it won't come true."

# COLLEEN

Colleen stood on a chair in front of Lark's doorless cabinets, staring at a row of punch glasses. The windowpanes vibrated with the noise of the log splitter, Rich tossing cordwood into the wheelbarrow.

"What do you think?" Marsha asked, scraping greasy dust off a plate with her fingernail. "I'll try soaking them."

Colleen handed down the etched crystal goblets, green tinted, relics of another century.

"Where did he get these, I wonder?" Marsha asked, keeping the talk going. "Must have been a wedding gift."

Chub emptied Sasquatches from the hutch, lining them up along the baseboards. He'd asked where Lark was and seemed to accept the answer, though he'd been more persistent about the squirrel, whose tail Rich had found in a mud wallow.

Colleen scrubbed out the cupboards. Marsha's cheery voice and Chub's shy replies faded into the background, until she realized she no longer heard Rich. The log splitter sat silent, wood piled neatly against the shed. The dogs had crawled underneath his truck, sheltering from the drizzle.

"You want more coffee?" Marsha asked. "I'll make some."

Rich streaked by the window, loping down to the river and hurling a rock out. He bent, bracing his arms on his knees, then turned and strode back up, past the house. After a few minutes, Rich streaked past again, like he could hurl the thoughts in his head out with the next rock, sink them to the bottom of the river.

"Took Lark years to carry those rocks up," Marsha said, handing her a steaming mug. "Carried one up out of the river every day, until he got hurt."

Colleen had seen the rock pile at the base of the giant stump on Knockdown Ridge. The tree that had killed Rich's father. They watched Rich stoop, hands braced against his knees, dark folds of forest disappearing into the mist on the other side of the river.

"What is it about men?" Marsha asked. "They'd be better off if they'd just cry and be done." Marsha picked invisible lint off her shoulder. "You ready for the living room? I'm afraid of what might be living under that couch."

Rich came up onto the porch, hesitated, not wanting to sully the mopped floors.

"Almost clean enough to eat in here," Marsha announced.

A lard can sat near the door, filled with cigarettes cut from the undersides of furniture.

"Liked hiding them more than he liked smoking them," Marsha said.

"You about ready?" Rich asked. Colleen nodded.

Chub had fallen asleep on the couch. Colleen touched his shoulder, waited for him to sit up. Rich stood in the kitchen alone for a moment. The last one out, he pulled the door shut behind them.

"You know," Marsha said, "I think that's the first time I've ever seen that door closed."

Rich clapped Killer and Banjo out from under the truck, hog nosing around Marsha's tires.

"Move it, you big lard-ass, before I fry you in your own grease." Marsha shooed him. "I'll come by and feed 'em tomorrow. Think we should take down his signs?"

Rich shrugged. "Tree's still here. Put a can out."

"You think? Maybe I will."

"Watch out for potholes," Colleen called.

"Honey, it's the assholes I never see coming."

# RICH

"Lark loaned me some money," Rich said, setting the pile of cash on the table. "Before he died. Should help tide us over, until the grove starts paying out."

Colleen looked at it, then at him. "I'll deposit it today," she said.

He nodded, grabbed his lunch pail and thermos.

She followed him out. "Be careful." She rose onto her tiptoes to peck him on the cheek. He turned his head, caught her lips instead.

A few miles south of the house: a single brake cherry in the distance. Rich slowed: a station wagon, front end accordioned, perpendicular across both lanes, ocean a flash of silver through the trees. Rich pulled off onto the narrow shoulder, eyed the blind curve ahead, walked around to the driver's side. Volvo. Washington plates. Sleeping bags, a cooler.

"Everybody okay?" he asked. A woman cupped a hand to her bleeding nose in the passenger seat. The husband turned, bewildered, still gripping the wheel.

"I told you to slow down," the wife said.

The man pried his hands off the wheel, pulled the door release, bashed Rich in the kneecaps, sat back. There was a divot in the windshield where his head had hit, egg rising on his forehead.

"Those needles get pretty slick when they're wet," Rich commiserated. "Will she start?"

Two kids in the backseat. The woman's nosebleed dripped down her chin. Rich offered his handkerchief. The man wouldn't move, so Rich stuck his arm through to her.

"Log truck comes around that bend, he'll cream you," Rich said. He reached in and tried the key. The starter clicked.

"Put her in neutral," Rich said. "Kids better hop out."

He got the wife behind the wheel. He and the husband pushed the car to the shoulder. The man faced north, probably the direction they'd been headed.

"I can give you a lift to town," Rich said.

They squeezed in, Volvo fading into the fog behind them. With the car out of sight, the man began to snap out of it.

"I couldn't see."

"Where you from?" Rich asked.

"Bellingham."

"You get fog up there?"

"Yes," the wife said, scrunching her nose, blotting experimentally.

The kids were spooked but unhurt. Be fine once they got a hot cocoa. Rich pulled in at the Beehive. Missed the crummy by now anyway.

"Dot bakes a mean bear claw," Rich said, holding the door for them. He ducked to avoid conking his head on the bell. Dot looked up, whisking the contents of a mixing bowl braced under her arm as though the motion were also powering the lights overhead. "These folks had a little car trouble," he said.

The wife pulled the kerchief away from her nose.

"Oof," Dot said. "Let's get some ice on that." Dot showed the wife to the toilet, set two cinnamon rolls on plates for the kids. The man stood like he was waiting to be told what to do next.

"Dot brews coffee to raise the dead," Rich told him. "Dot, I got to get to work. Can you call Harvey? We got it to the side, but somebody comes around that curve too fast, that'll be it."

"Where at?"

"North of Wilson Creek."

"Go on." She reached for the phone.

When Rich got to the mill lot, Marsha was hauling a box to her car. He rolled down the window.

"You moving?"

"You think I want to be here when they find out?"

"Find out what?"

"Grove's sold."

"Sold?" Rich asked. "What do you mean, sold? To who?"

"The park. Bought and paid for. Merle just called and told me himself."

"But—the harvest plans. They just finally—" Rich stammered.

"That's what he said." Marsha shrugged, wedging the box into her back-seat, Merle's Cadillac nowhere in sight.

"Where is he?" Rich asked.

"Home, I think."

*That sonofabitch.* Rich tore out of the lot, went flying back through town, up Requa Hill. The Cadillac's doors were thrown open, trunk crammed with suitcases. The debarked dog unleashed a hoarse volley when Rich set foot on the bottom step. The front door stood ajar. Gone were the hutches with their china eggs, the burl clock, four indents in the carpet where the coffee table once sat. Even the phony smells had dissipated, leaving only a damp, musty tang.

"Somebody rob this place?" Rich asked.

Merle looked over his shoulder, taping a carton shut. "She's on the market. You interested? I'll let you have her for a song."

Rich snorted. "So that's it?" Rich asked.

Merle hefted the carton. "Not much of a sendoff, is it?"

Rich followed him out onto the porch, watched him wedge the carton into the trunk and slam it, lean his weight to force it shut.

"Why'd you sell?" Rich asked.

"I didn't *sell* anything." Merle scratched his neck. "You got a problem, talk to Congress. Took the whole Damnation Creek drainage. Why do you think corporate wanted that timber down so bad? Have their cake and eat it too, just like in '68. Anything 'downed by the hand of man' as of January thirty-first they can haul out. And they got their proof right there in the newspaper." Merle leaned back against the car, catching his breath. "Laws are funny, aren't they?"

"What are you talking about?" Rich asked.

"That grove is park land now. Sanderson will get its salvage job, and then it'll be reclamation, restoration, all that environmental bullshit. By the end, won't know there was ever a road there. You want your logs off the 24-7, you'll need a goddamn helicopter, no other way you're getting them out."

"I thought they expanded the park down by Redwood Creek," Rich said.

"Rich." Merle smiled. "Read the fine print." He must have known this was coming for months.

"What do you mean?" Rich asked, his chest tightening.

"It's all Humboldt County, except for two parcels. Little spot known as Damnation Grove. It took some negotiating, I can tell you. It's not 'contiguous.' But I sold it hard, Rich. 'You ain't never seen redwoods like these, if they go, the Damnation Creek salmon run goes too.' I sold it so hard, shit, even *I* teared up. Those trees are *special*." Merle flicked an imaginary tear from his eye.

"You two-faced sonofabitch." Rich backed up, his vision blurring. "All this time you were stringing us along, getting us to fight for that grove, while you were selling it out from under us?"

"That's the way the cookie crumbles," Merle said. "Works out better for the company's bottom line. Is it my fault a bunch of rich city assholes want to spend their family vacations looking at trees? I didn't invent the cow, Rich, I just see how to milk it. Sure, it'll cost a few guys like you—well, it'll bury *you*, you can forget about using those access roads, you'd need a federal right-of-way to haul private timber across park land. With how long that environmental bullcrap takes, you'll be dead before you—"

Rich decked him, catching the hard ridge of his cheekbone, the fleshy bend of nostril. Merle stumbled back.

"That all you got, Gundersen? Come on." Merle smacked his other cheek.

Rich hit him again, then a third time. A thick rivulet of nose blood ran down over Merle's lips.

"Enough," Merle panted.

Rich's breath came and went, came and went. He shook the sting out of his knuckles.

Merle wiped his lip on his sleeve, leaned over, spat, blood smeared across his teeth. "Eugene cut a couple hundred grand worth of burls off that grove. Maybe he'll teach you."

"Cheat, bribe, stab, or steal," Rich said.

A look of satisfaction crossed Merle's face. "Always liked the sound of that."

Merle climbed heavily into his car and reversed out of the driveway. The husky came out from under the porch, whining.

"You forgot your dog," Rich called.

"Shoot him," Merle said. "We'll call it even."

The rear end of the Cadillac sank, rounded the bend, and slipped out of sight. Rich blew air out his nose and started the truck. The husky stretched to the end of his chain, white around the eyes.

Waste-of-a-bullet dog.

When he got back to the mill, Marsha's car was still in the lot.

"Figured you'd be back," she said, standing behind her counter when he came in. She laid out his check. Rich signed and Marsha tore off the voucher, a ripping he felt in his chest.

He fingered the corner, folded it in half, and tucked it into his breast pocket. "You know how much my first check was? Twelve dollars. Bought myself two pairs of denims and about a hundred chocolate bars."

Marsha smiled. "I'm mailing everybody else's." She nestled a stack of envelopes inside a carton of odds and ends. "Walk me out."

She stood for a moment in the doorway, surveying the front office, before turning the light out on twenty years of her life. In the parking lot, Marsha popped her trunk, reached in, and pulled out a framed picture—the crew, Lark and his dad. "You should take this."

"Nah."

"Go on." She dug in the trunk, came up with a wood box about the size of a King James Bible. "Lark said not to give it to you right away," Marsha said. "You know he liked to boss."

It was heavy: river carved into the lid, a heron lifting off at the water's edge, chinook leaping from the current, each fish scale angled and oiled to create the illusion of glistening. *Show-off.*

"I almost forgot." Marsha went around to her glove box and came back. "Here." She plonked Lark's bone-handled knife into Rich's hand.

It took most of the day, driving out to the grove, the crew a mob, Eugene kicking the rim of the crummy's tire hard enough to break a toe, then storming off in the direction of town, park service guys shifting nervously in their tan-and-greens, Harvey in between. At the end, Don got into Rich's truck and they rode back to the mill, following the crummy.

"Sold us out to the park. All the shit I've seen Merle pull over the years, and I still can't believe it." Don shook his head, like he was drunk and trying to sober himself up. "What are you going to do with your free time, Rich?"

"Travel."

Don snorted. They came up on Eugene limping along, fists balled, torso thrust forward.

"Should we let him walk it off?" Don asked.

Rich passed him, slowed, watched Eugene grow larger in the rearview.

Don slid out to let Eugene climb in the middle. Rich waited for him to let loose, but Eugene only clenched and unclenched his fists, the quietest Rich had ever seen him.

Rich dropped Don at his truck in the mill lot. Eugene slouched down and tilted his head back, staring at the truck's ceiling.

"I burned Carl's place down," he said. "Merle told me they wouldn't be home. Said not to worry about the truck in the driveway, they were up visiting her folks." Eugene shook his head. "All the shit he had me do. For what? What the hell do I do now?"

"I don't know," Rich admitted.

Eugene sat forward, hunched over his knees.

"He cleared out his place," Rich confided. "Probably halfway to Vegas by now."

Eugene ran his palms along both sides of his hat. "Shit," he said, and got out.

Rich watched him limp to his truck and climb in, head off home. Once he was out of sight, Rich headed back up to Merle's house.

"You going to bite me, you sonofabitch?" Rich asked, letting the husky off its chain. The dog bolted, moving fast, despite its hobble, scrambling up into the cab.

"Nah, you ride in back." Rich let the tailgate down. "Come on, now."

The dog refused, feinted when Rich reached for him, until finally Rich gave up. The husky whined, panting as they backed down the drive, wet nose tracing patterns in the glass, fogged with its god-awful breath. Rich reached across and cracked the passenger-side window. Together they rode, wind on their faces.

At the house, Rich hooked him to Scout's old chain around back.

"Whose dog is that?" Colleen asked, standing at the kitchen window when he came in.

"Nobody's."

She scrounged around for something to feed it. He sat down and laid the picture frame on the table: Lark on a giant stump, head tipped slightly back, Rich's father beside him, leaning an elbow on Lark's shoulder, stubborn, bashful, stupid with hope.

"What happened to your hand?" she asked.

His knuckles had swelled, a smear of Merle's blood dried across them. Elbows on the table, he bowed his head, pressed his fists into his forehead.

"Rich, what is it?"

"Nothing." He straightened up. His right hand throbbed. "Just tired."

"Rich. Tell me."

"I don't know what I'm going to do," he said.

"Tell me anyway."

*April 14*

# COLLEEN

Chub held the empty pickle jar in his lap. She parked in the dirt pullout above the path. Chub ran ahead through the brambles, a tunnel of green. He hadn't even noticed the old dog this morning. Just as well. It couldn't bark and might not live until dinner.

The path turned to sand. Chub disappeared into the light at the end, surf crashing.

"Chub, wait!"

She ran after him, bursting out onto the beach. Chub stood surveying a pile of driftwood, redwood pounded smooth but still orange, not salt or water enough in the ocean to bleed its color. The tide was still going out, foaming where it cut around sea stacks. Chub hung back, wary, that feeling of the ocean calling your name, ready to knock you down and drag you out.

They searched tide pools for something show-and-tell worthy. Wind whipped Colleen's hair, snapped her slicker, a wind to shake the change from your pockets.

"There's one!" Chub yelled. An orange starfish clamped to a rock.

Usually he dragged on the way back to the truck, but today he raced ahead, shaking the jar, watching the starfish slosh in the seawater.

"You'll make him seasick."

He buckled his seat belt and swung his legs, jumping down as soon as she pulled to the curb outside the school. She watched him go. Before he got to the main doors, kids were swarming him, jar emitting a light only they could see.

\* \* \*

That afternoon, she sat under the painted saw, waiting for Rich, when he came in. He set his keys in the burl bowl, as if he'd spent the day at work.

"Where's Chub?" he asked.

"Out back."

He went down the hall to their bedroom. She followed.

"Where were you today?" she asked.

"Don and me went down to Eureka to talk to a guy." He lowered himself onto the carpet, unbuttoning his shirt, lying facedown on the floor beside their bed.

After a moment, she peeled off her socks and stepped up onto the dips of his lower back. He groaned. The ribbing of his undershirt bunched under her toes.

"Sanderson's going to put out a contract," Rich explained, his voice compressed by her weight. "To haul out what's already down in the lower grove. I think me and some of the guys could bid it out. Found a gyppo trucker today who will haul it on commission. We could rent the equipment, clear out what's salvageable in a couple weeks."

"But I thought the park owned it now?"

"The land, but not the trees already down in Lower Damnation. That's why Merle wanted it in the paper—he wanted a record. It's 'downed tree property.' The company has the right to harvest it, but it'll be cheaper for them to contract it out."

Colleen balanced between Rich's shoulder blades, pivoted.

"How can the government just take it?" Colleen asked.

"Same way they made the park. The big dogs—Louisiana-Pacific, Arcata Redwood—they took the payout then, they'll take it again, just like Sanderson."

If Damnation Grove was park now, they'd leave it alone, never spray it again. She stopped, balancing all her weight on one foot. "Will they still let you use those roads to haul your 24-7 timber out?" she asked.

He let out a deep breath. "I'm trying to find that out."

She stepped off, sat on the bed. Rich rolled over onto his back.

"How am I ever going to pay that loan off?" he asked. He sat up. The flab at his stomach folded over in a soft roll, his arms so pale and vulnerable compared to the callused mitts of his empty hands. "I never should have bought it—" He shook his head. "I should have known. I should have thought—"

"Hey," Colleen said. He lifted his eyes. "The past isn't a knot you can untie. Remember?"

*May 25*

# RICH

Chains clanked, snapped tight, and the rented yarder's booms began to turn. *Easy, now.* The mainline creaked, dragging the last salvage logs out of Lower Damnation, up to the landing below No Name Road.

Rich threw his head back to gauge the hour. He, Lew, Don, and Pete had gotten together and won the contract Sanderson put out. They might have been an old-dog crew, but with Eugene and Quentin setting chokers they'd still gotten the downed timber bucked and yarded in under five weeks. Monday they'd rent the grappler and start loading logs onto the gyppo trucks that would deliver them to the mill in Eureka. If all went right, they'd walk away with fifteen grand apiece. That would hold Rich over while he figured out what the hell to do next. He'd skipped the May mortgage payment completely. He'd been avoiding stopping by the post office to check for the late notice, envelopes piling up in the cubby of his mind. He'd never dodged a debt in his life.

Snowmelt thundered from the culvert. Don hung out of the yarder's cab, looking downhill. Rich heard the scraps of an argument, spotted a pair of guys grappling in the creek. He loped down muddy skids gashed knee-deep. Lew and Quentin stood watching from the creek bank, Eugene hip-deep in the current, knee in the hump of a back, forcing a man under. A rucksack, some smashed jars, and a lone boot were scattered along the opposite bank. Eugene must have grabbed him by the leg and dragged him in.

"You like that?" Eugene jerked Dolores's son up by the hair; the man's arms windmilled as he choked for air. "More?" Eugene dunked him again. "How's that water taste? Clean enough for you?" Eugene yanked him up, the guy gasping so deep Rich felt it in his own chest. "Still thirsty?" Eugene forced him back under. The man thrashed, one arm twisted behind his back, Eugene turning his head to avoid getting splashed.

Quentin cast an uneasy glance up the hill, like Don might appear and put a stop to it. But Don had stayed up by the landing.

"Eugene," Quentin called. "Cut it out, man. Let him go."

Eugene hauled the guy up.

"What's the matter?" Eugene shook him. "Had enough? I thought you Yuroks were supposed to be good swimmers. You got so much of that damn salmon in you."

The man coughed, vomiting creek water.

"Let him go," Quentin commanded.

Eugene forced the guy's head under again until he bucked. Quentin unsnapped his shirt and whipped it off.

"You're gonna drown him?" Rich called across to Eugene. *Make him come to you.*

"You got a better idea? Hell, Rich, you're the one that should be doing this." Eugene yanked the man up by the hair, then shoved him back under.

Quentin started down the bank. Lew stuck out an elbow to block his path.

"Eugene," Lew yelled. "Knock it off."

"He's going to drown him," Quentin said.

"Relax," Lew said. "He'll tire himself out here in a minute."

Quentin pushed past Lew and plunged in, fighting the current.

"Eugene," Rich called.

Eugene looked at Quentin, skinny, but a head taller than he was, and dragged the guy over to Rich instead. Eugene cuffed him one last time in the face and spat into the current. "All yours," he said.

Quentin waded over and hoisted the man up onto the bank, since he didn't look to have the strength to do it himself. Blood ran down from his eyebrow, one foot bare. Water sluiced down his body, sticking his clothes to his skin.

Eugene climbed out after them. Rich stuck an arm out to fend him off.

"What, you're protecting him now?" Eugene asked. "For all you know he screwed your wife. Screwed with her head, that's for sure." Eugene wiped his forehead on his arm and lunged. Quentin jabbed him in the gut. Eugene grunted, jackknifed at the waist. He straightened up, eyes glinting, and, this time, Rich swung. Eugene stumbled, then lurched forward with a roar. Rich hit him again, and stood over Eugene, panting.

Dolores's son coughed. What the hell was his name? Rich had worked so hard to push it from his mind. Now it hovered just out of reach.

"Let's go," Rich said and started up the hill.

After a moment, the man followed. Quentin fell in behind them.

A strange calm came over Rich as he hiked up. His knuckles ached, blood thickening to fill the split skin. When they got to the road, Rich slid in behind the wheel. Dolores's son exchanged a few words with Quentin, then climbed into the cab.

"You stay here," Rich told Quentin when he tried to follow. "The two of us have some talking to do."

The man nodded to show it was okay, pulled the passenger door shut, leaned his head back, and shut his eyes.

Rich put the truck in gear, the pair of them bouncing over ruts, leaving Quentin behind. The guy shivered, lips bled of color, bruises on his face already swelling, darkening. He stank of puke and urine. Must have pissed himself. Rich turned the blower on.

"You okay?" Rich asked.

"Yeah," the man croaked.

When they got to the mill, Rich stopped the truck, pulled a dry shirt from under his seat, and tossed it at him.

The man caught it, turned it over in his hands. He peeled off his soaked shirt, hissing air through his teeth as he bent his arms out of it and threaded them through the too-long sleeves of Rich's spare, snapping it up. Colleen might have married this man, and Rich would still be living off boiled hot dogs and chocolate bars, hanging on in the Widowmaker until last call.

"Colleen said you were fair."

Rich ran his tongue along his bottom gums. "She told me," he said.

The man froze.

Rich kneaded the wheel, sore knuckles throbbing. "The first one she lost, I thought—it's just bad luck." He shook his head. "But watching it happen again, watching her—just over and over—not being able to protect her." Rich sucked in a breath. "The last one, I put my hand on that little tiny baby— I thought: Take me. Take me. I swear to God, I meant it." Rich looked off out the window. He cleared his throat, collected himself, eyed the rearview.

"When she told me about—you know . . ." he trailed off. "I thought: I'm going to kill that bastard." He nodded, remembering the feeling, the metallic taste of his own anger. He swallowed. "Colleen's everything I have."

"Look—I never meant—" The man jogged his right leg, knee bobbing, as though he might grab for the door release and haul ass. "I know—I shouldn't have—"

"You listened to her when I wouldn't . . ." He reached for the man's name again but couldn't recall it. "I'm not proud of that."

They rode in silence, truck pitching over ruts like a boat on rough surf until they reached the pullout where the man had stashed his van. Rich watched him climb out, hobbling on his bare foot. Rich tossed him the balled-up shirt Eugene had torn nearly in half.

"He'll lick his wounds, and then he'll come looking for you," Rich warned. Eugene's rage at Merle was still simmering, but here was a man he could blame—if he hadn't stirred the pot, forced Merle's hand, maybe none of them would be a few days away from unemployed, on the razor edge of broke.

The man turned his head slightly, listening, an engine in the distance. They waited, until the noise faded off in another direction. "I'm headed out in a week anyway," he said.

"I wouldn't wait a week, if I was you."

"What do you care?"

"I don't." Rich shook his head. "But Colleen does. She thinks you'll get to the bottom of all this—" Daniel—the name suddenly came back to him, a coin that had been spinning on edge in his mind for an hour finally falling flat. "She needs to believe that."

Daniel nodded and limped off toward his van.

# COLLEEN

She loaded the lemon bars into a Tupperware and grabbed her keys. No Name Road's ruts were troughed with rainwater. She rounded the bend where Rich and the guys were working, pickups pulled off on either side, flattening brush. Lew's green Ford with the toolbox in back, Eugene's Chevy so rusted it was hard to tell where the bronze ended and the white side stripes began. She didn't see Rich's truck. She pulled over, got out.

She heard voices downhill, the diesel purr of the rented yarder. Eugene climbed up onto the road in front of her.

"Where's Rich?" she asked.

Eugene smirked, a shiner darkening his swollen eye. "Your boyfriend came to visit. Rich took him for a little ride." Eugene crossed to his truck.

"He's not my boyfriend."

"Could have fooled me, hot buns." Eugene pulled open his passenger door. In the footwell sat a human skull. He waited, letting her get a good look, turned a finger in his ear, inspected a chunk of earwax.

"All Merle wanted was to buy a little time to talk the park into buying out the grove. Worth more on the stump than Sanderson ever would have made cutting it, meanwhile he's raking it in selling off those burls. That sonofabitch screwed me too, screwed us all, but damn if he didn't screw Rich a little bit extra, just for the fun of it. Shit, one little article in the paper, and they were showing up to protest. They did the work for him. I didn't even get to use this third one."

Eugene hooked two fingers through the skull's eyeholes. Colleen dropped the Tupperware, backing up.

"Rich?" she yelled.

"Relax." Eugene pitched the skull back into the truck and picked the container up, popped the lid off, and scooped out a lemon bar.

"Rich? Rich?!"

"I told you, he took him for a ride," Eugene said through a mouthful.

"Where?" Colleen asked.

Eugene tossed his head in the direction of Deer Rib. "Dead end. Where he belongs."

"You belong in jail."

Eugene snorted, selected another lemon bar. "It's a good thing we're family."

"You're not my family."

# CHUB

Chub balanced his lunch box on the brick wall, but his mom didn't come. He was the last one. He cupped his hands around his eyes and looked through the window into his empty classroom. Luke's desk sat abandoned in the front row, two more empty desks where Jake and Jason Gershaw, who were twins but not identical, had sat until their dad got a job in Oregon, and one more behind that, where a quiet girl named Talia who never talked, although she knew how, sat, but she hadn't come to school yesterday and today her name tag was gone.

He went back and sat on the wall.

"What are you still doing here?" Mrs. Porter asked, coming out with her purse.

The car felt big and cold without Luke. The ocean appeared and disappeared alongside the road. At home, the driveway was empty. It was cold in the house, creaky and strange. He'd never been alone in it.

"Hello?" Mrs. Porter called in the door. She found a pad and paper and wrote a note.

They went back outside. His dad's truck turned up the driveway.

"Well," Mrs. Porter said, crossing her arms. "Somebody took his sweet time."

# COLLEEN

She floored the gas, tires spinning, digging herself deeper. She elbowed out, cursing Eugene—no way had Rich taken this road. She wedged branches under the tires, tried again, until finally the truck lurched backward. She stomped the gas, afraid to lose momentum, reversing back to No Name Road.

She drove to the school—almost six o'clock—and found Miles Jorgensen mopping the floor in the cafeteria.

"Gail took him," Miles Jorgensen said, looking down at her muddy boots.

When she got home, Rich's truck was parked out front. Chub came running around the side of the house, barreling into her. She heard a pause in the ax's clatter, Rich stopping to catch his breath, and followed Chub around back.

"Gail brought him," Rich said, splitting a round in two. He set the halves upright.

"I got stuck." She felt a tug of shame—how stupid she'd been, to listen to Eugene.

"You want to take that guy the rest of those jars, you better do it now," Rich said, splitting the halves into quarters. "Eugene tried to drown him." Rich brought the ax down again. "If he's smart, he'll get out of town."

Colleen watched him set the quarters upright and split them into kindling. She'd made no attempt to hide the jars, but that Rich would think of them touched her.

She hurried in the back door, tracking mud, filled a last jar and labeled it, loaded it into a bag with a dozen others. When she came back out, Rich was around front, hosing the mud off her truck. He turned the nozzle off, watched her open her door and climb in.

"Be careful," he said.

The truck nosed down into the weeds, then shot up into Daniel's uncle's clearing, haze of smoke rising out of the dugout canoe that had emerged from the log she'd seen last time. Daniel's van was parked near the house. She tucked her keys up into the visor and climbed out, meadow thick with smoke. She coughed and the door to the house opened. Daniel came out, hauling a duffel bag.

His face was bruised and puffy, a wide gash in his eyebrow. He spotted her and cast a glance sidelong, his uncle detaching himself from the side of a shed, where Colleen hadn't noticed him. The old man leaned into the canoe, raking embers.

"What's he doing?" she asked when Daniel got close.

"Curing it. Fire brings the sap out. That's what makes it waterproof." Daniel hoisted the duffel into the van.

"Are you okay?" she asked.

"Sampled about a gallon of creek water." He coughed, stowed the duffel behind the driver's seat, pulled out a rolled-up flannel, and handed it to her— one of the extras she stored in Rich's pickup, so he wouldn't have to ride home in wet clothes.

"Where are you going?" she asked.

He tossed his head north. "My funding's up. I've got a year's worth of data to write up."

She held out the bag of jars. He snugged them in beside the duffel.

"It's a long process, to convince the EPA," he said.

Colleen nodded. The cut in his eyebrow was deep and would scar. It would change the look of his face. He coughed again, a wet, chesty cough.

"Danny!" The screen door whapped, and an old woman shuffled out, carrying a grocery bag.

"Ma, leave it. I'll get it," Daniel called, but the woman kept coming, stopping only when she rounded the front of the van and stood ten feet away, her eyes on Daniel, paper sack wider than she was. Dolores Bywater's face was gaunt, hollowed out by sickness, her turban hat set back on her head so that Colleen could make out several inches of bald scalp. "Ma, I'm coming back in." Daniel took the sack from her arms.

Once, after Daniel had been thrown against a locker and sent to the office for fighting, Colleen had sat waiting for Enid outside the principal's closed door, flinching with each smack of the paddle, when Dolores Bywater had blown in like a gust of furious wind. She'd streaked past Gail Porter's desk, straight into the principal's office. The principal, a short, pudgy, balding man, barely had time to look up, Enid bent over the desk, before Mrs. Bywater snatched the paddle from his hand.

*If you ever hit my son again*—she'd said, then turned on her heel, taking the paddle with her, Colleen's own heart welling with relief.

It seemed impossible that this was the same woman: frail, emaciated, surveying the contents of the van.

"I'll be in in a minute, Ma," Daniel promised. She turned and shuffled back to the house.

Colleen and Daniel stood for a moment in silence.

"I asked her to come with me. There are good doctors in Canada." Daniel swallowed. "She won't leave. She says it took her too long to get back here the first time." A pained look passed over Daniel's face. "It's just—what if it's the last time—?" Daniel pushed air out his nose. "She says if I need to go, go; it's okay to wander, as long as we always come home. She says she's sick of me waiting around for her to die."

"She's a good mother," Colleen said.

"Yeah." Daniel's eyes swept the clearing as though committing it to memory. She smelled smoke, mud, and, faintly, the musty spice of the shirt—Rich's smell.

"I should go," she said.

Daniel nodded. His Adam's apple bobbed in his throat. She hoped there was a woman waiting for him up north, that he wouldn't drive all night only to push through the door of an empty house.

"Take care," he said.

She crossed the yard to her truck, this huge white, unwanted truck that somehow, over the months, without her realizing it, had become hers. He gave a quick salute. She climbed up behind the wheel, closed her door, and pulled down the visor. The keys to her old life fell into her lap.

## *May 28*

# COLLEEN

Colleen pushed all the clothes hanging in the coat closet to one side. Where was Chub's slicker? She'd looked everywhere and finally let him go outside without it, since the morning drizzle had lifted, but it had to be here someplace.

The table saw whined out front, Rich running boards up against the blade with the practiced movement of a man feeding carrots to an old horse. The harvest work was done on the lower grove. Tomorrow, trucks would come to haul the logs to the mill, they'd return the rented equipment, and Rich would be finally, officially, unemployed.

She watched him set another board on the stack of finished ones. He'd stripped the bathroom walls down to the studs already, working to push the worry from his mind.

"Have you seen Chub's slicker?" she asked, going out.

"In the truck," Rich said, reaching for another board.

The balled-up slicker stuck out from under the seat. When she pulled it free, a wooden box slid out from behind it.

"Where'd this come from?" she asked after Rich finished the next board.

"Marsha."

She fingered the carved lid: curve of river, salmon midleap, a scene so lifelike she felt a pang of nostalgia for a time she didn't even remember.

"You want it in the truck?" she asked.

"Nah, take it in."

He reached for another board and she hugged the box to her chest, watching him guide the salvaged redwood into the blade, the spray of sawdust. He was still trying to sort out what to do about his 24-7, timber he owned but could not harvest, the worthless, wild backwoods he'd mortgaged everything they had for.

She went in, hung Chub's slicker from the hook, set the box on the table. Out back, Chub was trying to teach the old dog to fetch. She watched him wave a stick, hurl it across the yard, wait, then grab the dog by the collar and drag him over to it. She made sandwiches.

"Lunch," she called out the back door. "Chub, go tell your dad lunch is ready."

He dropped the stick and disappeared around the side of the house. The saw went quiet and they came in together, Chub chattering about the dog.

Rich leafed through the mail while he ate, half-listening.

"Is this today's?" he asked.

She shook her head. "Today's Sunday."

He tapped the end of an envelope against the tabletop, dropped it back onto the stack of bills.

"You keep at him," Rich told Chub. "He'll learn. Even an old dog can learn, if you're patient with him." He cast Colleen a playful glance, got up, and set his plate in the sink.

"You want a cup of coffee?" she asked.

"Nah. Need to finish up out there before it rains." He went out.

"I'm thirsty," Chub said.

Colleen handed him a glass and lifted her chin at the dispenser.

"Can I have juice?" he asked.

"Have water."

He sighed and shuffled over, struggling to hold the glass in place and press the spigot, the novelty worn off.

She watched Rich out the window.

When Chub went back to school, she would get a job. She would ask Gail Porter if she needed help in the office, or maybe Dot could use her at the register. If all else failed, she could find something up in Crescent City a few days a week. It might not be much, but it would be something. Of course she couldn't tell Rich, not yet. The hurt look he would give her. *You think I can't take care of us?*

*May 29*

# CHUB

His dad held the kitchen door and Chub slipped out, racing up the hill through the fog. It was a school day, but his dad had let him stay home. His dad swung him across Little Lost Creek and they hiked up and over, resting at the 24-7 tree, until finally they stood at the bottom of a muddy hill studded with stumps and broken logs. Water ran down the slope, washing dirt into a brown river.

"Where are we?" Chub asked.

"You know where we are."

Chub shook his head. Without the trees, it didn't look like any place he knew.

His dad carried him across and they climbed around steep cliffs where mud had fallen away. His dad let him ride on his back, so Chub could see over the maze of broken trees and rocks, once-underground springs now welling in the mud.

They hiked up to where giant logs were stacked. At the gravel road, the fog ended, like they'd walked through a white wall into a different day.

"When's your birthday again?" his dad asked.

"Tomorrow!"

"Tomorrow? Why do I keep forgetting that?" His dad grinned, full of mischief.

"What are we waiting for?" Chub asked.

"The trucks," Rich said. "They're coming to take these logs to the mill."

"Are these the last ones?" Chub asked.

"Yep," his dad said, squinting off into the distance. Chub tugged at his dad's pant leg until he lifted him up to see: the top of the 24-7 tree sticking up from a blanket of fog, bright orange in a beam of sun. "Last of the last," his dad said.

# COLLEEN

She turned up the driveway, pharmacy bag sliding across the seat. A man stood at the front door, like he had an appointment. She collected her groceries, the new spatula, and stepped out.

"Mrs. Gundersen?" The man eyed the spatula uneasily, as though it were a weapon. He was young and clean-cut. He looked familiar.

"Did something happen?" she asked. "Is Rich okay?"

The man wore a suit, as an undertaker might.

"Ma'am, is your husband home?" the man asked. "I'd like to talk to him if he has a few minutes."

"He's working."

She recognized him as the congressman's assistant only after he introduced himself. She remembered him standing off to the side when the congressman had stopped by the fish fry with his wife a few months back, moving from table to table, shaking hands. *Must be an election year*, Gail Porter had scoffed, crossing her arms, burying her hands in her armpits, safely beyond reach.

"I don't vote," Colleen told the young man, who was standing aside now to make room for her to open the door and invite him in.

He gave a tight smile. She shifted the bags in her arms. She wasn't letting him inside without Rich home.

"We're reaching out," the man began, "to all the landowners affected by the . . ." He paused, as though the next word were delicate. "Expansion."

"Our land wasn't taken," Colleen said, aware of how short she sounded. "It's the land next to ours."

"That must have been disappointing for your husband." He searched Colleen's face for a reaction.

"He needs a right-of-way."

"That's a question he'll have to broach with the park service," the assistant brushed her off. "If he has any questions, he can call the office." The man produced a business card.

"Questions about what?" she asked.

The man offered the same clenched smile. "We'd be happy to discuss with your husband what his . . . options might be."

"You want to make sure we won't make a stink, is that it?" Colleen asked.

The man stared at her, unblinking, as though she were a simpleton, not worth arguing with. "I understand you're upset, ma'am. Again, we'd be happy to discuss it with your husband."

The assistant looked to Colleen's full hands. She adjusted her load, fiddling with her keys. He dropped the business card into her grocery sack and stepped off the cement slab onto the driveway gravel.

Inside, she unpacked flour, sugar, Chub's birthday candles. She rubbed the corner of the man's card between her fingers, paper thick and expensive. She set it on top of the bill pile, then took the pharmacy bag and its contents down the hall to the bathroom and shut the door.

# RICH

Rich felt lighter, now that the timber had been loaded and hauled away. Chub ran ahead, galloping down their hill to greet the dog, throwing a stick, then grabbing the old husky by the collar and dragging him over to it, while Rich went inside to clean up.

"We're back," he called.

He pushed the bathroom door open and there on the toilet with her underwear around her ankles sat Colleen. He stank of sweat and diesel, but she didn't seem to notice him. He hesitated on the threshold.

"Honey?" he asked. "What is it?"

She looked up, tears streaming down her face, and held a clear tube out for him to see: a small brown disc, like an eye, at the bottom. She began to sob.

"Hey, it's okay." He squatted next to her, took her face in his hands, the smell of piss in the toilet.

She unrolled a wad of toilet paper and blew her nose.

"I went to get the candles," she said finally. "I was right there, by the pharmacy, so I thought, maybe—" She lifted her chin at the test.

"How far along?" Rich asked.

"Six. Maybe seven. What do we do?" she asked.

Rich swallowed. His back had cramped up from crouching, so he stood up.

"What do you want to do?"

Colleen shook her head, wiped herself, stood and rebuttoned her pants, flushed.

"I know it's stupid to think—" She washed her hands, leaned into the mirror and examined her eyes, blew air up from her bottom lip. "Why would this time be any different?" She breathed deep. "But I can't help it, you know? I just—I'm so happy."

The kitchen door whooshed, Chub tumbling in.

"Mo-om?!" he yelled.

"I'm coming." She palmed her cheeks and smiled at Rich. "I promised him he could help me make his cake."

*June 2*

# RICH

Rich sat parked, looking out the fogged windshield at the Widowmaker's heavy door. He drummed the wheel. He was early, still time to throw the truck in reverse. He'd been turning it over in his mind all week, but it wasn't until the last of the Lower Damnation logs were hauled off that the prospect of hanging up his hard hat for good really hit him. He couldn't afford just to sit on the 24-7 the rest of his life. Hell, once his share of the salvage contract check came through, he couldn't afford to sit more than a few months, after he back-paid the missed mortgage payments. He'd waited until Colleen herded Chub out the door to school this morning, then snatched the business card off the stack of mail, fumbling the numbers as he dialed. And now, here he was, hunched in his truck outside a bar on a Friday night, like a man about to cheat on his wife.

He stepped out. Rain speckled the arms of his coat. He heard music seeping out from inside, the after-work crowd. He pulled the door open and the full force of the band hit him. Randy tossed a coaster onto the bar and set a beer on top of it. Foam soaked Rich's mustache and he wiped it with the back of his hand. His back was to the door. Every time it opened, he felt a gust of cool air, a clench in his gut. Randy drew him another, the band loud, and then came the tap on his elbow. He followed the aide, young and clean-shaven like a missionary, into the back room, and there, sitting behind a rough-hewn dining table, a relic of the last century, was the man himself.

"This is Richard Gundersen," the aide said, eyeing the beer Rich had brought with him, the last inch slopping at the bottom of the glass.

"Mr. Gundersen." The congressman gestured for Rich to sit, as though they were in his house.

Rich pulled out a chair, its legs scraping the floor, a little slow from the beer, a belch stuck halfway up his windpipe.

The young man went out. Once they were alone, the congressman leaned back in his chair, a move that reminded Rich of Merle.

"So. I hear you've got some park-quality timber to sell."

"I did. Before that new park deal blocked us in," Rich said.

The congressman nodded. "You need a right-of-way, through the Damnation parcels, to get your harvest out."

"I need the road," Rich confirmed.

"A federal right-of-way can be . . . *costly*. Environmental assessments, public comment periods, enough red tape to run you from here to Sacramento and back," the congressman explained. "Bureaucracy. Takes a lot of grease to get the wheels turning sometimes."

"I wish somebody would have told me that a year ago," Rich said.

"A raw deal," the congressman agreed.

Rich tipped his glass to the side, watched the liquid slosh, waiting for the man to lay out whatever offer he'd brought him here to make.

"Would you do the work yourself?" he asked at last.

Rich nodded. "I've got a couple guys I used to work with. We had the contract on that 'downed tree property' on the lower grove."

"Let's see now, you got what?" The congressman mulled it over. "A hundred million board feet stranded up on that ridge? At a penny a board foot, that's——" He calculated, then shook his head. "I just don't see it, Mr. Gundersen, not with what jumping through all the hoops will cost you."

Rich downed the last sip of his beer, set his glass back on the table.

"What if I didn't want to cut it?" he asked.

The congressman gave a slow smile. "That's a funny question for a logger to ask."

"There's a lot of old-growth up on the top of that ridge," Rich reminded him.

"The League might be interested," the congressman conceded. "If you were willing to settle for less."

"How much less?" Rich asked.

"Oh, I don't know. Maybe they'd pay twenty percent of market. Maybe a little more if you found the right party to . . . *negotiate*." He eyed Rich, waiting for him to take his meaning.

Rich swallowed. Twenty percent on a million dollars—$200,000, less than he owed, minus whatever this joker had in mind for arranging it.

"That's pretty steep." Rich stalled, wondering how much of a cut the man would take.

"It is." His soft hands drummed the tabletop: the hands of a man who'd never done an honest day's work in his life. "A rock and a hard place, am I right?" The congressman pushed to his feet. "Take a few days, Mr. Gundersen. Think about it."

He hung his coat over his shoulder and left Rich there, alone at the table, the noise of the band picking up on the other side of the door.

*June 3*

# CHUB

Chub wore his new birthday boots, the ones his mom had bought him before school started. He didn't remember them until he opened the box. They were just like his dad's, except the laces kept coming undone. In the sandy lot above the beach, his dad crouched low with a groan, cinching Chub's rabbit ears tight.

The ocean was loud. His dad kicked through the driftwood, tossed a piece to the side, then another, making a pile. Chub scooped up a small log, bulky but light.

"That's a good one," his dad said.

For a while, there was just the lap of the tide, the clunk of wood. Chub watched waves through his binoculars. His dad sat down on a log to rest.

"Let me see that one there. By your feet," his dad said.

Chub picked up the driftwood, orange-red. His dad turned it over, shook it, held it to Chub's ear. "What do you think is in there?"

"A Sasquatch."

His dad shook it again, listened. "You know, I think you're right. Hand me another one."

Chub listened again. "Sasquatch."

His dad put it aside, dug through their pile.

"Here. Listen good now."

"An elephant."

His dad laughed. "Pretty small elephant."

His dad laid the wood on his knee, pulled a knife from his pocket, then took the knife off his belt and laid it beside the first; they matched. He tucked the first knife onto his belt instead and showed Chub how to dig the blade out of the one that was left, how to lock it straight. "You try." It was hard. "There you go."

Chub closed the knife and held it in both hands.

"My dad gave me this knife when I was about your age," his dad said. "And now I'm giving it to you."

Chub looked up, to see if he meant it.

"I have Lark's now." His dad patted the knife on his hip. "That one's yours. Open her back up."

It took Chub a few tries.

"Go ahead. Dig out your elephant."

His dad squinted down the beach. Chub gouged at the wood.

"I'm cold," he said after a while. His dad didn't stir, lost in his thoughts. "Daddy, I'm cold."

"Close that up then, we'll get going." His dad waited for him to drop the knife into his bib pocket and loaded Chub's arms with the driftwood they'd collected.

At home, his dad turned serious. He led Chub down the hall to the back bedroom. His dad's cheaters lay sprawled beside the alarm clock on the nightstand. His dad opened the nightstand drawer and waited for Chub to set the knife inside. "A knife is a tool, not a toy. You ask your mom when you want to get it out. You don't get it out on your own, you understand?"

Chub nodded. His mom watched from the doorway with her arms crossed. "This cookie-boy smells like seaweed," she said. Her tummy had been hurting before, but now she felt better.

His dad sniffed his hair. "Wowee, he does." His dad tickled him.

"Stop!" Chub squealed, squirming, but not too hard. Not hard enough to get free.

# RICH

Colleen zipped Chub into his slicker, Chub begging to bring the old dog along.

"Not this time," Rich said. When they'd let him off yesterday, he'd hobbled out onto the highway and stood in the middle of the pavement, braying. A chain can ruin a dog.

Chub ran ahead up Bald Hill and down the other side, ducked into the brambles to hide. Rich took Colleen's cold hand and squeezed three warm pulses. She squeezed back. She could keep ahead of the nausea as long as she got something in her stomach first thing.

"Chub?" Colleen called.

"Where'd he go?" Rich asked.

"I don't know."

"Maybe the bears ate him."

"Bears don't eat people," Chub called from the undergrowth.

Rich growled. Chub thrashed free, shrieking, giddy with terror.

Up at the 24-7, they rested, their backs against the big tree. Bark pressed into the knots in Rich's shoulders. What choice did he have, besides accepting the man's offer and walking away still owing more than twenty grand? Even if he could find someone else to buy the land, that might take months. And what would he do for work?

"What?" Colleen asked, eyeing him.

"Nothing."

Chub crawled into his lap.

"What are you going to be when you grow up?" Rich asked him.

"A carver. What did you want to be?" Chub asked, banging his head back against Rich's chest to look up into his face.

"Me?" Rich let out a breath, but it did nothing to loosen the tightness in his chest. The guys would have a field day when they found out. Selling out to the tree huggers at the League? They'd rib him for the rest of his life.

"Dad?"

"What?" Rich asked.

"What did you want to be when you growed up?"

"Grew," Colleen corrected him.

Rich looked down at the stumps of Lower Damnation Grove, muddy skid roads scarring the steep side.

"What did you want to be when you *grew* up?" Chub pressed him.

"Nobody ever asked me that," Rich said, putting an arm around Colleen. "A logger, I guess."

If he could jam a wedge in and stop the machine, cogs of time grinding to a halt, he would stop it here: the three of them together, the 24-7 stubborn, proud, and, for now—for another week or two, whatever short time was left—his.

Chub squirmed.

Rich groaned, lifting Chub off his lap. "Let's go home." He pulled Colleen to her feet.

"Race you," Chub said.

"I'm too old to race," Rich said, "I'm an old—" He sprinted, Chub shouting, *Cheater*, shouting, *Wait! Daddy! Wait!*


Colleen made peanut-butter-and-cheeses for lunch, though it was only ten o'clock. Rich got the table saw set up, pulled the tarp off the stack of salvage wood.

"I told Enid she could drop the kids off on her way," Colleen said when he came back in, buzz of the saw still ringing in his ears.

Chub sat at the table, newspapers spread out, working on his driftwood.

"I'm tired," Chub said.

"Go put that away," Colleen told him. Chub closed the knife and pushed back from the table.

Rich yawned. "I'm tired too," he said, padding down the hall after him. Chub returned the knife to the drawer, then threw himself down on the bed, pretending to sleep, his dimples giving him away. Rich flopped down beside him. Chub opened one eye, then rolled onto Rich's chest like he'd pinned him. Rich tickled him. Chub shrieked and wrestled until they both lay still, panting.

"One of my whale wishes came true," Chub said, picking at a button on Rich's shirt.

"What whale wishes?" Rich asked.

"I wished for you to get another Scout." Chub looked down at Rich through the thick fringe of his bangs, his green-blue eyes flecked with gold, his small, bony chest pressed against Rich's. "And for a goldfish." Chub bit his lip.

A horn blasted out front.

"They're here!" Chub sang. He sprang to his feet and ran out.

Rich watched Chub disappear around the corner and out of sight, then groaned, got to his feet, and followed.

"Where do you want her?" Enid asked Colleen, baby on her hip.

"I'll take her," Colleen said, and groaned. "She's getting so heavy."

"You're telling me," Enid said.

The girls plunked down in the entryway, kicking off their boots.

Through the front window, Rich saw Eugene sitting in the truck with Agnes. They were taking her to an eye specialist in Medford and would be gone all day. He and Eugene had orbited each other, finishing up the salvage job and parting ways without exchanging a word. Rich wasn't ready to see him yet: the fading bruises and scabbed-over cuts would shame him. Eventually Rich would hold out a hand and they'd shake, agree to put it behind them, but not now. Not yet.

"Wyatt! Be good!" Enid yelled down the hall. "Did you make a list?" she asked Colleen.

Another week or two until the timber was milled and they split the profits, Eugene and Enid running on fumes. Rich ducked out the back door, leaving Colleen to dig out her grocery list, her pocketbook, the extra twenty bucks she would slip into Enid's hand.

# CHUB

"I have to piss," Wyatt said, but he walked past the bathroom into Chub's parents' room.

"What are you doing?" Chub asked, following him.

"Just looking." Wyatt pulled open his mom's nightstand drawer and rifled through, then crawled across the bed to search his dad's.

Chub heard his mom talking to the girls in the front room. Wyatt reached his arm way back.

"Hey," Wyatt said, grinning. "Look what I found."

Wyatt held out the knife. Chub backed up.

"We're not allowed," Chub said.

"What are you going to do, tell?" Wyatt flicked Chub on the side of the head. He sat down on the bed and fiddled with the knife, trying to figure out how to open it. "Be right back," Wyatt said, dropping the knife on the bed.

Chub heard the sound of pee in the toilet. He looked at the knife—his knife. The toilet flushed. He snatched it, shoved it down inside his bib pocket.

"Chub," his mom said when he passed through the kitchen. "Put your slicker on if you're going outside, please." He pulled the slicker off its hook and slid his arms into the sleeves. "Don't go far, okay?"

He slipped out into the misting rain. The old dog waddled up. Chub scratched him under the chin—*Who's a good boy?* Then he heard Wyatt in the kitchen and he ran, knife clunking against his chest bones. The back door opened. Chub dove into the ferns.

"Chub?" Wyatt called. "Here Chubby-Chub-Chub."

From his hiding spot, crouched up the hill, Chub watched Wyatt in the yard.

Ferns tickled his ears. His rubber slicker squelched. He held his breath. Wyatt kicked through the grass as though searching for a dropped quarter. Carefully, so carefully, Chub lifted his binoculars to his eyes. The view went blurry with brambles until there, right in front of him, was Wyatt. Chub could see every freckle on his face. He stretched out his breath. Time stretched with it. If he breathed, Wyatt would see him. *One one thousand, two one thousand, three, four, five*—he gasped, Wyatt looked up, and time snapped, Wyatt catapulting into the tall grass.

Ferns thwacked Chub's face, brambles clawing at his overalls. He scrambled up the hill, tripping and running down toward Little Lost Creek.

"You're dead!" Wyatt yelled.

Chub took a running leap, landing with a splash in the shallows. He scissored his shoulders free of his heavy slicker, shrugged it off, and ran. He slid down the next ridge to Garlic Creek, got a running start, and landed with a giant splash, deep to his knees. He sloshed up the opposite bank, cold water running down his legs, socks squelching inside his too-big birthday boots, clawing his way up, up, up. His breath scraped the back of his throat. His side ached. He still heard Wyatt behind him. He climbed and climbed, his face hot, until finally he was up by the 24-7 tree. He pressed his hand to its bark the way he'd seen his dad do, wishing a door would open.

"Chub, wait up, you pussy," Wyatt called from below.

Chub tripped on his laces, caught himself, took off down the other side, slipping on wet needles, sliding on his butt, until he was down at the bottom of the gulch, standing at the edge of a muddy creek he'd never seen before, fast and brown, forking around chunks of mud and broken wood. This wasn't right. Farther up, he saw the stumps from the big trees the trucks had hauled away, but this wasn't the creek from last time. This creek was louder, thick as a chocolate milkshake, with foam and waves. He looked at his map, traced the line on his palm. Where was he?

"Chub!" Wyatt called. "Wait up!"

Chub turned and saw Wyatt staggering toward him, holding his side like he had a stitch. Chub knew this trick. He would fake it until he got close, then knock Chub over, pin him, and spit in his mouth. Chub looked back at the brown chop. His heart beat in his ears. He needed to pee.

"Chub!" Wyatt called. Wyatt's face was red from running. For a minute Chub thought he was going to call *truce*. But then Wyatt grinned, tilted his head back, and slit his throat with his finger.

Chub bolted up, following the edge of the creek, rhymes pounding in his head. *Damnation Creek leaks down from the spring, water so clean you could almost sing. You zag along Eel Creek, you follow the sound. On one side is town, and the other Knockdown. When you start to Shiver, you're close to the river.*

Beside him the muddy water thundered so loud he felt its vibration in his chest. He climbed and climbed until he came to the edge of a road pocked with bowls of rainwater. He looked back for Wyatt, but there was no Wyatt.

He didn't know where he was—nothing looked the same—but he crossed the road and started climbing the hill on the other side. His legs were tired. His heavy boots rubbed his wet heels. He tripped on his laces and fell hard on his chest. His palms stung.

Behind him, a twig snapped. He pushed to his knees.

"Wyatt?"

He listened, his own breathing loud in his ears, the *tok-tok* of a wood-pecker knocking on the door of his heart. He got up, backed away from the spot where he'd tripped, and kept going. He heard the tinkle of water, and suddenly there it was: Damnation Spring! *Water so clean you could almost sing.* He thrust his hands in, drank, patted his hot, itchy face. He looked down the hill for Wyatt, reached for his binoculars hanging from his neck. His hands touched air. They were gone! He spun around. He'd been holding them by the strap before, when he was running. He reached into his bib pocket but all it held was the cold, closed-up knife.

He sat down on a rock. He wanted to cry. He snapped the knife open and locked it. The forest was dimmer now. The air felt stiller, cooler. Big trees creaked overhead. His wet clothes clung. His fingers tingled. He wanted to go home. He wanted his mom to peel off his wet shirt and rub his shoulders with a towel warm from the dryer. Raindrops flicked his face. He would be in trouble for losing his slicker.

Cold sweat stuck his shirt to his back. Chub shivered. He got up, dragging his feet down the hill, following Damnation Creek. He knew the way home from here, but it was a long, long, way. He started to sniffle, nose leaking, plodding downhill to No Name Road. He crossed to the other side and tromped down through the mud and rocks and broken logs, too tall to see over, a maze he kept turning scary corners in, until he came to a clearing. Mud sucked at his boots as he crossed it and stood at the edge looking down where soil had caved away: a big drop.

Behind him, a stick snapped.

"Got you!" Wyatt yelled, slamming into his back. The knife flew from his hand. He watched it sail through the air, flipping end-over-end down toward the creek below, and then he was falling, falling, falling. His head conked against a rock. His eyelids felt heavy. It was getting dark. *Mama.* He wanted her to turn on his night-light.

"Get up, retard." Wyatt rolled Chub onto his back. He sounded far away.

Through his fluttering eyelashes, Chub saw Wyatt nudging his leg.

"Chub, get up." Wyatt squatted over him. Chub felt his head lifted up, warm water trickling behind his ear, then it dropped back, hitting the rock again. His eyes were hot and gluey, Wyatt blurring, backing up. And then he was gone.

*Where'd you get those beautiful green eyes?* he heard his mom ask. He felt the little puff of hot air the words made against his temple. *Chub, don't go far, okay? Stay where—Chub, don't go—*

He lay there. The light faded.

*Chu-ub?* his mom yelled.

Then his dad, in the distance. *Chu-ub?*

Their voices lapped over him. They were far away, but they were coming. They were coming to sweep him up in their arms and carry him inside.

# COLLEEN

He never went far. She couldn't recall exactly what time he'd gone out, though it seemed important now. Like if she could just remember the time, a buzzer would go off and Chub would walk in the front door. She heard the girls playing in the front room.

At first, she was sure Chub was crouched somewhere on the hill, hiding. *Stand up*, she'd commanded in her mind as Rich had waded up through chest-high sword ferns, calling his name. She'd stayed in the house, like they'd agreed, squinting out the kitchen window into the mist, watching for Rich to emerge, leading Chub by the hand, Wyatt trailing defiantly. She wiped her breath off each of the back door's nine wood-trimmed windowpanes with the cuff of her sweater, Bald Hill shrouded in fog.

*He never goes far. He knows to stay where he can see the house.*

If they'd gone and gotten lost, it was Wyatt's fault. Chub would never wander away on his own. Wyatt was a bully, just like his father; she would keep Chub away from him from now on.

Minutes peeled past on the kitchen stove clock, the seven rotating up to replace the six. She checked on the baby. It must have been around noon when Chub went out. He'd be cold, worn out. He'd want warm milk heated in a saucepan with a dash of brown sugar. He'd press his wet socks against the woodstove to hear them sizzle.

Colleen tapped her fingernail against the glass, but the old dog didn't budge from his post at the edge of the yard, chain taut, barking his silent bark. She flipped through it all again: Enid had dropped the kids off. She remembered making Chub come back for his slicker. He hadn't pulled the

kitchen door shut all the way. She'd heard him out there, talking to the dog—
*Who's a good boy?*

Colleen had given the girls cookies and sent them outside to play, brought
the portable radio into the living room and set up her sewing machine: a new
dress shirt to replace Chub's yellow one. She'd nudged the volume up until it
drowned out Rich's table saw, the occasional pop of pitch in the woodstove.
She'd held pins between her teeth, expecting Chub and Wyatt to come barging
in any minute to claim their rightful cookies, listening with half an ear for the
baby, thinking about names—*Pearl, Ruby, Marigold, Goldie for short*. By the
time she finished—just the buttonholes left—it was time to start supper. She'd
jabbed the extra pins into the cloth tomato, checked on Alsea, added the names
to the list on her nightstand, and gone to start the casserole. Salting the water
for the noodles, she'd looked out the window and realized she didn't see him.

Now, more than Chub's small form, his new overalls rolled in wide,
floppy cuffs up over the still too-big boots—she should have bought the next
size down, but oh well, he'd grow into them—it was the snap of the screen
door Colleen kept replaying.

*He's fine. Rich will find him. Stop worrying.* She touched her belly to reassure the baby.

She'd nestled the serrated lids down inside the empty tuna cans, grated
cheese. The radio sang. She'd slid a hand through the geranium leaves and
jerked the window open in its track.

"Chub!" she'd called over the drone of the table saw. She'd drained the
pasta, mixed everything together, slid the pan into the oven, and gone to feed
Alsea. The comforting aroma of casserole had filled the house.

"Dinner!" she'd called out the back door, though it was only five o'clock.
The girls had tromped in.

"Where's Chub?" she'd asked.

What had she done next? Gone to the back door and called him, then
Wyatt. A mosquito netting of mist hung in the yard. The top of the casserole
glistened, greasy skin of cheese clinging to her new spatula. The girls glugged
their milk.

"Rich, dinner!" She'd had to yell it twice more before he heard.

Rich came in and stood at the counter with his plate, Chub's seat empty.
Wyatt hadn't come back yet either.

"Chub!" Colleen had called out the back door. "I don't see him."

Rich drank off half his milk. "Maybe he smelled tuna."

She'd gone out, scanned for a disturbance in the ferns.

"Chub! Dinner!"

After a minute, Rich had come out behind her.

"I don't know where he is," she'd said, suddenly panicked. Wind had washed over them, carrying the roar of the chop.

"Chu-ub?" Rich had called. "Wy-att?"

"Chub?! I'm counting to three!" Colleen had warned. "Chub! I mean it!"

"Maybe they went down to the creek?" Rich had suggested.

"Chub wouldn't, not on his own." She'd felt a flash of anger at Wyatt.

"You stay here, in case they come back," Rich had said.

She'd wanted Rich to say Chub was okay, he was fine, don't worry, to squeeze her cold hands in his long enough for her to absorb his warmth, his certainty. Instead, he'd loped up through the brush at a speed she would have had to run to match.

Left behind, she'd kept calling him. *Chu-ub?!* The wind swept her voice away. The dog whined.

"Shht." She'd crouched, clamped her hands over the old mutt's snout, holding it shut. "Quiet. You be quiet."

The dog had begun to whimper, a vibration she'd felt in her hands.

"It's okay." She'd released him. "He's okay. He never goes far." To prove her point, she'd gone in. She'd stood at the window looking out, willing him to appear, forcing herself to stay calm, resting one hand on her belly.

And now the eight, peeling up on the stove clock.

She went out into the yard. In the distance, the echo of Rich's voice. *Chu-ub. Chu-u-ub.* Then suddenly, it stopped. Had he found him? In the fading light she saw Rich wading down through the undergrowth, a bundle bunched in one hand. She rushed to meet him. His face was drawn, deep lines in his forehead.

"Where was it?" she asked, grabbing Chub's slicker, hugging it to her chest.

"Across the creek." Rich swallowed, opening his fist. Chub's binoculars. "We'd better call Harvey. It's getting dark. There are tracks everywhere. We need more than one person."

Her fingers trembled as she dialed.

"Harvey?" she asked.

"Tell him to hurry," Rich said.

# RICH

Colleen stood in the rain in the backyard, yelling Chub's name. He heard tires on the gravel out front and went to meet Harvey. If they started at the creek and split up, they'd have a better chance of finding them before the rain melted their tracks. But it was Eugene's truck in the driveway, Enid heaving herself out.

"I have to get home and milk those goats," she said. "Another hour and they'll explode."

"We can't find Chub." Rich swallowed. It sounded worse aloud. "He and Wyatt are gone."

"Well. They've got about two minutes," Enid warned, and disappeared into the house.

Out back, Colleen had gone quiet.

"Enid's back—" he said, rounding the corner, and then he saw Wyatt, standing at the edge of the yard, soaked and shivering, his shirt smeared with blood.

"Where's Chub?" Colleen asked him.

Wyatt began to sob, and before Rich could move, she flew at him.

"What did you do?! What did you do!" She grabbed his shirt, pulling it up, checking he was intact, then shaking him.

"What the hell is going on out here?" Enid came out the back door.

Colleen was screaming now, smacking Wyatt, who cowered, shielding his head. Rich pulled her off him. "Chub?!" she yelled, fighting Rich's embrace. "Chu-ub?!"

Enid squatted before Wyatt, holding him by the shoulders, his cheeks tearstained. "Wyatt, what happened?" The gentlest voice Rich had ever heard her use. Wyatt bawled. "Wyatt, where's Chub?"

"Where is he?!" Colleen yelled.

Enid thrust an arm out to quiet her. There was the sound of rain pouring off the roof.

"Chub fell," Wyatt said. "We were playing and he fell. He hit his head—"

"Where?" Enid coaxed.

Colleen strained in Rich's arms.

Wyatt turned and pointed. "By the road," he said.

Colleen sprinted up Bald Hill, stumbling.

"Colleen! It's too far!" Rich yelled. "Get in the truck!"

"Go," Enid said, seeing Rich hesitate, and started up the hill after her.

Rich dashed through the house for his keys, sprinted to the truck, gravel skittering across the highway as he swung out. Rain pelted the windshield. His heart beat so loud in his ears it sounded like nothing more than Chub's name.

No Name Road was a muddy washboard. Rich gunned it, parked the truck at the culvert, and pushed out.

"Chub!" He stood at the road edge. Damnation Creek thundered below him.

His voice echoed down into the cut zone and he slid after it, detouring around busted logs and torn-up boulders until he reached the spot where the slide dropped off in a cliff edge. He surveyed the frothing creek, swollen with runoff.

He cupped his hands around his mouth. "Chu-ub?"

How easy it would be, standing here, for the side to calve off, churn him down into that mud. He backed up, turned, and tracked uphill at a diagonal, calling Chub's name all the way back up to the road. The rain had let up some. Out of breath, he started another sweep down the hill.

"Chu-ub?"

He hiked back up and cut down again, pushing through the ferns into the harvest zone. He followed the rutted Cat tracks and suddenly there in the mud were footprints. He crouched to inspect them, stood.

"Chub?"

He listened, scanning the hill. Dusk was falling. Ruined logs lay on their sides, berms as high as a house blocking his view. Rich made for a stump upslope, circled it, searching out handholds, until, straining and grunting, he heaved himself up onto the flat expanse of the cut and pushed to his feet.

"Chu-ub?" His voice warped. *Chu-u-u-ub.*

His eyes combed the steep slope, skid trails grooved deep into the mud, broken limbs, piles of dry-rotted timber busted to chips the size of matchbooks. He walked to the edge of the stump, a thirty-foot drop on the downhill side.

"Chub?" he called, hoarse. The crash of the creek grew louder in the silence that followed, his gaze raking through narrow passages between logs, blood pumping in his ears until suddenly—there, there in the low, gray light: boots.

"Chub!" Rich forgot himself, nearly vaulted over the edge. He turned, slid down the stump's lowest spot, bark scrubbing his side, and ran, dodging spears of splintered timber, weaving between wrecked logs until—there: Chub's little body. On his back in the mud.

"Chub?" Rich asked, approaching.

Chub lay pale and rain soaked, a gash in his forehead. Rich crouched beside him, took his hand, cold and still.

"Chub?" Rich's voice broke.

He touched Chub's throat, feeling for a pulse. His lips were blue, his hair matted with blood. Rain beaded on his cheeks, his nose. Despite the cut, he looked almost peaceful. *Please. God. Please. No.*

A sob loosed itself from deep inside Rich's rib cage.

*Take me. Please.*

He pressed harder, two fingers against the soft underside of Chub's jaw.

*Take me.*

Chub blinked.

"Chub?!" Rich's heart leapt. Chub's eyes tracked across the sky until they found Rich's. Chub stirred. "Stay still." Rich moved a hand to Chub's chest.

"Daddy?" he asked, confused. His lip wobbled.

"I'm here. You're okay. I'm here now."

Rich examined the cut on Chub's forehead. Chub winced. "Sorry, Grahamcracker," Rich said. "Let me just get a look." Rich followed the gash around, parting Chub's hair to inspect where the gap opened to the width of a knife blade on his scalp, jellied black with blood. "You're okay," he said, as much to himself as to Chub. He whipped off his coat and wrapped him in it.

"I'm cold," Chub said.

Rich rubbed the backs of Chub's arms through the fabric. His knees cracked as he pushed to his feet with Chub in his arms.

"Where's Mama?" Chub asked.

Rich heard a voice in the distance, Enid calling after Colleen.

"She's coming, Grahamcracker." Rich carried Chub up the hill. "She'll be here in a minute."

Rain speckled his neck and shoulders, Chub warm against his chest, water snaking down the hillside as they made their way through stumps and slash, up through the dark pillars of the big pumpkins that remained.

# COLLEEN

Chub sat in a kitchen chair, legs dangling. Colleen leaned over him, holding her breath as she eased the sticky edges of the bandage free.

Chub flinched. "Ow."

"Sorry, Grahamcracker." She was trying to be gentle when it would be better to be quick. She pulled. Chub yipped. "There, got it." She examined the yellow ooze on the pad, less than yesterday, swept his bangs up out of his eyes.

The stitches in his forehead were pink, crusted with dried blood.

"It itches," Chub complained.

"That's good, Grahamcracker. If it's itching, it's healing."

Another week and she would take him to get them out, then to the drugstore to pick out a new Matchbox car, a reward for holding still. They'd pinched the gash in his head—four inches long and a half-inch wide—closed with staples, shaved off his hair around the wound, prickle of new growth now as she dabbed the edges with the soapy cloth.

"That stings," Chub whined, tipping his head away from her.

"I know, Grahamcracker. I'll be quick." He whimpered a little. She squeezed out the rinse cloth and blotted the soap off. "One more time," she said, careful not to press too hard. When she finished, she tore a new bandage from its wrapper, pressed it carefully over his sewn-up forehead, and let his hair fall back, covering it. "All clean, my little miracle."

He slid off the chair and out the back door before she could stop him.

In the front room, Rich shoved the ash drawer back into the woodstove and stood. He'd spent the morning cleaning the stack. She took the bowl of soapy water to the sink and drained it, wrung the washcloth out, watching Chub in the backyard, talking to the dog, looking over his shoulder, the shadow of his accident still trailing him. She heard Rich come into the kitchen behind her.

"I shouldn't have let him wear those boots," she said. "They're too big."

"It wasn't your fault," Rich reminded her for the hundredth time. "Wyatt pushed him."

She hugged her elbows. "Still."

*Just a fluke*, the doctor had said. *He hit that rock just right.*

Rich washed his hands, dried them, rehung the towel.

"Colleen, he's fine," he said. "You don't have to watch him every minute of the day. He's okay." He slid his hands around her waist, cupped her belly, kissed the top of her head, and rested his chin there. "We're all going to be okay."

She let out a ragged breath, relaxed into him. When she looked back out the window, Chub was gone.

"It's past his bedtime," she said.

Rich gave her arms a squeeze. "I'll get him."

From the kitchen door, she watched Rich scan the yard, then walk up the hill to roust him from the ferns, clapping his hand to his chest when Chub leapt out, then herding him on ahead, up the path and out of sight.

# CHUB

From his hiding place in the ferns, Chub had fiddled with the dials, then brought the binoculars to his eyes. He'd watched his dad come up behind his mom. He'd watched him rest his chin on top of her head and twist a little, like they were dancing. It made Chub forget he was mad at his mom for washing his cuts with soap. It gave him a squirmy, happy feeling. It made him want to bury his face.

He'd squeezed the binoculars. He loved them because they came in a black leather case with red insides. He loved them because they were small and heavy, an adult thing. But what he loved most about the binoculars was this: how he could be so close he could see a crumb in his dad's mustache, the freckle below his mom's eye, so, so close, without them knowing.

Suddenly his dad had come out the back door.

"Chub?" he'd asked.

Chub crouched lower.

"Chu-ub?"

Chub had felt the urge to stand up. *Here I am*. The squeeze of excitement that came from hiding.

"Have you seen Chub?" his dad asked the old dog. "No? Me neither." His dad had shrugged. "I guess Bigfoot got him."

"There's no such thing as Bigfoot!" Chub had yelled.

"Who said that?" His dad had wheeled around, shading his eyes with his hand.

Chub had hunched lower. Through the binoculars, he'd watched the little smile play at the corner of his dad's mouth, felt it tug the corner of his own.

He was invisible for as long as he could hold his breath. *One one thousand. Two one thousand.*

His dad had narrowed his eyes, then started stomping up through the grass, ferns swishing.

"Ha!" Chub had shot up when his dad got close. His dad had reeled back.

"You scared me," his dad had said. "Come on."

Now Chub ran ahead up the path to the top of their hill and together they stood looking back down at the house, the yellow square of kitchen window casting its glow out into the yard.

His dad breathed deep, and Chub copied him, his breath burning in his chest, until finally his dad let it go, threw his head back, and stared up at the darkening sky.

Chub's neck got tired, so, after a while, he turned and looked out at the light going down through the forest instead, trees almost black in the dim. A figure appeared: hunched and shaggy, bigger than a man. Chub froze. Hairs rose on the back of his neck. It came closer, sniffing the air.

"Dad," Chub whispered.

For one long, impossible moment, Chub didn't move, didn't breathe.

"Dad." Chub tugged his dad's pant leg. His dad turned to look.

Slowly, the Sasquatch dropped to all fours, becoming a bear again. It sauntered off into the brush. Chub stood still. *Bear bear bear bear,* said his heart. Until finally his dad took his hand and, together, they walked down the dark path home.

*June 19*

# RICH

His hair wet-combed, Rich thumped himself in the breast to loosen the tight knot of dread.

"Where are you going?" Colleen asked.

"Bank," Rich said. When he'd finally stomached checking it, he'd found the post office box strangely empty, but surely if he showed up in person, he could work something out. The salvage job money would be here soon.

"Need anything?" he asked.

Colleen looked up from sewing the buttons onto Chub's new blue dress shirt.

"Saltines. And we're almost out of pickles. Could you put the new bottle on the dispenser before you go?" she asked. "I can't lift it."

He went into the kitchen and changed it, then scooped his keys from the burl bowl.

"Rich?" she asked, his hand on the knob, as if she could sense he wasn't telling her something.

He swallowed, turning. "Yeah?"

"Be careful." She smiled, dropped her eyes, raised them.

He came back and pecked her on the cheek. "Be back in a couple hours."

It had rained hard last night. The winding highway was slick with fallen needles, a white tunnel through the fog.

In the parking lot of the savings and loan, he popped the false bottom out of the glove box and removed his paperwork, checked his back pocket for his wallet. He stepped up onto the curb, filled his lungs, and pushed in the glass doors.

Wedged into a too-small chair in the too-small waiting area, he bounced his leg, keys jingling in his pocket. The receptionist scowled. After half an hour, the loan officer emerged, annoyed at being summoned without an appointment.

"Mr. Gundersen."

The hallway seemed shorter than last time and before Rich had a moment to wipe his sweating palms down his denims, he sat facing the man. He swallowed.

"What can I do for you?" the man asked, sounding tired, as though they'd already been through the whole song and dance.

Rich pulled at his collar. "I've uh—been a little short. I missed a payment. Two, actually." Rich pushed the loan papers across the desk. "I'm probably going to miss a third one here, coming up, but I'll have the money next month. I was hoping there might be some kind of—grace period—"

The man flipped the papers around, leafed through, forehead creased, as if he had no memory of drawing them up. He tapped the end of the stack against the desk and stood.

"Give me a minute," he said.

In the stillness, Rich listened to the ticking of the burl clock, the squeak of the chair, the jogging of his own leg. He rubbed his palms over his knees. *Take a few days. Think about it.*

Nobody was hiring climbers. He could pick up tree-trimming work, maybe—some people wanted only to keep their big trees standing, make sure they didn't fall on the house. He might make some kind of living, as long as his body held up, but then what? He rubbed a thumb along the edge of the man's massive desk, cheap mahogany veneer.

The loan officer returned, tossed the papers onto his desk along with a folder, and sat down with a sigh.

"You're all set, Mr. Gundersen," he said, pushing the papers back across.

Rich waited for him to lay out the terms, what kind of fee he was looking at, to deliver a warning of what the consequences might be next time.

"You're paid off," the man explained, opening the folder. "Paid in full . . . March twenty-fifth. I was off that day, so looks like one of my colleagues took care of it for you."

Rich choked on his own saliva, buried his cough in his elbow. "What?"

"It's paid off," the loan officer repeated.

"What do you mean?" Rich asked. "How?"

The man flipped the folder around. And there inside was a carbon copy of a cashier's check, the shaky scrawl of Lark's signature.

Rich's arms tingled.

"They should have sent a payoff notice, PO Box 43, Klamath." The loan officer took the folder back and stared at the check for a moment before closing it again.

"I took him to the bank that day." Rich sat back, stunned. "I didn't know he had that kind of money."

He shook the loan officer's hand when he offered it, somehow made his way back down the hall, until he stood outside again.

*Lark, you sonofabitch, how the hell did you ever pull that off?*

*Shit pays.*

He wanted to shout it across the empty parking lot. He found a pay phone. His hands shook as he dialed. *Colleen, pick up!* He tried again.

Across the way was the pet store, an aquarium in the window, phone still ringing in his ear. He hung up and crossed the street. A bell tinkled over his ducked head. A gray-haired woman looked up from behind the register and nodded. He walked to the wall of tanks: darting neons, a sucker fish with its whiskered mouth latched to the glass.

"Do you have any goldfish?" Rich asked, his chest nearly bursting with the good news.

The clerk shifted herself heavily off her stool and sauntered toward him. She took a clear plastic bag from a pile and a dip net from a hook on the wall.

"Which one?" she asked.

"It's for my son," he said, breathless, as she filled the bag with water and scooped the flopping fish inside.

"Anything else?" she asked, knotting the top.

The register chugged out the receipt. She nestled the plastic bag with the fish inside into the glass bowl along with the canister of fish flakes and handed it to him. He tucked it under one arm. Outside, he passed the jeweler's, and there in the display, a pendant: a single pearl.

When he got back to the truck, he pulled his door shut, set the fishbowl on the seat beside him, then popped open the blue velvet case to peek at the necklace on its silver chain. *Pearl*, he'd seen at the top of the list on her nightstand.

He started the truck and rolled out of the bank lot. Waves crashed against the crescent of beach as he hit the straightaway, rain sweeping in again as he got into the bends. He flicked on his headlights. After a year of worry, his whole body felt loose, wild with relief. The wipers swished. He swung around Last Chance curve and the fishbowl slid, dove off the seat. He reached after it, fingers grasping air, steering with one hand, road barely visible over the dash. He touched glass.

"Gotcha."

He brought the bowl up into his lap. Ahead, a horn blared. Headlights filled his windshield. He jerked the wheel to the right, swerving, the horn's pitch swelling, distorting, and then, in slow motion, he was tipping—

Down below, through the dark trees—snatches of silver, ripple of ocean.

Then he was upside down, flung against the passenger door, heavy *thunk-thunk* of wood denting metal.

His head cracked window glass, crash of rock, rolling—he was weightless, he was airborne, a snap in his neck—*Colleen*—and, now, he was falling—

# COLLEEN

The phone rang and rang. Colleen pushed in the kitchen door and stomped across the linoleum to grab it. Suddenly, it stopped. *Enid*. She'd ignored the first few rings, but when Enid hadn't given up, she'd sighed, shucked off her gardening gloves, and brushed the dirt from her knees. The door ajar, she heard Chub tag the old dog out back—*You're it!*—and twist away.

She picked up the receiver and dialed.

"What?" she demanded when Enid answered.

"What?" Enid asked back.

"Did you just call me?"

"No."

"Oh."

On the other end, Enid was quiet. They hadn't spoken since the day after Chub's fall, Enid checking to make sure he was okay.

"I bought strawberries," Colleen said. "I was going to make jam." She let the invitation hang in the air, stretched the phone cord so she could see out the window. There was Chub, crouched in the tall grass with his binoculars, cheeks round with his held breath, as though not breathing were the secret to invisibility.

"All right," Enid said finally.

It was past eleven by the time Enid pulled up out front in Eugene's truck. She came in carrying Alsea, Wyatt trailing behind.

"It's so sunny out all of a sudden," Enid said. "This day just can't make up its mind. Wyatt, what do you have to say to Aunt Colleen?"

Colleen saw the scratches on his face and neck, the bruises she'd made.

"I'm sorry," Wyatt said. He looked smaller, younger. He was only a little boy.

"You're sorry, what?" Enid demanded.

"I'm sorry I pushed Chub and he got hurt." Wyatt's lip wobbled. "I'm sorry—"

"It's okay, sweetie," Colleen said. He staggered into her, pressing his face against her stomach—he hadn't done that in years. She patted his back. "I'm sorry too. I'm sorry I hit you." He sucked snot in his nose, stepped back, and wiped his eyes.

"All right. Now, go tell Chub," Enid said.

Wyatt scampered out. Colleen saw Chub stand up from the grass, wary. Wyatt crossed the yard to him. They faced off, and then Chub led Wyatt to the pile of fetch sticks. He waved one in front of the old dog's face, hurled it across the yard, waited, took the dog by the collar and dragged him over to it, Wyatt trailing behind.

"They'll be okay," Enid said, coming up beside her. "They're boys."

Colleen washed the first flat of strawberries and Enid set Alsea down on a blanket, then sat at the table cutting the green tops off.

"Did you have lunch?" Colleen asked.

"Not yet."

Colleen heated tomato soup, fried grilled cheeses in a pan. Rich should be home any minute.

Chub and Wyatt chattered, pulling their breads apart to see how far they could stretch the cheese, then begged to be excused. Without them, it was quiet again.

"How's Marla?" Colleen asked at last.

Enid let out a long sigh, reaching for another handful of strawberries. "I don't know. She doesn't talk to me. It's like she can't wait to turn eighteen and get out of here."

"Neither could you," Colleen reminded her.

Enid snorted. "And look at me now."

Colleen stood over the stockpot, stirring.

"Eugene wants her to go to college. Her grades are good enough," Enid said.

"What would she do at college?" Colleen asked.

Enid shrugged. "Nurse? Teacher? What do I know about college? I don't even know why he thinks she'll want to—"

"I'm pregnant," Colleen blurted out.

Enid tilted her head. "That's great," she said. "Isn't it?"

Colleen nodded, then swallowed. She hadn't meant to tell her.

By the time the last of the jam jars were sealed, it was almost dinnertime. Enid nursed Alsea.

"I wonder where Rich is," Colleen said, clattering the dirty pot into the sink. The faucet sputtered.

Enid gathered up Alsea and went to get her boots on.

"Take some of these," Colleen called after her. "We can't eat all this."

She heard Rich turn in. She'd have to tell him the water was spitting again; he needed to check the new pipe.

"Hey," Enid said. "Harvey's out front."

Colleen dried her hands.

"What's he doing here?" Enid asked.

"Checking on Chub?" Colleen guessed, looking out the window.

Harvey rested a palm on the top of his squad car, looking out at the ocean, sun low in the sky, glinting off the water. He turned and walked slowly toward the house. She pulled open the front door, a tickle of dryness in her throat.

"Hi, Harvey," she called. *Chub's fine,* she was going to say. *I'm sorry we bothered you that night—*

Harvey took off his hat. With the sun in her eyes, she couldn't see his face clearly.

*July 1*

# ENID

The day Dad's body washed up, Mom came to get Colleen and me at school. Normally, the bus let us off at the Deer Rib fork and we walked the last two miles. By the time we got home, Mom was on her second mug. Bottom-shelf gin. Take the polish right off your nails.

That day though, we walked out the double doors and there she was, leaning against the fender of her beater Mercury still in her gutting apron, smoking a cigarette. We stepped off the curb. I was just a kid, happy not to have to walk those two miles, but Colleen grabbed my hand. Other kids moved around us. Dad had been missing for days. He'd disappeared before, gone on benders, come crawling back. But this time they'd found his truck abandoned in a pullout near the harbor.

I started for the car, but Colleen held me back. She squeezed my hand— *one, two, three*—kept us there at the edge, like if we just didn't cross to the other side of that parking lot. If we just stayed where we were. Here, on this side, he was still alive.

Later, after Colleen left for Arcata, she used to call the school. We didn't have a phone. That bitch Gail Porter used to make me spit out my gum and hand me the receiver.

"Enid?" Just my name, the sound of Colleen's voice, loosened the knot I worked so hard to keep tied inside. She was always more my mom than Mom.

Then Mom got sick. I got knocked up. I was scared. Kel let me use the phone at the Only. I called Colleen and she came home. Just like that. I called, and she came home.

Once, after Mom died, Eugene and me drove out to the cabin with Marla.

Colleen was so alone out there. I felt bad about it. Except, when we got there, she wasn't alone. Rich was up on the roof. She'd only just met him. Eugene had brought him along to dinner a couple times. But there were the worn-out old shingles strewn across the yard and Rich on his hands and knees with a pouch full of roofing nails, laying new ones.

I'm not proud of it, but I was jealous. It was nothing to him, fixing that roof. He'd have fixed a hundred roofs for her. I saw it when we sat down to dinner and later, when he stood at the sink, soaping our plates. I saw the way he watched her bouncing Marla on her knees—*giddyup, giddyup*. Already, his heart beat for her.

Don't get me wrong, I love my husband. But for Colleen—Rich—it was different. And if she had him, then what did she need me for?

It took me a while to come around. But then we sold the cabin, she had Chub, she had her own life there, with him, and she was happy. Colleen's so quiet, it's hard to tell, unless you really know her, but I saw it. This life she'd always, always wanted. With all the ups and downs, she was happy.

If I live to be a hundred, I'll never forget the look on her face when Harvey came up to the house. It was like some part of her knew. The way she'd known that day at school. This time though, it was me who grabbed her hand and held it. When Harvey got close, she backed up. With her free hand she was clutching her belly, shaking her head. *No. No. No.* And she was squeezing these quick, panicked pulses, like she was spelling out a message. *Rich! Rich! Rich!*

It would take a few days, Harvey said. To get a boat, divers.

*No.* Colleen shook her head. *No.* As if Harvey was mistaken.

*Someone saw it, Colleen.* Harvey tried to reason with her.

She tugged at my hand, backing up. Poor Harvey, I backed up too. I think some part of me still believed my big sister could undo it. That we could step back and the curb would be there. That we could turn around, and walk back in those doors.

*July 12*

# COLLEEN

The house smelled different, like firewood and fried eggs left on the stove, like it had smelled when she first came to live in Rich's house. The clink of her keys set down in the bowl of agates. The empty rooms. She was still expecting him to be here when she came home. To knock his boots against the back stoop and duck in. To ask her: *How was it?*

She helped Chub out of his funeral clothes, put him to bed. In the bathroom, she took off her earrings. A sob rose up from her belly. She turned on the faucet and let it run. All day she'd been holding it in. Now she sat on the toilet and cried.

When she was through, she washed her face and made toast. She took a pot from the kitchen out onto the front stoop and tipped the five-gallon bottle until water poured.

The little metal urn had reminded her of a cold thermos when they'd handed it to her. The grave was in the west corner, near his parents, below a weeping willow whose leaves swept the ground. She brought the good water inside.

In the backyard, she fed the old dog his dinner. Her nostrils were rubbed raw. Her swollen eyelids ached. She stroked the mutt's hackles while he ate, soothing him the way Rich had. She stared at the yellow square of window light. From outside, it looked like a normal house.

Tall grasses painted cold wet tails along her legs. Rich hadn't mowed since—

She pressed her palms against her eyes.

Finally, she went in. One by one, she turned off the lights, until she stood in the doorway of their dark bedroom.

*Will you be okay to drive?* they'd asked after the service. Not, *Will you be okay to chop wood, change your oil, raise your son without his father?* Not, *Will you be okay to live?* As though driving were the only thing she would have to learn to do without him.

She sat in the rocker. She didn't want to lie down. The phone rang and rang in her dreams. She'd wake with the gasp of the drowned, fling her arm out across his empty pillow. Sometimes, in the haze of waking, it took her a moment to remember.

She rocked to the same rhythm she'd once nursed Chub to—*Hush, little baby, don't say a word.* Any moment she'd hear Rich's tires on the gravel, his keys in the burl bowl. The chair creaked on its runners, keeping her quiet vigil.

Past midnight, she finally crawled into bed, took the last shirt he'd slept in—retrieved from the laundry basket—from under the covers. It still smelled like him.

*I'm twelve weeks today.* She slid her hands over her belly, as Rich might have. She buried her head in her elbows. *Rich, come back. Don't leave me here. I can't do this by myself. Please. Come back.*

*July 13*

# COLLEEN

Enid stopped by with a rotisserie chicken and the check for Rich's share of the salvage job. She brought a stack of mail up from the box.

"I could come stay for a while," she offered.

"We're okay," Colleen said.


There was paperwork. Waiting in line at the county health department for Rich's death certificate, a piece of paper she held in her hands, like a ticket she could trade for her husband, if she could just find the right office. There were casseroles. A banana cream pie left on the mat. Colleen covered the casseroles with tinfoil and stacked them in the refrigerator. When the freezer was full, she threw them away.

Harvey stopped by to check on her, sat with his hat between his knees.

"I can't sleep," she admitted. "I keep thinking—"

Ocean flooding in the window he kept cracked, his panic as the light faded overhead, his lungs burning, that final deep gasp.

"He was gone before he ever hit the water," Harvey assured her.

"How do you know?"

"I've patrolled that road for thirty years. Seen a lot of wrecks. He didn't feel a thing, Colleen. I promise you."

Colleen wiped her eyes.

"How's Chub?" he asked, to change the subject.

She shook her head. One hour he was fine. The next he climbed up into her lap and clung to her. When would this all be over?

* * *

Don and Gail Porter brought a gasoline can. Don went out back and mowed the lawn.

Dot brought a cobbler.

Pete brought a cord of firewood and stacked it for her.

The young, skinny man from Rich's crew, Quentin, brought back an old chainsaw Rich had loaned him.

"I can put it in the shed," he offered. "It's heavy."

"You should keep it," she said. "We won't use it."

"He might, when he's older?" The man lifted his chin at Chub.

She shook her head no.

"Can I see?" Chub asked, stepping around her, then peering at the different parts as the man explained them.

"Your dad taught me a lot," he said. "He was a good man." He set his hand on Chub's shoulder.

It wasn't until after Quentin left that Colleen noticed the two new water bottles sitting on the gravel below the stoop, as though Rich had delivered them in the night.

Marsha made coffee, the kitchen table heaped with unopened mail—sympathy cards, bills.

"Look at all this," Marsha said. "You ready for some help?"

Like the sputter of the kitchen faucet, the spider roaming the bathroom ceiling, what were her finances except one more thing waiting, waiting for Rich to return?

Marsha sat down and opened the bills. "Where's your bank book?"

Colleen brought it to her.

"Where's the loan bill on that 24-7 land?" Marsha asked.

Colleen shrugged.

"Did he pay it this month already I wonder?" Marsha thumbed through his checkbook, wrinkled her nose, talking to herself. "This here is a lifesaver." Marsha tapped the salvage check, which Colleen still hadn't deposited. "He had life insurance, didn't he?" Marsha asked. "Clive sold all the guys policies back in the day. Might not be a lot, but every little bit helps." Marsha flicked through the folder Colleen had brought her. "Come on now, Rich," Marsha mumbled. "Where did you put it?"

Colleen pressed her fingers to the spot in her chest where the ache had lodged. She wanted Rich to come home and sort out this whole mess. She wanted Rich.

After everyone had left and she was finally alone, after she'd turned on Chub's night-light and stood for a moment in its red glow, she went into their bedroom, took the stack of undershirts out of Rich's dresser, and pressed them to her face. The cloth was woven with his scent, soft with wear. It muffled the sound.

*July 18*

# CHUB

His mom slung the waders over her shoulder, took Chub's slicker off its hook, and held it out. Chub raced down the hall for his binoculars.

Outside, the old dog got to his feet.

"Can we bring him?" Chub begged. "Pleeease?"

His mom found a length of rope, tied it to the dog's collar, and set the other end in Chub's hands.

"You know the way?" she asked.

He found the path and followed it. At Little Lost Creek, the dog waded across, then shook. Chub squeezed his eyes shut.

"Come back!" he yelled, chasing the trailing rope.

He got up to the 24-7 tree first and ran around the back, jerking the dog's rope, pulling him along. He crouched, huffing too hard to hold his breath for long. *One one thousand, two one thousand.*

After a moment, he heard his mom. He clamped the old dog's snout shut so he wouldn't pant so loud.

"Chub?" his mom called.

He waited.

"Chu-ub?!" she shouted. Her voice boomeranged through the mist. "Chub!"

The old dog broke free. His mom appeared, stumbling toward him, pulling him to her chest, hugging him too tight.

"Please don't hide from me." She cupped his face in her hands. "I don't want to lose you, Grahamcracker. I can't lose you, okay?"

He nodded. She was squishing his cheeks. The old dog plopped down, panting.

When they finally got down to Damnation Creek, his mom stood at the edge. She toed a rock. It dropped off into the water and sank.

"Do you know how?" Chub asked.

"Sort of," she said. "I guess we'll learn, won't we?" She gave a sad smile.

"Sometimes Dad takes his shirt off," Chub offered.

His mom nodded, unbuttoned her cuffs, and rolled up her sleeves.

"I should have brought my bathing suit," she said, climbing into the waders, pulling the straps up over her shoulders. She stepped into the creek, looking down, watching her feet under the water, slowly crossing toward the new pipe his dad had laid.

"Here?" she asked, looking back over her shoulder at him.

"Farther," Chub said. "There."

She hissed when she reached her arm in. Her shoulder, her ear, the side of her head disappeared into the cold water. She took a breath and went under. The dog pulled, barking his ghost bark.

"Wait!" Chub yanked the dog's rope. "Mama!"

He watched the spot where she'd disappeared. The creek gurgled. Coins of sunlight played across the surface. She burst up again, gasping, took a deep breath and stuck her head back under.

Chub crouched at the creek edge, counting—*One one thousand, two one thousand*. Long grasses swayed in the current, velvet silt coating the rocks underwater, and there, between them, something glinted. He reached for it, stood up. His mom went underwater again. He tripped backward and sat on his butt. He forced the latch and pushed the flat side of the blade until the knife snapped closed into its handle, just like his dad had taught him.

"Chub?" his mom asked.

He looked up. She stood knee-deep in the creek, water running down her hair. In her hand was a wad of wet leaves, and—magically—she was smiling.

# July 30

# COLLEEN

She turned sideways in the bathroom mirror, cupping the little swell of her belly. Today she would do it. She would make a space.

One by one, she opened Rich's dresser drawers, piling his clothes on the bed. Denims, work shirts, half a dozen pairs of wool socks. She paused, making sure she still heard Chub in his room.

The bottom drawer was a jumble—boxer shorts, an old cap, two pairs of suspenders, a waxed paper envelope with a decayed tooth inside, the wooden box with the carved lid, wedged in so tightly she had to get down on her knees to maneuver it. She angled it this way and that, a light sweat on her brow, jolting backward when finally it came loose. She set it down on the floor beside her and there, underneath it, pressed against the bottom of the drawer, sat Rich's old handkerchief, navy blue embroidery in the corner: RG. It was folded so neatly that the creases held when she picked it up. She let it fall open: a smear of red lipstick. Tears sprang into Colleen's eyes. The smell of the bonfire—*Smoke follows beauty*—wafted out from the folds.

Her stomach lurched, a dry heave. She picked up the wooden box, got a sleeve of saltines from the kitchen cabinet, filled the kettle, and set it to boil. She sat at the table eating the crackers, lifted the carved lid off the box.

She'd removed the first few photographs when Chub tromped in.

"Are you hungry?" she asked.

Chub shook his head.

"Look at this." She held the image between her palms to keep from sullying it. "It's your uncle Lark, when he was young, see?" Lark stood beside a young woman seated with a dark-haired baby in her lap, a boy of four or five standing between them. "That must be his wife," she said, turning the photo over, as though something might be written there. She hadn't known Lark had had children.

"What else is in there?" Chub asked, reaching for a cracker.

She picked up a yellowed newspaper clipping: Rich young, ax midswing. *Del Norte County log-splitting champ Richard C. Gundersen.*

"Look, it's your dad. Look how young he is."

"His hair is all curly," Chub said, touching the old newsprint.

There was a thick stack of them clipped together—*Richard C. Gundersen, first place, tree-climbing competition. Richard C. Gundersen, grand prize, chainsaw competition.*

She examined each one gently. *You never told me this.* She leafed through the rest of the papers, pulled out a manila envelope.

The kettle whistled.

"Chub, could you turn that off, please?" Chub walked to the stove and turned the knob. "Other way. Thank you."

She stuck her hand in and slid an old photograph out of the envelope: a man holding a toddler up to a giant tree, the child's hands pressed to the bark, a lopsided grin on his face.

"Chub, look," she said. "It's your dad, when he was a baby. Look at him." She held the photo up beside Chub's face. He looked so much like him. Tears ran down her cheeks.

"What's wrong?" Chub asked.

"Nothing, Grahamcracker." She sniffed and wiped her eyes. "I'm just happy."

She turned the envelope over. There, in smudged carpenter pencil: Lark's herky-jerky scrawl, the writing of a man who, aside from signing his name, hadn't put more than a hundred words to paper in his life. *Not a lot of guys are born to do something.*

A piece of paper fell out into her lap. She unfolded it, read it once, then again.

"What's that?" Chub asked.

Her hands trembled. "It's a deed."

"What's a deed?" Chub asked.

"It means—your dad's land, it's—" she stammered, the paper so flimsy in her hands. "It doesn't matter." She picked up the clippings of Rich again, traced his profile with her finger. Chub leaned against her, waiting, though the box was empty.

"Where are your binoculars?" she asked.

Chub shrugged.

"Go get them."

They crossed the highway and followed the dirt path down the cliffside, wind bending the grasses, bowling them over. It whipped her hair, flapped the folds of her clothes. Chub reached for her hand. A rock ricocheted down, loosed by the memory of Rich walking ahead.

The sides of the path glowed electric, the lit-from-within green of new life. Wind snapped her hair from behind her ears, an effort just to open her eyes into it.

Here was Rich, leading her down to Diving Board Rock the first time, the stone slab jutting out over the gray ocean.

They came to the end of the path and here was Rich, lowering himself to one knee, so nervous he dropped the ring in the grass and crawled around, looking for it.

Here was Rich, hands around her belly, when she was pregnant with Chub.

Flashes of memory, Polaroids pinned to a clothesline, moments that would end always with the feeling of having missed the last step: he is not here.

She sat down in the grass. Chub climbed into her lap.

"What do you see?" she asked, batting at the binoculars until he lifted them to his eyes and looked out at the water.

She bounced him in her lap, as she had when he was small, inventing their singsongs.

"I was walking down the street, and I saw a man with green eyes." She bobbed her knees to the old rhythm. "I said, 'Hey, mister, where'd you get those beautiful green eyes?'"

Chub was quiet.

"Hey, mister," she whispered. "Where'd you get those beautiful green eyes?"

Chub lowered his binoculars and tipped his head back against her. His bangs fell away, exposing the pink scar, his forehead, his sharp little chin, his cheeks with their dimples, and there, looking up at her, were those eyes, serious and changing, Rich's eyes, flecked with bits of brown and gold, leaves floating in a pool of green water—his beautiful, beautiful eyes.

# ACKNOWLEDGMENTS

My mom trekked, through forests and clear-cuts, down to the ocean with me on research trips, and showed me the way to our creek. My dad taught me to use a chainsaw. But outside of family anecdotes, I knew very little about the long shadow herbicides had cast across timber country. I'm grateful to Patty Clary at Californians for Alternatives to Toxics, who first pointed me in the right direction and recommended *A Bitter Fog*, Carol Van Strum's true account of the grassroots struggle to stop the spraying of 2,4,5-T. David Harris's *The Last Stand: The War Between Wall Street and Main Street over California's Ancient Redwoods* and James LeMonds's *Deadfall: Generations of Logging in the Pacific Northwest* offered a window into timber-industry politics and life working in the woods. I'm grateful to Lucy Thompson's 1916 history of Yurok life along the Klamath from before genocide and colonization, *To the American Indian: Reminiscences of a Yurok Woman*; to *Grave Matters: Excavating California's Buried Past* by Tony Platt for background on the legacy of massacre, plunder, and grave robbing in the region; to the work of a number of journalists, especially Anna V. Smith at *High Country News* for her reporting on the Yurok Tribe's continuing legal work on behalf of the Klamath; and to *Yurok Today: The Voice of the Yurok People* for making their informative newsletter available online. Rangers at Redwood National and State Parks provided information on burl poaching, and Neil Levine talked me through the legal basics of takings. Thank you to Jan Wortman and the Requa Inn for a wealth of knowledge and useful tips, a view of the river, a quiet meeting place, and the best pancakes on the North Coast. I owe a kidney to Amy Cordalis for her generosity, expertise, and careful review, and for taking time away from her writing and her life's work—carrying on her family's legacy of defending Yurok sovereignty and protecting the Klamath River and Yurok lifeways—to help me see what I was missing. My deepest gratitude to the loggers, mill workers, and community members of Klamath and Requa, California, who helped me find my way, especially the late Yurok advocate Robley Schwenk and Stace Fisher, for patiently answering my questions and for sharing knowledge and experiences I couldn't find in any book. Any and all errors are my own.

I got two miracles: my agent, Chris Parris-Lamb, a true marathoner, whose guidance and sharp eye improved every page, and the honorable Kathryn Belden, this book's editor and its midwife, who says the hard thing in the gentlest way. The two of them, with Nan Graham, changed my life. At the Gernert Company, I'm indebted to Rebecca Gardner and to Sarah Bolling for her insights and her expertise in the art of summary, and to Rebekah Jett at Scribner, editorial chiropractor, whose adjustment brought a key plot point into alignment.

It took me a while to get here, and I racked up debts along the way:

To the Flinn Foundation, for opening the door to the world, and to the Iowa Writers' Workshop, the Arizona Commission on the Arts, and MacDowell, for giving me the space and the freedom to write like it was my job.

To my teachers at Iowa: Kevin Brockmeier, Ethan Canin, James Alan McPherson, and especially Lan Samantha Chang, who builds us all up, and to Deb West, Jan Zenisek, Kelly Smith, and Connie Brothers, who ran a tight ship despite an unruly passenger list.

To Dr. Karen Butterfield, Dr. Penelope Wong, Janeece Henes, Gloria Elio, Kelly Shushok, Fletcher Lathrop, and a number of generous writers who also taught, especially Mike Levin at FALA, and Paige Kaptuch, Kate Leary, and the late Jon Anderson at the University of Arizona.

To the staff of Prairie Lights, the Java House, Late for the Train, and the Tourist Home (Shelby!), where chunks of this book took shape, and to Gary at Technology Associates in Iowa City, who recovered what I lost.

To the magazine editors who first plucked me out of the slush, especially Valerie Vogrin at Sou'wester and Paul Ketzle at Quarterly West.

To the writers who took time away from their own books to help me with this one: Shabnam Nadiya, Christa Fraser, Greg Brown, and the ruthless Aamina Ahmad. To Erica Martz, Bryan Castille, Andrés Carlstein, and Madhuri Vijay for many hours of shop talk and for reminding me, through their work, what I love about fiction. And to fierce and fearsome writers Ted Kehoe, J. Scott Smith, Don Waters, Jordan Glubka, Merritt Tierce, Arna Bontemps Hemenway, E. J. Fischer, and Amy Parker, who offered a kind word when I really needed one.

To the prolific Melissa Sevigny and to Chris Sevigny, for poker games and pots of chili.

To the Café Léa writers, Hannah Holtzman and Caroline Sandifer, and to Shakespeare and Company, for hosting a motley crew.

To Christopher Merrill, Kelly Morse, Susannah Shive, Kelly Bedeian, Lisa Dupree (cupcake artist!), and Maria Bertorello at the UI International Writing Program, and especially to Nataša Ďurovičová, who uplifts writers around the globe and who treated this book like a real thing before it was one.

To the good people of the Grand Canyon Trust, who give my day life a sense of direction, and especially to Darcy Allen for "Drive fast and take lots of chances" and Rick Moore for "potholes and assholes" and other gems.

To the staff and clients of the IRC/Suburban Washington Resettlement Center 2007–2010, especially Taameem Al-Maliki, Selena Cetino, Abeje Chumo, Kate Evans, Katy Frank, Elsabet Gerbi, Simret Goitam, Marshall Hallock, Chelsea Kinsman, Rachel Mogga, Myat Lin, Tin Tin Oo (and Vanessa Lin), Mina Mulat, and Dr. Beeletsega Yeneneh—the very best of humanity.

For good stories and good company: Cassalyn David, Dr. Megan Johnson, Omar Naseer, Issa Naseer, Mustafa Naseer, Tenmay, Mahmud Rahman, Karen Eason (and Marty), Michelle Hertzfeld, Maya Abela, Emily Musta, Audrey Belliard, Pearl Buniger, Alia El Khatib, Natasha Hale, Anne Mariah Tapp, and Ashley Sheen.

To Rebecca Buntman, Laurah Hagen, and Dr. Whitney Sheen James, who pursue their dreams and believe in mine.

To Greg McLaskey, for good counsel, and many letters, over many years.

To Harold Jacobson. I miss you every time I open the mailbox.

To my sister, Anne, my best person.

And, above all, to my parents, Susan and Dean, storytellers both, whose memories of Klamath got this book started and whose faith, humor, and big-heartedness kept it alive, the whole long way.

And to you who made it this far, for reading.

# ABOUT THE AUTHOR

Ash Davidson was born in Arcata, California, and attended the Iowa Writers' Workshop. Her work has been supported by the Arizona Commission on the Arts and MacDowell. She lives in Flagstaff, Arizona.